PENGUIN POETS

The Penguin Book of Homosexual Verse

Dr Stephen Coote was educated at
Magdalene College, Cambridge, where
he was an exhibitioner, and at Birkbeck
College, University of London, where he
was Sir William Bull Memorial Scholar.
He has edited *The Vicar of Wakefield* for
the Penguin English Library. He now
lives and works in Oxford.

THE PENGUIN BOOK OF

Homosexual Verse

EDITED BY STEPHEN COOTE

PENGUIN BOOKS

Penguin Books Ltd, Harmondsworth, Middlesex, England
Penguin Books, 625 Madison Avenue, New York, New York 10022, U.S.A.
Penguin Books Australia Ltd, Ringwood, Victoria, Australia
Penguin Books Canada Ltd, 2801 John Street, Markham, Ontario, Canada L3R 1B4
Penguin Books (N.Z.) Ltd, 182–190 Wairau Road, Auckland 10, New Zealand

First published 1983
Published simultaneously by Allen Lane

Made and printed in Great Britain by
Richard Clay (The Chaucer Press) Ltd,
Bungay, Suffolk

for

David

Contents

9 Contents

14 *Contents*

Acknowledgements

For permission to reprint the poems in this anthology acknowledge-
ment is made to the following: David Higham Associates Ltd, for J. R.
Ackerley, 'After the Blitz', from *Michael Dever and Other Poems*;
Penguin Books Ltd, for Fleur Adcock (trans.), 5:116, from *The Greek
Anthology*; Jonathan Cape Ltd, for Kingsley Amis, 'An Ever-Fixed
Mark', from *A Look Round the Estate*; Faber and Faber, and Random
House Inc., for W. H. Auden, 'Uncle Henry', from *Collected Poems*;
University of California Press, for Mary Barnard (trans.), Sappho, 'I
have had not one word', 'It was you, Atthis', 'Be kind to me', from
Sappho: A New Translation; Naiad Press, for Sandia Belgrade (trans.),
Renée Vivien, 'Toward Lesbos', 'The Pillory', 'Words to My Friend',
from *At the Sweet Hour of Hand in Hand*; Thirteenth Moon Press and the
author, for Ellen-Marie Bissert, 'The Most Beautiful Woman',
'Another', from *The Immaculate Conception of the Blessed Virgin Dyke*;
University of Chicago Press, for James Boswell (trans.), Anon., 'A
Perverse Custom', from *Christianity, Social Tolerance and Homo-
sexuality*; Panjandrum Books, for Perry Brass, 'I Think the New
Teacher's a Queer', from Winston Leyland (ed.), *Angels of the Lyre*; Yale
University Press, for Olga Broumas, 'Leda and her Swan', from *Start-
ing with O*; Anthony Reid, Esq., for R. N. Chubb, extracts from *The
Book of God's Madness, Song of My Soul, The Sun Spirit*; Interim Books
and the author, for Kirby Congdon, 'Daredevil', from *Juggernaut*;
Duckworth Ltd, for G. L. Dickinson (trans.), Theognis, 'Lo, I have
given', 'I never asked', from *Autobiography*; Edward Colman, Esq., for
Lord Alfred Douglas, 'Two Loves', 'The Poet', from *Poems*; Penguin
Books Ltd, for Alistair Elliot (trans.), 10:20, from *The Greek Anthology*;
Gay Sunshine Press, for Jim Everhard, 'Cute', from *Cute*; Gay
Sunshine Press, for Steven Finch (trans.), Genet, from 'The Man
Sentenced to Death', from *Treasures of the Night*; Druid Heights Books,
for Elsa Gidlow, 'For the Goddess Too Well Known', from *Sapphic
Songs*; Gay Sunshine Press, for Allen Ginsberg, 'Maybe Love';
Random House, for Paul Goodman, 'Lines: His cock is big and red',
'Long Lines: Youth and Age', from *Collected Poems*, ed. Stoehr; Diana

Press, for Judy Grahn, 'Carol in the Park', 'A History of Lesbianism', 'in the place where', from *The Work of a Common Woman*; Penguin Books Ltd, for Peter Green (trans.), Juvenal, from 'Satire VI', from *Juvenal: The Sixteen Satires*; Faber and Faber, for Thom Gunn, 'Modes of Pleasure – I jump with pleasure', from *My Sad Captains*, and 'Fever', from *Jack Straw's Castle*; Methuen and Co., for Radclyffe Hall, 'Poem 32', from *Forgotten Island*; Penguin Books Ltd, for Tony Harrison (trans.), 12:30, 12:185, from *The Greek Anthology*; Penguin Books Ltd, for Teddy Hogge (trans.), 12:192, 12:213, 12:222, from *The Greek Anthology*; the Estate of A. E. Housman and the Society of Authors, and Holt, Rinehart & Winston, for A. E. Housman, 'Look not in my eyes for fear', 'Shot? So quick, so clean an ending?', 'The laws of God, the laws of man', 'Because I liked you better', 'Half-way, for one commandment broken', 'He would not stay for me; and who can wonder', 'Oh who is that young sinner with the handcuffs on his wrists?'; Simon and Schuster, for Christopher Isherwood, 'On His Queerness', from *Exhumations*; Penguin Books Ltd, for Peter Jay (trans.), 7:99, 7:100, 7:669, 7:670, 7:714, 12:44, from *The Greek Anthology*; Gay Sunshine Press, for Simon Karlinsky (trans.), G. Trifonov, 'For three swift days'; Estate of Walter Kaufman, for Walter Kaufman (trans.), Erich Kastner, 'Ragoût fin de siècle', from *Twenty German Poets*, ed. and trans. Walter Kaufman; Hogarth Press Ltd and the translators, for Edmund Keeley and Philip Sherrard (trans.), C. P. Cavafy, 'The Window of the Tobacco Shop', 'In Despair', 'In the Twenty-fifth Year of His Life', 'Days of 1896', 'Two Young Men', 'The Mirror', 'He Asked About the Quality', from *Collected Poems of C. P. Cavafy*; Gay Sunshine Press, for Dennis Kelley, 'Chicken', from *Chicken*; the author, for James Kirkup, 'Gay Boys,', 'The Love of Older Men', from *Refusal to Conform*; Gay Sunshine Press, for E. A. Lacey, 'Ramon', 'Abdelfatteh', and E. A. Lacey (trans.), Cassiano Nunes, 'Episode'; Jonathan Cape and Doubleday, for T. E. Lawrence, 'To S.A.', from *Seven Pillars of Wisdom*; Jay Landesman Ltd, for Eddie Linden, 'A Sunday in Cambridge', from *City of Razors*; Oxford University Press, for Edward Lucie-Smith, 'Caravaggio Dying', from *Confessions and Histories*; Shameless Hussey Press and the author, for Paul Mariah, 'Quarry/Rock' from *Personae Non Gratae*; Hogarth Press Ltd, for J. Mavrogordato (trans.), C. P. Cavafy, 'The Next Table', 'Their Beginning', from *Poems of C. P. Cavafy*; Penguin Books Ltd, for Alan Marshfield (trans.), 5:19, 12:3, 12:4, 12:22, 12:136, from *The Greek Anthology*; Granada and James Michie, for Catullus, 9, 16, 33, from 61, 99, from *The Poems of Catullus*; Penguin Books Ltd, for Andrew Miller (trans.), 5:232, from *The Greek Anthology*; Penguin Books Ltd, for Edwin Morgan (trans.), 11:36, from *The Greek Anthology*; Gay Sunshine Press, for J. Murat and W. Gunn (trans.), Verlaine and Rimbaud, 'Ode to My Lovers', 'Sonnet: To the Asshole', from *A Lover's Cock*; Chatto and Windus Ltd, for Ralph Nichols, 'Burial in Flanders', from *Ardours and Endurances*; Panjandrum Books, for Harold Norse, 'Behind the Glass Wall', 'Breathing the Strong Smell', from Winston Leyland (ed.), *Angels of the Lyre*; Random House, for Frank O'Hara, 'Homosexuality', from *The Collected Poems of Frank O'Hara*; Panjandrum Books, for Charles Ortleb, 'Some Boys', from Winston Leyland (ed.), *Angels of the Lyre*; Sea Horse Books, for Felice Picano, 'The Gilded Boys', 'The Heart Has Its Reasons', from *The Deformity Lover*; Gay Sunshine Press, for Valery Pereleshin (trans.), Pushkin, 'Sweet Boy'; Jonathan Cape Ltd, for William Plomer, 'The Playboy of the Demi-world', 'Ganymede', from *Collected Poems*; the author, for Ralph Pomeroy, 'A Tardy Epithalamium', 'The Leather Bar'; W. W. Norton and Co. Inc., for Adrienne Rich, poems I, XII, XVI from 'Twenty-one Love Poems', from *The Dream of a Common Language, Poems 1974–1977*; the translator, for Joanna Richardson (trans.), Baudelaire, 'Women Damned'; Curtis Brown Ltd, for Victoria Sackville-West, 'Butterflies', from *The Land*; G. T. Sassoon Esq. and Viking Press Inc., for Siegfried Sassoon, 'At Daybreak', from *Collected Poems*; David Higham Associates Ltd, for Dorothy L. Sayers (trans.), Dante, *Inferno*, Canto XV; Penguin Books Ltd, for W. G. Sheppherd (trans.), 12:205, from *The Greek Anthology*; the author, for David R. Slavitt, 'In the Seraglio'; Faber and Faber and Random House, for Stephen Spender, 'How strangely this sun', 'To T.A.R.H.', from *Collected Poems, 1928–1953*; Panjandrum Books, for Jack Spicer, 'Central Park West', from Winston Leyland (ed.), *Angels of the Lyre*; Random House, for Carol North Valhope and Ernst Morowitz (trans.), Stefan George, 'The Lyre Player', from *Stefan George: Poems*; Constable and Co. and W. W. Norton and Co. Inc., for Helen Waddell (trans.), 'To Ausonius', 'Written on an Island off the Breton Coast', 'Lament for the Cuckoo', 'To His Friend in Absence', 'David's Lament for Jonathan', from *Medieval Latin Lyrics*; Penguin Books Ltd, for Peter Whigham (trans.), 12:23, 12:41, 12:127, 12:133, 12:159, 12:164, from *The Greek Anthology*; New Directions Ltd, for Tennessee Williams, 'Life Story', from *In the Winter of Cities*; Perigree Books, for Fran Winant, 'Christopher Street Liberation Day'; S. A. Woodley, for F. S. Woodley, 'The Beautiful', 'I love this boy', from *A Crown of Friendship*; the author, for Ian Young, 'Double Exposure', 'Honi Soit'.

Every effort has been made to trace copyright holders but the publishers would be interested to hear from anyone not here acknowledged.

Introduction

This is a collection of poems by and about gay people. It ranges in time and place from classical Athens to contemporary New York. It ranges in tone and content from celebration to satire. While the collection can, I hope, be read for pleasure, I would like to think of it also as a record, a history of the different ways in which homosexual people have been seen and have seen themselves. Only if we know something about the past is there a chance we can do something about the future. To that extent I would like to think of the voices collected here as voices of encouragement.

Our history is usually looked on as a history of persecution. Within limits, this is true. But it is important to define our terms, important to realize, for example, that the word 'homosexual' has no exact equivalent in the major founding languages of our culture: Greek, Latin and Hebrew. It was invented in 1869, in that period when, having hacked a limb from the body of love, it was thought necessary to call it diseased. The modern 'homosexual', when legally defined and clinically separated, is a Victorian bogeyman seeking a new identity. Nonetheless, persecution of gay people and gay love is not a recent phenomenon. Minorities have been picked on by emperors and street boys since the beginning of time. A change in the law in sixth-century Byzantium is a paradigm case.

Homosexual love was first universally outlawed by the Emperor Justinian in 533 A.D. This move was sanctioned in the usual way of Byzantine emperors by an appeal to the Christian faith. But the church, it seems, did not lend him its support. Perhaps the clerics realized that the law was not part of a morality drive but of a campaign against the Emperor's old enemies, including themselves. The Empress certainly used it as such. She indicted a youth who had been rude about her, dragged him from the altar where he was seeking sanctuary, and then, without benefit of trial, ordered him to be castrated. No doubt Theodora was as pleased as her husband to have so ready a way of removing her critics, but when she tried the ruse again the judges refused to hear the charges, and, after the young man's release, the city celebrated with a public holiday.

A number of interesting points emerge from this: first, the fact that the Emperor was more interested in revenge than morality. The law was one of several passed against Samaritans, astrologers, heretics and pagans, and it was used very largely to punish those known to be 'guilty' *before* the law was made. It was an act of expediency which, to raise money and eliminate critics, made gay love, as Gibbon observed, 'the crime of those to whom no crime could be imputed'. Throughout, in so far as the origins of prejudice can be traced, gay love has been accepted or despised to the degree to which it supports (or at least does not threaten) the values of those in charge. It is for this reason that gay people must be politically aware.

Ancient Greece

The ancient Greeks had neither a word for a 'homosexual' nor a belief that their priests should interpret a highly proscriptive and super-natural sexual code. What they did recognize was that many people prefer now members of their own sex, now those of the other, and, having recognized the fact, they celebrated it.

But we should avoid too sentimental a reverence for gay life in ancient Athens. To be sure, all around them their art glorified the body and their poets and philosophers wrote vividly of homosexual passion. They believed the father of their gods transformed himself into an eagle to abduct a beautiful youth. The pots in their houses celebrated scenes of gay courtship and sex. One of these, preserved in Oxford, shows a bearded man imperiously erect and holding a slim youth between his thighs. There is a look of intense pleasure on the man's face as the willing boy puts his arm round his neck and allows his genitals to be fondled; but, significantly. the boy himself is not excited. This, and the position the two have adopted, tell us a great deal.

While the Greeks regarded certain forms of homosexual love as perfectly natural, they were little interested in mutual love between people of the same age and gender. For them, the legitimate, the socially acceptable form of gay love, involved a man and a youth: the *erastes* and the *eromenos*. It was the sort of relationship they could tolerate, indeed promote and transform into great art, precisely because it enhanced the values of their ruling elite: the well-to-do, Athenian male citizen. Because boys (along with women, slaves and foreigners) did not possess the all-important qualification of citizen status, the relation was absolutely not one between equals. The god of love, as Plato declared, was in the lover, the *erastes*, but he did not possess the youth at all. Falling in love with a beautiful *eromenos*, what the man prized were his budding strength, his speed, endurance and masculinity, in other words the values most to be prized in a land of fragmented and aggressive city states where strong personal relationships were found perhaps less in the family than between active, military men and the boys who would replace them in the *polis*.

These up and coming warriors were not expected to initiate sex. When Strato declared that it was not worth going through an elaborate charade to chat up one Menèdemos, he was doing more than labelling the boy a tart. He was satirizing him as one who was trying to subvert the whole ethos of love between males; and, incidentally, he was exposing the lad to grave dangers.

The proper response of the *eromenos* to his man was one of compassion, chastity and eventual compliance. After a long period of courtship in which the *eromenos* tested his lover's sincerity by refusing his favours, he might, because he admired him and had grown to feel rather sorry for him, allow him the sex for which he was so obviously burning. But the boy himself should not in the least enjoy this. Cold sober, as Xenophon declared, he was to look on the other as drunk with desire. To relieve him was a deed of kindness, an act of respect to an older and a better, but to have relished or initiated too passive a role would have been womanly and so wrong. Hence the boy in the vase painting: affectionate yet unexcited.

But the picture tells us more. It is a common misconception that male love centres around sodomy. While this may be an attendant pleasure, it is evidently not what is happening here. And with good reason. The Greeks believed that while an active gay role is natural, males have no inherent desire to be the passive partner. To allow oneself to be sodomized was the extreme expression of passivity and hence of disgrace. Males who willingly let themselves be sodomized could be deprived of their citizen status, and that in a society where citizenship meant everything. Provided he did not mind being classed with the powerless, with women, slaves and foreigners, there was little to prevent an Athenian citizen from becoming a prostitute; but the boy in the vase is not in this category. His acceptance of intercrural sex, the fact that he is standing, the flaccid state of his small genitals, all these indicate a youth of moral and physical excellence. The picture is a model of the 'perfect' relationship.

The *erastes* may first have seen his boy in the gymnasium. It was a recognized and obvious place for contact, and a number of poems from *The Greek Anthology* relate to the sort of things that happened there. Obviously, the special interest of the *erastes* would fairly quickly become a matter of common knowledge and he was expected to behave himself with decorum. After first sight, modest ogling, presents and poems were expected to follow. It is courtship's oldest pattern.

The poems of courtship that remain to us are highly attractive: witty, sometimes smutty, hopelessly romantic or hopelessly despairing, they offer a picture of a way of love at once formal yet fresh every time. There are poems of pursuit, poems about eyes flickering over bodies on a hot afternoon. A number of the epigrams describe glimpses of the *eromenos* (in the street or getting out of the bath, perhaps), spasms of desire in the long pursuit. Others describe despair at parting or rejection. One anonymous poet gets drunk and goes to serenade his boy. Meleager, visited in dreams by a vision of perfect beauty, writhes in divine anguish and learns he is a man.

But such decorum was not always the case. Fights seem to have broken out in the gymnasia, while the poem by Strato on page 70 makes it clear that there were ways of taking advantage of familiar situations. Evidently the father in this poem was a worldly wise man, perfectly aware of the abuses that went on, but it is doubly difficult for us to imagine how the situation could have been tolerated at all. First, we are led to think that those whom we put in a position of trust over our children commit a serious offence if they break that bond. The Greek ideal of an older male's combining a benevolent and more or less educational interest in a boy with an overt and accepted sexual one fills most people with horror. On the other hand, we are so used to thinking of gay relationships as abnormal, particularly when one of the partners is very young, that to imagine ourselves back into the Greek model is exceptionally difficult. And again, despite such relationships being traditional, even conventional, the boy involved put himself at some risk. Too liberal with his favours and he could be ranked and perhaps condemned as a prostitute. Too sexually responsive and his manhood was in peril. And what about presents? Surely there is a dangerously fine distinction between accepting these and being bought.

Perhaps the traditional nature of these affairs brought with it a certain inertia, while discretion, for obvious reasons, was much prized. The educational ideal was, at its purest, a noble one. No doubt many boys derived much from it. But how far the ideal was preserved, how far a teenager, a boy avid for experience, could truly maintain the modesty and discretion required, it is difficult to say. Perhaps, in the end, the ruling classes of Athens veiled their pleasures with a double standard. On the secrets of the bedroom History modestly closes the door.

Rome

Or at least she usually does. The gossiping Naevolus of Juvenal's Ninth Satire forces it a little ajar; not, of course, that we should take the details of his plight as a serious personal history. What he shows us is Juvenal's view of a Rome gone to ruin, Nero's Rome and that of Vespasian, Domitian and Nerva.

It is interesting that Juvenal shows virtually no contempt for Naevolus' way of life: interesting, but not surprising. Juvenal condemns him neither for being gay (or predominantly gay) nor for being a gigolo. Sexual morality was, for the Roman male, largely a matter of personal preference and, as at all times, convention. Gay prostitution, for example, had become so wholly an accepted part of normal life that not only was it taxed but the boys were given an annual public holiday. Marriages between men seem to have been recognized, and the section included here from Catullus' *Hymeneal* shows that young bachelors kept male slaves for their sexual release as a matter of course. Interestingly, Catullus seems to have regarded heterosexuality as more 'grown up', but the tenderness such relationships could inspire is charmingly evoked in the poem by Statius.

The Romans preserved a Greek indifference to the gender of those they loved. Horace moved with guiltless urbanity from boy to girl, while Virgil could write of the love of Nisus and Euryalus (too long for inclusion here) as an example of heroic patriotism. His second Eclogue is an exquisite picture of an affair that happened to be gay. Nevertheless, like the Greeks, the passively inclined citizen was, in earlier periods at least, viewed with disgust and despised for his aura of supposed political impotence. A man's slave remained his slave, his preferences were unimportant; but to refer to Catullus again, while it was highly amusing and no doubt enjoyable to sodomize the boy he surprised laying a girl (page 80), to threaten the adult Aurelius with the same was to threaten to humiliate him utterly.

But the easy-going, pick-your-own-morality way of the Romans led to famous excess, and not only under the Empire. Cicero mentions juries being bribed by the offer of noble youths, and we know from the historian Polybius that these could be extremely expensive. Yet it is the later period, the age of Martial and Juvenal, which, more richly documented, seems to offer us the Romans' distinctive contribution.

Juvenal and Martial, both of Spanish origin and friends, moved through a world wracked with disillusion and titivated by excess, a world made the more bitter to them by their poverty.

The older Martial is a various poet and, carefully used, a mine of information. Some of his epigrams, that to Dindymus for example, are lovely, delicate things; but Martial was able to write not only with affecting sentiment but with a coarse-grained and salacious wit which is probably more significant for its cleverness than its moral outrage.

This is not the case with Juvenal, the greatest poet of righteous indignation. A dream of ancient rectitude forced him to pour scorn on coterie faggots, effeminates and lesbians. In Satires Two, Six and Nine he gives a clear view of this but conveys also the impression that Roman culture was both protracted and diffuse. Many elements in Roman poetry and Roman attitudes to gay love were imported from the Greeks, and the similarities between the gay poems of both cultures are obvious. But Juvenal in particular gives us a vivid picture (comparatively rare in European poetry) of a densely populated, highly differentiated city. For him, as for Martial, gay life was chiefly an urban one, and at the close of Satire Nine we are shown how gay people are necessarily attracted to cities. But for Juvenal, the city of Rome had turned her back on a simple past and her modern vices were essentially those of a complex metropolis. Rome was no more the city that stood for rectitude, for a whole way of life, and those who abused her through gay sex wrongly conceived abused a whole morality. Just as in Satire Nine he is not outraged by Naevolus *per se*, so in Satire Two Juvenal is horrified less at homosexual marriage than at the pathic role of a Roman aristocrat, one who nonetheless played his part in great public functions. For Juvenal the juxtaposition is incongruous, irreconcilable. Gay love, wrongly conceived and wrongly lived, shows a society gone to the dogs, and for all its strength as rhetoric, the appeal that closes this section, the appeal to an old and manly Rome, is horribly in the mode of queer-bashers in all ages.

Lesbians in Classical Poetry

Both Martial and Juvenal write scathingly of lesbians. They seem to have been people the Romans did not find easy to accept. Lesbian activities may have carried with them a suggestion of adultery and the elder Seneca recommended that such women should be executed if caught *in flagrante*, a procedure quite legal when it involved heterosexual adultery. But it is clear also that lesbianism deeply upset the views of both Martial and Juvenal as to how women should behave. Both created cartoon images of the 'butch dyke' with a slightly hysterical, almost zoological fascination. They were horrified by the thought that such women could rouse the sexuality of others like a man. Martial can only envisage some bizarre form of clitoral intercourse, Juvenal imagines himself watching with horrified amazement a scene which he describes as searingly pornographic – for men. Simple heterosexual concepts of active and passive could be transferred to love between men because, legitimately practised, the passive partner was no more important than a woman: he was a boy, a slave, a foreigner. When it came to love between women, the inappropriate use of the same model with its emphasis on dominance and penetration could only rouse horror or the sniggers of a freak show.

Ovid is particularly important in this respect. He could write with great charm about the love of gods for boys, but when it came to lesbians the absence of a penis resulted in a Whitehall farce.

The story of Iphys and Ianthee takes place in one of those poor rural communities where surplus women are a luxury. The mother, reluctant to kill her daughter (who has already been given a name appropriate to either gender), is told by Isis to preserve the child and all will be well. Iphys is brought up as a boy. Puberty occurs and she falls in love with a girl. Iphys goes through an agony of thwarted gender expectation. She is unnatural, horrible, inadequate. Ovid does not deny the force of the love but cruel nature, it seems, denies it a means of expression. What can be done? A unique case, this calls for special remedies. Mother and daughter go back to the temple where the kindly Isis provides muscles, beard and a brand new penis. Armed with these, especially the latter, all is now for the best in the best possible of all worlds: the phallocentric one.

To be fair to Ovid, he was not being serious. This is men's-room wit and his literary interest was paradox. Nonetheless, the belief that love without a penis cannot be love at all is fundamental to the history of lesbianism and only in the most fragmentary Greek remains do we find what are probably vestiges of a more mature attitude.

Alkman may be expressing these in remains too incomplete for this book, but in the remaining scraps of Sappho we have the voice of a woman and a poet who as far as one can see (and that is not very far) showed love between women as passionate, sensuous, and, perhaps, a relation between equals. Sappho is, however, a very early poet, and while it is tempting to make too much of what remains, it is important to note that no literature whatsoever from the later period celebrates lesbian love. Not even the comedies satirize it. The subject may well have been taboo in Greece (given the lives of women in classical Athens it is unlikely to have been forgotten), but it is clear that while both the Latin and the Greek authors could, under certain circumstances, celebrate love between males, that between women became for the poets a matter at once so bizarre and so troubling that it had to be suppressed under rumbling disapproval or sniggering laughter.

The Making of Prejudice

Ausonius is a key figure: a Christian and a classicist, a collector of pornography and the beloved of a saint. He seems to have united in himself some of the contradictory strands of his complex age: the fourth century. After the era of excess came both a narrowing of attitudes and the increasing absolutism of an empire run largely by provincials. The pleasures of sex were played down. In their place came an emphasis on duty, on procreation and a separation of body and soul to the detriment of the former. The legal status of gay marriage was denied in 342.

Into this world Christianity was born, absorbing elements of other creeds to become the means by which a narrowed morality spread across Europe. Anti-gay attitudes began to be formulated by desert fathers who associated it with child-molesting, paganism and pleasure. Looking to the apocryphal *Epistle of Barnabas*, they learned that to eat hares made one a paedophile, while hyenas (which, as everyone knows, change sex every year) made one an adulterer and a homosexual. Such notions passed into manuals of popular science just as the crucial 'Alexandrian rule' that moral sex is purely procreative passed into handbooks on child-rearing. While looking at wildlife, the concept of an ideal Nature was worked out. In sum, the theological ammunition that was to be fired at homosexuals from the thirteenth century to the early twentieth was here being created and stockpiled.

But for the moment it was not used, at least not widely. Ausonius (possibly from the effects of too much hare pie) wrote his lovely sixty-second epigram; the man in whom he inspired such love, Saint Paulinus of Nola, wrote him the poem on page 111. And indeed for the next 800 years the clerics' attitude towards homosexuality was distinctly positive. Alcuin, light of the court of Charlemagne, wrote poems of strong gay sentiment to his pupils whom he knew by such pet names as 'Cuckoo'. In a letter to an absent bishop he fantasized about flying to cover him with passionate kisses. For gays at least, the Dark Ages were not pitch black.

And from the tenth through the twelfth century, with the rebirth of cities and the wonderful eroticizing of life that broke like sudden spring, there was a major flowering of European gay subculture. While the Troubadours (including a lesbian one) sang in the courts of Provence, love in the monasteries became a cornerstone of theology. There are love letters to males among the correspondence of Anselm, and it was he who prevented the first anti-gay legislation being passed in England. He became Archbishop of Canterbury and a saint. Another saint and Englishman, Aeldred of Rievaulx, made gay love the basis of monastic life. While he did not wholly approve of such relationships being genital, he did not forbid them from being so because 'such great joy is experienced' in them. It was he who wrote of Christ and Saint John that 'the closer they were, the more copiously did the fragrant secrets of the heavenly marriage impart the sweet smell of spiritual chrism to their virgin love'.

It was against a world as accepting as this, a world in which such poems as *Spirit of Venus* were widely copied and sung, a world in which hunting was for clerics a more serious sin than sodomy, that *Ganymede and Helen* was written. Couched in the form of a love debate, the poem is an example of a popular medieval form. And this in itself is significant. Evidently the work, which is found in copies from the Vatican to Cambridge, was produced in a world almost as indifferent to gender as the classical one.

Almost, but not quite. Ganymede's beauty is frankly admitted and enjoyed, he upholds the idea that sex is for pleasure and declares that many great clerics, men who arbitrate morals, are not averse to loving boys. The argument gets heated and many familiar gambits are used before Ganymede is straightened out and married off. Homosexuality goes with prostitution, says Helen, with callow adolescence, it is unnatural, non-procreative and, to clinch the matter (when used a second time), a waste of sperm. Heterosexuality wins out. Nature, Reason and Providence wished it to do so. The poem is not to be read as pro-gay, but what is so positive about it is its suggestion of a tolerant and sophisticated audience, of a group of people who were prepared to listen.

What went wrong? Why in the last fifty years of the thirteenth century did gay love change from being a cornerstone of monasticism to a capital crime for which in England hanging was too good and burying alive was recommended?

The causes are difficult to ascertain and are probably many. It is important to remember that poems from the heyday of tolerance were those of a relatively small, highly educated and international elite. They are representative not of the majority but of the best. Lower down the scale, those with a different sort of influence were trying to get things done. In 1102 the Council of London wanted to make the public aware of how serious 'sodomy' was (evidently they weren't) and to insist on its being confessed as a sin. This was the edict Anselm quashed, declaring, rather oddly for an archbishop, that sodomy was so widespread that nobody was embarrassed by it anyway. This argues a certain indifference to homosexuals on the part of the people, but it was an indifference born of ignorance, something that would soon be changed.

Given an artillery of theological argument, some popular prejudice and, in certain quarters at least, a willingness to act, what was needed to pervert a vague tolerance to fanatical hatred? The answer was intellectual change and a common enemy. The thirteenth-century Church had both.

Saint Thomas Aquinas gave the High Middle Ages its definitive theology. In so doing he fixed the Catholic Church's teaching on gay love: it is more than wrong, it is to be ranked with cannibalism, bestiality and eating dirt. Such extremism was really no more than a concession to popular bigotry, no more than the official wording of points made a century before in *A Perverse Custom*, that anti-gay poem read and copied from Oxford to Leipzig. Homosexuality is shown here to be against nature and worse than bestial since animals do not go in for it. (They do.) It is unreasonable, non-procreative, and particularly despised by God. It is a heresy and a passport to Hell.

While such attitudes had a long evolution, it is the political use of them, their sudden galvanizing, that is so significant. Gays were now being violently attacked because their sort of love was practised by the two great enemies of the closing ranks of Christian society: Turks and heretics. After the failure of repeated crusades, goggle-eyed Europeans were told of how beautiful Christian boys were bought up by Saracens aflame with lust; of how, oblivious to human dignity, the Infidel lived with 'effeminates' in open marriage. (That Moorish gay poetry of the Middle Ages was exquisite is illustrated by the two examples included here.) As for the heretics, weeping and silent papal legates were shown the fleshless arms, the skinned belly and testicles of Jacques de Molay, Grand Master of the powerful, wealthy and supposedly homosexual Templars.

The stockpile of arguments had been turned on the Church's enemies and the souls of the straight had been saved.

Renaissance and Enlightenment

Rather than wither as the love that dared not speak its name, gay emotion rechristened itself 'Friendship'. One of the literary traditions of the Middle Ages, it received support from the classical concept of *amicitia* and found its Renaissance prose-poet in Montaigne. It was he who wrote of an 'inexplicable and fatal force' in his love for Estienne de la Boëtie, a love which Montaigne was careful to differentiate from the pederasty of the Greeks and to show as that between mature equals. Englishmen wrote of an affection between themselves that was 'neither separated at bourde, nor severed at bed'. It is highly likely that such relationships were sometimes genital, but if they were, this side to them was not discussed. Classical Friendship gave such affairs a conventional safety but they were fed by other sources, as the passage from Cowley shows.

The *Davideis* is no great shakes as poetry, but it is interesting that Cowley (an ambitious poet) should have gone some way with writing an epic that included a gay theme. Classical convention sanctioned this, of course, but the principal reason he could do so was that he saw no necessary connection between love and sex. Indeed, the friendship of David and Jonathan is so beautiful to him precisely because it is so 'pure'. The couple are compared to doves and share a relation of equality superior to both marriage and courtship. Freed from sex, they are like angels in a Christian and neo-Platonic Heaven. In post-Freudian days it is difficult not to be a little sceptical of this: difficult but important if we are truly to value the very genuine ideals of certain poets writing on gay themes. We may think of such passion as sublimation and perhaps look down on it; Michelangelo called it love and looked Heavenwards.

Because by convention such poetry did not discuss genital sex and relied instead on traditions of love centred around Friendship, beauty and the soul, it could afford to be relatively indifferent to gender. Michelangelo, Shakespeare, Barnfield, Gray and Platen could write about males neither because in real life gender choice did not matter (as far as sex was concerned it mattered terribly) nor because they were 'out' homosexuals (the term is meaningless applied to them). They could write as they did because their literary interest was the religion of love rather than the pursuit of sex, contact with the soul rather than the genitals. In this respect it is interesting that the poems they wrote to males are mainly sonnets, for the sonnet is pre-eminently the form for such ideal love from Petrarch onwards.

Hence the inclusion of Shakespeare. All the great commonplaces of love are here: presence and absence, youth and age, jealousy, disillusion and the belief that love somehow partakes of eternity. Against these, all poems are measured.

But this was not the only form of gay awareness in the Renaissance. The charm of Barnfield's sonnets is more obviously sensuous, while the passage from Marlowe's *Hero and Leander* is a picture of attempted rape. Heywood's poem is a clever send-up; the two verses by Aretino are jokes by the first modern master of pornography. But it is in the Latin epigrams that we find elements of all these combined: sensuality, classicism and wit. These are the poems of a highly educated coterie at once suave and outrageous, and, in the case of Poliziano, flippant yet tragic.

Poliziano was a leading platonist who got sacked for not being sufficiently platonic with the boys of Lorenzo de' Medici. No doubt it served him right, but he was lucky. Drayton's account of the love of Edward II and Gaveston is a picture of what could happen. Love between two men is frankly celebrated here, celebrated with the beauty of epithet that came so naturally to the Elizabethans. What is celebrated however is 'Virtue': emotion and states of the soul. Its opposite, 'Lust', is the cause of the couple's downfall and the consequent political confusion of the country.

This association of homosexuality with political unrest is persistent in Renaissance literature. We find it strongly marked in Agrippa d'A'ubigné where the notorious court of Henri III, its absolutism and gender confusion, are directly linked to the tragic state of France. The theme is repeated in *Sodom: or the Quintessence of Debauchery*, a piece of erotica from the court of Charles II and close in time to the writing of the *Davideis*. Here gay sex is again equated with political absolutism because both are unnatural. In all times and places gay people have had a close and often painful relation to politics.

They have also tried to create some form of subculture. Charles Churchill's picture of cruising in eighteenth-century London, a satire written from the most sexist and reactionary position (as the best satire often is), gives a jaundiced view of a capital in which many familiar traits appear: cruising areas, gay bars (there were about twenty of these around Covent Garden and Lincoln's Inn), gay clubs and gay brothels. It seems also that another sign of a coherent minority group was developing: a common slang.

But all this, of course, was for men. Because it viewed love between women as sexless, society condoned and even encouraged lesbianism. The virtuous love of men celebrated in Cowley finds its female voice in Katherine Philips.

And it is a voice of some poetic force. The love poems of the 'matchless Orinda' use the conventions of the day as it is only natural they should. What is so refreshing is that one remarkably able woman applied them to another. The verses to Lucasia transcend mere historical interest. They develop what is called there 'friendship's mystery' to offer the picture of a whole world centred around the love of women. It was a world of great beauty, great dignity. Evidently it was a world of inspiration, too. The second stanza of *Orinda to Lucasia* ranks with the best late Metaphysical verse, and in Philips's time this status was acknowledged.

What was not acknowledged was an equal status for women in general. In a society confident that the full expression of love required the men who were so keen to preserve the market price of chastity, intelligent and sensitive women were not only obliged to develop relations between themselves but were, if they were surplus, encouraged to do so. There was no stigma attached to such love. It was harmless and it was convenient. In novel after eighteenth-century novel we see how such affairs could be passionate and deep. No doubt for many women sold into loveless marriage such friendship was a lifeline to sanity. That it could absorb other fashionable traits not only gave it breadth but a body of values to be developed and enriched.

Danebury is an epitome of this. A poem of sentiment, of fashionably refined and generous feeling, it has also its full complement of the Gothick: war, hostile Danes and a hermit in the wood. Deeply in love with each other, Emma and Elfrida's idyll is lived far from the madding crowd until war comes and Elfrida's father goes off to fight. Resolved to defend his patriarchal values with her life (a not insignificant matter), Elfrida is wounded by an arrow meant for him. Emma, who has meanwhile rushed to be at her friend's side, sucks this poison out, determined to die in Elfrida's place. Joy and pain are woven pretty fine here, but the dilemma is solved by the friendly hermit who has been sent by God and is armed with medical knowledge. Heaven clearly approves of such virtuous and heroic friendship, approves, that is, of its patriotism and dutiful daughter-hood. Never far from politics, a gay relationship is seen here as supporting the *status quo*.

Danebury is more interesting as a document than as a poem, but that such relationships as it portrays were not merely conventional is clear from the lives of the Ladies of Llangollen: Sarah Ponsonby and Eleanor Butler, who ran off with each other and created a very real arcadian bliss for themselves in which they were visited by characters as diverse as Josiah Wedgwood and Lady Caroline Lamb. Wordsworth wrote a poem on these 'sisters in love', Anna Seward wrote others.

Anna Seward was a gay woman whose works were edited by Sir Walter Scott. The great love of her life was Honoria Sneyd, a woman nine years younger, with whom she shared a passionately celebrated friendship broken by Honoria's eventual marriage. She still felt the cruelty of this many years later. The sonnet on page 180 is a bitter torrent from a gay person condemned to loneliness by all-powerful heterosexual norms.

But the finest poet of lesbian friendship is one of the great English language poets: Emily Dickinson. Her passion for Sue Gilbert was poured into her letters and her poems. Both are the works of a lover and a genius.

So unique, so absolute, was Emily Dickinson's vision that she forced language into a new pattern and created a combination of paradox and physical acuteness of imagery that is without parallel except among others of the very great. Her language is a scalpel. It lays bare the finest nerves of love. With her, the oldest images, nesting birds, bridehood, June, are transmogrified. 'Her sweet Weight on my Heart a Night' is at once sensuous and dryly certain. A poem like 'The Stars are old, that stood for me' has that fresh, slightly ironic perception of what has always been which is so pre-eminently Emily Dickinson's. Adoring, physical and absolute in their analysis, these difficult, awesome poems express a radical syntax of the heart. We do not read them to remain unchanged.

It is clear from such poems, these lives and novels, not only that gay relations between women were looked on unbashfully but that (and this is the significant qualification), because they did not threaten a heterosexual male world, they could be absorbed, tolerated and seen as harmless and even useful. They could be passionate and were inspiring. Why, we must ask ourselves, did they become interpreted as a threat, a rent in the fabric of society?

The Making of the 'Homosexual'

Women in the novels of Friendship cry out to each other for relief, for escape from men. In the poems of nineteenth-century decadence their cries echo hollowly back. Baudelaire, Swinburne, Aleister Crowley and, to a certain extent, Pierre Louys, present lesbians as passionate but deprived. Luxuriously sinful, they are a delight to the voyeur. And the voyeur, of course, was a man.

To certain men lesbianism is deeply erotic, particularly when coupled with sin, death and destruction. Many lesbian scenes take place in Hell or the brothels and boudoirs that became its social equivalent. Torrid sex combines here with moral horror (it is difficult to decide which is the more silly), and the general emphasis is on social degradation, sado-masochism and the alluring sight of infinite passion forever unfulfilled. What had been latent in the Romans but was little discussed in the periods between (except as a joke or an aphrodisiac) becomes here a heightened thrill. It is the penis myth combined with fashionable titillation and evident terror.

If lesbians are shown in these works to be unable to get full satisfaction without a penis, it is also clear that they did not want the penis of the poet. Condemned to sterility, they were nonetheless reckoned to know esoteric techniques that were sexier than heterosex. Swinburne's Faustine is an adept in these. Yet what would she give the man who offered her the 'real' thing? Poison. Obsessed with power, with wealth and pleasure, the modern woman would kill him off. In other words she would castrate him. This, for male readers, is the *frisson* of the whole poem.

For his own period at least we may adopt a Freudian model and see the fear of symbolic castration in many reactions to the emerging 'New Woman' with her demands for education, work and political equality; her commitment to emasculating the phallocentric universe.

But something was joined to this which is of the greatest importance not only to lesbians but to all gay people: the creation of new psychological theories which categorized gay love for the first time and found it a disease. The sickness was named 'homosexuality'. The approach of the 'scientists' who coined it was often as sensational as that of the novelists who in a number of instances provided them with their inspiration and even their case histories. The two most influential, Krafft-Ebing and Havelock Ellis, declared lesbianism to be a 'functional sign of degeneration' and related it to nervous disorders and psychotic behaviour in a manner which, about as scientifically valid as Swinburne's poem, shows less art and no imagination. The trouble was, of course, that Krafft-Ebing, Havelock Ellis and later Sigmund Freud were tremendously influential. By 1895, less than ten years after the death of Emily Dickinson, one partner of an American lesbian menage was writing of love between women as an 'abnormal condition'. It says a great deal that a highly intelligent woman, a university teacher, could so wholly internalize these new ways of thought and make the enemy without the enemy within.

By the time of Baroness von Putkammer, this internalizing of a guilt that is nonetheless strongly defied, a Swinburnian sadism and a sense of eternal suffering, are the bases of poems by lesbians themselves. Their lust nails them to crosses, their passion is a scarlet bloom of sin in the gardens of winter. Driven into a harsh world, priests will pray for them in vain and nice people will avoid them.

For once the position was little better for men. After the Wilde scandal it was worse.

The trial of Oscar Wilde took place in 1895, ten years after the passing of the Labouchère amendment which made all gay acts between males 'grossly indecent'. Gross indecency remains to this day an ill-defined term, but so hysterical was legal and political thinking that men could be sentenced to death under buggery laws for practising fellatio; in the House, Peel had to refer to homosexuals by a Latin circumlocution; in court at the Wilde committal, the magistrate (who had presumably seen a few murderers in his time) stated that there was no worse crime than that of which Wilde was accused. It was into this sort of world that new definitions of the 'homosexual' (derived largely from the study of other 'criminal' types) were thrown for general use.

The pioneers who tried to do something about this were very brave men. One of them, John Addington Symonds, was also a fine poet. In common with Richard Burton, Havelock Ellis (far more mature in his attitude to gay men than to lesbians) and Edward Carpenter, Symonds cavilled at Victorian prudery and worked hard at the history of gay people to prove that despite repression they have existed at all times and in all places, and to show them further as neither pathological nor effeminate. Finally he tried to disseminate his findings and feelings. For Symonds this was the most difficult part of the process, and his reluctance is understandable in an age when the alternative to the closet was often the cell. Many of his poems were printed in limited and often anonymous editions, but for all that they are fine works. The close of *Ithocles* is truly moving.

The Victorian pioneers were united in admiration for Walt Whitman, who seemed to combine radical innocence with a directness that made him the epitome of what they were seeking: the healthy homosexual. While they and their contemporaries felt 'doomed by . . . timidity and ignorance to a repression which amounts to death', Whitman appeared as a figure gloriously uninhibited. His democratic spirit, his expansiveness, were widely written about; but when Symonds at length asked Whitman about his gayness he received a dusty answer. Whitman knew himself a prophet, he did not feel called on to be a martyr.

The left-wing appeal of Whitman is clear in the work of Edward Carpenter, a social and sexual visionary (and, incidentally, the editor of the first major modern anthology of gay verse). In *Towards Democracy*, love between gays becomes a way of breaking down barriers of class, a form of real affection, a liberation of the spirit beyond roles forced by a capitalist society. It is a brave and potent vision of the happy body and contented soul. It was widely influential. Wholly uninfluential but more visionary and more physical are the poems of Ralph Chubb, whose works, laboriously but beautifully hand-illustrated, show at once a Blakeian delight in the body of joy and a cranky, increasingly sentimental emphasis on the liberating effect of sex with boys.

This is something often but by no means always denied in the poetry of boy love that had a sudden flowering in the work of the nineteenth-century Uranians. Much of their verse is guilt-ridden, apologetic and tedious. It is also deeply ambivalent. In a poet like John Barford there is at once a clear sexual interest and a resolute sublimation. Other poets worked the thinning vein of Friendship that had allowed Tennyson, the poet laureate, to write of one man's feeling for another that it is better to have loved and lost than never to have loved at all. For the diverse whole we can perhaps most usefully say that such variety does indeed prove Symonds's point about the irrepressible voice of the gay community even under the most adverse conditions.

Socialism, both the modern and the older handwoven-vegetarian type, was and continues to be a vital force in relieving these conditions. So does sheer protest. There is no more powerful nor angry a gay poem than *Don Leon*. The naturalness of homosexuality is asserted here (in the 1860s), and through the figure of Byron, romantic passion and sexual exploration are both described. The poem lashes a hypocritical England of half-hidden brothels and place-seeking politicians. It expresses the harmlessness of gay people and pours no inconsiderable scorn on the narrow-minded Victorianism that was to lead to the passing of the Labouchère amendment.

But just as the lesbian poets internalized guilt and reinforced their own suffering, so did many males. The best of Housman is bitter melancholy, anger at the arbitrariness of law and near despair in the face of irremediable gayness. From recalling Oscar Wilde, taunted as he was taken to prison, from a newspaper cutting about the suicide of a soldier, Housman created poems of terse, delicate anguish. His victims are diseased, brave, despairing souls closeted by the laws of God and man which the poet himself despised.

How the 'disease' may be caught is the subject of Rimbaud's *The Tortured Heart*, a description of rape (or imagined rape) in which the presiding fear is that such an outrage may have been enjoyable. A similar ambiguity is again clear both in the gay poems of Verlaine, Rimbaud's lover, and in the *Sonnet: To the Asshole* on which Rimbaud and Verlaine collaborated. But in these works there is a rage and relish that has little to do with gay liberation. These powerful poems are a defiant celebration of internalized guilt, a vigorous attempt to *épater le bourgeois* who, in Verlaine's case, may well have been chiefly himself.

True liberation, the breakdown of models of sickness and the celebration of the health and diversity of the whole body of love, is the work of this century. It must be our work.

Gay Today

The twentieth century has been more massively brutal to gay people than any other. It has also, very recently, been better informed and more humane. Thirty years (less than half a lifetime) separate the mass exterminations of Belsen from the first marches of Gay Lib. Our freedom, partial, perilously young and threatened on all sides, still has something of the adolescent's quest for a lifestyle. In that lie hope and great danger.

Among the century's greatest gay poems are those from the two world wars: Sassoon, Nichols and Owen wrote love poems to men that are wholly untroubled by gender. The same is true of Ackerley's *After the Blitz, 1941*, a masterpiece of pathos, one of the very greatest of gay love poems precisely because it is a love poem first and a gay poem second. Of course, the lost love, the thwarted joy that Ackerley mourns were wholly illegal. Gay men were still hemmed in by narrow legal and clinical pictures of 'homosexuals', were still seen as sick creatures to be forced into a schizophrenic life of public face and private torment, but by a sheer effort of poetic imagination Ackerley broke away from the furtive to write with a strength that needed no excuse. His poem is one solution to the great problem: the experience of love rather than the details of gender.

This is also central to Lorca's *Ode to Walt Whitman*.

It is interesting that Lorca, like the nineteenth-century English pioneers, turned to Whitman for his ideal. It is highly significant that he set Whitman in the exploited landscape of modern capitalism. Lorca's subject is love: the intuition of a natural repose, a fulfilment of the soul which is every person's unique quest in the shortness of life:

> Man may, if he wishes, lead his desire
> through the veins of the coral or celestial nudes.
> Love by the morning will be as the rocks. Time's
> but a sleeping breeze that creeps through the branches.

Indifference to the intuition of love is, for Lorca, the origin of the living-death capitalism of modern society. It is the origin of soul-destroying labour, of cities of the dead, of bankrupt trivialization and of war. But its most vicious product is the urban faggot, the self-emasculated gay cruising for high-octane thrills and living off nothing more nourishing than the gilded loneliness of cocktail bars. For Lorca, it is gay people such as these who are the most dangerous enemies of love. His observation is not without point.

Three other great gay poets, largely from the early part of the century, must also be mentioned. Cavafy, while still using the model of the gay 'disease', is a poet whose sophisticated directness and recreation of the numinous body of sex in sad surroundings voice the experiences of many. Seediness redeemed by remembered joy makes these works poems of an international stature. A lesser poet, Jean Cocteau, wrote a beautiful elegy to a sleeping boyfriend whom he knows he has lost. Waves of love and regret mingle in the poet's dream. This is a difficult poem of great insight, so different in its Mediterranean ethos from the darkened cell, the relished nightmare of our third poet, Jean Genet.

But for voices more typical of the post-war period, of Gay Lib and the freedom flowering of the sixties and early seventies, we must turn increasingly to America. In poems such as that by Michael Rumaker we have for the first time in centuries voices of the possibility of hope, a record of actions taken and freedoms won. These are poems discussing the ways of a new love freeing itself from sexism, from spurious scientific definition and the dreadful inheritance of an unreal guilt.

The verse by Fran Winant expresses much of the early spirit of this: its pride and protest, its joining of women's freedom to the movement as an inseparable part of gay rights and the radical freedom of the body of love.

The enormous energy of the American gay scene, its organization and diversity, created this freedom against the odds and by some-times violent protest. In the year previous to Winant's poem, in the Stonewall riot, harassed gays fought back against police raids and, as a result, the New York Gay Liberation Front was born. A similar group was founded in England in 1970 to develop the possibilities opened up by the eventual decriminalizing of male gay activities, possibilities limited to private acts for those adult males who happen to be over twenty-one.

It is these possibilities of diversity that recent gay poets celebrate as they write either about themselves and other gay people or against the deeply ingrained prejudice that still remains. Adrienne Rich has beautifully celebrated lesbian/feminist love. Judy Grahn has fought against oppression. Among the variety of men, Harold Norse has celebrated the physical aspects of love, Felice Picano and Ralph Pomeroy have written movingly about relationships, Thom Gunn has described as no other the atmosphere of a gay bar.

There is still an enormous amount to do: more freedoms to be won, more people to educate, more lifestyles to develop, more maturities to achieve. Much was gained in a period of affluence: we must guard against losing it in poverty. Gay freedom is young and youth is potent. It is also easily sold short. All the time we are subject to oppression we can and must band together, but in banding together we should avoid the lethal closets of the stereotype. True freedom does not lie in being a tolerated minority but in being seen and knowing ourselves as part of the whole and indivisible body of human love. I hope the poems collected here may be of some use in this task of keeping ourselves aware, developing and diverse.

For me, a gay poem is one that either deals with explicitly gay matters or describes an intense and loving relationship between two people of the same gender. In putting this anthology together I have tried to be as representative of these criteria as possible. But in the end this is a personal collection. I do not see that it could have been anything else. From an enormous amount of material, I have selected what I found most interesting, most pleasing. It follows that the book does not set out to be a canon of gay verse.

The title – *The Penguin Book of* Homosexual *Verse* – was agreed after much discussion. For some, 'homosexual' is an emotive term still loaded with implications of 'unnatural vice'; for others, 'gay' is seen as an effete and transitory usage. Lexicographically, both words are unsatisfactory: 'homosexual' is an ugly fusion of Greek and Latin, 'gay' threatens to narrow the range of a useful adjective. The associations of both words tend to make them poor historical tools, and European culture developed largely without either. Perhaps 'homoerotic' is the proper term here, but it is both unfamiliar and rather pompous.

In the Introduction I have used 'gay' and 'homosexual' interchangeably, first because I do so in conversation, secondly because I needed variety: a variety of sound and absolutely not one of sense. In the end, 'homosexual' was chosen for the title because it can be employed relatively neutrally, analytically, and has survived in acceptable liberal usage. 'Gay', being closer to slang, will, I suspect, date.

I have worked within the Western tradition because that is the one I know best. There are vast resources elsewhere, from the Babylonian *Epic of Gilgamesh*, the Arab cultures and the Far East. Not all of these have been translated, and where they have the pronouns have often been dishonestly changed. Even in the West much material has not been 'Englished', and there is more of my own work in this book than I would have wished. In many cases it was a question of translate it yourself or leave it out. All of the unacknowledged translations are my own. In other instances, where a number of translations do exist, I have gone not just for the most accurate but also for older versions. This not only removes too twentieth-century a bias, but in such charming cases as Creech's versions of Theocritus the translations are a witness to gay interests in other periods and hence an aspect of gay history.

In putting this collection together I have been greatly helped by others. My oldest friend, Rod Hall, suggested making this book when it was just a collection of photocopies in green folders. To Donald McFarlan who had the courage to commission and the professionalism to support this project I am especially grateful. I received much help from the bibliographies of Ian Young, Barbara Grier and Jeannette Foster. Timothy D'Arch Smith generously gave me copies of rare poems by Symonds and others. Alison Hennegan kindly offered the benefit not only of her wide scholarship but also of her insight and commitment to the gay movement. I was given access to Anthony Reid's remarkable collection of paedophiliana in his fine library at Lake Dawn. The staffs of both the University of London Senate House and the British Libraries gave their customarily courteous and efficient help.

Further reading

Boswell, John: *Christianity, Social Tolerance and Homosexuality: Gay People in Western Europe from the Beginning of the Christian Era to the Fourteenth Century*, University of Chicago Press, 1980.

Bray, Alan: *Homosexuality in Renaissance England*, Gay Men's Press, 1982.

Dover, K. J.: *Greek Homosexuality*, Harvard University Press, 1978; rept. Vintage Books, 1980.

Faderman, Lillian: *Surpassing the Love of Men: Romantic Friendship and Love Between Women from the Renaissance to the Present*, Junction Books, n.d.

Weeks, Jeffrey: *Coming Out: Homosexual Politics in Britain, from the Nineteenth Century to the Present*, Quartet Books, 1977.

HOMER
(between 850 and 1050 B.C.)

from *Iliad*, Book 23
lines 70–123

'The Ghost of Patroclus'

. . . great *Pelides*,[1] stretch'd along the Shore
Where dash'd on Rocks the broken Billows roar,
Lies inly groaning; while on either Hand
The martial *Myrmidons* confus'dly stand:
Along the Grass his languid Members fall,
Tir'd with his Chase around the *Trojan* Wall;
Hush'd by the Murmurs of the rolling Deep
At length he sinks in the soft Arms of Sleep.
When lo! the Shade before his closing Eyes
Of sad *Patroclus* rose, or seem'd to rise;
In the same Robe he living wore, he came,
In Stature, Voice, and pleasing Look, the same.
The Form familiar hover'd o'er his Head,   ⎞
And sleeps *Achilles*, (thus the Phantom said) ⎬
Sleeps my *Achilles*, his *Patroclus* dead?   ⎠
Living, I seem'd his dearest, tend'rest Care,
But now forgot, I wander in the Air:
Let my pale Corse the Rites of Burial know,
And give me Entrance in the Realms below:
Till then, the Spirit finds no resting place,
But here and there th' unbody'd Spectres chace
The vagrant Dead around the dark Abode,
Forbid to cross th' irremeable Flood.
Now give thy Hand; for to the farther Shore
When once we pass, the Soul returns no more.
When once the last Funereal Flames ascend,
No more shall meet, *Achilles* and his Friend,
No more our Thoughts to those we lov'd make known,
Or quit the dearest, to converse alone.
Me Fate has sever'd from the Sons of Earth,

---

1. Achilles

The Fate fore-doom'd that waited from my Birth:
Thee too it waits; before the *Trojan* Wall
Ev'n great and god-like Thou art doom'd to fall.
Hear then; and as in Fate and Love we joyn,
Ah suffer that my Bones may rest with thine!
Together have we liv'd, together bred,
One House receiv'd us, and one Table fed;
That golden Urn thy Goddess Mother gave
May mix our Ashes in one common Grave.
      And is it thou (he answers) to my Sight
Once more return'st thou from the Realms of Night?
Oh more than Brother! Think each Office paid,
Whate'er can rest a discontented Shade;
But grant one last Embrace, unhappy Boy!
Afford at least that melancholy joy.
      He said, and with his longing Arms essay'd
In vain to grasp the visionary Shade;
Like a thin Smoke he sees the Spirit fly,
And hears a feeble, lamentable Cry.
Confus'd he wakes; Amazement breaks the Bands)
Of golden Sleep, and starting from the Sands,   }
Pensive he muses with uplifted Hands.   )

[ALEXANDER POPE, 1720]

SAPPHO
(7th century B.C.)

42

I have had not one word from her

Frankly I wish I were dead.
When she left, she wept

a great deal; she said to
me, 'This parting must be
endured, Sappho. I go unwillingly.'

I said, 'Go, and be happy
but remember (you know
well) whom you leave shackled by love

'If you forget me, think
of our gifts to Aphrodite
and all the loveliness that we shared

'all the violet tiaras,
braided rosebuds, dill and
crocus twined around your young neck

'myrrh poured on your head
and on soft mats girls with
all that they most wished for beside them

'while no voices chanted
choruses without ours,
no woodlot bloomed in spring without song . . .'

[MARY BARNARD]

43

It was you, Atthis, who said

'Sappho, if you will not get
up and let us look at you
I shall never love you again!

'Get up, unleash your suppleness,
lift off your Chian nightdress
and, like a lily leaning into

'a spring, bathe in the water.
Cleis is bringing your best
purple frock and the yellow

'tunic down from the clothes chest;
you will have a cloak thrown over
you and flowers crowning your hair . . .

'Praxinoa, my child, will you please
roast nuts for our breakfast? One
of the gods is being good to us:

'today we are going at last
into Mitylene, our favorite
city, with Sappho, loveliest

'of its women; she will walk
among us like a mother with
all her daughters around her

'when she comes home from exile . . .'

But you forget everything

[MARY BARNARD]

93

Be kind to me

Gongyla; I ask only
that you wear the cream
white dress when you come

Desire darts about your
loveliness, drawn down in
circling flight at sight of it

and I am glad, although
once I too quarrelled
with Aphrodite
                to whom
I pray that you will
come soon

[MARY BARNARD]

SOLON
(*c.* 638–558 B.C.)

'Boys and Sport'

Blest is the man who loves and after early play
   Whereby his limbs are supple made and strong,
   Retiring to his house, with wine and song
Toys with a fair boy on his breast the livelong day!

[J. A. SYMONDS]

THEOGNIS
(*c.* 550 B.C.)

'To Kurnos'

   Lo, I have given thee wings wherewith to fly
Over the boundless ocean and the earth;
Yea, on the lips of many shalt thou lie
The comrade of their banquet and their mirth.
Youths in their loveliness shall make thee sound
Upon the silver lute's melodious breath;
And when thou goest darkling underground
Down to the lamentable house of death
Oh yet not then from honor shalt thou cease,
But wander, an imperishable name,
Kurnos, about the isles and shores of Greece!

[G. LOWES DICKINSON]

PINDAR
(*c.* 522–442 B.C.)

'Ode on Theoxenos'

O soul, 'tis thine in season meet,
To pluck of love the blossom sweet,

When hearts are young:
But he who sees the blazing beams,
The light that from *that* forehead streams,
    And is not stung: –
Who is not storm-tost with desire, –
Lo! he, I ween, with frozen fire,
Of adamant or stubborn steel,
Is forged in his cold heart that cannot feel.

Disowned, dishonoured, and denied
By Aphrodite glittering-eyed,
    He either toils
All day for gold, a sordid gain,
Or bent beneath a woman's reign,
    In petty broils,
Endures her insolence, a drudge,
Compelled the common path to trudge;
But I, apart from this disease,
Wasting away like wax of holy bees,

Which the sun's splendour wounds, do pine,
Whene'er I see the young-limbed bloom divine
Of boys. Lo! look you well; for here in Tenedos,
Grace and Persuasion dwell in young Theoxenos.

[J. A. SYMONDS]

EPIGRAMS FROM THE GREEK ANTHOLOGY
(*c.* 429 B.C.–A.D. 600)

PLATO

7,99

For Hekabé and the women of Ilion
Tears were fated from the day of their birth.
But in your moment of glorious triumph, Dion,
The Gods spilt all your far-flung hopes. Now earth
Cloaks you with civic honour in your hometown,
You who maddened my heart with love, my Dion!

[PETER JAY]

7, 100

All I said was – Alexis is gorgeous. Now
Everyone stares, ogles him everywhere.
Dear heart, why show the dogs a bone? You'll care
Later. Remember? Phaidros went that way too.

[PETER JAY]

7, 669

'Aster'

My star,[1] star-gazing? – if only I could be
The sky, with all those eyes to stare at you!

[PETER JAY]

7, 670

'Aster'

You were the morning star among the living:
But now in death your evening lights the dead.

[PETER JAY]

RHIANUS
12, 93

Most inexplicable the wiles of boys I deem,
Like to an endless labyrinth their strange charms seem;
Whene'er upon a lovely youth a glance I cast,
Entangled in the bird-lime beauty holds me fast.

Here Thèodòrus with his rounded body's grace,
And with the flower of his unsullied limbs and face
My fancy claims; then golden Theocles doth shine,
Though not full-grown, in matchless bloom of grace divine.

1. *Aster*: Greek for 'a star'

Yet if you Leptines in all his beauty viewed,
Your limbs like adamant would stay with footsteps glued,
So great a light he blazes from his eyes to greet
Us all; so fair is he from head to dainty feet.

Hail! lovely boys, soon ruthless time shall fade away
The bloom of youth from all, and fair curls turn to grey.

[SYDNEY OSWALD]

ALKAIOS
12,30

Nicander, ooh, your leg's got hairs!
Watch they don't creep up into your arse.
Because, darling, if they do, you'll soon know
How the lovers flee you, and years go.

[TONY HARRISON]

MELEAGER
12,23

And now I, Meleager, am among them,
     those whom I mocked,
the young men crying through the evening
     to their señoritas.
For Cupid has nailed me to your gates,
     Myiscus,
on my brow cut mocking words:
     'Lo! The Fruit of Favours long Preserved.'

[PETER WHIGHAM]

12,41

It is true that I held Thero fair,
     Apollodatus a torch of love –
not so no longer:
     that light is out.

Mine now woman's love.
The delights of hirsute sex
let us leave to Welsh shepherds.

[PETER WHIGHAM]

12,49

Drink, unhappy lover, drink.
Let Bacchus bring forgetfulness
And drown your passion for the boy.
Drink and drain the brimming cup
Till wine drives out the anguish.

12,52

Listen, you who know the pains of love:
The South wind that the sailors bless
Has borne off half my soul,
Has borne away Andragathus –
Thrice happy ship,
Thrice happy waves
And four times happy wind.

Would I were a dolphin
To bear him on my back to Rhodes,
The home of beautiful boys.

12,59

The boys of Tyre are beautiful,
But Myiscus is a sun
Whose blazing forth extinguishes the stars.

12,94

Diodorus is nice, isn't he, Philocles?
Everyone is looking at Heraclitus.
Dion has a lovely voice,

And Uliades a beautiful behind.
Go on, touch the soft-skinned one,
Drool over the second, speak to the third,
As to the fourth . . . and so on.
You see, I'm not jealous.
But if you cast your greedy eyes on Myiscus,
I'll scratch them out.

12, 106

One boy alone in all the world for me,
Yea, only one my loving eyes can see
And he, Myiscus, I love constantly.

In all the other youths no charms I find,
He is my all, to others I am blind;
Then can it be my eyes, with love afire,
Can flatter him who is my soul's desire.

[SYDNEY OSWALD]

12, 110

Lo! Beauty flashed forth sweetly; from his eyes
The flames of love abroad he casts as fire;
Has Eros taught the boy to win the prize
Of love with thunderbolts? Hail, then, desire
To mortals bringing beams that dazzle sight.
Shine forth, Myiscus fed with quenchless fire,
Which burns for me alone with friendly light.

[SYDNEY OSWALD]

12, 125

Love brought me quietly in the dreaming night
A softly laughing boy of just eighteen.
I pressed him to me and I hugged despair.
Memory burns me
And my eyes still see what they saw.

Ill-starred lover,
You must forget the warmth of beauty
Even in your dreams.

12, 127

At 12 o'clock in the afternoon
    in the middle of the street –
        Alexis.

Summer had all but brought the fruit
    to its perilous end:
        & the summer sun & that boy's look

did their work on me.
    Night hid the sun.
        Your face consumes my dreams.

Others feel sleep as feathered rest;
    mine but in flame refigures
        your image lit in me.

[PETER WHIGHAM]

12, 133

I was thirsty.
It was hot.
I kissed the boy
with girl-soft skin.
My thirst was quenched.
I said: Is that what
upstairs you're up
to Papa Zeus,
is that what strip-
ling Ganymede
at table serves,
under Hera's
watchful eye?

Lip-spilt wine
from soul to soul
as honeyed-sweet
as these vast draughts
Antiochus
pours now for me!

[PETER WHIGHAM]

12,159

The breath of my life – no less,
    this rope that constrains
me, Myiscus, to you
    – you have me fast.

Sweet boy,
    even a deaf-mute
could *hear* what you *look*!
    Look blackly at me,
winter breaks out in clouds.
    Smile with clear eyes,
& spring giggles
    coating me with petals.

[PETER WHIGHAM]

12,164

As honey in wine / wine, honey
    Alexis in Cleobulus
Cleobulus in Alexis
    sweet-haired & lovely each
as he with whom the other
    mingles . . . product
of such two entwined
    potent
as vineyards of deathless Cypris.

[PETER WHIGHAM]

GLAUKOS

12,44

Time was when once upon a time, such toys
As balls or pet birds won a boy, or dice.
Now it's best china, or cash. Lovers of boys,
Try something else next time. Toys cut no ice.

[PETER JAY]

ANONYMOUS

7,714

I celebrate Rhegion, Italy's tip, licked by
    shoals of Sicilian water, because
Ibykos, who loved both boys and his lyre, is buried
    there, his many pleasures spent, under
an elm-tree whose leaves cast shade on his tomb, piled high
    with
    thick ivy and a bed of white reed.

[PETER JAY]

12,116

Since I'm completely drunk
I'll go and serenade him.
Here, boy, take this wreath,
It's bathed in my tears.
I've a long walk and the night is black,
But I shan't get lost
For Themison is a torch.

12,136

Why all the racket, you chattering birds?
Don't bother me here, warméd by the boy's

delicate flesh. You nightingales in leaves,
sleep, I beg you, you babbling women,
shut up!

[THOMAS MEYER]

MARCUS ARGENTARIUS

5,116

Hetero-sex is best for the man of a serious turn of mind,
But here's a hint, if you should fancy the other:
Turn Menophila round in bed, address her peachy behind.
And it's easy to pretend you're screwing her brother.

[FLEUR ADCOCK]

PHILIP OF THESSALONICA

11,36

You were a pretty boy once, Archestratus, and
    young men burned for your wine-rosy cheeks;
you had no time for me then, on the game with those
    who took your bloom away. Now bristly and black
you push your friendship in my face, holding out
    straw after others have got your harvest.

[EDWIN MORGAN]

FLACCUS

12,12

Just as he is growing a beard,
The beautiful Lado
(He who despised us all)
Has fallen in love –
With a boy!
Fate is quick to revenge.

ADAIOS

10,20

If you see someone beautiful
   hammer it out right then.
Say what you think; put your hands full
   on his bollocks: be a man.

But if 'I admire you' is what you say
   and 'I'll be a brother to you' –
shame will bar the only way
   to all you want to do.

[ALISTAIR ELLIOT]

ANONYMOUS

12,17

I don't care for women,
But men make me burn with desire.
As men are stronger than women,
So are the loves they inflame.

AUTOMEDON

12,34

I dined with Demetrius last night –
That lucky teacher.
One boy lay on his lap,
One leaned over his shoulder,
One brought in the dishes
And one filled his cup –
A pretty sight!
'Tell me,' I said with a laugh,
'Do you teach these boys at night as well?'

STRATO

12,3

Boys' cocks, Diodore,
have three phases,
or so those in the know say.
Leave 'em alone & they babble,
let 'em swell & they wail,
but when a hand·yanks 'em,
those pricks talk;

that's all you need to know.

[THOMAS MEYER]

12,4

I delight in the prime of a boy of twelve,
but a thirteen-year-old's better yet.

At fourteen he's Love's even sweeter flower,
& one going on fifteen's even more delightful.

Sixteen belongs to the gods, & seventeen . . .
it's not for me, but Zeus to seek.

If you want the older ones, you don't play
any more, but seek & *answer back*.

[THOMAS MEYER]

12,5

I like them pale, fair or honey-skinned.
I like dark·hair and hazel eyes,
But when a glance is sparkling black
It drives me wild.

12,8

Passing the flower-stalls there did I perceive
A boy intent upon a wreath to weave;
Such chance I let not slip, but by him stayed,
And whispering soft I to him offer made,
'For how much will you sell to me your crown?'
Redder than rose he blushed, and looking down,
   In sweet affright, he made me answer low,
    'Before my Father see, I pray you go.'
As pretext garlands from the boy I bought,
Then, leaving him, my house I lonely sought;
Where round the gods did I the garlands twine
With fervent prayers the boy might soon be mine.

[SYDNEY OSWALD]

12,9

Now art thou fair, Diodorus,
And ripe for love thou art,
E'en should'st thou wed a woman,
From thee we'll not depart.

[SYDNEY OSWALD]

12,15

When Graphicus sat by the baths,
The seat pinched his behind.
What will happen to me
If even wood is stirred?

12,21

Stolen kisses, wary eyes –
How long are we going on talking?
We're wasting time.
You'll grow a beard.
Come on Phidon, add deeds to words!

12,177

At even, when the hour drew nigh at which we say farewell,
My Moeris kissed my lips, in dream or truth I cannot tell;
   All else he said and asked, all else to me is clear,
   But if he kissed my lips, in truth I cannot swear;
But if the kiss divine were real, then this indeed I know,
My joyous soul no more on earth can wander to and fro.

[SYDNEY OSWALD]

12,178

Like when the burning sun doth rise,
And drives the stars from out the skies,
My very soul was turned to flame,
When 'mongst the youths first Thendis came.
And still I burn and Thendis seek,
Though thick the hair upon his cheek.
E'en though the sun of youth shall wane,
To me sole light he'll e'er remain.

[SYDNEY OSWALD]

12,184

Oh! trouble not Menèdemos by guile
To win, but give him but a passing smile,
With wand'ring eye but throw a glance upon
The boy; then without shame he'll cry, 'Lead on.'
   Then no delay he'll make,
   But swift he'll overtake:
Lo! swifter far, not than a tiny stream,
But than a river vast his haste will seem.

[SYDNEY OSWALD]

12,185

Those snooty boys in all their purple drag!
We'll never get our hands on one of those!

They're like ripe fig trees stuck up on a crag –
food only for vultures and high-flying crows.

[TONY HARRISON]

12,192

Long hair, endless curls trained by the devoted
'Artistry' of a stylist beyond the call of
Nature, do nothing for me. What I like's a
Boy's body hot from the park, all grimy
And the sight of his flesh rubbed down with oil.
Nice, and artless; none of the pretty 'enchantment'
Laid on by your merchants of the romantic.

[TEDDY HOGGE]

12,196

Thy eyes are sparks, Lycines, god-like made,
   Or rather rays, O Lord, that send forth flame;
   To look thee in the face I cannot claim,
So fierce a fire thy eyes have on me played.

[SYDNEY OSWALD]

12,205

I am provoked
by the delicious boy next door.
His laugh of complicity is not
that of a novice.
He is twelve years old.
Green grapes may be touched, but his ripe
chastity will be guarded.

[W. G. SHEPHERD]

12,207

But yesterday, when from the bath he stept,
   Young Diocles his wondrous limbs laid bare,

And standing naked, lo! he did appear
    Fairer than she, who from the ocean leapt.

On Ida, years agone, when Paris deemed
    It meet to judge 'twixt goddesses, and gave
The prize to her, who sprang from out the wave,
    Thrice fairer e'en would Diocles have seemed.

[SYDNEY OSWALD]

12,213

'To Kyris'

You recline that magnificent pair of buttocks
Against the wall . . . why tempt
The stone, which is incapable?

[TEDDY HOGGE]

12,222

There was this gym-teacher
Who took his chance while giving
A lesson to a smooth lad –
He whisked him over his knee, and started
Doing his press-ups there right up him, hand
Working his balls. At which moment the father
Comes looking for his son; the gym-teacher
Throws the boy flat on his back,
Leaps on top and grips him tight round the neck.
Father knows a thing or two about wrestling
And says, 'Easy, please! You'll have it right off.'

[TEDDY HOGGE]

12,226

All through the night my eyes have streamed with rain
Of ceaseless tears, striving relief to gain
From that distress, which thralls my sleepless brain
Alway since my dear comrade went away.

For yesterday my lover, leaving me,
Set out for Ephesus, and now if he
Return not swift and end this misery,
Alone upon my couch I cannot stay.

[SYDNEY OSWALD]

12,227

Even if I try not to ogle a boy in the street,
He passes by and I turn round.

12,248

How shall I know if my love lose his youth,
Who never for a day hath left my sight?
He, who but yesterday was my delight.
I needs must love today if love be truth,
And if I love today, tomorrow's light
Against our love will e'en forbear to fight.

[SYDNEY OSWALD]

12,256

Gathering the bloom of all the fairest boys that be,
Love wove this varied crown, Venus, for thee.
A lily sweet, Diodorus, there he set;
Asclepiades breathed an odorous violet;
Like rose amid the thorns, Heraclitus next he placed,
While Dion's form, close-clinging vine, the garland graced;
A saffron crocus Theron blazed, the flame-haired lad,
And, bunch of mountain-thyme, Andiades did he add;
Myiscus of the girlish locks a bunch of olive made,
While all the charms of Aretas as foliage round he laid;
    O holy Isle of Tyre, thrice blessèd mayst thou be,
Since, like a fragrant grove, these boys all flower in thee.

[SYDNEY OSWALD]

12,258

Perchance some coming after,
   Hearing my songs will say
That these were all the verses
   Of love I gave away.

But 'tis for you boy-lovers
   That I will write alway,
Whene'er some god shall hold me
   Caught in Love's restless sway.

[SYDNEY OSWALD]

SKYTHINOS

12,22

Great woe, fire & war come on me:
Elissus, filled with love's ripe years
(sixteen, that deadly age) has all charms
& a voice & lips that read & kiss like honey.

What am I to do? He tells me: just look.

So I lie awake & let my hands fight unfilled love.

[THOMAS MEYER]

RUFINUS

5,19

boy-mad no longer
         as once before
               I am called
woman-mad now
               from scabbard to thimble
   instead of boys' unalloyed skin
                         I go in for

chalky complexions
        and the added-on crusts
                of cochineal
dolphins shall pasture
        in the Black Forest
and nervous deer
        in the grey sea

[ALAN MARSHFIELD]

PAULOS

5,232

Kissing Hippomenes, I crave
    Leander's touch;
while clinging to Leander's lips
  my fancy dwells as much

on Xanthus; locked in his embrace
    my heart strays back,
restless, toward Hippomenes.
      Yearning for what I lack,

shrinking in turn from those I hold
    in shifting arms,
contentedly I taste the wealth
  of Cytherea's charms.

May she who lifts opprobrious brows
    to censure me
lie cursed between the stale sheets of
  paupered monogamy.

[ANDREW MILLER]

ANONYMOUS

12,145

Cease your labours, lovers of boys,
Wish no more your hopeless hopes.

Can any man dry the flowing sea
Or count the desert sand?
For that's what it's like to love a boy
Who's proud of a beauty sweet to gods and men.

Look at me you lovers:
My toils after a boy
Were as water on desert sand.

12,151

When 'mongst the youths you lately came,
And saw a flower transcending fair;
Then having seen, you must declare
Apollodòtus is his name.

If now the blazing flame has sown
No seeds of love; nor has desire
Unceasing strength to overpower,
A god thou art or made of stone.

[SYDNEY OSWALD]

12,156

O Diodorus, in a storm of spring,
My love is striving on a restless sea;
For now thy eyes are charged with rain, and next they fling
Glances serene abroad, and laugh most tenderly.
As one who shipwrecked on the sea's fierce whirl,
I strive to mount the waves, which o'er me swirl,
But lo! the storm drives on yet wantonly.
On friendship's rock or hate's, I pray me throw,
So in which sea I swim my heart may know.

[SYDNEY OSWALD]

THEOCRITUS
(3rd century B.C.)

Idyllium 23: A scorn'd Shepherd hangs himself, the cruel fair is kill'd by the Statue of Cupid

To Mr Rily, Painter to his Majesty

An Amorous Shepherd lov'd a charming Boy,
As fair as thought could frame, or wish enjoy;
Unlike his Soul, illnatur'd and unkind,
An Angell's body with a Fury's mind:
How great a God Love was, He scorn'd to know, ⎞
How sharp his arrows, and how strong his bow, ⎬
What rageing wounds he scatters here below. ⎠
In his address and talk fierce, rude, untame,
He gave no comfort to the Shepherd's flame:
No cherry Lips, no Rose his Cheeks did dÿe,
No pleasing Fire did sparkle in his Eye,
Where eager thoughts with fainting Vertue strove,
No soft discourse, nor Kiss to ease his love:
But as a Lion on the Lybian Plain
Looks on his Hunters, he beheld the Swain:
His Lips still pouting, and his Eyes unkind,
His Forehead too was rough as was his Mind;
His Colour gone, and every pleasing Grace
Beset by Fury had forsook his face;
Yet midst his passion, midst his frowns he mov'd,
As these were Charms He was the more belov'd:
But when o'recome he could endure no more,
He came and wept before the hated door,
He wept and pin'd, he hung his sickly head,
The threshold kisst, and thus at last he said:
Ah cruel fair, and of a Tigress born!
Ah stony Boy, compos'd of frowns and scorn:
Unworthy of my love, this Rope receive,
The last, and wellcomst Present I can give:
I'le never vex thee more, I'le cease to wo,
And whether you condemn'd, I'll freely go,
Where certain Cures for Love, as Stories tell,

Where dismal shades, and dark Oblivion dwell:
Yet did I drink the whole forgetful Stream,
It would not drown my Love, nor quench my flame:
Thy cruel doors I bid my last Adieu,
Know what will come, and you shall find it true:
The Day is fair but quickly yields to shades,
The Lilly white, but when 'tis pluckt it fades:
The Violet lovely, but it withers soon,
Youth's beauty charming, but 'tis quickly gone:
The time shall come when you, proud Boy, shall prove
The heat of Passion, and the rage of Love:
Then shall thy Soul melt thro thy weeping Eye,
Whilst all shall smile, and you unpitty'd dye.
Yet grant one kindness, and I ask no more,
When you shall see me hanging at the door
Do not go proudly by, forbear to smile,
But stay, sweet Boy, and gaze, and weep a while;
Then take me down, and whilst some tears are shed,
Thy own soft garment o're my body spread,
And grant one Kiss, one Kiss when I am dead:
Nere fear, for you may safely grant me this,
I shalln't revive tho you could Love and Kiss:
Then dig a Grave, there let my Love be laid,
And when you part, say thrice, 'my friend is dead,'
Or else go further on to please my Ghost,
And cry, 'my best, my dearest friend is lost':
And on my Monument inscribe this Rhime,
The witness of my Love and of thy Crime,
'This shepherd dy'd for Love, stay Stranger here,
And weep, and cry, He lov'd a cruel fair':
This said, he roll'd a Stone, a mighty Stone,
Fate lent a hand behind, and pusht it on:
High by the Wall, on this he panting rose,
And ty'd, and fitted well the fatal noose:
Then from the place on which before he stood
He slipt, and hung the Door's unhappy load:
The Boy came forth, and with a scornful Meine
And smiling look beheld the tragick Scene;
Hang there said He, but O how I despise
So base, so mean a Trophy of my Eyes!
The proudest Kings should fall by my disdain,

Too noble to be lost upon a Swain:
This said, he turn'd, and as he turn'd his head
His Garments were polluted by the Dead,
Thence to the Plays and to the Baths did move,
The Bath was sacred to the God of Love;
For there he stood in comely Majesty
Smiles on his Cheeks, and softness in his Eye,
That part of th' Marble wrought into his Breast
By Power divine was softer than the rest,
To show how Pitty did exactly suit
With Love, and was his darling Attribute:
The God leapt forth, and dasht the Boy, the Wound
Let out his Soul, and as it fled He groan'd.
    Hail Lovers, hail, see here the scornful dyes,
A just, and acceptable Sacrifice,
Be kind, and Love for mutual Love return,
For see the God takes vengeance on my scorn.

[T. CREECH, 1684]

Idyllium 26: An Advice to a Friend to be constant in his Love

To Charles Viner of Wadham College, Esquire

Wine, Friend, and Truth, the Proverb says, agree,
And now I'me heated take this Truth from me;
The Secrets that lay deep and hid before
Now rais'd by Wine swim up, and bubble o're;
Then take this riseing Truth I can't controul:
Thou dost not Love Me, Youth, with all thy Soul;
I know it, for this half of Life I boast
I have from you, the other half is lost:
When e're you smile I rival Gods above,
Grown perfect, and exulted by thy Love;
But when you frown, and when dislike you show,
I sink to Hell, more curst than all below;
Yet how can this with common sense agree
To torture one that loves, and dyes for Thee?
But Youth, could my Advice thy thoughts engage,
Mine who have learn'd Experience by my Age,
The Counsell's good, and when a numerous store

Of Blessings Crown Thee, Thou wilt praise me more:
On one Tree build one Nest, and build it strong,
Where no fierce Snake can creep, and seize thy young:
Now here you stand, and suddenly are gone,
You leap from Bough to Bough, and fix on none.
If any views thy Beauty, and Commends,
You straight enroll him midst your antient friends,
Whilst all your old Acquaintance laid aside,
Dear youth this smells of Vanity and Pride:
Love One, your Equal, love whilst Life remains,
This pleases all, and Commendation gains,
By this your Passion will but light appear
Which conquers all, and all are forc't to bear;
Love seizes all; and doth all Minds controul,
It melts the stubborn temper of my Soul;
But O I must embrace, Dear, grant one Kiss,
And thus reward, and practise my Advice.

[T. CREECH, 1684]

CATULLUS
(*c*. 84–*c*. 54 B.C.)

9

Veranius, my dear friend, the friend worth
More to me than three hundred thousand others,
Is it true that you've come back to home and hearth,
To your old mother and affectionate brothers?
It's true. Wonderful news! In a short while
I'll see you safe and well, hear you describe
In your inimitable traveller's style
The sights of Spain, a landscape or a tribe,
Put my arms around you, draw you close and then
Plant on the mouth and eyes I love a kiss.
Of all the world's supremely happy men
Who is as happy as Catullus is?

[JAMES MICHIE]

15

I entrust my all to you, Aurelius,
And I ask this modest favour in return:
If ever you have wished to keep something pure
Then guard this darling of my heart from danger.
I don't mean protect him from the common herd
Who wander through the streets involved in themselves,
But save him rather from your own great penis
Which is lethal to any boy, good or bad.
You can display yourself wherever you please
And indulge your lust whenever you want to.
I only ask this modest request: spare *him*.
But if you commit that most heinous of crimes,
Then I pity the lust that drives you to it,
For I'll fetter your feet and shove through the gate
Of your arse radishes and the fins of mullet,
Punishing you like a common adulterer.

16

I'll have you by the short and curly hair,
Furius and Aurelius, horrible pair,
Bugger and bum-boy! So you dare conclude
Because my verse is wanton that I'm lewd?
Fools! Though the sacred poet should abjure
Grossness himself, his work need not be pure;
Indeed, it will taste dry and dull unless
It's sauced and salted with licentiousness
And has the power to tickle and provoke
Some action – not in boys, I mean old folk
With grey hairs and rheumaticky, stiff hips.
Do you think that just because you read of 'lips'
And 'a thousand kisses' I'm no man? Take care,
Or I shall 'man' you both, horrible pair!

[JAMES MICHIE]

33

Of all our bath-house thieves the cleverest one
Is you, Vibennius, with your pansy son.
(The old man's fingers suffer from a heinous
Itch, but the boy's as grasping with his anus.)
Why not deport yourselves, go anywhere
The weather's horrible? For all Rome's aware
Of Father's pilferings, and believe me, Sonny,
That hairy rump won't make you any money.

[JAMES MICHIE]

38

Your Catullus is depressed, Cornificus,
And his angst and despair get worse by the hour;
And though it is the easiest thing in the world,
Have you sent one word to console him at all?
No. I am angry that you treat my love thus.
Send me only some little line of comfort
Though it be as sad as Simonides' tears.

48

If I could go on kissing your honeyed eyes
Juventius, then I would kiss each of them
Three hundred thousand times and not be sated –
No, even if the harvest of our kissing
Were richer than the ripe gold ears of the corn.

56

I have something for you to laugh at, Cato,
Something worthy for you to hear and laugh at.
Cato, laugh as much as you love Catullus –
The thing is so ridiculous and funny.
Just now I saw a young lad fucking his girl,
So I arose, and, by the grace of Venus,
Transfixed him then and there with my own stiff prick!

from *Hymeneal*, 61

Unmuzzle the broad joke,
Let bawdy comment flow,
Let the pet slave who shared
His master's pillow throw
Nuts to the boys: he's heard
The news that she's preferred.

You pampered bedroom pet,
Throw walnuts to the boys.
You've played for long enough
With nuts, you've outgrown toys.
Throw walnuts: you must bow
To Hymen's mastery now.

Slave-boy, the other day
No simple bailiff's wife
Seemed good enough for you.
But now the barber's knife
Scrapes off your beard. Too bad!
Scatter the nuts, poor lad!

And you, spruce, perfumed groom –
They say that you can't trust
Yourself to give your smooth-
Cheeked boys up: yet you must.
Sing 'Hymen, Hymen', sing
The god of marrying!

[JAMES MICHIE]

80

Gellius, what reason can you give why those ruddy lips of yours
    Are whiter than winter snow when you get up in the morning
And when you rise from your soft siesta in the long hours after lunch?
    I don't know if it's true what the gossips say:
That you are friends with men who are really no better than they
        ought to be,
    But *this* is certain: Virro's strained thighs
And those white lips of yours have *something* in common.

81

Juventius, could you not find in this great crowd of men
  A handsome example that you could learn to like
Other than that squalid friend of yours from wretched Pisarum
  Who, though he is paler than a statue, is dear to you,
And whom you prefer to me, though you don't know how much it
    hurts?

99

Juventius, my honey, while you played
I stole a little kiss from you. It was
Sweeter than sweet ambrosia. I paid
The penalty, though; for, nailed to the high cross
Of your displeasure, I remember spending
More than an hour feebly excusing it,
While all the tears I shed for the offending
Act didn't soften your fierce mood one bit.
As soon as it was done you washed the place
With water, then you wiped it with each finger
In turn, meticulously, just in case
Any contagion from my mouth might linger –
As though you'd been infected on the lips
By some foul whore's saliva! Now, moreover,
You've sentenced me to the racks, the screws, the whips
Reserved by Love for the tormented lover;
So that, ambrosial once, that kiss became
Bitterer than the bitterest hellebore.
If that's the sort of punishment you claim,
I shan't steal kisses from you any more.

[JAMES MICHIE]

VIRGIL

(70–19 B.C.)

The Second Pastoral, or, Alexis

The Argument

The Commentators can by no means agree on the Person of *Alexis*, but are all of opinion that some Beautiful Youth is meant by him, to whom *Virgil* here makes Love; in *Corydon's* Language and Simplicity. His way of Courtship is wholly Pastoral: He complains of the Boys Coyness, recommends himself for his Beauty and Skill in Piping; invites the Youth into the Country, where he promises him the Diversions of the Place; with a suitable Present of Nuts and Apples: But when he finds nothing will prevail, he resolves to quit his troublesome Amour, and betake himself again to his former Business.

Young *Corydon*, th' unhappy Shepherd Swain,
The fair *Alexis* lov'd, but lov'd in vain:
And underneath the Beechen Shade, alone,
Thus to the Woods and Mountains made his moan.
Is this, unkind *Alexis*, my reward,
And must I die unpitied, and unheard?
Now the green Lizard in the Grove is laid,
The Sheep enjoy the coolness of the Shade;
And *Thestilis* wild Thime and Garlike beats
For Harvest Hinds, o'respent with Toyl and Heats:
While in the scorching Sun I trace in vain
Thy flying footsteps o're the burning Plain.
The creaking Locusts with my Voice conspire,
They fry'd with Heat, and I with fierce Desire.
How much more easie was it to sustain
Proud *Amarillis*, and her haughty Reign,
The Scorns of Young *Menalcas*, once my care,
Tho' he was black, and thou art Heav'nly fair.
Trust not too much to that enchanting Face;
Beauty's a Charm, but soon the Charm will pass:
White Lillies lie neglected on the Plain,
While dusky Hyacinths for use remain.
My Passion is thy Scorn; nor wilt thou know
What Wealth I have, what Gifts I can bestow:
What Stores my Dairies and my Folds contain;
A thousand Lambs that wander on the Plain:
New Milk that all the Winter never fails,

And all the Summer overflows the Pails:
Amphion sung not sweeter to his Herd,
When summon'd Stones the *Theban* Turrets rear'd.
Nor am I so deform'd; for late I stood
Upon the Margin of the briny Flood:
The Winds were still, and if the Glass be true,
With *Daphnis* I may vie, tho' judg'd by you.
O leave the noisie Town, O come and see
Our Country Cotts, and live content with me!
To wound the Flying Deer, and from their Cotes
With me to drive a-Field, the browzing Goats:
To pipe and sing, and in our Country Strain
To Copy, or perhaps contend with *Pan*.
Pan taught to joyn with Wax unequal Reeds,
Pan loves the Shepherds, and their Flocks he feeds:
Nor scorn the Pipe; *Amyntas*, to be taught,
With all his Kisses would my Skill have bought.
Of seven smooth joints a mellow Pipe I have,
Which with his dying Breath *Damaetas* gave:
And said, This, *Corydon*, I leave to thee;
For only thou deserv'st it after me.
His Eyes *Amyntas* durst not upward lift,
For much he grudg'd the Praise, but more the Gift.
Besides two Kids that in the Valley stray'd,
I found by chance and to my fold convey'd.
They drein two bagging Udders every day;
And these shall be Companions of thy Play.
Both fleck'd with white, the true *Arcadian* Strain,
Which *Thestilis* had often beg'd in vain:
And she shall have them, if again she sues,
Since you the Giver and the Gift refuse.
Come to my longing Arms, my lovely care,
And take the Presents which the Nymphs prepare.
White Lillies in full Canisters they bring,
With all the Glories of the Purple Spring:
The Daughters of the Flood have search'd the Mead
For Violets pale, and cropt the Poppy's Head:
The Short *Narcissus* and fair Daffodil,
Pancies to please the Sight, and Cassia sweet to smell:
And set soft Hyacinths with Iron blue,
To shade marsh Marigolds of shining Hue.

Some bound in Order, others loosely strow'd,
To dress thy Bow'r, and trim thy new Abode.
My self will search our planted Grounds at home,
For downy Peaches and the glossie Plum:
And thrash the Chesnuts in the Neighb'ring Grove,
Such as my *Amarillis* us'd to love.
The Laurel and the Myrtle sweets agree;
And both in Nosegays shall be bound for thee.
Ah, *Corydon*, ah poor unhappy Swain,
Alexis will thy homely Gifts disdain:
Nor, should'st thou offer all thy little Store,
Will rich *Iolas* yield, but offer more.
What have I done, to name that wealthy Swain,
So powerful are his Presents, mine so mean!
The Boar amidst my Crystal Streams I bring;
And Southern Winds to blast my flow'ry Spring.
Ah, cruel Creature, whom dost thou despise?
The Gods to live in Woods have left the Skies.
And Godlike *Paris* in th' *Idean* Grove,
To *Priam*'s Wealth prefer'd *Oenone*'s Love.
In Cities which she built, let *Pallas* Reign;
Tow'rs are for Gods, but Forrests for the Swain.
The greedy Lyoness the Wolf pursues,
The Wolf the Kid, the wanton Kid the Browze:
Alexis thou art chas'd by *Corydon*;
All follow sev'ral Games, and each his own.
See from afar the Fields no longer smoke,
The sweating Steers unharnass'd from the Yoke,
Bring, as in Triumph, back the crooked Plough;
The Shadows lengthen as the Sun goes Low.
Cool Breezes now the raging Heats remove;
Ah, cruel Heaven! that made no Cure for Love!
I wish for balmy Sleep, but wish in vain:
Love has no bounds in Pleasure, or in Pain.
What frenzy, Shepherd, has thy Soul possess'd,
Thy Vinyard lies half prun'd, and half undress'd.
Quench, *Corydon*, thy long unanswer'd fire:
Mind what the common wants of Life require.
On willow Twigs employ thy weaving care:
And find an easier Love, tho' not so fair.

[JOHN DRYDEN, 1697]

HORACE
(65 – 8 B.C.)

from *Odes*

4, 1

Again? New tumults in my breast?
Ah spare me, Venus! let me, let me rest!
    I am not now, alas! the one
Who made Cinara both his queen and sun.
    Ah sound no more thy soft alarms,
Nor circle sober fifty with thy charms.
    Mother too fierce of dear desires!
Turn, turn to willing hearts your wanton fires:
    To Paulus' house direct your doves
And there more properly inflame your loves.
    He noble, handsome and still young,
For all his clients has a nimble tongue.
    He, with a hundred arts refined,
Shall stretch thy conquests over half the kind:
    To him rich rivals shall submit,
But freed, when presents fail, shall bless their wit.
    Then shall thy form in marble grace,
Near Alba's lake, some shaded, holy place.
    The thickest incense you'll inhale
– 'Tis sweet to you – and music shall regale
    Your ears from silver sounding lyres
That call the smiling Loves and young Desires.
    There Youths and Nymphs in consort gay,
Shall hail the rising, close the parting day.
    With me, alas! those joys are o'er;
For me, the vernal garlands bloom no more.
    Adieu! fond hope of mutual fire
With boy or girl in still-renewed desire!
    – But Ligurinus, why, my dear,
Steals down my cheek th' involuntary tear?
    Why words so flowing, thoughts so free,
Stop, or turn nonsense at one glance of thee?
    And why through all my dreams at night
Do I or grasp you or pursue your flight

    Across the boundless Martian field,
And chase through waves a boy who will not yield?

[*Adapted from an 'Imitation' by* ALEXANDER POPE]

4, 10

                O Ligurinus:
Still cruel,
        still proud,
            still powerful,
When flaunting your gifts from Venus –
You'll learn despair when your beard begins to grow.
That hair,
        rippling over your shoulders
                      will fall out.
Your skin,
        the fairest flower in a bed of roses,
                      will fade.
You'll see your altered face and say:
'This mind I have now,
            why did I not train it as a boy?
How can I return
        loveliness
            to my cheeks?'

TIBULLUS
(*c.* 60–19 B.C.)

from *Odes*, 1,4

1
lines 11–20

    Far from the tender Tribe of Boys remove,
For they've a thousand ways to kindle Love.
This, pleases as he strides the manag'd Horse,
And holds the taughten'd Rein with early Force;
This, as he swims, delights the Fancy best,
Raising the smiling Wave with snowy Breast:
This, with a comely Look and manly Airs;
And that with Virgin Modesty ensnares.

But if at first you find him not inclin'd
To Love, have Patience, Time will change his Mind.

2
lines 53-72

    And you, whate'er your Fav'rite does, approve,
For Condescension leads the Way to love.
Go with him where he goes, tho' long the Way,
And the fierce Dog-star fires the sultry Way;
Or the gay Rainbow girds the bluish Sky,
And threatens rattling Show'rs of Rain are nigh.
If sailing on the Water be his Will,
Then steer the Wherry with a dext'rous Skill:
Nor think it hard Fatigues and Pains to bear,
But still be ready with a willing Cheer.
If he'll inclose the Vales for savage Spoils,
Then on thy Shoulders bear the Nets and Toils;
If Fencing be the Fav'rite Sport he'll use,
Take up the Files, and artlessly oppose;
Seem as intent, yet oft expose your Breast,
Neglect your Guard, and let him get the best;
Then he'll be mild, then you a Kiss may seize,
He'll struggle, but at length comply with ease;
Reluctant, tho' at first you'll find him grow
Ev'n fond, when round your Neck his Arms he'll throw.

[JOHN DART, 1720]

OVID
(43 B.C.—A.D. 18)

from *Metamorphoses*, Book 9
lines 792-938

'*Iphys and Ianthee*'

. . . in the Shire of Phestos hard by Cnossus dwelt of yore
A Yeoman of the meaner sort that Lyctus had to name:
His stock was simple and his wealth according to the same.
Howbeit his life so upright was, that no man could it blame.

He came unto his wife then big and ready downe to lye,
And sayd: two things I will with thee. T'one that when thou out
    shalt crye,
Thou mayst dispatch with little paine: the other that thou have
A Boay. For Girles to bring them up a greater cost do crave
And I have no abilitie, and therefore if thou bring
A wench (it goes against my heart to thinke upon the thing)
Although against my will, I charge it straight destroyed be.
The bond of nature needs must beare in this behalfe with me.
This sed: both wept exceedingly, aswell the husband who
Did give commandement, as the wife that was commanded to.
Yet Telethusa earnestly at Lyct her husband lay,
(Although in vaine) to have good hope, and of himselfe more
    stay.
But he was full determined. Within a while the day
Approached that the fruit was ripe, and she did looke to lay
Her belly every minute: when at midnight in her rest
Stood by her (or did seeme to stand) the Goddesse Isis, drest
And trayned with the solemne pompe of all her Kites.[1] Two
    hornes
Upon her Forehead like the Moone, with eares of ripened
    cornes
Stood glistering as the burnisht gold. Moreover she did weare
A rich and stately Diademe. Attendant on her were
The barking bug[2] Anubis, and the saint of Bubast and
The pydecote Apis, and the God that gives to understand[3]
By finger holden to his lippes that men should silence keepe,
And Libian Wormes[4] whose stinging doth enforce continuall
    sleepe,
And thou Osyris who the folke of Aegypt ever seeke,
And never can have sought enough, and Kittlerattles[5] eke.
Then even as though that Telethuse had fully beene awake
And seene these things with open eyes, thus Isis to her spake.
My servant, Telethusa, cease this care, and breake thy charge
Of Lyct. And when Lucina[6] shall have let thy fruite at large,
Bring up the same what ere it be I am a Goddesse who

1. birds of prey 2. bogey, hobgoblin 3. Harpocrates 4. snakes 5. sacred rattles
6. goddess of childbirth

Delights in helping folke at neede. I hither come to do
Thee good. Thou shalt not have a cause hereafter to complaine
Of serving of a Goddesse that is thanklesse for thy paine.
When Isis had this comfort given, she went her way againe.
  A joyfull wight rose Telethusa, and lifting to the skie
  Her hardened hands, did pray her dreame might worke
    effectually.
Her throwes increast, and forth alone anon the burthen came,
A Wench was borne to Lyctus, who knew nothing of the same.
The mother making him beleeve it was a boy, did bring
It up, and none but she and nurse were privie to the thing.
The father thanking God, did give the child the Grandsires
    name,
The which was Iphys. Joyfull was the mother of the same,
Because the name did serve alike to man and woman both,
And so the lye through godly guile forth unperceived goth.
The garments of it were a boyes. The face of it was such
As either in a boy or girle of beauty uttered much.
When Iphys was of thirteen yeares, her father did insure
The browne Ianthee unto here a wench of looke demure,
Commended for her favor and her person more than all
The maydes of Phestos: Telest, men her fathers name did call.
He dwelt in Dyctis. They were both of age and favor leeke,
And under both one Schoolmaster they did for nurture seeke.
And heereupon the hearts of both the dart of love did streeke.
And wounded both of them alike. But unlike was their hope.
Both longed for the wedding day together for to cope.
For whom Ianthee thinkes to be a man, shee hopes to see
Her husband. Iphys loves whereof she thinkes she may not
    bee
Partaker, and the selfe same thing augmenteth still her flame.
Herself a mayden with a mayde (right strange) in love became.
  She scarce could staye her teares. What end remains for me
    (quoth she)
  How strange a love: how uncoth: how prodigious raignes in
    me:
If that the Gods did favour me, they should destroy me quight.
Or if they would not me destroy, at leastwise yet they might
Have given me such a maladie as might with nature stond
Or nature were acquainted with. A Cow is never fond
Upon a Cow, nor Mare on Mare. The Ram delights the Eawe,

The Stage the Hinde, the Cock the Hen. But never man could
    shew,
That female yet was tane in love with female kinde. I would
To God I never had beene borne. Yet least that Candye[7] should
Not bring forth all that monstrous were, the daughter of the
    Sonne
Did love a Bull. Howbeit there was a Male to dote uppon.
My love is furiouser than hers, if truth confessed bee.
For she was fond of such at least as might be compast. Shee
Was served by a Bull, beguild by Arte in Cow of tree,
And one there was for here with whom advowtrie to commit.
If all the cunning in the world and slights of suttle wit
Were here, or if that Daedalus himselfe with uncouth wing
Of war, should hither flye againe, what comfort should he
    bring:
Could he with all his cunning crafts now make a Boy of mee?
Or could he, O Ianthee change the native shape of thee?
Nay, rather Ithys settle thou thy minde and call thy wits
About thee: shake thou off these flames that foolishly by fits,
Without all reason reigne. Thou seest what nature hath thee
    made
(Unlesse thou wilt decieve thy selfe.) So farreforth wisely wade
As right and reason may support, and love as women ought.
Hope is the thing that breedes desire, hope feedes the
    amorous thought.
This hope thy sex denieth thee. Not watching doth restraine
Thee from embracing of the thing whereof thou art so faine.
Not yet the Husband's jelousie, nor roughnesse of her Sire,
Nor yet the coynesse of the Wench doth hinder thy desire,
And yet thou canst not her enjoy. No though that God and
    man
Should labor to their uttermost and do the best they can
In thy behalfe, they could not make a happier wight of thee.
I cannot with the thing but that I have it. Franke and free
The Gods have given me what they could. As I will so will hee
That must become my father in law. So wils my father too,
But nature stronger than them all, consenteth not theretoo.
This hindereth me and nothing els. Behold the blissfull time,

7. Crete

The day of marriage is at hand. Ianthee shall be mine,
And yet I shall not her enjoy. Amid the water wee
Shall thirst. O Juno president of marriage, why by thee
Comes Hymen to this wedding, where no bridegrome you
    shall see,
But both are birds that must that day together coupled bee?
  This spoken she did hold her peace. And now the tother
    Mayde
  Did burne as hot in love as she. And earnestly she prayed
The bridale day might come with speede. The thing for which
    she longd.
Dame Telethusa fearing sore, from day to day prolongd
The time, oft feigning sicknes, oft pretending she had seene
Ill tokens of successe: At length all shifts consumed beene.
The wedding day so oft delayd was now at hand. The day
Before it, taking from her head the kercheefe quite away,
And from her daughter's head likewise, with scattered haire
    she layd
Her hands upon the Alter, and with humble voyce thus prayd.
  O Isis who dost haunt the towne of Paretonie, and
  The fieldes by Maraeotis Lake, and Pharos which doth stand
By Alexandria, and the Nile divided into seven
Great channels, comfort thou my feare, and send me help
    from heaven,
Thy selfe O Goddesse, even thy selfe and these thy relickes I
Did once behold, and knew them all: as well thy companie
As eke thy sounding rattles, and thy cressets burning by,
And mindfully I marked what commandement thou didst
    give.
That I escape unpunished that this same wench doth live,
The counsell and thy hest it is. Have mercie now on twaine,
And helpe us. With that the teares ran downe her cheeks
    amayne.
  The Goddesse seemed for to move her Alter: and in deede
  She moved it that the temple doores did tremble like a reede.
And hornes in likeness to the Moone about the Church did
    shine,
And Rattles made a raughtish[8] noyse. At this same luckie
    signe,

8. rattling

Although not wholy carelesse, yet right glad she went away,
And Iphys followed after her with larger pace than aye
She was accustomd. And her face continued not so whight.
Her strength encreased, and her looke more sharper to the
    sight.
Her haire grew shorter, and she had a much more lively
    spright,
Than when she was a wench. For thou O Iphys who right now
A moother wert art now a boay With offrings both of yow
To Church retyre, and rejoyce with faith unfearefull. They
With offrings went to church againe, and there their vowes
    did pay.
They also set a table up, which this breefe meeter had.
The Vowes that Iphys vowde a wench, he hath perfourme'd a
    Lad.
Next morrow over all the world did shine with lightsome
    flame,
When Juno and Dame Venus, and Sir Hymen joyntly came
To Iphys marriage, who as then transformed to a boy,
Did take Ianthee to his wife, and so her love enjoy.

[ARTHUR GOLDING, 1565–7]

STATIUS
(*c.* A.D. 40–*c.* 96)

from *Sylvae*, Book 2

6

Too harsh the man who setting bounds to grief
Can make the period of mourning brief.
Sad is the father kindling the flame
For rip'ning boys who died e'er manhood came;
Bitter the husband sundered from his wife
Who on a lonely bed weeps out his life;
Wretched the sighs for sisters breathed with pain
Or tears for brothers shed, but shed in vain;
Yet men of other stock than ours we love
And lighter pains a greater grief can move.

'Tis for your slaveboy, Ursus, that you mourn
(No slave by nature though to service born.)
His loyalty and love both merited
These bitter tears by his survivor shed,
And better than unspotted pedigree
Was his expansive soul: then, tears, flow free!
Be not ashamed a worthy grief to show
When such a fate's decreed to one below;
For you, a man (alas, I rub the smart)
Bewail the brother of your very heart.
Fain would he serve who ruled himself so well.
Then blame not tears that on his gravestone fell.
The Parthian weeps his horse in battle slain;
For his dead hounds the huntsman feels pain;
E'en cherished birds have had their fun'ral fire;
And for a deer great Virgil tuned his lyre.
Was he within his heart a very slave?
My own eyes marked him, marked his bearing brave,
Saw you alone he would as lord allow,
Yet marked the prouder bearing of his brow.
High character his boyish looks proclaimed.
Glad for such sons were ancient mothers famed.
Less noble was proud Theseus when the maid
The secret of the labyrinth displayed;
Less comely Paris when a queen to save
He launched reluctant ships upon the wave.
Don't think I lie to you nor softly say
Poetic licence leads my song astray.
I saw and see him still, a finer shape
Than young Achilles when, that he might 'scape
The noise of battle, Thetis, singing war,
Hid her beloved on the maidens' shore;
And fairer too than Troilus when the spear
Of that Achilles stopped his life so dear.
How beautiful you were, handsomer far
Than all our youths save your dear master's star
Which as the moon, hung in the midst of night,
Outshines on earth each every lesser light,
Or Hesperus who dims the fires of Heaven so bright.
There was no maiden's beauty in your face,
No soft effeminacy to your grace

As those we bid leave love when looks divine
Are gone. A handsome manliness was thine;
A gaze not insolent, yet gently strong
As those of ancient heroes praised in song.
Simple the comliness of locks so sleek
And bloom of youth on your unbearded cheek;
Such guiless grace Eurotian boyhood fames
Or youths competing in Olympic games.
How may I sing the honours of his soul,
The calm and wisdom that made up the whole?
Sometimes he'd chide, or aid with counsil deep,
Partake of joy or pain, yet never keep
Himself apart but answer to your look
Patroclus-like. But come, we may not brook
Praise that o'er steps his rank. He was a slave ⟩
As loyal as he whose patient ardour grave ⟩
Long waited for Odysseus erring on the wave. ⟩
    What god or chance makes choice of wounds so fell?
Why do the Fates their powers use too well?
Ah, how much braver, Ursus, you'd have stood
Stripped of your wealth, deprived of Fortune's good;
If smoking ruin had o'erwhelmed your farm
Or swelling rivers wrecked their utmost harm;
If prosp'rous Crete her harvest had denied
Or bounty all her goods had not supplied.
But baleful Envy, ever skilled to wound,
The surest way to your heart's weakness found.
Just at the gate of manhood stood the boy,
A peerless youth of fifteen summers' joy,
When grim-looked Fate her glances cast at him,
Gave first a greater lustre to his trim,
Filled out his muscles and raised high his head, ⟩
But finding that her heart with envy bled ⟩
With her deceitful favours crushed the poor boy dead; ⟩
And then with hooked, relentless fingers sure
At his unsullied flesh and visage tore.
The dripping horses of the morning star
Were barely harnessed to his heav'nly car
When your Beloved, glimpsing Charon's shore
Beheld Death's bitter river stretch before.
With what a grief your master called your name;

Not your dead mother nor your father's frame
Could mourning's lacerations better show;
While e'en your watching brother's cheek did glow ⎱
With shame that they his mourning should outgo. ⎰
Your body rested on no slaveboy's pyre,
Incense and saffron mixing in the fire
With spices from the Phoenix' balmy nest
And herbs by Assyrian druggists pressed
Fed the devouring flames, while ashes dear
Drank only of the master's treasured tear.
Such grief's more precious to a fleeting shade
Than wine or onyx on dull embers laid.
    But what use tears? Why do we yield to grief?
Treasuring our sorrow against relief?
Where is the eloquence you oft have shown
To pris'ners brought before the judge's throne?
Why torture his loved ghost with your despair?
'Tis true he had a soul beyond compare
And worthy to be mourned, but that debt's paid
And now through Elysium stalks his shade.
Perchance enobled parents there resort
Or by still Lethe fountain fairies sport
With him, by Proserpine observed. Then cease;
The Fates or he may yet bring your soul peace;
A new Beloved may be offered you
As rich of heart and lovely to the view
As he who with a joyous, loving art
Will teach the handsome lad to win your heart.

MARTIAL
(*c*. A.D. 40 – 104)

Epigrams
1, 40

'On Bassa'

Insomuch, Bassa, as I never saw
    You join male company, nor yet, in truth,
Has rumour e'er asserted that you draw
    In happy slavery one favoured youth;

But for each duty crowds of women press
  Around you, hidden from man's impure eye;
I thought you a Lucretia I confess;
  Yet meanwhile you were fucking on the sly.
Oh, horrible! You dare two cunts unite!
  To play the man, unnatural dreams you nourish!
Only the Sphinx could read this riddle right:
  With males renounced, adultery can flourish.

[ANONYMOUS]

2,26

'New Love'

Charm of my life, my dearest care,
Never, O never here I swear,
Within my cradling arms has lain
Your like, nor ever will again.
Give me your willing lips that I
May taste the honey of the vine,
And give me when I ask for wine
The cup in which your kisses lie.

And if – ah, if – my sweetest sweet,
With love as true my love you greet,
A greater joy than mortals know
Within my heart will flame and grow;
O not so rapt in godlike bliss
In his high halls is Jove indeed
When in his arms young Ganymede
Snuggles and lifts warm lips to kiss.

[BRIAN HILL]

2,59

'On a Slanderer'

Before your mouth was fringed with hair,
All pricks might find a haven there,
Till hangmen loathed a boy so common,
And deadcart men preferred a woman.

When gamahuche no longer paid,
Your tongue was still your stock in trade,
No more to suck, but to discharge
Its venom on mankind at large;
On characters base slurs to fix,
As once it had polluted pricks.
Oh filthy tongue, you'd better far
Be what you were than what you are.

[ANONYMOUS]

2,62

'To Labienus'

Labienus, each hair on your bosom that grows,
  On your arms, on your legs, with much trouble
You shave, and your belly's appurtenance shows
  Like a newly mown field with its stubble.
Thus blooming and sweet as the breath of the morn,
  Your mistress entwines you, fond boy,
But you've something behind, neatly shaven and shorn,
  That's scarcely a mistress's toy.

[ANONYMOUS]

3,73

'To Phoebus'

Lying with unstable pego 'twixt a brace of vigorous boys,
Phoebus what's the little game that all your leisure time employs?
I should guess, but contradicting rumours from your friends, odd rot
  'em,
Check the surmise that you open to these vigorous youths your
  bottom;
Rumour with its hundred tongues, that tells us you're not up to
  fucking,
Tells us that you are not buggered; what's then left for you but
  sucking?

[ANONYMOUS]

4,7

'A Riddle'

Young Hyllus, why refuse today
   What yesterday you freely granted,
Suddenly harsh and obdurate,
   Who once agreed to all I wanted.

You plead your beard, your weight of years,
   Your hairy chest in mitigation?
To turn a boy into a man
   How long then was the night's duration?

Why, Hyllus, do you mock at me,
   Turning affection into scorning?
If last night you were still a boy,
   How can you be a man this morning?

[BRIAN HILL]

4,48

'To Papilus'

What! want to be buggered, and cry when it's done!
   Here clear contradictions seem blended!
Do you grieve that the sodding was ever begun,
   Or lament that the pleasure is ended?

[ANONYMOUS]

6,37

'To Charinus, a Catamite'

Cracked is the very foundation
   Of joys that Charinus must mourn,

Still worshipped in deep admiration,
   Though the seat of enjoyment is gone;
No more blessings the gods dream of granting,
   With curses the poor wretch enclasp,
Leaving luckless Charinus still panting
   For pleasures he's no power to grasp.

[ANONYMOUS]

7,67

'To Philaenis'

Abhorrent to all natural joys
Philaenis sodomizes boys,
And like a spouse whose wife's away
She drains of spend twelve cunts a day.
With dress tucked up above her knees
She hurls the heavy ball with ease,
And, smeared all o'er with oil and sand,
She wields a dumb bell in each hand,
And when she quits the dirty floor,
Still rank with grease, the jaded whore
Submits to the schoolmaster's whip
For each small fault, each trifling slip:
Nor will she sit her down to dine
Till she has spewed two quarts of wine:
And when she's eaten pounds of steak
A gallon more her thirst will slake.
After all this, when fired by lust,
For pricks alone she feels disgust,
These cannot e'en her lips entice
Forsooth it is a woman's vice!
But girls she'll gamahuche for hours,
Their juicy quims she quite devours.
Oh, you that think your sex to cloak
By kissing what you cannot poke,
May God grant that you, Philaenis,
Will yet learn to suck a penis.

[ANONYMOUS]

7,89

'Go, Happy Rose'

Go, happy rose, and wreathe my dear friend's brow;
Not only now,
But when his shining locks have turned to grey,
(Though distant be that day!)
So, from this hour,
Be love's own flower.

[BRIAN HILL]

9,58

'On Hedylus'

Friend Hedylus' cloak is a sight to behold,
It's ragged, it's tattered, it's battered, it's old,
Not the handles of flaggons grown smoother from wear,
Not the legs of chained asses more mangy and bare,
Not the ruts of a highway where market carts meet,
Not the round shining pebbles on which the waves beat,
The rags of dead paupers, spades ground by the soil,
Nor the cart wheel made bright in its circular toil,
Not the flank of the bison, rubbed raw in his lair,
   Not an old boar's white tusk ground down to a stump,
Are so worn as old Hedylus' cloak, yet I'd swear
   That his cloak's much less worn than the hole in his rump.

[ANONYMOUS]

9,69

'To Polycharmus'

When you lie with a woman, at least so girls say,
   You shit the same moment you come.
But what do you do, Polycharmus, I pray,
   When a lover's stiff prick stops your bum?

[ANONYMOUS]

10,32

'The Likeness'

This portrait which I treasure so
Is Marcus painted long ago
When he was young and gay and fair,
Who now is old with silvered hair.

Would that the artist's brush could bind
In paint the beauties of his mind,
For then, I swear, the world today
No rarer picture could display.

[BRIAN HILL]

10,42

'To Dindymus'

Your face reveals a down so light
    A breeze might steal it, or a breath;
    Soft as a quince's bloom that might
    Find in a finger's touch its death.
Five kisses – and your face is cleared
While mine has grown another beard.

[BRIAN HILL]

11,43

My better half, why turn a peevish scold,
When round some tender boy my arms I fold,
And point me out that nature has designed
In you as well a little hole behind?
Has Juno ne'er said this to lustful Jove?
Yet graceful Ganymede absorbs his love.
The stout Tirynthian left his bow the while, as
The lusty hero drove his shaft in Hylas.
Yet think you Megara had not her bulls-eye?

And starting Daphne turning round to fly,
Her bottom lit a lust for virile joys
Phoebus needs quench in the Oebalian boy's:
However much Briseiris towards Achilles
Turned her white buttocks, fairer than twin lilies,
He found below the smooth Patroclus' waist
Enjoyment more congenial to his taste.
Then give no manly names to back or front,
A woman everywhere is only cunt.

[ANONYMOUS]

11,63

'To Lygdus'

You swear you'll come, you name the time and place,
Whene'er I ask of you one fond embrace:
The livelong night I wait, racked with desire,
Rigid with lust, and all my veins on fire,
And ofttime thinking of your girlish frame
My left hand quenches the devouring flame.
In bitterness of heart I'll ask my god
To curse you, lying and deceitful sod.
May you ne'er stir from out your threshold's door,
Save at the heels of some damned one eye'd whore.

[ANONYMOUS]

12,75

Me Polytimus vexes and provokes,
He always leaves me for insipid pokes;
Hypnus is so retiring, shy and coy,
He swears he'll not be called my darling boy:
Secundus fills his well gorged arse with cream,
And to the dregs he drains each amorous stream;
The pathic Dindymus affects disgust
For Sodom and Gomorrah's manly lust:
Modest Amphion blushes when I toy —

Nature was mad to make so shy a boy.
For all their faults and their annoying ways
With darling Ganymedes I'd pass my days,
Rather than lead a sumptuous tinselled life
With twenty million dollars and a wife.

[ANONYMOUS]

15,205

Give me a boy whose tender skin
Owes its fresh bloom to youth, not art;
And for his sake may no girl win
A corner in my heart.

[BRIAN HILL]

JUVENAL
(? A.D. 55–? 140)

from *Satire Two*
'Faggots in Ancient Rome'

I want to flee to the frozen north when cliques who prattle
About ancient virtue live like beasts and talk of morals.
For a start they are pig ignorant, though their houses are stuffed with
    busts
Of Stoic philosophers. Their great hero is one who has bought
A picture of Aristotle or one of the sages, or keeps an original of
    Cleanthes.
You can't judge a man by his looks – there are gloomy debauchees
    everywhere.
You chastise sodomy, *you*, the most notorious Socratic fairy!
A body bristling with hair, hirsute arms, give promise
Of a manly soul, but your arse is sleek when the laughing doctor
Comes to lance your piles. You 'philosophers' are taciturn,
But you cut your hair to match your eyebrows. At least Peribombus
Is candid – his face and walk reveal all his inclinations,
And I call those Destiny's fault. His honest flaunting

And self-exposure are pardonable really and worthy our pity.
But you, with Herculean tongues, denounce his weakness and chatter about
Virtue while preparing to practise vice. 'How can I respect *you*?' shouts one
Notorious queen. 'You do what I do. Why am I worse?'
Hypocrites, all of them . . . A famous lawyer dresses in chiffon . . .
Everyone marvels as he launches out against all the vices.
Who'd dress like that? 'But darling, it's so hot on July afternoons!'
. . . Careful, this will spread and you'll get involved in worse, you'll slip by degrees
And propitiate the Mother Goddess with the other queers, be welcomed
In homes where men wear heavy necklaces and fillets round their heads.
You'll sacrifice the stomach of a pig and a vast bowl of wine while ensuring
That only males come in. 'Clear out! Women are profane!
No music from she-minstrels here!' Such were the cries and the rites
In Athens . . . One queen is using an eyebrow pencil,
A needle stained with damp soot. She puts on mascara.
Another drinks from a phallic cup and ties her hair
In a glittering net. Her cheeks are blue or smooth and green.
The servant, following the master, swears only by Juno . . .
No decent language, no elegant manners, but high-pitched voices
And a gluttonous old grey-haired priest – a master who should teach the vice . . .
Gracchus has given his cornet – perhaps he played a 'straight' horn –
Four thousand pounds as a dowry! The contract's signed,
The blessings are pronounced, the banqueters are seated, and the male bride
Reclines at ease on the bosom of her new-found husband.
Oh, nobles of Rome, what do we need, a soothsayer or a moralist?
Would you find it worse, would you be more moved if a woman gave birth
To a calf or a cow or a lamb? The man who is now a 'husband'
Carried a shield in the procession of Mars, sweating with the burden!
Oh, father of our city, how came our shepherds so full of vice?
Oh, Lord of War, where did our pastoral grandsires learn this?
An aristocrat marries a man and you sit idly by –
Go, go from the martial plain which you have forgotten!

from *Satire Six*
lines 301–349

What conscience has Venus drunk? Our inebriated beauties
Can't tell head from tail at those midnight oyster suppers
When the best wine's laced with perfume, and tossed down neat
From a foaming conch-shell, while the dizzy ceiling
Spins round, and the tables dance, and each light shows double.
Why, you may ask yourself, does the notorious Maura
Sniff at the air in that knowing, derisive way
As she and her dear friend Tullia pass by the ancient altar
Of Chastity? and what is Tullia whispering to her?
Here, at night, they stagger out of their litters
And relieve themselves, pissing in long hard bursts
All over the Goddess's statue. Then, while the Moon
Looks down on their motions, they take turns to ride each other,
And finally go home. So you, next morning,
On your way to some great house, will splash through your wife's
    piddle.
    Notorious, too, are the ritual mysteries
Of the Good Goddess,[1] when flute-music stirs the loins,
And frenzied women, devotees of Priapus,
Sweep along in procession, howling, tossing their hair,
Wine-flown, horn-crazy, burning with the desire
To get themselves laid. Hark at the way they whinny
In mounting lust, see that copious flow, the pure
And vintage wine of passion, that splashes their thighs!
Off goes Saufeia's wreath, she challenges the call-girls
To a contest of bumps and grinds, emerges victorious,
But herself is eclipsed in turn – an admiring loser –
By the liquid movements of Medullina's buttocks:
So the ladies, with a display of talent to match their birth,
Win all the prizes. No make-belief here, no pretence,
Each act is performed in earnest, and guaranteed
To warm the age-chilled balls of a Nestor or a Priam.

[PETER GREEN]

---

1. the daughter or wife of Faunus whose devotees were women

Satire Nine

JUVENAL:

Why do you look so gloomy, Naevolus? Every time I meet you your
    face is as wretched
As Marsyas's when he was beaten at music by Apollo and knew
    he'd be flayed
Or Ravolus's when caught *in flagrante* between the legs of Rhodope.
When a slave licks a pie we give him a thrashing, but you look like a
    stock-broker
When he offers a triple rate of interest and nobody trusts him.
What are these wrinkles? You used to be an easy-going man,
The local squire, the urbane wit with the pointed tale.
You've changed! Why this hang-dog look and unkempt hair?
You used to have bird-lime beauty packs, but your skin's all dry
And your legs are dirty and covered with matted hair.
Why, you're like a man who's been suffering a terrible fever for
    months.
Joy and woe can both be read on a sickly face,
And it's my opinion that something's happened and your old life has
    changed.
I can remember that not so long ago you could be found
In the temple of Isis or hanging round the statue of Ganymede
In the temple of Peace, not to mention the secret courts
Of Cybele and Ceres where anyone can easily pick up a girl.
You were a more notorious adulterer than Aufidius himself –
And, though you never admitted it, you buggered the husbands as
    well.

NAEVOLUS:

Many men have done well from my way of life,
But I've got precious little out of it. Sometimes I've been given
An old, greasy cloak to cover my toga –
Some coarsely woven, coarsely dyed rag made by a peasant in
    France –
And sometimes I get a hand-me-down geegaw made out of low grade
    silver.
But Destiny's our master! Fate even rules what's under our clothes,
And if the stars are against you the fantastic size of your cock gets you
    nowhere.
Even if Virro did slobber when he saw your naked charms

And sent love letters by the hundred, lewdly misquoting Homer for
    fun:
'A man is attracted by the very sight of – a pansy or queen.'
There is nothing worse than a tight-fisted, debauched old queer.
'I gave you *this* much,' he says, 'and then I gave you *that* amount
    afterwards,
And then I gave you ever so much more.' Lust at piece-rate!
'Well,' I said, 'let's do the thing properly and call in an accountant.
Cough up five thousand miserly sesterces and *I'll* say what *I've*
    earned.
I suppose you think it's fun, stuffing my prick up so far
That it hits your dinner. *Real* ploughboys earn far more!'
'You used to call yourself handsome,' he said, 'and the Ganymede *de
    nos jours.'*
'But when will a man like you (who won't even pay for his pleasures)
Show kindness to a poor follower? *And* you want presents,' I added.
'Who expects green sunshades and amber beads when his birthday
    comes round
And lolls on his day-bed, counting his gifts at Ladies' Day?
What are those hill farms at Apulia for, you lecherous sparrow,
And all those acres of meadow that would tire a kite to cross?
Your stores are filled with plump grapes from your vineyard slopes
At Cumae, Gaurus and Trifoli – enough for a lifetime's drinking!
Would it be too much to give a few acres to these exhausted loins?
Do you really think it's better to give a countrywoman, her cottage,
    her baby and her dog
To some cymbal-clashing boyfriend?' 'How rude you are!' you
    scream.
'Yes, but I've got to pay my rent and my single slaveboy.
(That's right. Just the one. I need another, and that's two to feed.)
I suppose I'm expected to pray when winter howls around!
But what about their frozen bodies when December's north wind
    blows?
Shall I tell the lads: 'OK, hang on, wait till summer and the cicadas
    come'?
If you ignore my other services, how do you price this one:
Were I not your faithful servant, your wife would still be a virgin?
How often have you asked *that* of me and what promises you made!
She'd be near to doing a bunk when I bedded her for you
And would have torn up the marriage licence if it hadn't been for my
    hard work

When you were crying outside the door. The bed – and you
Who heard the groaning inside – are witnesses to these facts.
There's many a household been saved by a timely adultery, you
    know.
So what are you going to do? Which was the best of my services?
Is it nothing to a bastard like you that I have given you a son and a
    daughter?
No – *you* rear the children and publish your virility in the papers,
Hang garlands at your door! You're a father! No one can spread
    rumours.
And you have paternal rights and all that tax relief through me!
Your children make you heir to a fortune, and there's more if I get you
    a third.'

JUVENAL:
You've reason to complain, Naevolus, but what does *he* say?

NAEVOLUS:
He takes no notice and looks for another two-legged donkey,
Another just like me. But this must stay a secret, please.
These pumice-smoothed queens make the worst enemies – and he
    suspects.
He'd stop at nothing: the sword, a clubbing or burning my house.
And just you remember that poison is cheap for a wealthy man.
So don't split on me. This matter is highly confidential.

JUVENAL:
Oh, Corydon, Corydon! Do you think a rich man *has* any secrets?
His slaves may hold their tongues, but his mules and his dogs will
    talk.
His doorposts and marble columns will tell tales, you know.
Let him shut all his windows, fasten the doors, cover every crack with
    a curtain,
Extinguish the light, turn every person out of the house
And let no one sleep nearby – yet the landlord at the corner will know
What he was up to before the dawn. The rich man will hear
The tales that the baker's made up and what the cooks and the
    servingmen said.
They'll say anything to be revenged for a beating, and the drunk at the
    crossroads
Will belch his story in your unwilling ear. Ask *them* to be quiet,
For they'd bleat out stories more readily than a high class tart

Swills her stolen wine at a public sacrifice.
There are many reasons for right living, but the chief of all
Is that there's no need to fear your gossiping slaves. They're bad,
But worse is the plight of a man who cannot escape from their chatter.

NAEVOLUS:
Your advice is wise but vague. What can I do now
With so much time gone already and my hopes forever unfulfilled?
The short, sad span of life hastes like a flower to its close.
We drink, we call for chaplets, for perfumes and girls,
Yet old age creeps up unperceived.

JUVENAL:
There's nothing to worry about. As long as the Seven Hills
Stand in Rome, fairies will come from every quarter
And carriages will bring gentlemen who will show they're gay by
        secret signs.
Besides, there are always aphrodisiacs, you know – colewort and
        things.

NAEVOLUS:
These are maxims for those who are lucky. I'm content
If I can fill my belly with the earnings of my prick. Oh little gods
That I keep by the ancestral hearth and supplicate with a pinch of
        incense
And sometimes with a tiny garland, when can I be really sure
That I won't have to go begging with a crutch and a mat when I am
        old?
I want twenty thousand sesterces wisely invested and safe,
Some modest silver tableware and a couple of porters
To carry my sedan to the bawling circus on their stout shoulders.
That's enough for a poor man like me. But when will it happen?
Whenever Fortune's invoked for Naevolus she plugs up her ears
With the same wax that Ulysses used when he passed the sirens.

AUSONIUS
(*c.* 310–390)

Epigrams
62

Glad youth had come thy sixteenth year to crown,
To soft encircle thy dear cheeks with down

And part the mingled beauties of thy face,
When death too quickly came to snatch your grace.
But thou'll not herd with ghostly, common fools,
Nor, piteous, waft the Stygian pools;
Rather with blithe Adonis shalt thou rove
And play the Ganymede to highest Jove.

77

'Reincarnating Pythagoras, say:
How shall the new-shaped Marcus greet his day?'
'Who's he?' 'That kidnapper of scoundrel mind,
That late seducer of the male kind,
That "pilfering, perverted paedophile",
To borrow Lucilius' lofty style.'
'Oh, him. No bull nor hippocamel he;
A dung-beetle shall nasty Marcus be!'

PAULINUS OF NOLA
(353–431)

'To Ausonius'

I, through all chances that are given to mortals,
    And through all fates that be,
So long as this close prison shall contain me,
    Yea, though a world shall sunder me and thee,

Thee shall I hold, in every fibre woven,
    Not with dumb lips, nor with averted face
Shall I behold thee, in my mind embrace thee,
    Instant and present, thou, in every place.

Yea, when the prison of this flesh is broken,
    And from the earth I shall have gone my way,
Wheresoe'er in the wide universe I stay me,
    There shall I bear thee, as I do today.

Think not the end, that from my body frees me,
    Breaks and unshackles from my love to thee;

Triumphs the soul above its house in ruin,
    Deathless, begot of immortality.

Still must she keep her senses and affections,
    Hold them as dear as life itself to be.
Could she choose death, then might she choose forgetting:
    Living, remembering, to eternity.

[HELEN WADDELL]

VENANTIUS FORTUNATUS
(*c.* 530–*c.* 603)

'Written on an Island off the Breton Coast'

You at God's altar stand, His minister,
    And Paris lies about you and the Seine:
Around this Breton isle the Ocean swells,
    Deep water and one love between us twain.

Wild is the wind, but still thy name is spoken;
    Rough is the sea: it sweeps not o'er thy face.
Still runs my love for shelter to its dwelling,
    Hither, O heart, to thine abiding place.

Swift as the waves beneath an east wind breaking
    Dark as beneath a winter sky the sea,
So to my heart crowd memories awaking,
    So dark, O love, my spirit without thee.

[HELEN WADDELL]

ALCUIN
(*c.* 735–804)

'Lament for the Cuckoo'

O cuckoo that sang to us and art fled,
    Where'er thou wanderest, on whatever shore
Thou lingerest now, all men bewail thee dead,
    They say our cuckoo will return no more.

Ah, let him come again, he must not die,
   Let him return with the returning spring,
And waken all the songs he used to sing.
   But will he come again? I know not, I.

I fear the dark sea breaks above his head,
   Caught in the whirlpool, dead beneath the waves.
Sorrow for me, if that ill god of wine
   Hath drowned him deep where young things find their graves.
But if he lives yet, surely he will come,
   Back to the kindly nest, from the fierce crows.
Cuckoo, what took you from the nesting place?
   But will he come again? That no man knows.

If you love songs, cuckoo, then come again,
   Come again, come again, quick, pray you come.
Cuckoo, delay not, hasten thee home again,
   Daphnis who loveth thee longs for his own.
Now spring is here again, wake from thy sleeping,
   Alcuin the old man thinks long for thee.
Through the green meadows go the oxen grazing;
   Only the cuckoo is not. Where is he?

Wail for the cuckoo, every where bewail him,
   Joyous he left us: shall he grieving come?
Let him come grieving, if he will but come again,
   Yea, we shall weep with him, moan for his moan.
Unless a rock begat thee, thou wilt weep with us.
   How canst thou not, thyself remembering?
Shall not the father weep the son he lost him,
   Brother for brother still be sorrowing?

Once were we three, with but one heart among us.
   Scarce are we two, now that the third is fled.
Fled is he, fled is he, but the grief remaineth;
   Bitter the weeping, for so dear a head.
Send a song after him, send a song of sorrow,
   Songs bring the cuckoo home, or so they tell.
Yet be thou happy, wheresoe'er thou wanderest.
   Sometimes remember us. Love, fare you well.

[HELEN WADDELL]

ANONYMOUS
Latin
(*c.* 800)

O spirit of Venus whom I adore,
Whose body is perfect, quite without flaw,
He will protect you who stars and the shore,
The sun and the ocean rules evermore.
You shall be saved from the Furies' shrill roar,
And the Fates have promised you richest store.

Boy, I do not hail you rhetorically,
And I pray to the Fates respectfully
That those three sisters watch protectingly,
Though thou hast the sea gods abetting thee
While crossing the waves. Unforgetfully
I love and feel your loss affectingly.

He who made men and in the old earth's bones
Found his material (the hardest stones)
He made this boy who causes all my groans,
Who stands unmoved while listening to my moans.
This perfect boy my hated rival owns.
A stricken deer, I seek the forest zones.

WALAFRID STRABO
(809–849)

'To His Friend in Absence'

When the moon's splendour shines in naked heaven,
    Stand thou and gaze beneath the open sky.
See how that radiance from her lamp is riven,
    And in one splendour foldeth gloriously
Two that have loved, and now divided far,
Bound by love's bond, in heart together are.

What though thy lover's eyes in vain desire thee,
   Seek for love's face, and find that face denied?
Let that light be between us for a token;
   Take this poor verse that love and faith inscribe.
Love, art thou true? and fast love's chain about thee?
Then for all time, O love, God give thee joy!

[HELEN WADDELL]

AT TALIQ
(*c.* 961–*c.* 1009)

I took leave of my beloved one evening: how I wish
I had rather tasted death than been away from him!
I find that even the sun complains of love for him,
And the doves weep with the pain of loving him:
The evenings seem so feeble after he has left,
As if they also felt the pain of what I now suffer,
The breeze began to carry the feelings of our love,
And became soft with love, its breath grew fragrant,
The dew of the garden was mixed in the morning
With the sweet fragrance of remembrance of him,
The flowers are his mouth, the breeze his breath,
The rose has been moistened by the dew of his cheeks:
Therefore I love gardens so madly, for at all times
They make me remember the one whom I adore!

[A. R. NYKL]

IBN AL-ABBAR
(died 1041/2)

You know not how deep was the love your eyes did kindle
Within my soul, or how great was my suffering!
Bless my beloved! He wished to visit me, but could not
Come near me because of his tear-drowned eyes;
He feared the watchers, so he came to me quickly,
Taking all adornments off his neck, except his beauty:

I offered cups of wine to him: the wine was put to shame
By those honey-like lips, those pearly teeth!
His eyelids were at last vanquished by slumber,
Wine made him obedient to all my wishes;
I wanted to make my cheek his pillow, but he found
It too small and said: Your arm is the best pillow for me!
Thus he slept safely, not frightened by treachery:
I spent the night in thirst, not touching the pure spring:
The moon appeared: it was nearly its last,
The firmament was dark, because of envy:
The night was perplexed: Where will the moon rise?
Did it not know that she was sleeping on my arm?

[A. R. NYKL]

PETER ABELARD
(1079–1144)

'David's Lament for Jonathan'

Low in thy grave with thee
        Happy to lie,
Since there's no greater thing left Love to do;
        And to live after thee
            Is but to die,
For with but half a soul what can Life do?

So share thy victory,
        Or else thy grave,
Either to rescue thee, or with thee lie:
        Ending that life for thee,
            That thou didst save,
So Death that sundereth might bring more nigh.

Peace, O my stricken lute!
        Thy strings are sleeping.
Would that my heart could still
        Its bitter weeping!

[HELEN WADDELL]

GODFREY THE SATIRIST
Latin
(12th century)

'To Grosphus'

Who sees you, G, surprises two in one:
A boy behind, your front as man must rate.
You play the lad for your illicit fun,
But on the turn, you're virile, true and straight!

BERNARD OF MORLAS
Latin
(*c.* 1150)

from *'Contempt for the World'*, Book 3

Scarcely believe things shameful to utter which yet I shall speak of:
  sins of dire name and sins beyond sin.
Alas! the fires of Sodom flicker around us
  and none strikes down the error, conceals nor laments of his crime.
Close your eyes to bestial sin, you who are here:
  for impious rage bursts forth when it is known of and heard.
Fruitlessly, furiously, he becomes she:
  marriage is rejected and virtue despised.
Weep for the time, weep for each part of it, cram full of sin.
  Oh rage, oh terror, when man forgets manhood to be as the hyena.
Behold the multitude, filthy and barren:
  of what order is their sin and who may name it? Surely the grave.
Alas! this crime re-echoes its horror to the stars,
  the deed is open and is noised abroad. Chastity, tremble!
This man learns it of that man, that man of this
  and your law as your voice and your prophecy come near to their
    death, oh Christ.
The law of Sodom obtains in a world that is teeming with Ganymedes,
  and showing forth his crime, the beast is in every dwelling.
Every couch and the high places belong to the boy;
  marriage is rejected, oh madness, as the she-goat gives way to the
    kid.

Ask me to number the flock and quickly I shall tell it,
   quickly proclaim and readily unfold it in tragic speech:
It is as common as grains of barley in harvest, as oysters in the sea
   or sands on the shore, as Adriatic Cyclades[1] or as incense in India,
   as wild oats at Tibur.
The castle, the villa and the holy places are ripe with it;
   and everywhere, oh shame, flows over with this plague.
The world in impotence perishes, wants what is horrible, does what is
      dire;
   all feeds on brimstone and is become one Gomorrah.

ANONYMOUS
Latin
(12th century)

'Love-Letter One'

To C—
   her lover,
      sweeter than honey or honeycomb,
B—
   sends her loving.
Uniquely special,
Why do you delay
                  so long,
                  so far?
Why do you want your only one to die,
me,
your soul and body lover,
me,
your little starveling bird,
Sighing for you
                  every hour,
                  every second?
Without your honied presence

1. thus in the original

I want
       to hear no one,
       to see no one.
Like the turtle on its shrivelled branch
Forever mourning for its mate
I
  too
     endless
            mourn
Until I have your love again.
I look
       but do not find
                        HER.
And there's not the comfort of a single word.
Loving and loveliness of speech and face:
                        despair
For now there's no such love.
What similes for love?
                        Sweeter than honey,
                        Brighter than gold,
                        Brighter than silver.
More?
                        You are gentle,
                        You are perfect,
                        Sweeter than milk,
                        Sweeter than honey.
                        Perfectly gentle,
                        Perfectly perfect.
My spirit fails
                        perpetually
                                   without you.
You are without
                        bitterness,
                        faithlessness.
You are
                        sweeter than milk.
                        sweeter than honey,
                        peerless, among millions.
I love you
           and
              you alone

> my love,
> my longing,
> the sweet cooling of my brain.

Joyless,
> without you;
All that was delightful
> dark
> without you.

Truly
> If my life would buy yours,
> I'd sell it
for YOU,
> woman of my heart.
(Please God,
> don't let me die before I see her again.)
Farewell,
> all my love.
I send you my constancy.
Take it,
> please.

ANONYMOUS
Latin
(12th century)

'Love-Letter Two'

To G, her one and only rose,
Her A this bond of true love shows.
Ah, how can I endure the pain
Or patience to the utmost strain
Till you have come back home again?
Am I a stone that should not yearn,
Do you believe, for your return?
All day, all night, I'm anguish-tossed
Like one who foot and hand has lost.
Without you, all that joys my blood
Is little more than trampled mud.
Far from rejoicing, I shed tears

And never happiness appears.
When I recall how you caressed
So joyously, my little breast
I want to die. Since we can't greet,
What for the most unhappy's meet,
And where should I, the poorest, turn?
Oh, that the earth could me inturn
Until your long-desired return,
Or that, like Habbakuk in trance,
I might come once your face to glance!
That happy hour could be my last;
You, by none of the world surpassed,
So lovable, so dear to sense,
So true, so void of all pretence!
I shall not cease from endless pain
Till I win sight of you again.
A sage said greatest misery
Comes when a man is far from he
Without whose sight he cannot be;
While this world lasts you'll never part
From the true centre of my heart,
So there's no need to say yet more.
Return, oh thou whom I adore!
No longer distant from me dwell,
Absence is a mastering hell.
And so, remember me! Farewell.

ANONYMOUS
Latin
(12th century)

Ganymede and Helen

In Taurus was the sun and flowery Spring
Had reared her lovely, many blossomed head
When I 'neath olives on a grassy bed
Rejoiced at sweetest love remembering.

The perfumed flowers and freshness of the day,
The birds in chorus and the gentle breeze

Caressed my mind into a dreaming ease.
Oh, that such dreams should ever pass away!

I saw where Ganymede with Helen went
On summer grass beneath a lovely pine:
Serene their faces' so majestic line
That shamed the rose and lily in them blent.

Then seemed they both to sit upon the ground
Which to their lovely looks did often smile.
Such beauty gods alone have to beguile,
Yet both did wonder at the grace they found.

There they discussed a host of things, I ween,
And then about their beauties did debate;
They seemed two gods competing in their state,
The boy comparing him unto the queen.

She, longing for a man and fit for bed,
Could feel the goading pangs of cruel sex;
The comeliness of Ganymede did vex
And inner fires did glow an outward red.

Though Shame will turn her from love's place of rest,
The woman had no more a virgin's ice,
And, since she was not asked, she dared entice,
Off'ring the boy her lap, her mouth, her breast.

Though both were stretched upon the grass so free
And union been blessed between the two,
Young Ganymede, not knowing what to do,
Pressed close to her that he might passive be.

She senses something's wrong and in amaze
She pushes him aside, she weeps, she rails,
She curses nature and the gods bewails
That so unnatural had so fair a gaze.

The argument develops to a fight:
She praises womankind, the male he,
Till Nature and Reason are called to be
The judges and determiners of right.

Each therefore mounts a steed without delay
And spurs him on until three dawns are run
When they are greeted by the rising sun
At Nature's palace whence they made their way.

Dame Nature in the house of highest Jove,
While ruminating futures she can see,
In surest scales created things to be
And thread into uncounted figures wove.

Near stood companion Reason 'neath whose eyes
She causes growth and sows the future's seeds;
A mixture of the sexes there she kneads
Whence manifold fertilities arise.

Providence also, lofty to the view,
Whom God created from his purest thought,
Stood there beside, her vision missing naught;
Both past and present are in her purlieu.

'Hither,' she says, 'two lovely humans pace,
Of greatest beauty and astounding fair,
I wonder much that Earth could breed the pair
For Heaven's self would joy in such a race.

I hear the accusations of each one
But wish I didn't know their argument.
However, call the gods to parliament.'
And as she ordered, so they saw it done.

The tale arouses Jove and all his race.
Some with Ganymede, some with Helen side.
The seats are set, the palace opened wide
And heav'nly halls are filled with god-like grace.

As the two humans summoned to appear
Tie their horses and to the threshold go
(Their golden accoutrements all a-glow)
At once they're sighted as the gate they near.

The unexpected youth now ent'ring there
Shone like the Morning Star before the dawn.

All that he glimpsed his eyes appeared to scorn:
Mortality's disdained by one so fair.

His locks were like a royal golden train
In purest saffron by the Chinese dyed,
While those which round his lovely forehead tried
To touch his brows curled coyly back again.

Those brows were parted by a comely space,
His wide eyes sparkled with a lovely light,
His mouth demanded kisses as of right,
His whole expression radiated grace.

The lightly blushing Helen followed there –
Yet unknown to mankind and shy and grave
As virgin Cynthia rising from the wave –
Nor comes she second with a face so fair.

Part of her locks loose hanging did appear
While part were bound and beautifully spread
Back from her hairline to her coiffured head
Which was held high as one unused to fear.

Proud was her brow yet playful was her glance
And beautifully delicate her nose;
Her kiss had Venus scented with a rose,
Her god-smoothed chin did beauty more enhance.

And lest her hair her beauty should disguise
Spare locks were tamed and round her ears were drawn,
And then her face showed lovely as the dawn
Which pink and white each morning does arise.

And now the gods were squirming all around:
Apollo's hot while Mars his sighs were spent
As if he held Dame Venus closely pent.
He did not try to hide the beastly sound.

And shameless Jove calls Ganymede the fair
While for his queen had Nature set a place;
The presence of the boy she called disgrace
And would not name him either son or heir.

HELEN: 'Alas,' says Helen, 'much my pity runs
          Since womankind cold-heartedly you spurn
          And so the natural order overturn.
          Why had you father if you'll have no sons?'

GANYMEDE: 'Sons from old men will please a young man's zest
          For he has lust to pleasure youthful May.
          The gods' invention is the game we play
          Which still is followed by the bright and best.'

HELEN: 'But merely ornamental is your face
          And hastes to perish since you have no wife.
          If you should marry and beget new life
          A son's fresh form his father's would replace.'

GANYMEDE: 'I have no wish my features to repair;
          I pleasure men with me uniquely made.
          I hope with time your beauties all will fade
          For I am less beloved since you are fair.'

HELEN: 'How lovely are the different sexes' loves
          When men and women mutually entwine;
          By natural attraction they combine
          As do the beasts, the boars and e'en the doves.'

GANYMEDE: 'But mankind should not rut like pigs and birds
          For humans have the power of thought divine,
          And only peasants – those we may call swine –
          Are born as men to loose to female herds.'

HELEN: 'No love has ever touched a boyish heart,
          That's man and woman's coupled in one bed;
          For proper union's achieved, it's said,
          When both the sexes are distinct, apart.'

GANYMEDE: 'But things are sundered by disparity;
          More elegant are men joined each to each.
          Perhaps you're ignorant of rules of speech:
          The adjective and noun must both agree.'

HELEN: 'When first the great Creator formed the male
          He tried to make the woman yet more fair

So drawn to her the man might have an heir
And men's regard for men would not prevail.'

GANYMEDE: 'The love of women I might have agreed
Was good if manners went with looks by right,
But married women sully love's delight,
While those unmarried serve the public need.'

HELEN: 'Then let men blush and Nature grieve as well;
That men should join was never yet her mind.
Men yoked by Venus fruitless coupling find.
This boy, despite his sex, his charms will sell.'

GANYMEDE: 'Such worthy love each worthy man employs,
The highly placed such passion highly rate,
And men who moral matters arbitrate
Are not averse to loving soft-thighed boys.'

HELEN: 'I don't count those whom frenzied lusts deprave.
No reasons can for your defence conspire.
This youngster here has never felt desire
And so his wickedness is yet more grave.'

GANYMEDE: 'The smell of profit is a pleasing one
Whose sure appeal many men acclaim;
To gather riches most go on the game,
For men who want a boy will pay for fun.'

HELEN: 'Even if this were not a sin for youth,
For older men there's simply no excuse;
I have to laugh at their absurd abuse.
It *is* a sin in dotage, that's the truth.'

GANYMEDE: 'Your accusations of the old are just.
It seems disgraceful when their hairs are grey
To join the pleasures of the young and gay.
But they should not discourage boyish lust.'

HELEN: 'But tell me, lad, when youthful good looks fade,
With wrinkled face and beard that's more than fluff,
With chest turned bushy and your arsehole tough,
Will you be still the prize whence dreams are made?'

GANYMEDE: 'When by the years your virgin charms are marred,
Your lips have thickened and your skin is dry,
When crowsfoot's drooping round your misty eye,
Won't your most ardent lover be half-hard?'

HELEN: 'You try to keep as hairless as a sylph
And imitate a woman with your ass;
Defying nature you become a lass
And war on her with such unnatural filth.'

GANYMEDE: 'I'd like to be both soft and smooth, 'tis true,
But God forbid I had a woman's fane.
My softness puts off girls whom I disdain.
What difference between a mule and you?'

HELEN: 'Oh, were I not restrained by modesty
I'd not be mincing words with you, my son;
But I'll not be heard swearing, it's not done,
For foul words are a slight to modesty.'

GANYMEDE: 'But we came here to speak of vulgar acts,
This is no place to show the modest mind,
For piety and shame were left behind
And I shan't spare nor maiden's airs nor facts.'

HELEN: 'I don't know where to turn, for I must prate
With equal viciousness or loser be,
But if I strive for an equality
My virtue with a prostitute's will rate.'

GANYMEDE: 'Go try your lies on someone more naive!
Flat on your back you've propositioned men.
Where was such a dove-like innocence then?
This sudden change am I meant to believe?'

HELEN: 'But when a man a boy in congress meets
(The sort of man who rashly gelds his males)
The horrid sin o'er both of them prevails
And, shame to say, the morning shows stained sheets.'

GANYMEDE: 'The man into whose bed a strumpet slinks
And whose delight is filthy woman's quim,

When tarts recumbent open up to him
Learns all too well how their bilge water stinks.'

HELEN: 'Tarts smell like tarts and they are bound to cloy,
But girls excel the balsam's fragrant bliss;
There's honey on their lips and in their kiss,
And blest the man who virgins can enjoy.'

GANYMEDE: 'When Jupiter divides him in his bed
And turns to Juno first then to his boy,
He swiftly leaves his wife for proper joy,
Returns to quarrel, then takes me instead.'

HELEN: 'Your wretched Venus' fruitless, sterile art
Causes the love of women to decay;
When man mounts man in this disgraceful way
A monstrous Venus fakes the woman's part.'

GANYMEDE: 'It is not monstrous monsters to avoid:
The sticky bush, the darkly yawning cave,
The hole whose stink all others will outbrave;
Nor pole nor oar will e'er come near that void.'

HELEN: 'Be quiet, be quiet, such words are a disgrace!
Just talk more decently, you filthy pup!
If for a modest girl you won't shut up,
At least to Nature and the gods give place.'

GANYMEDE: 'If such things in cloaks of words you'd cover,
By such a tricked out truth you may beguile,
But I'll not help in gilding what is vile:
Words and actions both must suit each other.'

HELEN: 'Then I'll put by the cloak of shame and fear
Since now I am obliged to speak so plain:
When impure coupling you entertain
Between your thighs you lose the precious tear.

There's the unutterable disgrace:
My words are nasty but your deeds are base.'

The youth hears the unmentionable crime,
A stupor stops his speech and blushes rise
And furtive tears steal warmly from his eyes.
Lacking defence, he does not speak this time.

Now in his silence Reason from her throne
Speaks prudently with fitting words though few:
'Here needs no judge, the matter's plain to view.
I say: "Enough. The boy is overthrown." '

He says: 'I don't seek to refute my blame,
I recognize my error and what's right.'
'While I,' Apollo says, 'have seen the light.'
Jupiter declares: 'For Juno I'm aflame.'

On ancient heresies the gods thus frown,
Virgins rejoice and Juno offers prayers,
While Reason celebrates with Nature's heirs,
And public honours do the maiden crown.

Young Ganymede now asks if she will wed:
All the attendant gods approve of this
Since blessed union promises bliss,
While joy resounding woke me on my bed.

At God's desire this vision came to me;
Let Sodomites blush and Gomorrhans weep,
While all who sin thus show repentance deep.
And if ever I should sin so, Lord, have mercy!

ANONYMOUS
(12th century)

'A Perverse Custom'

A perverse custom it is to prefer boys to girls,
Since this type of love rebels against nature.
The wildness of beasts despises and flees this passion.
No male animal submits to another.

Animals curse and avoid evil caresses,
While man, more bestial than they, approves and pursues such
    things.
The irrational obeys reason's law;
The rational strays far from reason.
When the Lord blessed the first parents on earth,
He ordered them to be fruitful, to farm and fill the earth.
They were not both created men but a man and a woman,
And thus multiplied, filling the earth.
If both had been men and had favored this passion,
They would have died out without posterity.
Although he hates all vices, God despises this one particularly:
Of which – if you are doubtful – the destruction of Sodom is proof,
Where we read that sulfur and fire annihilated
The residents of Sodom and that an evil people perished with fit
    penalties.
Those who follow this heresy had better reconsider now
Or face condemnation to flames and sulfur.
Let them perish and go to hell, never to return,
Who wish to have tender youths as spouses.

[JOHN BOSWELL]

BIEIRIS de ROMANS
Provençal
(first half of 13th century?)

Lady Maria, in you merit and distinction,
joy, intelligence and perfect beauty,
hospitality and honor and distinction,
your noble speech and pleasing company,
your sweet face and merry disposition,
the sweet look and the loving expression
that exist in you without pretension
cause me to turn toward you with a pure heart.

Thus I pray you, if it please you that true love
and celebration and sweet humility
should bring me such relief with you,
if it please you, lovely woman, then give me

that which most hope and joy promises
for in you lie my desire and my heart
and from you stems all my happiness,
and because of you I'm often sighing.

And because merit and beauty raise you high
above all others (for none surpasses you),
I pray you, please, by this which does you honor,
don't grant your love to a deceitful suitor.

Lovely woman, whom joy and noble speech uplift,
and merit, to you my stanzas go,
for in you are gaiety and happiness,
and all good things one could ask of a woman.

[MAUD BOGIN]

DANTE ALIGHIERI
(1265–1321)

from *Inferno*
Canto XV

Now the hard margin bears us on, while steam
    From off the water makes a canopy
    Above, to fend the fire from bank and stream.

Just as the men of Flanders anxiously
    'Twixt Bruges and Wissant build their bulwarks wide
    Fearing the thrust and onset of the sea;

Or as the Paduans dyke up Brenta's tide
    To guard their towns and castles, ere the heat
    Loose down the snows from Chiarentana's side,

Such fashion were the brinks that banked the leat,
    Save that, whoe'er he was, their engineer
    In breadth and height had builded them less great.

Already we'd left the wood behind so far
   That I, had I turned back to view those glades,
   Could not have told their whereabouts; and here,

Hurrying close to the bank, a troop of shades
   Met us, who eyed us much as passers-by
   Eye one another when the daylight fades

To dusk and a new moon is in the sky,
   And knitting up their brows they squinnied at us
   Like an old tailor at the needle's eye.

Then, while the whole group peered upon me thus,
   One of them recognized me, who caught hard
   At my gown's hem, and cried: 'O marvellous!'

When he put out his hand to me, I stared
   At his scorched face, searching him through and through,
   So that the shrivelled skin and features scarred

Might not mislead my memory: then I knew:
   And, stooping down to bring my face near his,
   I said: 'What, you here, Ser Brunetto? you!'

And he: 'My son, pray take it not amiss
   If now Brunetto Latini at thy side
   Turn back awhile, letting this troop dismiss.'

'With all my heart I beg you to,' I cried;
   'Or I'll sit down with you, as you like best,
   If he there will permit – for he's my guide.'

'Oh, son,' said he, 'should one of our lot rest
   One second, a hundred years he must lie low,
   Nor even beat the flames back from his breast.

Therefore go on; I at thy skirts will go,
   And then rejoin my household, who thus race
   Forever lost, and weeping for their woe.'

I durst not venture from the road to pace
    Beside him, so I walked with down-bent head,
    Like some devout soul in a holy place.

He thus began: 'What chance or fate has led
    Thy footsteps here before thy final day?
    And who is this that guides thee?' So I said:

'Up in the sunlit life I lost my way
    In a dark vale, before my years had come
    To their full number. Only yesterday

At morn I turned my back upon its gloom;
    This other came, found me returning there,
    Stopped me, and by this path now leads me home.'

And he made answer: 'Follow but thy star;
    Thou canst not fail to win the glorious haven,
    If in glad life my judgement did not err.

Had I not died so soon, I would have given
    Counsel and aid to cheer thee in thy work,
    Seeing how favoured thou hast been by heaven.

But that ungrateful, that malignant folk
    Which formerly came down from Fiesole,
    And still is grained of mountain and hewn rock,

For thy good deeds will be thine enemy –
    With cause; for where the bitter sloes are rooted
    Is no fit orchard for the sweet fig-tree.

A blind people, and always so reputed,
    Proud, envious, covetous, since times remote;
    Cleanse off their customs lest thou be polluted.

Fortune has honours for thee – of such note,
    Both sides will seek to snatch thee and devour;
    But yet the good grass shall escape the goat.

Let Fiesole's wild beasts scratch up their sour
  Litter themselves from their rank native weed,
  Nor touch the plant, if any such can flower

Upon their midden, in whose sacred seed
  Survives the Roman line left there to dwell
  When this huge nest of vice began to breed.'

I answered him: 'Might I have had my will
  Believe me, you'd not yet been thrust apart
  From human life; for I keep with me still,

Stamped on my mind, and now stabbing my heart,
  The dear, benign, paternal image of you,
  You living, you hourly teaching me the art

By which men grow immortal; know this too:
  I am so grateful, that while I breathe air
  My tongue shall speak the thanks which are your due.

Your words about my future I'll write fair,
  With other texts, to show to a wise lady
  Who'll gloss them, if I ever get to her.

This much I'd have you know: I can stand steady,
  So conscience chide not, facing unafraid
  Whatever Fortune brings, for I am ready.

Time and again I've heard these forecasts made;
  The whims of Luck shall find me undeterred,
  So let her ply her wheel, the churl his spade.'

And when my master's ear had caught that word
  He turned right-face-about, and looked me straight
  In the eyes and said: 'Well-heeded is well-heard.'

Yet none the less I move on in debate
  With Ser Brunetto, asking him whose fame
  In all his band is widest and most great.

'Some,' he replies, 'it will be well to name;
   The rest we must pass over, for sheer dearth
   Of time – 'twould take too long to mention them.

All these, in brief, were clerks and men of worth
   In letters and in scholarship – none more so;
   And all defiled by one same taint on earth.

In that sad throng goes Francis of Accorso,
   And Priscian; could thy hunger have been sated
   By such scabbed meat, thou mightest have seen also

Him whom the Servant of servants once translated
   From Arno to Bacchiglione, where he left
   The body he'd unstrung and enervated.

I would say more, but must not; for a drift
   Of fresh dust rising from the sandy ground
   Warns me to cease and make my going swift;

Here come some folk with whom I mayn't be found;
   Keep handy my *Thesaurus*, where I yet
   Live on; I ask no more.' Then he turned round,

And seemed like one of those who over the flat
   And open course in the fields beside Verona
   Run for the green cloth; and he seemed, at that,

Not like a loser, but the winning runner.

[DOROTHY L. SAYERS]

'PANORMITANUS'
[ANTONIO BECCADELLI]
Latin
(15th century)

'Epitaph on Pegasus, a Limping Gay'

Oh, passer-by, should you inquire
About my name or my desire

Then know that buried 'neath this sod
Halt Pegasus awaits his God.
Learn his request now you've his name
And then you'll satisfy the same:
Whene'er a willing boy you'd lay,
Oh, screw him on my tomb, I pray.
'Tis not incense but coition
Eases souls in their perdition,
Such requiems a ghost desires
As sweetest respite 'midst Hell's fires.
Our ancestors on this truth seized:
Achilles Chiron's ghost appeased
When blond Patroclus' bottom knew
The pleasures of a well-wrought screw,
While Hercules first pierced his lad
When at the fun'ral of his dad.
So, like the ancients, I advise
You too should make this sacrifice.

'To Corydon'

This Quintus, Corydon, for whom you lust,
Dry, hollow-boned boy as saffron yellow,
He has no blood, his veins are filled with dust,
There is no sweating passion to the fellow!
An Ethiope usurped his father's place
Engendering some dusky offspring there.
Provoke his smile and you'll get a grimace
As if you'd shown the cunt of some old mare.
Go smell his mouth. 'It is an arse,' you'll say,
But sure an arse is cleaner than that gob.
Your dick will shrink for ever and a day
If once you try to kiss the putrid slob.
So, clear off, Quintus, you clapped, poxy whore,
Go where you please, you poisoner of cocks,
As many men are lost in your great maw
As ships are wrecked on the Sicilian rocks.
Yet publicly he does what women do,
This common tart gives every man the goods,
And he who such a boy would wish to screw
Would let the wild beasts shag him in the woods!

ANDREA POLIZIANO
Latin
(1454–1495)

'Unto the Breach'

Haste, haste my verses with your sharpened teeth
And seize my randy fundament beneath,
Which, swelling, lustful, both on heat and rank
Is made a balding corpse whose flesh is lank.
Behold its hairless brows and dribbling lips,
Its wrinkled cheeks on which a red eye drips,
All toothless save a pair of fangs that rot
Below two nostrils running o'er with snot;
Its foul-breathed, open lips with mucus flow
While ancient, useless tits like cobwebs show;
Beneath a sagging gut and scabby quim
Dry, skimpy buttocks wormy to the rim;
Both legs, both arms are shrivelled up and dried,
The joints stick out, the heels are one kibe.
Be sure there's nothing worthier rebuke
Or aught more guaranteed to make you puke.
But here all hucksters, carters once you'd find,
While butchers, hangmen, millers here would grind,
Here soldiers, servants, porters joined the band
And mule-drivers got a one night stand.
Now no one sees me, no one wants to talk,
They all deride me and my arsehole baulk,
Which, red with misprised lust, yet hotly burns,
And, shameless wanton, for still others yearns.
But now 'tis less a bum than corpse to rot;
Whene'er it itches (and when does it not?)
Is it to ask that I restrain desire
Or that I should myself put out the fire
As if I were an ass, a dog, a boar?
Be off, be off, abominable whore!
You either are a real anus or
Some wretched hobgoblin or graveyard muck;
And, if the choice were mine, I'd rather fuck
A sow than you, or satisfy my itch
Upon some farmyard ass or common bitch.

MICHELANGELO
(1475–1564)

To Luigi del Riccio, after the Death of Cecchino Bracci

Scarce had I seen for the first time his eyes
which to your living eyes were life and light,
when closed at last in death's injurious night
he opened them on God in Paradise.

I know it and I weep, too late made wise:
Yet was the fault not mine; for death's fell spite
robbed my desire of that supreme delight,
which in your better memory never dies.

Therefore, Luigi, if the task be mine
to make unique Cecchino smile in stone
for ever, now that earth hath made him dim,

if the beloved within the lover shine,
since art without him cannot work alone,
you must I carve to tell the world of him.

[J. A. SYMONDS]

To Tommaso de' Cavalieri

With your fair eyes a charming light I see,
for which my own blind eyes would peer in vain;
stayed by your feet the burden I sustain
which my lame feet find all too strong for me;

wingless upon your pinions forth I fly;
heavenward your spirit stirreth me to strain;
e'en as you will I blush and blanch again,
freeze in the sun, burn 'neath a frosty sky.

Your will includes and is the lord of mine;
life to my thoughts within your heart is given;
my words begin to breathe upon your breath:

like to the moon am I, that cannot shine
alone; for lo! our eyes see nought in heaven
save what the living sun illumineth.

[J. A. SYMONDS]

To Tommaso de' Cavalieri

Why should I seek to ease intense desire
with still more tears and windy words of grief,
when heaven, or late or soon, sends no relief
to souls whom love hath robed around with fire?

Why need my aching heart to death aspire,
when all must die? Nay, death beyond belief
unto these eyes would be both sweet and brief,
since in my sum of woes all joys expire!

Therefore because I cannot shun the blow
I rather seek, say who must rule my breast,
gliding between her gladness and her woe?

If only chains and bands can make me blest,
no marvel if alone and bare I go
an armèd Knight's[1] captive and slave confessed.

[J. A. SYMONDS]

From thy fair face I learn, O my loved lord,
that which no mortal tongue can rightly say;
the soul, imprisoned in her house of clay,
holpen by thee to God hath often soared:

and though the vulgar, vain, malignant horde
attribute what their grosser wills obey,
yet shall this fervent homage that I pay,
this love, this faith, pure joys for us afford.

1. a pun on the surname of the dedicatee

Lo, all the lovely things we find on earth
resemble for the soul that rightly sees,
that source of bliss divine which gave us birth:

nor have we first-fruits or remembrances
of heaven elsewhere. Thus, loving loyally,
I rise to God to make death sweet by thee.

[J. A. SYMONDS]

Thou knowest, love, I know that thou dost know
that I am here more near to thee to be,
and knowest that I know thou knowest me:
what means it then that we are sundered so?

If they are true, these hopes that from thee flow,
if it is real, this sweet expectancy,
break down the wall that stands 'twixt me and thee;
for pain in prison pent hath double woe.

Because in thee I love, O my loved lord,
what thou best lovest, be not therefore stern:
souls burn for souls, spirits to spirits cry!

I seek the splendour in thy fair face stored;
yet living man that beauty scarce can learn,
and he who fain would find it, first must die.

[J. A. SYMONDS]

PIETRO ARETINO
(1492–1556)

1

Brother Astolfo sated appetite
    By rubbing off against a choirboy's bum
    Until the ground was all a-wash with cum.
Was he, therefore, a sinful sodomite?

No, he was not. Brother Astolfo went
   Not *in* the bum but *on* the surface skin
   And since such friction is not deemed a sin
It constitutes no cause for punishment.

2

Brother Alberto, one hot summer day,
   Tried banishing his sloth and other smarts
   By flashing novices his private parts.
Was this profane or proper, would you say?

Since idleness will lead us to bad ways,
   Showing the boys his tool so each one starts
   Was good; but had he tried the bugger's arts
Alberto would have earned a hero's praise.

ANONYMOUS
Latin
(16th century)

'To Bellinus'

That Priapus with big divining rod
– From oak new-wrought this likeness of the god –
Has begged of me to answer in his name
Those verses you hacked out to his ill fame:
Reprobate, debauched and shady clown
Whom empty snail shells and weeds should crown,
Why do you, dog-like, gnaw me with your song?
If chance has made you perpetrate this wrong
My sesquipedalian, oaken dong
Will, when I catch you, horribly repay,
For this my frightful, bloody shaft will splay
Your arsehole open and then reach inside
To nudge your penis and tear up your hide,
Wherefore be warned thus far and henceforth cease,
Both you and yours leave Priapus in peace,
And, pathic poet, you revive that strain
No prick will bore your flabby arse again!

THÉODORE AGRIPPA D'A'UBIGNÉ
(1552–1630)

from *Les Tragiques*, Book II
lines 773–796

'*A Portrait of Henri III*'

Henri was suited to appraise the arts,
The finery and passion of court tarts
What with his barbered chin and whitened face,
His pathic eye and falsely girlish grace;
Indeed, once on a Twelfth Night, this queer beast,
Low-browed and brainless, decked the wonted feast
With pearl tricked ribbons in his flowing hair
Which 'neath a brimless bonnet debonair
Was done up in two arcs. He'd plucked his beard,
While's face with powder and with rouge besmeared
Made every courtier shudder and grimace:
A painted whore usurped their prince's place.
Think what a sight this was, how good to see
A king in corsets, satin finery
All black, cut Spanish fashion, slashes made
To cunningly reveal the golden braid;
While, to ensure an over-all effect,
His half-sleeves with white satin were bedecked;
These, mingling with others slashed and meet,
Were lost in frothing fancy round his feet!
Day-long sporting in this monstrous fashion
(The sickly costume equalling his passion)
For some long time all wondered if they'd seen
A womanly king or a male queen.

MICHAEL DRAYTON
(1563–1631)

from *Piers Gaveston*
lines 211–270

Gaveston describes his seduction of Edward, Prince of Wales

This *Edward* in the Aprill of his age,
Whil'st yet the Crowne sate on his fathers head,

My *Jove* with me, his *Ganimed*, his page,
Frolick as May, a lustie life we led:
　　He might commaund, he was my Soveraigns sonne,
　　And what I saide, by him was ever done.

My words as lawes, Autentique he alloude,
Mine yea, by him was never crost with no,
All my conceite as currant he avowde,
And as my shadowe still he served so,
　　My hand the racket, he the tennis ball,
　　My voyces echo, answering every call.

My youth the glasse where he his youth beheld,
Roses his lipps, my breath sweete *Nectar* showers,
For in my face was natures fayrest field,
Richly adornd with Beauties rarest flowers.
　　My breast his pillow, where he laide his head,
　　Mine eyes his booke, my bosome was his bed.

My smiles were life, and Heaven unto his sight,
All his delight concluding my desier,
From my sweete sunne, he borrowed all his light,
And as a flie play'd with my beauties fier,
　　His love-sick lippes at every kissing qualme,
　　Cling to my lippes, to cure their griefe with balme.

Like as the wanton Yvie with his twyne,
Whenas the Oake his rootlesse bodie warmes,
The straightest saplings strictly doth combyne,
Clipping the woodes with his lacivious armes:
　　Such our imbraces when our sporte begins,
　　Lapt in our armes, like *Ledas* lovely Twins.

Or as Love-nursing *Venus* when she sportes,
With cherry-lipt *Adonis* in the shade,
Figuring her passions in a thousand sortes,
With sighes, and teares,or what else might perswade,
　　Her deere, her sweete, her joy, her life, her love,
　　Kissing his browe, his cheeke, his hand, his glove.

My bewtie was the Load-starre of his thought,
My lookes the Pilot to his wandring eye,
By me his sences all a sleepe were brought,
When with sweete love I sang his lullaby.
   Nature had taught my tongue her perfect time,
   Which in his eare stroake duely as a chyme.

With sweetest speech, thus could I syranize,[1]
Which as strong *Philters* youthes desire could move,
And with such method could I rhetorize,
My musik plaied the measures to his love:
   In his faire brest, such was my soules impression,
   As to his eyes, my thoughts made intercession.

Thus like an *Eagle* seated in the sunne,
But yet a *Phenix* in my soveraigns eye,
We act with shame, our revels are begunne,
The wise could judge of our *Catastrophe*:
   But we proceede to play our wanton prize,
   Our mournfull Chorus was a world of eyes.

The table now of all delight is layd,
Serv'd with what banquets bewtie could devise,
The *Sirens* singe, and false *Calypso* playd,
Our feast is grac'd with youthes sweete comœdies,
   Our looks with smiles, are sooth'd of every eye,
   Carrousing love in boules of Ivorie.

lines 313–324

And thus like slaves we sell our soules to sinne,
Vertue forgot by worldes deceitfull trust,
Alone by pleasure are we entred in,
Now wandring in the labyrinth of lust,
   For when the soule is drowned once in vice,
   The sweete of sinne, makes hell a paradice.

O Pleasure thou, the very lure of sinne,
The roote of woe, our youthes deceitfull guide,

1. to be as deceptively harmonious as the Sirens

A shop where all confected poysons been,
The bayte of lust, the instrument of pride,
    Inchanting *Circes*, smoothing cover-guile,
    Aluring *Siren*, flattering Crockodile.

lines 403–444
Gaveston relates his downfall

Why doe I quake my down-fall to reporte?
Tell on my ghost, the storie of my woe,
The King commaunds, I must depart the court,
I aske no question, he will have it so:
    The Lyons roring, lesser beastes doe feare,
    The greatest flye, when he approacheth neare.

My Prince is now appointed to his guarde,
As from a traytor he is kept from me,
My banishment already is preparde,
Away I must, there is no remedie:
    On paine of death I may no longer stay,
    Such is revenge which brooketh no delaye.

The skies with cloudes are all invelloped,
The pitchie fogs eclipse my cheerfull Sunne,
The geatie night hath all her curtaines spred
And all the ayre with vapours overrun:
    Wanting those rayes whose cleernes lent me light,
    My sun-shine day is turn'd to black-fac'd night.

Like to the birde of *Ledaes*[2] lemmans[3] die,
Beating his breast against the silver streame,
The fatall prophet of his destinie,
With mourning chants, his death approching theame:
    So now I sing the dirges of my fall,
    The Anthemes of my fatall funerall.

Or as the faithfull Turtle[4] for her make
Whose youth enjoyed her deere virginitie,

2. swan 3. lover, i.e. Jove 4. dove

Sits shrouded in some melancholie brake
Chirping forth accents of her miserie,
  Thus halfe distracted sitting all alone,
  With speaking sighs, to utter forth my mone.

My bewtie s'dayning to behold the light
Now weather-beaten with a thousand stormes,
My daintie lims must travaile day and night,
Which oft were lulde in princely *Edwards* armes,
  Those eyes where bewtie sate in all her pride,
  With fearefull objects fild on every side.

The Prince so much astonisht with the blowe,
So that it seem'd as yet he felt no paine,
Untill at length awakned by his woe,
He sawe the wound by which his joyes were slaine,
  His cares fresh bleeding fainting more and more,
  No Cataplasma[1] now to cure the sore.

lines 469–515
Edward's lament

O breake my hart quoth he, O breake and dye,
Whose infant thoughts were nurst with sweete delight;
But now the Inne of care and miserie,
Whose pleasing hope is murthered with despight:
  O end my dayes, for now my joyes are done,
  Wanting my *Peirs*, my sweetest *Gaveston*.

Farewell my Love, companion of my youth,
My soules delight, the subject of my mirth,
My second selfe if I reporte the truth,
The rare and onely *Phenix* of the earth,
  Farewell sweete friend, with thee my joyes are gone,
  Farewell my *Peirs*, my lovely *Gaveston*.

1. plaster

What are the rest but painted Imagrie,
Dombe Idols made to fill up idle roomes,
But gaudie anticks, sportes of foolerie,
But fleshly coffins, goodly gilded tombes,
    But puppets which with others words replie,
    Like pratling ecchoes soothing every lie?

O damned world, I scorne thee and thy worth,
The very source of all iniquitie:
An ougly damme that brings such monsters forth,
The maze of death, nurse of impietie,
    A filthie sinke, where lothsomnes doth dwell,
    A labyrinth, a jayle, a very hell.

Deceitfull *Siren* traytor to my youth,
Bane to my blisse, false theefe that stealst my joyes:
Mother of lyes, sworne enemie to truth,
The ship of fooles fraught all with gaudes and toyes,
    A vessell stuft with foule hypocrisie,
    The very temple of Idolatrie.

O earth-pale Saturne most malevolent,
Combustious Planet, tyrant in thy raigne,
The sworde of wrath, the roote of discontent,
In whose ascendant all my joyes are slaine:
    Thou executioner of foule bloodie rage,
    To act the will of lame decrepit age.

My life is but a very mappe of woes,
My joyes the fruite of an untimely birth,
My youth in labour with unkindly throwes,
My pleasures are like plagues that raigne on earth,
    All my delights like streames that swiftly run,
    Or like the dewe exhaled by the Sun.

O Heavens why are you deafe unto my mone?
S'dayne you my prayers? or scorne to heare my misse?
Cease you to move, or is your pittie gone?
Or is it you that rob me of my blisse?
    What are you blinde, or winke and will not see?
    Or doe you sporte at my calamitie?

CHRISTOPHER MARLOWE
(1564–1593)

from *Hero and Leander*, Book 1
lines 51–90

Amorous Leander, beautiful and young,
(Whose tragedy divine Musaeus sung)
Dwelt at Abydos; since him dwelt there none
From whom succeeding times make greater moan.
His dangling tresses that were never shorn,
Had they been cut, and unto Colchos borne,
Would have allur'd the vent'rous youth of Greece
To hazard more than for the golden Fleece.
Fair Cynthia wish'd his arms might be her sphere;
Grief makes her pale, because she moves not there.
His body was as straight as Circe's wand;
Jove might have sipt out nectar from his hand.
Even as delicious meat is to the taste,
So was his neck in touching, and surpast
The white of Pelops' shoulder: I could tell ye,
How smooth his breast was, and how white his belly,
And whose immortal fingers did imprint
That heavenly path with many a curious dint,
That runs along his back; but my rude pen
Can hardly blazon forth the loves of men,
Much less of powerful gods: let it suffice
That my slack muse sings of Leander's eyes,
Those orient cheeks and lips, exceeding his
That leapt into the water for a kiss
Of his own shadow, and despising many,
Died ere he could enjoy the love of any.
Had wild Hippolytus Leander seen,
Enamoured of his beauty had he been:
His presence made the rudest peasant melt,
That in the vast uplandish country dwelt;
The barbarous Thracian soldier, mov'd with naught,
Was mov'd with him, and for his favour sought.
Some swore he was a maid in man's attire,
For in his looks were all that men desire,

A pleasant smiling cheek, a speaking eye,
A brow for love to banquet royally;
And such as knew he was a man would say,
'Leander, thou art made for amorous play:
Why art thou not in love, and lov'd of all?
Though thou be fair, yet be not thine own thrall.'

lines 153–226
Leander swims the Hellespont

With that he stripp'd him to the ivory skin,
And crying, 'Love, I come,' leapt lively in.
Whereat the sapphire-visag'd god grew proud,
And made his capering Triton sound aloud,
Imagining that Ganymede, displeas'd,
Had left the heavens; therefore on him he seiz'd.
Leander striv'd, the waves about him wound,
And pull'd him to the bottom, where the ground
Was strew'd with pearl, and in low coral groves
Sweet singing mermaids sported with their loves
On heaps of heavy gold, and took great pleasure
To spurn in careless sort the shipwrack treasure.
For here the stately azure palace stood,
Where kingly Neptune and his train abode.
The lusty god embrac'd him, call'd him 'love,'
And swore he never should return to Jove.
But when he knew it was not Ganymede,
For under water he was almost dead,
He heav'd him up, and looking on his face
Beat down the bold waves with his triple mace,
Which mounted up, intending to have kiss'd him,
And fell in drops like tears because they miss'd him.
Leander being up, began to swim,
And looking back, saw Neptune follow him;
Whereat aghast, the poor soul 'gan to cry,
'O let me visit Hero ere I die.'
The god put Helle's bracelet on his arm,
And swore the sea should never do him harm.
He clapp'd his plump cheeks, with his tresses play'd,

And smiling wantonly, his love bewray'd.
He watch'd his arms, and as they open'd wide,
At every stroke, betwixt them would he slide,
And steal a kiss, and then run out and dance,
And as he turn'd, cast many a lustful glance,
And throw him gaudy toys to please his eye,
And dive into the water, and there pry
Upon his breast, his thighs, and every limb,
And up again, and close beside him swim,
And talk of love. Leander made reply,
'You are deceiv'd, I am no woman, I.'
Thereat smil'd Neptune, and then told a tale,
How that a shepherd sitting in a vale
Played with a boy so lovely fair and kind,
As for his love both earth and heaven pin'd;
That of the cooling river durst not drink,
Lest water-nymphs should pull him from the brink.
And when he sported in the fragrant lawns,
Goat-footed Satyrs and upstarting Fauns
Would steal him thence. Ere half this tale was done,
'Aye me,' Leander cried, 'th' enamoured sun,
That now should shine on Thetis' glassy bower,
Descends upon my radiant Hero's tower:
O that these tardy arms of mine were wings!'
And as he spake, upon the waves he springs.
Neptune was angry that he gave no ear,
And in his heart revenging malice bare:
He flung at him his mace, but as it went,
He call'd it in, for love made him repent.
The mace returning back his own hand hit,
As meaning to be 'veng'd for darting it.
When this fresh bleeding wound Leander viewed,
His colour went and came, as if he rued
The grief which Neptune felt. In gentle breasts
Relenting thoughts, remorse and pity rests.
And who have hard hearts, and obdurate minds,
But vicious, hare-brain'd, and illit'rate hinds?
The god seeing him with pity to be moved,
Thereon concluded that he was beloved.
(Love is too full of faith, too credulous,
With folly and false hope deluding us.)

Wherefore, Leander's fancy to surprise,
To the rich Ocean for gifts he flies:
'Tis wisdom to give much, a gift prevails,
When deep persuading Oratory fails.

WILLIAM SHAKESPEARE
(1564–1616)

Sonnets

20

A woman's face with nature's own hand painted,
Hast thou the master mistress of my passion,
A woman's gentle heart but not acquainted
With shifting change as is false women's fashion,
An eye more bright than theirs, less false in rolling:
Gilding the object whereupon it gazeth,
A man in hue all hues in his controlling,
Which steals men's eyes and women's souls amazeth.
And for a woman wert thou first created,
Till nature as she wrought thee fell a-doting,
And by addition me of thee defeated,
By adding one thing to my purpose nothing.
　　But since she pricked thee out for women's pleasure,
　　Mine be thy love and thy love's use their treasure.

29

When in disgrace with Fortune and men's eyes,
I all alone beweep my outcast state,
And trouble deaf heaven with my bootless cries,
And look upon my self and curse my fate,
Wishing me like to one more rich in hope,
Featured like him, like him with friends possessed,
Desiring this man's art, and that man's scope,
With what I most enjoy contented least,
Yet in these thoughts my self almost despising,
Haply I think on thee, and then my state,

(Like to the lark at break of day arising
From sullen earth) sings hymns at heaven's gate,
    For thy sweet love remembered such wealth brings,
    That then I scorn to change my state with kings.

35

No more be grieved at that which thou hast done,
Roses have thorns, and silver fountains mud,
Clouds and eclipses stain both moon and sun,
And loathsome canker lives in sweetest bud.
All men make faults, and even I in this,
Authorizing thy trespass with compare,
My self corrupting salving thy amiss,
Excusing thy sins more than thy sins are:
For to thy sensual fault I bring in sense,
Thy adverse party is thy advocate,
And 'gainst my self a lawful plea commence:
Such civil war is in my love and hate,
    That I an accessary needs must be,
    To that sweet thief which sourly robs from me.

36

Let me confess that we two must be twain,
Although our undivided loves are one:
So shall those blots that do with me remain,
Without thy help, by me be borne alone.
In our two loves there is but one respect,
Though in our lives a separable spite,
Which though it alter not love's sole effect,
Yet doth it steal sweet hours from love's delight.
I may not evermore acknowledge thee,
Lest my bewailéd guilt should do thee shame,
Nor thou with public kindness honour me,
Unless thou take that honour from thy name:
    But do not so, I love thee in such sort,
    As thou being mine, mine is thy good report.

53

What is your substance, whereof are you made,
That millions of strange shadows on you tend?
Since every one, hath every one, one shade,
And you but one, can every shadow lend:
Describe Adonis and the counterfeit,
Is poorly imitated after you,
On Helen's cheek all art of beauty set,
And you in Grecian tires are painted new:
Speak of the spring, and foison of the year,
The one doth shadow of your beauty show,
The other as your bounty doth appear,
And you in every blesséd shape we know.
    In all external grace you have some part,
    But you like none, none you for constant heart.

55

Not marble, nor the gilded monuments
Of princes shall outlive this powerful rhyme,
But you shall shine more bright in these contents
Than unswept stone, besmeared with sluttish time.
When wasteful war shall statues overturn,
And broils root out the work of masonry,
Nor Mars his sword, nor war's quick fire shall burn:
The living record of your memory.
'Gainst death, and all-oblivious enmity
Shall you pace forth, your praise shall still find room,
Even in the eyes of all posterity
That wear this world out to the ending doom.
    So till the judgement that your self arise,
    You live in this, and dwell in lovers' eyes.

57

Being your slave what should I do but tend,
Upon the hours, and times of your desire?
I have no precious time at all to spend;
Nor services to do till you require.

Nor dare I chide the world-without-end hour,
Whilst I (my sovereign) watch the clock for you,
Nor think the bitterness of absence sour,
When you have bid your servant once adieu.
Nor dare I question with my jealous thought,
Where you may be, or your affairs suppose,
But like a sad slave stay and think of nought
Save where you are, how happy you make those.
　So true a fool is love, that in your will,
　(Though you do any thing) he thinks no ill.

60

Like as the waves make towards the pebbled shore,
So do our minutes hasten to their end,
Each changing place with that which goes before,
In sequent toil all forwards do contend.
Nativity once in the main of light,
Crawls to maturity, wherewith being crowned,
Crookéd eclipses 'gainst his glory fight,
And Time that gave, doth now his gift confound.
Time doth transfix the flourish set on youth,
And delves the parallels in beauty's brow,
Feeds on the rarities of nature's truth,
And nothing stands but for his scythe to mow.
　And yet to times in hope, my verse shall stand
　Praising thy worth, despite his cruel hand.

67

Ah wherefore with infection should he live,
And with his presence grace impiety,
That sin by him advantage should achieve,
And lace it self with his society?
Why should false painting imitate his cheek,
And steal dead seeming of his living hue?
Why should poor beauty indirectly seek,
Roses of shadow, since his rose is true?
Why should he live, now nature bankrupt is,

Beggared of blood to blush through lively veins,
For she hath no exchequer now but his,
And proud of many, lives upon his gains?
   O him she stores, to show what wealth she had,
   In days long since, before these last so bad.

87

Farewell! thou art too dear for my possessing,
And like enough thou know'st thy estimate,
The charter of thy worth gives thee releasing:
My bonds in thee are all determinate.
For how do I hold thee but by thy granting,
And for that riches where is my deserving?
The cause of this fair gift in me is wanting,
And so my patent back again is swerving.
Thy self thou gav'st, thy own worth then not knowing,
Or me to whom thou gav'st it, else mistaking,
So thy great gift upon misprision growing,
Comes home again, on better judgement making.
   Thus have I had thee as a dream doth flatter,
   In sleep a king, but waking no such matter.

94

They that have power to hurt, and will do none,
That do not do the thing, they most do show,
Who moving others, are themselves as stone,
Unmovéd, cold, and to temptation slow:
They rightly do inherit heaven's graces,
And husband nature's riches from expense,
They are the lords and owners of their faces,
Others, but stewards of their excellence:
The summer's flower is to the summer sweet,
Though to it self, it only live and die,
But if that flower with base infection meet,
The basest weed outbraves his dignity:
   For sweetest things turn sourest by their deeds,
   Lilies that fester, smell far worse than weeds.

104

To me fair friend you never can be old,
For as you were when first your eye I eyed,
Such seems your beauty still: three winters cold,
Have from the forests shook three summers' pride,
Three beauteous springs to yellow autumn turned,
In process of the seasons have I seen,
Three April perfumes in three hot Junes burned,
Since first I saw you fresh which yet are green.
Ah yet doth beauty like a dial hand,
Steal from his figure, and no pace perceived,
So your sweet hue, which methinks still doth stand
Hath motion, and mine eye may be deceived.
  For fear of which, hear this thou age unbred,
  Ere you were born was beauty's summer dead.

110

Alas 'tis true, I have gone here and there,
And made my self a motley to the view,
Gored mine own thoughts, sold cheap what is most dear,
Made old offences of affections new.
Most true it is, that I have looked on truth
Askance and strangely: but by all above,
These blenches gave my heart another youth,
And worse essays proved thee my best of love.
Now all is done, have what shall have no end,
Mine appetite I never more will grind
On newer proof, to try an older friend,
A god in love, to whom I am confined.
  Then give me welcome, next my heaven the best,
  Even to thy pure and most most loving breast.

116

Let me not to the marriage of true minds
Admit impediments, love is not love
Which alters when it alteration finds,
Or bends with the remover to remove.

O no, it is an ever-fixéd mark
That looks on tempests and is never shaken;
It is the star to every wand'ring bark,
Whose worth's unknown, although his height be taken.
Love's not Time's fool, though rosy lips and cheeks
Within his bending sickle's compass come,
Love alters not with his brief hours and weeks,
But bears it out even to the edge of doom:
    If this be error and upon me proved,
    I never writ, nor no man ever loved.

144

Two loves I have of comfort and despair,
Which like two spirits do suggest me still,
The better angel is a man right fair:
The worser spirit a woman coloured ill.
To win me soon to hell my female evil,
Tempteth my better angel from my side,
And would corrupt my saint to be a devil:
Wooing his purity with her foul pride.
And whether that my angel be turned fiend,
Suspect I may, yet not directly tell,
But being both from me both to each friend,
I guess one angel in another's hell.
    Yet this shall I ne'er know but live in doubt,
    Till my bad angel fire my good one out.

ANONYMOUS
French
(*c.* 1570)

'Epitaph for Jean Maillard'

Jean Maillard lies buried here,
Less a wide-boy than a queer
Who believed that if desire
Set a tutor's flesh on fire

Then a true-born Sorbonite
Could become a sodomite
Without any fear of vice
Because the action was so nice.
But, afraid that woman's lip
Just might let his secret slip
And so scandalize the rest,
Our good master thought it best
In case he was discovered
To ensure he was covered
By this fair expedient:
She could borrow him for rent.

THOMAS HEYWOOD
(1574?–1641)

Jupiter and Ganimede

The Argument of the Dialogue intituled Iupiter and Ganimede

Iove's Masculine love this Fable reprehends,
And wanton dotage on the Trojan Boy.
Shap'd like an Eagle, he from th'earth ascends,
And beares through th'aire his new *Delight* and *Joy*.
  In Ganimed's exprest a simple Swaine
  Who would leave Heaven, to live on Earth againe.

The Dialogue

Iupiter. Now kisse me, lovely *Ganimed*, for see,
Wee are at length arriv'd where wee would bee:
I have no crooked beak, no tallons keen,
No wings or feathers are about me seen;
I am not such as I but late appear'd.
Ganimed. But were you not that Eagle who late fear'd,
And snatcht me from my flocke? where is become
That shape? you speak now, who but late were dumbe.
Iupit. I am no man, faire Youth, as I appeare,
Nor Eagle, to astonish thee with feare:
But King of all the gods, who for some reason

Have by my power transhap't me for a season.
Ganim. What's that you say? you are not *Pan*, I know:
Where's then your pipe? or where your horns, should grow
Upon your temples? where your hairy thighes?
Iupiter. Thinks *Ganimed* that godhood only lies
In rurall *Pan*?
Gan. Why not? I know him one:
We shepheards sacrifice to him alone.
A spotted Goat into some cave we drive,
And then he seiseth on the beast alive.
Thou art but some Childe-stealer, that's thy best.
Iupit. Hast thou not heard of any man contest
By *Iove's* great Name? nor his rich Altar view'd
In Gargarus, with plenteous showres bedew'd?
There seen his fire and thunder?
Ganim. Do you then
Affirme your selfe the same who on us men
Of late pour'd haile-stones? he that dwells above us,
And there makes noise; yet some will say doth love us?
To whom my Father did observance yeeld,
And sacrific'd the best Ram in the field.
Why then (if you of all the gods be chiefe)
Have you, by stealing me, thus play'd the thiefe;
When in my abscence the poore sheep may stray,
Or the wilde ravenous Wolves snatch them away?
Iupit. Yet hast thou care of Lambs, of Folds, of sheep;
That now art made immortall, and must keep
Societie with Us.
Ganim. I no way can
Conceive you. Will you play the honest man,
And beare me backe to Ida?
Iup. So in vaine
I shap'd me like an Eagle, if againe
I should returne thee backe.
Ganim. My father, he
By this hath made inquirie after me;
And if the least of all the flocke be eaten
I in his rage am most sure to be beaten.
Iup. Where shall he finde thee?
Ganim. That's the thing I feare,
He never can clime up to meet me here,

But if thou beest a good god, let me passe
Into the mount of Ida where I was:
And then I'le offer, in my thankfull piety,
Another well fed Goat unto thy deity,
(As price of my redemption) three yeares old,
And now the chief and prime in all the fold.
Iup. How simple is this innocent Lad? a meere
Innocuous childe. But *Ganimed* now heare:
Bury the thoughts of all such terren drosse,
Thinke Ida and thy fathers flocks no losse:
Thou now art heavenly, and much grace mayst do
Unto thy father and thy country too.
No more of cheese and milke from henceforth thinke,
Ambrosia thou shalt eat, and Nectar drinke,
Which thy faire hands in flowing cups shalt fill
To me and others, but attend us still;
And (that which most should moove thee) make thy abode
Where thou art now, thou shalt be made a god,
No more be mortall, and thy glorious star
Shine with refulgence, and be seen from far.
Here thou art ever happy.
Ganim. But I pray,
When I would sport me; who is here to play?
For when in Ida I did call for any,
Both of my age and growth it yeelded many.
Iup. Play-fellowes for thee I will likewise finde,
Cupid, with divers others to thy minde,
And such as are of both thy yeares and size,
To sport with thee all what thou canst devise:
Only be bold and pleasant, and then know
Thou shalt have need of nothing that's below.
Ganim. But here no service I can do indeed,
Unlesse in heaven you had some flocks to feed.
Iup. Yes, thou to me shalt fill celestiall wine,
And wait upon me when in state I dine:
Then learne to serve in banquets.
Ganim. That I can
Already, without help of any man:
For I use ever when we dine or sup,
To poure out milke, and crowne the pastorall cup.
Iup. Fie, how thou still remember'st milke and beasts,

As if thou wert to serve at mortall Feasts:
Know, this is heaven, be merry then and laugh;
When thou art thirsty thou shalt Nectar quaffe.
Ganim. Is it so sweet as milke?
Iup. Pris'd far before,
Which tasted once, milke thou wilt aske no more.
Ganim. Where shall I sleep a nights? what, must I ly
With my companion *Cupid*?
Iup. So then I
In vaine had rap'd thee: but I from thy sheep
Of purpose stole thee, by my side to sleep.
Ganim. Can you not lie alone? but will your rest
Seeme sweeter, if I nuzzle on your brest?
Iup. Yes, being a childe so faire:
Ganim. How can you thinke
Of beauty, whil'st you close your eies and winke?
Iup. It is a sweet inticement, to increase
Contented rest, when our desire's at peace.
Ganim. I, but my father every morne would chide,
And say, those nights he lodg'd me by his side
I much disturb'd his rest; tumbling and tossing
Athwart the bed, my little legs still crossing
His: either kicking this way, that way sprawling,
Or if hee but remov'd me, straightwaies yawling:
Then grumbling in my dreams, (for so he sed)
And oft times sent me to my mothers bed:
And then would she complaine upon me worse.
Then if for that you stole me, the best course
Is even to send me backe againe; for I
Am ever so unruly where I lie,
Wallowing and tumbling, and such coile I keep,
That I shall but disturb you in your sleep.
Iupit. In that the greater pleasure I shall take,
Because I love still to be kept awake.
I shall embrace and kisse thee then the ofter,
And by that means my bed seem much the softer.
Ganim. But whilst you wake I'le sleepe.
Iup. Mercury, see
This lad straight taste of immortalitie;
And making him of service capable,
Let him be brought to wait on us at table.

RICHARD BARNFIELD
(1574–1627)

Sonnets

1

Sporting at fancie, setting light by love,
  There came a theefe, and stole away my heart,
  (And therefore rob'd me of my chiefest part)
Yet cannot Reason him a felon prove.
For why his beauty (my hearts thiefe) affirmeth,
  Piercing no skin (the bodies fensive wall)
  And having leave, and free consent withall,
Himselfe not guilty, from love guilty tearmeth,
Conscience the Judge, twelve Reasons are the Jurie,
  They finde mine eies the beutie t' have let in,
  And on this verdict given, agreed they bin,
Wherefore, because his beauty did allure yee,
  Your Doome is this; in teares still to be drowned,
  When his faire forehead with disdain is frowned.

4

Two stars there are in one faire firmament,
  (Of some intitled *Ganymedes* sweet face),
  Which other stars in brightnes doe disgrace,
As much as *Po* in clearenes passeth *Trent*.
Nor are they common natur'd stars: for why,
  These stars when other shine vaile their pure light,
  And when all other vanish out of sight,
They adde a glory to the worlds great eie.
By these two stars my life is onely led,
  In them I place my joy, in them my pleasure,
  Love's piercing Darts, and Natures precious treasure
With their sweet foode my fainting soule is fed:
  Then when my sunne is absent from my sight
  How can it chuse (with me) but be dark night?

6

Sweet Corrall lips, where Nature's treasure lies,
  The balme of blisse, the soveraigne salve of sorrow,
  The secret touch of loves heart-burning arrow,
Come quench my thirst or els poor *Daphnis* dies.
One night I dream'd (alas twas but a Dreame)
  That I did feele the sweetnes of the same,
  Where-with inspir'd, I young againe became,
And from my heart a spring of blood did streame,
But when I wak't, I found it nothing so,
  Save that my limbs (me thought) did waxe more strong
  And I more lusty far, and far more yong.
This gift on him rich Nature did bestow.
  Then if in dreaming so, I so did speede,
  What should I doe, if I did so indeede?

7

Sweet *Thames* I honour thee, not for thou art
  The chiefest River of the fairest Ile,
  Nor for thou dost admirers eies beguile,
But for thou hold'st the keeper of my heart,
For on thy waves, (thy Christal-billow'd waves),
  My fairest faire, my silver Swan is swimming:
  Against the sunne his pruned feathers trimming:
Whilst *Neptune* his faire feete with water laves,
Neptune, I feare not thee, nor yet thine eie,
  And yet (alas) *Apollo* lov'd a boy,
  And *Cyparissus* was *Silvanus* joy.
No, no, I feare none but faire *Thetis*, I
  For if she spie my Love, (alas) aie me,
  My mirth is turn'd to extreame miserie.

8

Sometimes I wish that I his pillow were,
  So might I steale a kisse, and yet not seene,
  So might I gaze upon his sleeping eine,
Although I did it with a panting feare:

But when I well consider how vaine my wish is,
　　Ah foolish Bees (thinke I) that doe not sucke
　　His lips for hony; but poore flowers doe plucke
Which have no sweet in them: when his sole kisses,
Are able to revive a dying soule.
　　Kisse him, but sting him not, for if you doe,
　　His angry voice your flying will pursue:
But when they heare his tongue,what can controule,
　　Their back-returne? for then they plaine may see,
　　How hony-combs from his lips dropping bee.

10

Thus was my love, thus was my *Ganymed*,
　　(Heavens joy, worlds wonder, natures fairest work,
　　In whose aspect Hope and Dispaire doe lurke)
Made of pure blood in whitest snow yshed,
And for sweete *Venus* only form'd his face,
　　And his each member delicately framed,
　　And last of all faire *Ganymede* him named,
His limbs (as their Creatrix[1]) her imbrace.
But as for his pure, spotles, vertuous minde,
　　Because it sprung of chaste *Dianaes* blood,
　　(Goddesse of Maides, directresse of all good,)
Hit wholy is to chastity inclinde.
　　And thus it is: as far as I can prove,
　　He loves to be beloved, but not to love.

11

Sighing, and sadly sitting by my Love,
　　He ask't the cause of my hearts sorrowing,
　　Conjuring me by heavens eternall King
To tell the cause which me so much did move.
Compell'd: (quoth I) to thee will I confesse,
　　Love is the cause; and only love it is
　　That doth deprive me of my heavenly blisse.
Love is the paine that doth my heart oppresse.
And what is she (quoth he) whom thou do'st love?

1. Nature

Looke in this glasse (quoth I) there shalt thou see
   The perfect forme of my faelicitie.
When, thinking that it would strange Magique prove,
   He open'd it: and taking of the cover,
   He straight perceav'd himselfe to be my Lover.

12

Some talke of *Ganymede* th' *Idalian* Boy,
   And some of faire *Adonis* make their boast,
   Some talke of him whom lovely *Laeda* lost,
And some of *Ecchoes* love that was so coy.
They speake by heere-say, I of perfect truth,
   They partially commend the persons named,
   And for them, sweet Encomions[1] have framed:
I onely t'him have sacrifized my youth.
As for those wonders of antiquitie,
   And those whom later ages have injoy'd,
   (But ah what hath not cruell death destroide?
Death, that envies this worlds felicitie),
   They were (perhaps) lesse faire then Poets write.
   But he is fairer then I can indite.

14

Here, hold this glove (this milk-white cheveril glove)
   Not quaintly over-wrought with curious knots,
   Not deckt with golden spangs,[2] nor silver spots,
Yet wholesome for thy hand as thou shalt prove.
Ah no; (sweet boy) place this glove neere thy heart,
   Weare it, and lodge it still within thy brest,
   So shalt thou make me (most unhappy), blest.
So shalt thou rid my paine, and ease my smart:
How can that be (perhaps) thou wilt reply,
   A glove is for the hand not for the heart,
   Nor can it well be prov'd by common art,
Nor reasons rule. To this, thus answere I:
   If thou from glove do'st take away the g,
   Then glove is love: and so I send it thee.

1. poems of praise   2. spangles

17

Cherry-Lipt *Adonis* in his snowie shape,
   Might not compare with his pure Ivorie white,
   On whose faire front a Poets pen may write,
Whose rosiate red excels the crimson grape,
His love-enticing delicate soft limbs,
   Are rarely fram'd t'intrap poore gazing eies:
   His cheekes, the Lillie and Carnation dies,
With lovely tincture which *Apolloes* dims.
His lips ripe strawberries in Nectar wet,
   His mouth a Hive, his tongue a hony-combe,
   Where Muses (like Bees) make their mansion.
His teeth pure Pearle in blushing Correll set.
   Oh how can such a body sinne-procuring,
   Be slow to love, and quicke to hate, enduring?

19

Ah no; nor I my selfe: though my pure love
   (Sweete *Ganymede*) to thee hath still beene pure,
   And even till my last gaspe shall aie endure,
Could ever thy obdurate beuty move:
Then cease oh Goddesse sonne (for sure thou art,
   A Goddesse sonne that canst resist desire)
   Cease thy hard heart, and entertaine loves fire,
Within thy sacred breast: by Natures art.
And as I love thee more then any Creature,
   (Love thee, because thy beautie is divine:
   Love thee, because my selfe, my soule is thine:
Wholie devoted to thy lovelie feature),
   Even so of all the vowels, I and U,[1]
   Are dearest unto me, as doth ensue.

20

But now my Muse toyled with continuall care,
   Begins to faint, and slacke her former pace,
   Expecting favour from that heavenly grace,

1. I (or J) and U are the boy's initials

That maie (in time) her feeble strength repaire.
Till when (sweete youth) th'essence of my soule,
   (Thou that dost sit and sing at my hearts griefe.
   Thou that dost send thy shepheard no reliefe)
Beholde, these lines; the sonnes of Teares and Dole.
Ah had great *Colin* chiefe of sheepheards all,
   Or gentle *Rowland*, my professed friend,
   Had they thy beautie, or my pennance pend,
Greater had beene thy fame, and lesse my fall:
   But since that everie one cannot be wittie,
   Pardon I crave of them, and of thee, pitty.

EDMUND WALLER
(1606–1687)

On the Friendship Betwixt Two Ladies

Tell me, lovely, loving pair!
Why so kind, and so severe?
Why so careless of our care,
Only to yourselves so dear?

By this cunning change of hearts,
You the power of love control;
While the boy's deluded darts
Can arrive at neither soul.

For in vain to either breast
Still beguiled love does come,
Where he finds a foreign guest,
Neither of your hearts at home.

Debtors thus with like design,
When they never mean to pay,
That they may the law decline,
To some friend make all away.

Not the silver doves that fly,
Yoked in Cytherea's car;

Not the wings that lift so high,
And convey her son so far;

Are so lovely, sweet, and fair,
Or do more ennoble love;
Are so choicely matched a pair,
Or with more consent do move.

ABRAHAM COWLEY
(1618–1667)

from *Davideis*, Book 2
lines 94–119

'David and Jonathan'

Still to one end they both so justly drew,
As courteous *Doves* together yok'd would do.
No weight of *Birth* did on one side prevaile,
Two *Twins* less even lie in *Natures Scale*.
They mingled Fates, and both in each did share,
They both were *Servants*, they both *Princes* were.
If any Joy to one of them was sent,
It was most his, to whom it least was meant,
And fortunes malice betwixt both was crost,
For striking one, it wounded th'other most.
Never did *Marriage* such true *Union* find,
Or mens desires with so glad violence bind;
For there is still some tincture left of *Sin*,
And still the *Sex* will needs be stealing in.
Those joys are full of dross, and thicker farre,
These, without matter, clear and liquid are.
Such sacred *Love* does he'avens bright *Spirits* fill,
Where *Love* is but to *Understand* and *Will*,
With swift and unseen *Motions*; such as We
Somewhat express in heightned *Charitie*.
O *ye blest One*! whose *Love* on *earth* became

So pure that still in *Heav'en* 'tis but the same!
There now ye sit, and with mixt souls embrace,
Gazing upon great *Loves* mysterious Face,
And pity this base world where *Friendship's* made
A *bait* for sin, or else at best a *Trade*.

KATHERINE PHILIPS
(1631–1664)

To My Excellent Friend Lucasia, on Our Friendship

I did not live until this time
   Crown'd my felicity,
When I could say without a crime
   I am not thine, but Thee.

This Carcass breath'd, and walkt, and slept,
   So that the World believ'd
There was a Soul the Motions kept;
   But they were all deceiv'd.

For as a Watch by art is wound
   To motion, such was mine:
But never had *Orinda* found
   A Soul till she found thine;

Which now inspires, cures and supplies,
   And guides my darkened Breast:
For thou art all that I can prize,
   My Joy, my Life, my Rest.

No Bridegroom's nor Crown-conqueror's mirth
   To mine compar'd can be:
They have but pieces of this Earth,
   I've all the World in thee.

Then let our Flames still light and shine,
   And no false fear controul,
As innocent as our Design,
   Immortal as our Soul.

Lucasia, Rosania and Orinda Parting at a Fountain, July 1663

Here, here are our enjoyments done,
· And since the Love and Grief we wear
   Forbids us either word or tear,
And Art wants here expression,
See Nature furnish us with one.

The kind and mournful Nimph which here
   Inhabits in her humble Cells,
   No longer her own sorrow tells,
Nor for it now concern'd appears,
But for our parting sheds these tears.

Unless she may afflicted be,
   Lest we should doubt her Innocence;
   Since she hath lost her best pretence
Unto a matchless purity;
Our Love being clearer far than she.

Cold as the streams that from her flow
   Or (if her privater recess
   A greater Coldness can express)
Then cold as those dark beds of Snow
Our hearts are at this parting blow.

But Time that has both wings and feet,
   Our Suffering Minutes being spent,
   Will Visit us with new Content.
And sure, if kindness be so sweet,
'Tis harder to forget than meet.

Then though the sad adieu we say,
   Yet as the wine we hither bring,
   Revives, and then exalts the Spring;
So let our hopes to meet allay,
The fears and Sorrows of this day.

Parting with Lucasia: A Song

Well, we will do that rigid thing
   Which makes Spectators think we part;

Though absence hath for none a sting
  But those who keep each other's heart.

And when our Sense is dispossest,
  Our labouring Souls will heave and pant,
And gasp for one another's breast
  Since their Conveyances they want.

Nay, we have felt the tedious smart
  Of absent Friendship, and do know
That when we die we can but part;
  And who knows what we shall do now?

Yet I must go: we will submit,
  And so our own disposers be;
For while we nobly suffer it,
  We triumph o're Necessity.

By this we shall be truly great,
  If having other things o'recome,
To make our victory compleat
  We can be Conquerors at home.

Nay then to meet we may conclude,
  And all Obstructions overthrow,
Since we our Passion have subdu'd,
  Which is the strongest thing I know.

Orinda to Lucasia

Observe the weary birds e're night be done,
How they would fain call up the tardy Sun,
  With Feathers hung with dew,
  And trembling voices too,
They court their glorious Planet to appear,
That they may find recruits of spirits there.
  The drooping flowers hang their heads,
  And languish down into their beds:
While Brooks more bold and fierce than they,
  Wanting those beams, from whence
  All things drink influence,
Openly murmur and demand the day.

Thou my *Lucasia* art far more to me,
Than he to all the under-world can be;
From thee I've heat and light,
Thy absence makes my night.
But ah! my Friend, it now grows very long,
The sadness weighty, and the darkness strong:
My tears (its dew) dwell on my cheeks,
And still my heart thy dawning seeks,
And to thee mournfully it cries,
That if too long I wait,
Ev'n thou may'st come too late,
And not restore my life, but close my eyes.

Friendship's Mystery: To My Dearest Lucasia

Come, my *Lucasia*, since we see
That Miracles Men's faith do move,
By wonder and by prodigy
To the dull angry world let's prove
There's a Religion in our Love.

For though we were design'd t'agree,
That Fate no liberty destroyes,
But our Election is as free
As Angels, who with greedy choice
Are yet determin'd to their joyes.

Our hearts are doubled by the loss,
Here Mixture is Addition grown;
We both diffuse, we both ingross:
And we whose minds are so much one,
Never, yet ever are alone.

We court our own Captivity
Than Thrones more great and innocent:
'Twere banishment to be set free,
Since we wear fetters whose intent
Not Bondage is, but Ornament.

Divided joyes are tedious found,
And griefs united easier grow:

We are ourselves but by rebound,
   And all our Titles shuffled so,
   Both Princes, and both Subjects too.

Our Hearts are mutual Victims laid,
   While they (such power in Friendship lies)
Are Altars, Priests, and off'rings made:
   And each Heart which thus kindly dies,
   Grows deathless by the Sacrifice.

JOHN WILMOT, EARL OF ROCHESTER
(1648–1680)

Song

Love a woman? You're an ass!
   'Tis a most insipid passion
To choose out for your happiness
   The silliest part of God's creation.

Let the porter and the groom,
   Things designed for dirty slaves,
Drudge in fair Aurelia's womb
   To get supplies for age and graves.

Farewell, woman! I intend
   Henceforth every night to sit
With my lewd, well-natured friend,
   Drinking to engender wit.

Then give me health, wealth, mirth, and wine,
   And, if busy love entrenches,
There's a sweet, soft page of mine
   Does the trick worth forty wenches.

attrib. ROCHESTER
(*c.* 1680)

from *Sodom, or The Quintessence of Debauchery*

To Love and Nature all their rights restore –
Fuck women and let buggery be no more:
It doth the procreative end destroy,
Which Nature gave with pleasure to enjoy.
Please her, and she'll be kind: if you displease,
She turns into corruption and disease.

GEORGE LESTEY
(*c.* 1680)

from *Fire and Brimstone; or the Destruction of Sodom*
lines 426–471

'Lament of the Sodomites'

Oh Heav'ns! I'm choack'd with Smoak, I'm burn'd with fire,
Brimston, Brimston! Where shall we retire?
We dye, we dye, O may this be the last
Of Heav'ns dreadful Sentence on us past!
We're burn'd and damn'd, there is no remedy;
We would not hear *Lot*, when he bid us fly
From wrath to come. O how our Limbs crack
With fire! Our Conscience is upon the rack
For by-past Crimes; our beastly Lusts Torment
Us, as the pretious time that we have spent.
O wretched Nature, whither hast thou brought
Us fools, and made us sell our Souls for nought?
Luxurious Eyes, why wer ye so unkind
To dote on objects, who have made you blind?
And you Tenacious hands, why did you grasp
The Poyson of the Spider? Why from Wasp
Did you seek Honey? did not Heav'n bestow,
As upon *Lot*, so also upon you,
The Lawful helps, and remedies for lust?

Was not all this enough? but that you must
In spite of Heav'n, lay hold on all that came,
Although they man his members had or name.
Could not a lawful Wedlock satisfie
Thy burning flame, proud flesh? No, thou must cry
Bring out thy handsome Guests, them we must know,
Not knowing that they were not from below:
Whose Just revenge doth make us miserable,
To bear these scorching flames we are not able.
And yet alas! our wo doth but begin,
The vengeance is Eternal that's for sin.
O that *Lot's* God would grant us a reprieve
But for one hour, that wretched we might live,
To wail our by-past sins; and beg his aid,
Who never yet to humble sinners said,
I scorn your plaints, but always graciously
Prepar'd a bottle for a melting Eye,
And piece-meal Pray'rs made whole with his own merit,
Sa'ing be comforted, 'tis you must inherit
My endless Joy; which sentence now doth pierce
Our Souls so much, that we cannot rehearse
Our woes, though Oh! alas! it is too late,
We must expect nought but Almightie's hate.
See how the Devils laugh, whom we have serv'd:
O cursed Sp'rits is't this we have deserv'd
From you, for all those things that we have done
At your Command?

THOMAS GRAY
(1716–1771)

Sonnet on the Death of Mr Richard West

In vain to me the smiling mornings shine,
And reddening Phoebus lifts his golden fire:
The birds in vain their amorous descant join,
Or cheerful fields resume their green attire:
These ears, alas! for other notes repine,
A different object do these eyes require.
My lonely anguish melts no heart but mine;

And in my breast the imperfect joys expire.
Yet morning smiles the busy race to cheer,
And new-born pleasure brings to happier men:
The fields to all their wonted tribute bear;
To warm their little loves the birds complain.
I fruitless mourn to him that cannot hear,
And weep the more because I weep in vain.

CHARLES CHURCHILL
(1731–1764)

from *The Times*
lines 293–334

Go where We will, at ev'ry time and place,
SODOM confronts, and stares us in the face;
They ply in public at our very doors
And take the bread from much more honest Whores.
Those who are mean high Paramours secure,
And the rich guilty screen the guilty poor;
The Sin too proud to feel from Reason awe,
And Those, who practise it, too great for Law.

  Woman, the pride and happiness of Man,
Without whose soft endearments Nature's plan
Had been a blank, and Life not worth a thought;
Woman, by all the Loves and Graces taught,
With softest arts, and sure, tho' hidden skill
To humanize, and mould us to her will;
Woman, with more than common grace form'd *here*,
With the persuasive language of a tear
To melt the rugged temper of our Isle,
Or win us to her purpose with a smile;
Woman, by fate the quickest spur decreed,
The fairest, best reward of ev'ry deed
Which bears the stamp of honour, at whose name
Our antient Heroes caught a quicker flame,
And dar'd beyond belief, whilst o'er the plain,
Spurning the carcases of Princes slain,

Confusion proudly strode, whilst Horrour blew
The fatal trump, and Death stalk'd full in view;
Woman is out of date, a thing thrown by
As having lost its use; No more the Eye
With *female* beauty caught, in wild amaze,
Gazes entranc'd, and could for ever gaze;
No more the heart, that seat where Love resides,
Each Breath drawn quick and short, in fuller tides
Life posting thro' the veins, each pulse on fire,
And the whole body tingling with desire,
Pants for those charms, which Virtue might engage
To break his vow, and thaw the frost of age,
Bidding each trembling nerve, each muscle strain,
And giving pleasure which is almost pain.
Women are kept for nothing but the breed;
For pleasure we must have a GANYMEDE,
A fine, fresh HYLAS, a delicious boy,
To serve our purposes of beastly joy.

ANNA SEWARD
(1747–1809)

from *Llangollen Vale*, inscribed to the Right Honourable Lady
Eleanor Butler and Miss Ponsonby
lines 84–234

Now with a vestal lustre glows the Vale,
   Thine, sacred Friendship, permanent as pure;
In vain the stern authorities assail,
   In vain persuasion spreads her silken lure,
High-born, and high-endow'd, the peerless twain,
Pant for coy Nature's charms 'mid silent dale, and plain.

Thro' ELEANORA, and her ZARA's mind,
   Early tho' genius, taste, and fancy flow'd,
Tho' all the graceful arts their powers combin'd,
   And her last polish brilliant life bestow'd,
The lavish promiser, in youth's soft morn,
Pride, pomp, and love, her friends, the sweet enthusiasts scorn.

Then rose the fairy palace of the Vale,
   Then bloom'd around it the Arcadian bowers;
Screen'd from the storms of Winter, cold and pale,
   Screen'd from the fervours of the sultry hours,
Circling the lawny crescent, soon they rose,
To letter'd ease devote, and Friendship's blest repose.

Smiling they rose beneath the plastic hand
   Of energy, and taste; – nor only they,
Obedient Science hears the mild command,
   Brings every gift that speeds the tardy day,
Whate'er the pencil sheds in vivid hues,
Th' historic tome reveals, or sings the raptured Muse.

How sweet to enter, at the twilight grey,
   The dear, minute Lyceum of the dome,
When, thro' the colour'd crystal, glares the ray,
   Sanguine and solemn 'mid the gathering gloom,
While glow-worm lamps diffuse a pale, green light,
Such as in mossy lanes illume the starless night.

Then the coy scene, by deep'ning veils o'erdrawn,
   In shadowy elegance seems lovelier still;
Tall shrubs, that skirt the semi-lunar lawn,
   Dark woods, that curtain the opposing hill;
While o'er their brows the bare cliff faintly gleams,
And, from its paly edge, the evening-diamond streams.

What strains Aeolian thrill the dusk expanse,
   As rising gales with gentle murmurs play,
Wake the loud chords, or every sense intrance,
   While in subsiding winds, they sink away!
Like distant choirs, 'when pealing organs blow,'
And melting voices blend, majestically slow.

'But ah! what hand can touch the strings so fine,
   'Who up the lofty diapason roll
'Such sweet, such sad, such solemn airs divine,
   'Then let them down again into the soul!'
The prouder sex as soon, with virtue calm,
Might win from this bright pair pure Friendship's spotless palm.

What boasts tradition, what th'historic theme,
    Stands it in all their chronicles confest
Where the soul's glory shines with clearer beam,
    Than in our sea-zon'd bulwark of the west,
When, in this Cambrian Valley, Virtue shows
Where, in her own soft sex, its steadiest lustre glows?

Say, ivied Valle Crucis, time-decay'd,
    Dim on the brink of Deva's wandering floods,
Your riv'd arch glimmering thro' the tangled glade,
    Your grey hills towering o'er your night of woods,
Deep in the Vale's recesses as you stand,
And, desolately great, the rising sigh command,

Say, lonely, ruin'd pile, when former years
    Saw your pale train at midnight altars bow;
Saw Superstition frown upon the tears
    That mourn'd the rash irrevocable vow,
Wore one young lip gay ELEANORA's smile?
Did ZARA's look serene one tedious hour beguile?

For your sad sons, nor Science wak'd her powers;
    Nor e'er did Art her lively spells display;
But the grim idol vainly lash'd the hours
    That dragg'd the mute, and melancholy day;
Dropt her dark cowl on each devoted head,
That o'er the breathing corse a pall eternal spread.

This gentle pair no glooms of thought infest,
    Nor Bigotry, nor Envy's sullen gleam
Shed withering influence on the effort blest,
    Which most should win the other's dear esteem,
By added knowledge, by endowment high,
By Charity's warm boon, and Pity's soothing sigh.

Then how should Summer-day or Winter-night,
    Seem long to them who thus can wing their hours!
O! ne'er may pain, or sorrow's cruel blight,
    Breathe the dark mildew thro' these lovely bowers,
But lengthen'd life subside in soft decay,
Illumed by rising Hope, and Faith's pervading ray.

   May one kind ice-bolt, from the mortal stores,
      Arrest each vital current as it flows,
That no sad course of desolated hours
      Here vainly nurse the unsubsiding woes!
While all who honour Virtue, gently mourn
LLANGOLLEN's vanish'd Pair, and wreath their sacred urn.

Elegy Written at the Sea-side, and Addressed to Miss Honoria Sneyd

I write, HONORA, on the sparkling sand! –
The envious waves forbid the trace to stay:
HONORA's name again adorns the strand!
Again the waters bear their prize away!

So Nature wrote her charms upon thy face,
The cheek's light bloom, the lip's envermeil'd dye,
And every gay, and every witching grace,
That Youth's warm hours, and Beauty's stores supply.

But Time's stern tide, with cold Oblivion's wave,
Shall soon dissolve each fair, each fading charm;
E'en Nature's self, so powerful, cannot save
Her own rich gifts from this o'erwhelming harm.

Love and the Muse can boast superior power,
Indelible the letters they shall frame;
They yield to no inevitable hour,
But will on lasting tablets write thy name.

Sonnet 32

To the Departing Spirit of an Alienated Friend

Behold him now his genuine colours wear,
      That specious false-one, by whose cruel wiles
      I lost thy amity; saw thy dear smiles
      Eclips'd; those smiles, that used my heart to cheer,
Wak'd by the grateful sense of many a year
      When rose thy youth, by Friendship's pleasing toils

Cultured; – but Dying! – O! for ever fade
The angry fires. – Each thought, that might upbraid
Thy broken faith, which yet my soul deplores,
    Now as eternally is past and gone
    As are the interesting, the happy hours,
Days, years, we shared together. They are flown!
    Yet long must I lament thy hapless doom,
    Thy lavish'd life and early hasten'd tomb.

JOHANN WOLFGANG VON GOETHE
(1749–1832)

from *West-Easterly Divan*, Book 9: 'The Book of the Cupbearer'

The Cupbearer Speaks

Prithee leave me, crafty hussy,
    Take thy ringlets brown away:
To my master suits my waiting
    And his kisses are my pay.

Therefore thou, I'm free to wager,
    Hast no love on me to spend:
And thy cheeks, thy breasts, would only
    Be fatiguing to my friend.

Dost thou really think to trick me
    Thus to leave as if so shy?
I will lie upon the threshold,
    Watching lest thou slippest by.

[JOHN WEISS]

The market square's admiring throngs
    Witness to your great repute,
But I can praise the well-wrought songs
    Heard by me when you are mute.

Silent songs of love I cherish,
    Kisses that shall never fade.
Words are words and they may perish,
    Kisses ever were repaid.

Rhymes on rhymes fair meaning carry,
    Thoughts to think bring deeper joy;
Sing to others if you'll tarry
    Silent with your serving boy.

The Poet to the Sleeping Saki

He slumbers well and has a right to slumber.
    Dear child, thou hast indeed decanted wine
For me, thy teacher: without strain and cumber
    The thought that ages him dost thou divine.
Now sleep is pouring out for thee, health-bringer
    That keeps thy limbs in full and glorious plight:
Still quaffing, to my lip I place a finger,
    Lest waking he should freshen my delight.

[JOHN WEISS]

WILLIAM WORDSWORTH
(1770–1850)

To Lady Eleanor Butler and the Honourable Miss Ponsonby, Composed in the grounds of Plas-Newydd, Llangollen

A stream to mingle with your favorite Dee
Along the Vale of Meditation flows;
So styled by those fierce Britons, pleased to see
In Nature's face the expression of repose,
Or, haply there some pious Hermit chose
To live and die – the peace of Heaven his aim,
To whom the wild sequestered region owes
At this late day, its sanctifying name.
Glyn Cafaillgaroch, in the Cambrian tongue,
In ours the Vale of Friendship, let this spot

Be nam'd, where faithful to a low roof'd Cot
On Deva's banks, ye have abode so long,
Sisters in love, a love allowed to climb
Ev'n on this earth, above the reach of time.

SAMUEL TAYLOR COLERIDGE
(1772–1834)

from *Christabel*
lines 236–277

'Christabel and Geraldine'

Her gentle limbs did she undress,
And lay down in her loveliness.

But through her brain of weal and woe
So many thoughts moved to and fro,
That vain it were her lids to close;
So half-way from the bed she rose,
And on her elbow did recline
To look at the lady Geraldine.

Beneath the lamp the lady bowed,
And slowly rolled her eyes around;
Then drawing in her breath aloud,
Like one that shuddered, she unbound
The cincture from beneath her breast:
Her silken robe, and inner vest,
Dropt to her feet, and full in view,
Behold! her bosom and half her side –
A sight to dream of, not to tell!
O shield her! shield sweet Christabel!

Yet Geraldine nor speaks nor stirs;
Ah! what a stricken look was hers!
Deep from within she seems half-way
To lift some weight with sick assay,
And eyes the maid and seeks delay;

Then suddenly, as one defied,
Collects herself in scorn and pride,
And lay down by the Maiden's side! –
And in her arms the maid she took,
      Ah wel-a-day!
And with low voice and doleful look
These words did say:
'In the touch of this bosom there worketh a spell,
Which is lord of thy utterance, Christabel!
Thou knowest tonight, and wilt know tomorrow,
This mark of my shame, this seal of my sorrow;
      But vainly thou warrest,
        For this is alone in
      Thy power to declare,
        That in the dim forest
      Thou heard'st a low moaning,
And found'st a bright lady, surpassingly fair;
And didst bring her home with thee in love and in charity,
To shield her and shelter her from the damp air.'

MATILDA BETHAM-EDWARDS
(1776/7–1852)

A Valentine

What shall I send my sweet today,
   When all the woods attune in love?
   And I would show the lark and dove,
That I can love as well as they.

I'll send a locket full of hair, –
   But no, for it might chance to lie
   Too near her heart, and I should die
Of love's sweet envy to be there.

A violet is sweet to give, –
   Ah, stay! she'd touch it with her lips,
   And, after such complete eclipse,
How could my soul consent to live?

I'll send a kiss, for that would be
  The quickest sent, the lightest borne,
  And well I know tomorrow morn
She'll send it back again to me.

Go, happy winds; ah, do not stay,
  Enamoured of my lady's cheek,
  But hasten home, and I'll bespeak
Your services another day!

ANONYMOUS
(1777)

Danebury

In ancient times e'er peace with lenient smile
Had shed her blessings o'er Britannia's isle:
When our bold fathers felt the patriot flame
Nerve the strong arm and urge them on to fame.
Unskill'd, Deceit, in all thy subtile arts,
A rude Sincerity inform'd their hearts:
Meek-ey'd Simplicity in rustic vest,
And Hospitality their souls possest;
Uncultur'd virtues, which too oft decay
Beneath Prosperity's enfeebling ray.

'Twas then retir'd on Brige's[1] peaceful plains,
The friend, the father of the neighb'ring swains;
The good old Egbert trod life's humble vale,
Where noise, nor care, nor vanity assail.
A little farm his every want supply'd,
Enough for happiness, though not for pride:
From Fashion's splendid slavery exempt,
Secur'd alike from envy and contempt.
Though small his fortune and his viands plain,
Never did want accost his ear in vain.
'Twas his to seek the lone obscure recess,
Where want and woe the virtuous mind oppress,

1. Roman settlement founded by Antonine in Hampshire

His pity and his bounty to impart,
And taste the transports of the feeling heart.

   Though of his much-lov'd partner long depriv'd,
One lovely copy of her worth surviv'd;
Oft as he view'd her beauty-beaming form,
What mix'd sensations his fond bosom warm!
Paternal transport trembling in his eye,
Allay'd by recollection's tender sigh!

   Sweetness and sense adorn'd Elfrida's mind,
By Nature's fostering hand alone refin'd.
His hoary age her filial duty chear'd,
His evening hours enliven'd and endear'd;
Her watchful tenderness his care beguil'd,
Supremely happy when her father smil'd.

   Thus blooms some violet in her native vale,
And sheds untainted fragrance on the gale;
Though unadmir'd she drops her modest bloom,
No garden flower excells her sweet perfume.

   Kind Providence ordains the friendly mind
Shall seldom fail a kindred soul to find;
For friendship form'd, Elfrida found that friend,
In Emma's mind unnumber'd graces blend.
Left to the world in youth's unfolding bloom,
Her early tears bedew'd her parents tomb.
That shelter Egbert's humble roof supplies
Which oft to innocence the world denies:
Ev'n in the dawn of childhood's sportive years,
Virtue's instinctive sympathy appears;
Fair Friendship smil'd upon their natal hour,
And ere they knew its name, they felt its power.

   If Emma's bosom heav'd a pensive sigh,
The tear stood trembling in Elfrida's eye;
If pleasure gladden'd her Elfrida's heart,
Still faithful Emma shar'd the larger part.
Successive years the tender tie endear'd,
And each to each a dearer self appear'd.
With social steps they rang'd the verdant fields,

(For Nature there her sweetest pleasure yields,)
And oft beneath some spreading shade reclin'd,
Pour'd forth the warm effusions of the mind:
Uncheck'd by fear, the rising thought impart,
And catch the glowing transport of the heart.
Or seated with their venerable sire,
In social converse round their evening fire;
With fond attention on his words they hung,
And learn'd the lore of wisdom from his tongue.

Thus peaceful stole the hours of life away,
And fancy painted all the future gay.

Oh human bliss! thou transitory flower
That springs, and blooms, and withers in an hour!
How vain the scenes by flattering hope pourtray'd!
How soon Life's fairest landscapes sink in shade!
Discord and war assum'd their baleful reign,
And blood and carnage stain'd the neighbouring plain.
On those wide Downs, in living verdure gay,
Where now the fleecy tribes securely stray;
Our brave forefathers met their haughty foes,
And arm'd with freedom, dar'd their deathful blows.
The direful scene arises full to view,
And Fancy peoples all the plain anew!
Loud shrieks of woe my frighted ears assail,
And Death's deep groan breathes horror through the vale!

Though in the scenes, where meek-ey'd Quiet strays,
The venerable Egbert spent his days:
Though prone to pity ev'n a foe distrest,
Fair Freedom's fire enlarg'd his glowing breast:
The neighbouring Swains his dauntless steps attend,
Those fields which late they cultur'd to defend.
Abandon'd now, each life-sustaining art,
They lift the spear or hurl the missile dart.
Yet though above each vulgar care's controul
The patriot passion lifts th'expanding soul:
Still Nature's, Friendship's ties, will oft be felt,
And ev'n the Hero's breast to anguish melt,

Ah then! what tortures wrung Elfrida's heart!
Imagination only can impart!
When to the fatal field she saw him fly,
Bravely resolv'd to conquer or to die!
She follow'd, filial love absorb'd each fear,
Check'd each fond tremor, dried each selfish tear:
Resolv'd, should Fate a Father's life demand,
To close his swimming eyes with duteous hand,
Pour the warm tear, catch the last fleeting breath,
And share or soften ev'n the pangs of death.

While round the feather'd Deaths promiscuous flew,
One well aim'd arrow caught Elfrida's view!
Instant she mov'd to meet the fatal dart,
Design'd to pierce the aged Hero's heart!
Her gentle breast receiv'd the fatal wound,
And her pale form sunk bleeding on the ground!
Youth's lovely bloom forsook her fading face!
And death-like languor crept o'er every grace!

Expressive silence only can reveal,
Those pangs, a Parent's breast alone can feel!
With feeble steps, and faltering oft with pain,
Scarce could he bear her from th' ensanguin'd plain;
How sunk his heart! when first appear'd in sight
The dear domestic scene of past delight!
What pungent sorrows Emma's bosom knew!
When all the woes imagination drew
Fatally real, met her startled eye,
Shook her whole frame and heav'd the bursting sigh!

Elfrida's Nurse, a venerable Dame!
Who almost merited a Mother's name,
Soon came, with anxious haste the wound to view,
(For nature's healing simples well she knew,)
From her full heart burst forth the honest tear,
That spoke, more forcibly than words, her fear.
A strong, somnific poison ting'd the dart,
Which mock'd the skilful Matron's utmost art.

Sweetly serene, the lovely sufferer smil'd!
While lost in anguish, o'er his dying child

The Father hung! too big the swelling woe,
The kind relief of friendly tears to know.

　Sad Emma strove to hide her grief in vain!
The fruitless effort but increas'd the pain.
Elfrida in their sorrows, lost her own,
Suppress'd each sigh and stifled every groan:
In faltering accents breath'd this last request,
'Oh check my Friend the anguish of thy breast!
'Support my Father! – cheer his life's decline!
'Fulfil the pleasing task that once was mine!
'Wipe, wipe that tear – since I have sav'd my Sire
'With gratitude and pleasure I expire!
'Protect them Heav'n!' – th' unfinish'd accents fail'd,
And Sleep, the Harbinger of Death prevail'd.

　Egbert withdrew to weep (a poor relief
That while it seems to lessen feeds our grief.)
Emma, alone remain'd to watch her Friend,
And o'er the bed in silent anguish bend.
While thought on thought distract her troubled mind,
Friendship a bold, a generous act design'd.
While death-like sleep her Friend's sensations drown'd,
She suck'd the poison from the throbbing wound!
Resign'd herself a victim to the grave,
A life far dearer than her own to save.

　Nature soon felt the change, no more with pain
The vital flood creeps cold through every vein.
Elfrida wakes, – the death-like slumber flies
As night retreats when morning glads the skies!

　The Father's heart with grateful transport glows!
Unknown the source from whence that transport flows.
But ah! from Emma's cheek the roses fly,
Joy beam'd a smile, while pain awak'd a sigh:
Too soon she felt her sickening spirits fail,
And languor o'er life's active springs prevail!
But loth to damp the joy she had inspir'd,
To the cool air she unobserv'd retir'd.

Beneath an ancient elm's romantic shade,
Where rustic toil an humble seat had made;
When day departing crimson'd o'er the sky,
And glitter'd on the stream that wander'd by.
The little friendly groupe would oft repair,
(While breathing woodbines sweeten'd all the air)
Each blameless feeling of their hearts unfold,
Or listen to the tale of times of old.
Ah happy moments! ever, ever fled!
Now Emma there reclines her dying head!
While o'er her pallid face creeps death's cold dew,
And all the landscape swims before her view.

When near approach'd a venerable Sage,
In all the hoary Majesty of Age!
Complacent dignity his looks express,
Sedate his smile and simple was his dress.
His silver hair, all loosely graceful flow'd,
And on his cheek the rose of temperance glow'd.
I come, he cries, commission'd from on high!
Heaven views thy virtues with approving eye.
Far from the busy world's tumultuous strife
The mingled cares and vanities of life,
Retir'd, I live; within my humble cell,
Where Peace, Content, and Contemplation dwell.

When sable Night her raven-pinions spread,
And Sleep had shower'd his poppies, o'er my head:
A heavenly vision warn'd me of thy fate;
And bade me hasten e'er it was too late!
Cultur'd with care, within my little field,
Salubrious herbs their useful fragrance yield:
With studious care, I long have sought to know
What healing virtues from their juices flow;
And warn'd by Heaven, prepar'd within my cell,
Such as have power all poison to expel.
Oh take the health-restoring draught and live!
With heart-felt pleasure, I the cordial give.

Amazement, gratitude, o'erwhelm her soul!
And motion, speech, and every power controul!

Silence, more eloquent than words, exprest
The strong emotions of her labouring breast.
At length the grateful transport forc'd its way,
Such thanks but few can feel, and fewer pay.
In her meek eye, the trembling lustre shone,
And health and beauty reassum'd their throne.

The moving tale soon reach'd Elfrida's ear,
The moving tale, stole many a rapturous tear.
Ah! who can paint the feelings of her mind?
Love, wonder, gratitude, and joy combin'd!
Or the calm bliss that beam'd in Egbert's eye,
Mild as the radiance of the evening sky!
From every heart, enraptur'd praise ascends,
And Heaven approving smiles on Virtue's friends.

And now return'd in peace, the warrior-train
With shouts of victory gladden all the plain.
Th'invading Danes before their valour yield,
And press, in slaughter'd heaps, the ensanguin'd field.

Though Time, with rapid wing, has swept away
Forgotten ages, since that well-fought day;
Ev'n now, their rising graves the spot disclose,
And Shepherds wonder how the hillocks rose!
Ev'n now, the precinct of their camp remains,
And DANEBURY HILL the name it still retains.

O'er those romantic mounds, whene'er I stray,
And the rude vestiges of war survey;
Fair gratitude shall mark, with smile serene
The alter'd aspect of the pleasing scene.
There, where the crouded camp spread terror round,
See! waving harvests cloath the fertile ground!
See! smiling villages adorn the plain,
Where desolation stretch'd her iron reign!
How fair the meads, where winding waters flow,
And never-fading verdure still bestow!
While stretch'd beyond, wide cultur'd fields extend
And wood-crown'd hills, those cultur'd fields defend!

But ah! too faint my numbers to display
The various charms that rise in rich array!
One peaceful spot detains my longing sight,
There, Fancy dwells with ever-fond delight,
Recalls the scenes of Childhood to her view,
And lives those pleasing moments o'er anew.

LORD BYRON
(1788–1824)

The Cornelian[1]

No specious splendour of this stone
   Endears it to my memory ever;
With lustre *only once* it shone,
   And blushes modest as the giver.

Some, who can sneer at friendship's ties,
   Have, for my weakness, oft reprov'd me;
Yet still the simple gift I prize,
   For I am sure, the giver lov'd me.

He offer'd it with downcast look,
   As *fearful* that I might refuse it;
I told him, when the gift I took,
   My *only fear* should be, to lose it.

This pledge attentively I view'd,
   And *sparkling* as I held it near,
Methought one drop the stone bedew'd,
   And, ever since, *I've lov'd a tear.*

Still, to adorn his humble youth,
   Nor wealth nor birth their treasures yield;
But he, who seeks the flowers of truth,
   Must quit the garden, for the field.

1. The cornelian was given to Byron by Eddlestone, a choirboy.

'Tis not the plant uprear'd in sloth,
   Which beauty shews, and sheds perfume;
The flowers, which yield the most of both,
   In Nature's wild luxuriance bloom.

Had Fortune aided Nature's care,
   For once forgetting to be blind,
His would have been an ample share,
   If well proportioned to his mind.

But had the Goddess clearly seen,
   His form had fix'd her fickle breast;
Her countless hoards would *his* have been,
   And none remain'd to give the rest.

from *Childe Harold's Pilgrimage*
stanzas 95–96

'To Eddleston'

Thou too art gone, thou loved and lovely one!
   Whom Youth and Youth's affections bound to me;
   Who did for me what none beside have done,
   Nor shrank from one albeit unworthy thee.
   What is my Being! thou hast ceased to be!
   Nor staid to welcome here thy wanderer home,
   Who mourns o'er hours which we no more shall see –
   Would they had never been, or were to come!
Would he had ne'er returned to find fresh cause to roam!

Oh! ever loving, lovely, and beloved!
   How selfish Sorrow ponders on the past,
   And clings to thoughts now better far removed!
   But Time shall tear thy shadow from me last.
   All thou couldst have of mine, stern Death! thou hast;
   The Parent, Friend, and now the more than Friend:
   Ne'er yet for one thine arrows flew so fast,
   And grief with grief continuing still to blend,
Hath snatched the little joy that Life had yet to lend.

JAMES FENIMORE COOPER, Jʀ
(1789–1851)

To a Friend

Thy voice, as tender as the light
That shivers low at eve –
Thy hair, where myriad flashes bright
Do in and outward weave –
Thy charms in their diversity
Half frighten and astonish me.

Thine eyes, that hold a mirth subdued
Like deep pools scattering fire –
Mine dare not meet them in their mood,
For fear of my desire,
Lest thou that secret do descry
Which evermore I must deny.

Hard is the world that does not give
To every love a place;
Hard is the power that bids us live
A life bereft of grace –
Hard, hard to lose thy figure, dear,
My star and my religion here!

KARL AUGUST GEORG MAX,
GRAF VON PLATEN-HALLERMÜNDE
(1796–1835)

To Schmidlein – 2

Believe me, every hour e'en yet I dream
   Of those in which I first revealed to thee
   The tender secret of thy victory,
Perplexed in speech, yet daring in my theme.
Now thy designs unfathomable seem:
   Since they consort not with such modesty,
   Thou dost lament our love's degeneracy,
And thy desires too bold and sinful deem.

Mid flowery perfumes Oh here let us lie,
　　Cheek against cheek, at dusk beneath the trees,
Breast pressing close to breast and thigh to thigh.
　　Hark how the old elms rustle in the breeze!
Perchance an elfin choir is swarming nigh,
　　To whisper soft, sweet bridal melodies.

[REGINALD BANCROFT COOKE]

To Rotenham – 3

As one abandoned on a barren shore,
　　I look about me, crying in despair:
　　Where is a glance that can with thine compare,
And where are lips which hold such gifts in store?
And when I hoped or when I knew that more
　　Than one regarded me with smile so fair,
　　Scarce would I upward glance at him, or stare
With eyes that statue-like expression bore.

Though I the goal of earthly life attain
　　Never again rejoicing thee to view,
And all my love unrecompensed remain,
　　Fret not thyself but I may prove untrue;
New charms shall ever lure my love in vain;
　　Eternal beauty is for ever new.

[REGINALD BANCROFT COOKE]

To Bülow – 2

Of those around thee there is none who heeds,
　　And that I love thee thou hast never guessed;
　　My whole life hath one purpose unexpressed,
And softly throbs my heart because it bleeds.
Whether it calmly rests or restless speeds,
　　Thy sympathy would ne'er be manifest;
　　And that thy friends my slender worth attest
Oft feeds my pain, yet oft my courage feeds.

Whatsoe'er, good or ill, befell, 't would seem,
   While upward ardently my spirit strove,
As though I were enshrouded in a dream,
   And therefore will I cherish this new love
With heartfelt fervency, which I should deem
   It far less rash to praise than to reprove.

[REGINALD BANCROFT COOKE]

To Liebig – 6

Who feels a growing hunger for fair eyes
   And pretty hair, I warn him to refrain,
   I, who have learned too well what grief and pain
Are the reward of futile enterprise.
Scarcely escaped whence chasms steeply rise,
   Of perils without end what signs remain?
   Of years of weeping in my eyes the stain
And in my breast anxiety and sighs.

Young hearts, shun cliffs precipitous as these!
   With treach'rous flame their border-lilies shine,
For Ah! they lure us into mournful seas.
   Only to these is life precious and fine
Who share its merriment, frankly, at ease,
   And unto them God calls: The world is thine.

[REGINALD BANCROFT COOKE]

To Liebig – 7

Longing for that true comrade of my need
   Who can my thoughts so richly amplify,
   Oft have I felt false hopes my heart belie,
And oft deception dealt me wounds that bleed,
Then in thine eyes fair messages I read,
   And, that I miss them not, to thee draw nigh;
   As though by swift enchantment, thee and I
In one short hour feel ourselves friends indeed.

When scarce this new attraction brings delight,
　　Parting already dims our happiness,
　　　Decreed for us by fate so sternly testing.
Yet joyfully our spirits may unite
　　In cordial intimacy none the less,
　　　On golden times to come our vision resting.

[REGINALD BANCROFT COOKE]

Sonnets to Karl Theodor German

1

When shall I master this anxiety
　　Which seizes me when thou, dear friend, art nigh?
　　I seek thy presence even as a spy,
Hoping yet fearing to discover thee.
How can I fear 'fore one I fain would see
　　Folded in my embrace? Oh tell me why
　　So swift my blood is checked, and what can tie
My spirit as with bonds of slavery.

Is it the dread lest thou thine heart shouldst close,
　　Lest on the crags of thy false pride I steer,
Ever avowed the foremost of love's foes?
　　Is it the godliness of bonds so dear,
Since love, as before God, for ever shows
　　Before its object reverence and fear?

[REGINALD BANCROFT COOKE]

22

How shall I still mankind's good will retrieve,
　　Since there is no one who can comfort me?
　　Let me be wholly plunged in misery,
To weep in silence and in silence grieve.
No longer am I worthy of reprieve,
　　Since I have perished in his memory;
　　And in these joints that ache so wearily
The seeds of dissolution I perceive.

But O ye Heavenly Powers, to him allow
  Entire happiness. Do not deny
Whatever wishes his heart may avow.
  Never again my glance shall meet his eye;
The form of one he hates no longer now,
  Alas! even in dreams, shall he espy.

[REGINALD BANCROFT COOKE]

ALEXANDER PUSHKIN
(1799–1837)

Sweet boy, gentle boy,
Don't be ashamed, you are mine forever:
The same rebellious fire is in both of us,
We are living one life

I am not afraid of mockery:
Between us, the two have become one,
We are precisely like a double nut
Under a single shell.

[VALERY PERELESHIN]

ALFRED, LORD TENNYSON
(1809–1892)

from *In Memoriam*

7

Dark house, by which once more I stand
  Here in the long unlovely street,
  Doors, where my heart was used to beat
So quickly, waiting for a hand,

A hand that can be clasped no more –
  Behold me, for I cannot sleep,

And like a guilty thing I creep
At earliest morning to the door.

He is not here; but far away
    The noise of life begins again,
    And ghastly through the drizzling rain
On the bald street breaks the blank day.

9

Fair ship, that from the Italian shore
    Sailest the placid ocean-plains
    With my lost Arthur's loved remains,
Spread thy full wings, and waft him o'er.

So draw him home to those that mourn
    In vain; a favourable speed
    Ruffle thy mirrored mast, and lead
Through prosperous floods his holy urn.

All night no ruder air perplex
    Thy sliding keel, till Phosphor, bright
    As our pure love, through early light
Shall glimmer on the dewy decks.

Sphere all your lights around, above;
    Sleep, gentle heavens, before the prow;
    Sleep, gentle winds, as he sleeps now,
My friend, the brother of my love;

My Arthur, whom I shall not see
    Till all my widowed race be run;
    Dear as the mother to the son,
More than my brothers are to me.

13

Tears of the widower, when he sees
    A late-lost form that sleep reveals,
    And moves his doubtful arms, and feels
Her place is empty, fall like these;

Which weep a loss for ever new,
   A void where heart on heart reposed;
   And, where warm hands have prest and closed,
Silence, till I be silent too.

Which weep the comrade of my choice,
   An awful thought, a life removed,
   The human-hearted man I loved,
A Spirit, not a breathing voice.

Come Time, and teach me, many years,
   I do not suffer in a dream;
   For now so strange do these things seem,
Mine eyes have leisure for their tears;

My fancies time to rise on wing,
   And glance about the approaching sails,
   As though they brought but merchants' bales,
And not the burthen that they bring.

27

I envy not in any moods
   The captive void of noble rage,
   The linnet born within the cage,
That never knew the summer woods:

I envy not the beast that takes
   His license in the field of time,
   Unfettered by the sense of crime,
To whom a conscience never wakes;

Nor, what may count itself as blest,
   The heart that never plighted troth
   But stagnates in the weeds of sloth;
Nor any want-begotten rest.

I hold it true, whate'er befall;
   I feel it, when I sorrow most;
   'Tis better to have loved and lost
Than never to have loved at all.

80

Thy voice is on the rolling air;
    I hear thee where the waters run:
    Thou standest in the rising sun,
And in the setting thou art fair.

What art thou then? I cannot guess;
    But though I seem in star and flower
    To feel thee some diffusive power,
I do not therefore love thee less:

My love involves the love before;
    My love is vaster passion now;
    Though mixed with God and Nature thou,
I seem to love thee more and more.

Far off thou art, but ever nigh;
    I have thee still, and I rejoice;
    I prosper, circled with thy voice;
I shall not lose thee though I die.

HENRY THOREAU
(1817–1862)

Lately, Alas, I Knew a Gentle Boy

Lately, alas, I knew a gentle boy,
    Whose features all were cast in Virtue's mould,
As one she had designed for Beauty's toy,
    But after manned him for her own strong-hold.

On every side he open was as day,
    That you might see no lack of strength within,
For walls and ports do only serve alway
    For a pretence to feebleness and sin.

Say not that Caesar was victorious,
    With toil and strife who stormed the House of Fame,

In other sense this youth was glorious,
   Himself a kingdom wheresoe'er he came.

No strength went out to get him victory,
   When all was income of its own accord;
For where he went none other was to see,
   But all were parcel of their noble lord.

He forayed like the subtile haze of summer,
   That stilly shows fresh landscapes to our eyes,
And revolutions works without a murmur,
   Or rustling of a leaf beneath the skies.

So was I taken unawares by this,
   I quite forgot my homage to confess;
Yet now am forced to know, though hard it is,
   I might have loved him had I loved him less.

Each moment as we nearer drew to each,
   A stern respect withheld us farther yet,
So that we seemed beyond each other's reach,
   And less acquainted than when first we met.

We two were one while we did sympathize,
   So could we not the simplest bargain drive;
And what avails it now that we are wise,
   If absence doth this doubleness contrive?

Eternity may not the chance repeat,
   But I must tread my single way alone,
In sad remembrance that we once did meet,
   And know that bliss irrevocably gone.

The spheres henceforth my elegy shall sing,
   For elegy has other subject none;
Each strain of music in my ears shall ring
   Knell of departure from that other one.

Make haste and celebrate my tragedy;
   With fitting strain resound ye woods and fields;
Sorrow is dearer in such case to me
   Than all the joys other occasion yields.

Is't then too late the damage to repair?
   Distance, forsooth, from my weak grasp hath reft
The empty husk, and clutched the useless tare,
   But in my hands the wheat and kernel left.

If I but love that virtue which he is,
   Though it be scented in the morning air,
Still shall we be truest acquaintances,
   Nor mortals know a sympathy more rare.

WALT WHITMAN
(1819–1892)

We Two Boys Together Clinging

We two boys together clinging,
One the other never leaving,
Up and down the roads going, North and South excursions making,
Power enjoying, elbows stretching, fingers clutching,
Arm'd and fearless, eating, drinking, sleeping, loving,
No law less than ourselves owning, sailing, soldiering, thieving,
    threatening,
Misers, menials, priests alarming, air breathing, water drinking, on
    the turf or the sea-beach dancing,
Cities wrenching, ease scorning, statutes mocking, feebleness
    chasing,
Fulfilling our foray.

A Glimpse

A glimpse through an interstice caught,
Of a crowd of workmen and drivers in a bar-room around the stove
    late of a winter night, and I unremark'd seated in a corner,
Of a youth who loves me and whom I love, silently approaching and
    seating himself near, that he may hold me by the hand,
A long while amid the noises of coming and going, of drinking and
    oath and smutty jest,
There we two, content, happy in being together, speaking little,
    perhaps not a word.

Vigil Strange I Kept on the Field One Night

Vigil strange I kept on the field one night;
When you my son and my comrade dropt at my side that day,
One look I but gave which your dear eyes return'd with a look I shall
    never forget,
One touch of your hand to mine O boy, reach'd up as you lay on the
    ground,
Then onward I sped in the battle, the even-contested battle,
Till late in the night reliev'd to the place at last again I made my way,
Found you in death so cold dear comrade, found your body son of
    responding kisses, (never again on earth responding,)
Bared your face in the starlight, curious the scene, cool blew the
    moderate night-wind,
Long there and then in vigil I stood, dimly around me the battle-field
    spreading,
Vigil wondrous and vigil sweet there in the fragrant silent night,
But not a tear fell, not even a long-drawn sigh, long, long I gazed,
Then on the earth partially reclining sat by your side leaning my chin
    in my hands,
Passing sweet hours, immortal and mystic hours with you dearest
    comrade – not a tear, not a word,
Vigil of silence, love and death, vigil for you my son and my soldier,
As onward silently stars aloft, eastward new ones upward stole,
Vigil final for you brave boy, (I could not save you, swift was your
    death,
I faithfully loved you and cared for you living, I think we shall surely
    meet again,)
Till at latest lingering of the night, indeed just as the dawn appear'd,
My comrade I wrapt in his blanket, envelop'd well his form,
Folded the blanket well, tucking it carefully over head and carefully
    under feet,
And there and then and bathed by the rising sun, my son in his grave,
    in his rude-dug grave I deposited,
Ending my vigil strange with that, vigil of night and battle-field dim,
Vigil for boy of responding kisses, (never again on earth responding,)
Vigil for comrade swiftly slain, vigil I never forget, how as day
    brighten'd,
I rose from the chill ground and folded my soldier well in his blanket,
And buried him where he fell.

O Tan-Faced Prairie-Boy

O tan-faced prairie-boy,
Before you came to camp came many a welcome gift,
Praises and presents came and nourishing food, till at last among the
  recruits,
You came, taciturn, with nothing to give – we but look'd on each
  other,
When lo! more than all the gifts of the world you gave me.

'The Beautiful Swimmer'

I see a beautiful gigantic swimmer swimming naked through the
  eddies of the sea,
His brown hair lies close and even to his head, he strikes out with
  courageous arms, he urges himself with his legs,
I see his white body, I see his undaunted eyes,
I hate the swift-running eddies that would dash him head-foremost
  on the rocks.

What are you doing you ruffianly red-trickled waves?
Will you kill the courageous giant? will you kill him in the prime of his
  middle-age?

Steady and long he struggles,
He is baffled, bang'd, bruis'd, he holds out while his strength holds
  out,
The slapping eddies are spotted with his blood, they bear him away,
  they roll him, swing him, turn him,
His beautiful body is borne in the circling eddies, it is continually
  bruis'd on rocks,
Swiftly and out of sight is borne the brave corpse.

CHARLES BAUDELAIRE
(1821–1867)

Women Damned

Like ruminating cattle on the sands,
They turn their eyes towards the line of sea;

Their feet, which seek each other, and their hands,
Are sweet and languid, quiver bitterly.

Some of them, longing, loving to confide,
Deep in the groves where streams run chattering,
Spell out the love of childhoods terrified,
And delve into the green woods burgeoning.

Others, like sisters, grave and slow of pace,
Cross rocks peopled by apparitions;
St Anthony saw there, like lava, rise
The purple, bare breasts of temptations.

Some of them, in the light of torches wan,
In silent hollow caves, pagan retreats,
Ask you for help in their delirium,
O Bacchus, who can lull the old regrets!

And there are some whose breast loves scapulars,
Who hide a whip beneath their long attire,
And, lonely, under heavens with no stars,
Mingle the foam of joy with torment's tears.

O virgins, demons, monsters, martyrs all,
Great spirits scornful of reality,
Who seek the infinite, believers, trulls,
Enraptured, or in utter misery,

You whom my soul pursues into your hell,
Poor sisters, I both love and pity you,
For your sore griefs, your thirsts insatiable,
The love with which your great hearts overflow!

[JOANNA RICHARDSON]

W. J. CORY
(1823–1892)

Heraclitus

They told me, Heraclitus, they told me you were dead,
They brought me bitter news to hear and bitter tears to shed.

I wept, as I remembered, how often you and I
Had tired the sun with talking and sent him down the sky.

And now that thou art lying, my dear old Carian guest,
A handful of grey ashes, long long ago at rest,
Still are thy pleasant voices, thy nightingales, awake;
For Death, he taketh all away, but them he cannot take.

EMILY DICKINSON
(1830–1886)

1

Her breast is fit for pearls,
But I was not a 'Diver' –
Her brow is fit for thrones
But I have not a crest.
Her heart is fit for *home* –
I – a Sparrow – build there
Sweet of twigs and twine
My perennial nest.

2

Her sweet Weight on my Heart a Night
Had scarcely deigned to lie –
When, stirring, for Belief's delight,
My Bride had slipped away –

If 'twas a Dream – made solid – just
The Heaven to confirm –
Or if Myself were dreamed of Her –
The power to presume –

With Him remain – who unto Me –
Gave – even as to All –
A Fiction superseding Faith –
By so much – as 'twas real –

3

Going – to – Her!
Happy – Letter! Tell Her –
Tell Her – the page I never wrote!
Tell Her, I only said – the Syntax –
And left the Verb and the Pronoun – out!
Tell Her just how the fingers – hurried –
Then – how they – stammered – slow – slow –
And then – you wished you had eyes – in your pages –
So you could see – what moved – them – so –

Tell Her – it wasn't a practised writer –
You guessed –
From the way the sentence – toiled –
You could hear the Boddice – tug – behind you –
As if it held but the might of a child!
You almost pitied – it – you – it worked so –
Tell Her – No – you may quibble – there –
For it would split Her Heart – to know it –
And then – you and I – were silenter!

Tell Her – Day – finished – before we – finished –
And the old Clock kept neighing –'Day'!
And you – got sleepy – and begged to be ended –
What could – it hinder so – to say?
Tell Her – just how she sealed – you – Cautious!
But – if she ask 'where you are hid' – until the evening –
Ah! Be bashful!
Gesture Coquette –
And shake your Head!

4

Ourselves were wed one summer – dear –
Your Vision – was in June –
And when Your little Lifetime failed,
I wearied – too – of mine –

And overtaken in the Dark –
Where You had put me down –
By Some one carrying a Light –
I – too – received the Sign.

'Tis true – Our Futures different lay –
Your Cottage – faced the sun –
While Oceans – and the North must be –
On every side of mine

'Tis true, Your Garden led the Bloom,
For mine – in Frosts – was sown –
And yet, one Summer, we were Queens –
But You – were crowned in June –

5

Precious to Me – She still shall be –
Though She forget the name I bear –
The fashion of the Gown I wear –
The very Color of My Hair –

So like the Meadows – now –
I dared to show a Tress of Their's
If haply – She might not despise
A Buttercup's Array –

I know the Whole – obscures the Part –
The fraction – that appeased the Heart
Till Number's Empery –
Remembered – as the Milliner's flower
When Summer's Everlasting Dower –
Confronts the dazzled Bee.

6

The Stars are old, that stood for me –
The West a little worn –
Yet newer glows the only Gold
I ever cared to earn –
Presuming on that lone result
Her infinite disdain
But vanquished her with my defeat
'Twas Victory was slain.

7

Now I knew I lost her –
Not that she was gone –
But Remoteness travelled
On her Face and Tongue.

Alien, though adjoining
As a Foreign Race –
Traversed she though pausing
Latitudeless Place.

Elements Unaltered –
Universe the same
But Love's transmigration –
Somehow this had come –

Henceforth to remember
Nature took the Day
I had paid so much for –
His is Penury
Not who toils for Freedom
Or for Family
But the Restitution
Of Idolatry.

8

Frigid and sweet Her parting Face –
Frigid and fleet my Feet –
Alien and vain whatever Clime
Acrid whatever Fate.

Given to me without the Suit
Riches and Name and Realm –
Who was She to withold from me
Penury and Home?

9

To see her is a Picture –
To hear her is a Tune –
To know her an Intemperance
As innocent as June –

To know her not – Affliction –
To own her for a Friend
A warmth as near as if the Sun
Were shining in your Hand.

CHRISTINA ROSSETTI
(1830–1894)

from *Goblin Market*
lines 183–197

'Laura and Lizzie Asleep'

Golden head by golden head,
Like two pigeons in one nest
Folded in each other's wings,
They lay down in their curtained bed:
Like two blossoms on one stem,
Like two flakes of new-fall'n snow,
Like two wands of ivory
Tipped with gold for awful kings.
Moon and stars gazed in at them,
Wind sang to them lullaby,
Lumbering owls forbore to fly,
Not a bat flapped to and fro
Round their nest:
Cheek to cheek and breast to breast
Locked together in one nest.

ALGERNON CHARLES SWINBURNE
(1837–1909)

Faustine

Ave, Faustina Imperatrix, morituri te salutant[1]

Lean back, and get some minutes' peace;
    Let your head lean
Back to the shoulder with its fleece
    Of locks, Faustine.

1. Hail, Empress Faustine, those who are about to die salute thee

The shapely silver shoulder stoops,
    Weighed over clean
With state of splendid hair that droops
    Each side, Faustine.

Let me go over your good gifts
    That crown you queen;
A queen whose kingdom ebbs and shifts
    Each week, Faustine.

Bright heavy brows well gathered up:
    White gloss and sheen;
Carved lips that make my lips a cup
    To drink, Faustine.

Wine and rank poison, milk and blood,
    Being mixed therein
Since first the devil threw dice with God
    For you, Faustine.

Your naked new-born soul, their stake,
    Stood blind between;
God said 'let him that wins her take
    And keep Faustine.'

But this time Satan throve, no doubt;
    Long since, I ween,
God's part in you was battered out;
    Long since, Faustine.

The die rang sideways as it fell,
    Rang cracked and thin,
Like a man's laughter heard in hell
    Far down, Faustine.

A shadow of laughter like a sigh,
    Dead sorrow's kin;
So rang, thrown down, the devil's die
    That won Faustine.

A suckling of his breed you were,
    One hard to wean;
But God, who lost you, left you fair
    We see, Faustine.

You have the face that suits a woman
    For her soul's screen –
The sort of beauty that's called human
    In hell, Faustine.

You could do all things but be good
    Or chaste of mien;
And that you would not if you could
    We know, Faustine.

Even he who cast seven devils out
    Of Magdalene
Could hardly do as much, I doubt,
    For you, Faustine.

Did Satan make you to spite God?
    Or did God mean
To scourge with scorpions for a rod
    Our sins, Faustine?

I know what queen at first you were,
    As though I had seen
Red gold and black imperious hair
    Twice crown Faustine.

As if your fed sarcophagus
    Spared flesh and skin,
You come back face to face with us,
    The same Faustine.

She loved the games men played with death,
    Where death must win;
As though the slain man's blood and breath
    Revived Faustine.

Nets caught the pike, pikes tore the net;
    Lithe limbs and lean
From drained-out pores dripped thick red sweat
    To soothe Faustine.

She drank the steaming drift and dust
    Blown off the scene;
Blood could not ease the bitter lust
    That galled Faustine.

All round the foul fat furrows reeked,
    Where blood sank in;
The circus splashed and seethed and shrieked
    All round Faustine.

But these are gone now: years entomb
    The dust and din;
Yea, even the bath's fierce reek and fume
    That slew Faustine.

Was life worth living then? and now
    Is life worth sin?
Where are the imperial years? and how
    Are you, Faustine?

Your soul forgot her joys, forgot
    Her times of teen;
Yea, this life likewise will you not
    Forget, Faustine?

For in the time we know not of
    Did fate begin
Weaving the web of days that wove
    Your doom, Faustine.

The threads were wet with wine, and all
    Were smooth to spin;
They wove you like a Bacchanal,
    The first Faustine.

And Bacchus cast your mates and you
    Wild grapes to glean;
Your flower-like lips were dashed with dew
    From his, Faustine.

Your drenched loose hands were stretched to hold
    The vine's wet green,
Long ere they coined in Roman gold
    Your face, Faustine.

Then after change of soaring feather
    And winnowing fin,
You woke in weeks of feverish weather,
    A new Faustine.

A star upon your birthday burned,
    Whose fierce serene
Red pulseless planet never yearned
    In heaven, Faustine.

Stray breaths of Sapphic song that blew
    Through Mitylene
Shook the fierce quivering blood in you
    By night, Faustine.

The shameless nameless love that makes
    Hell's iron gin
Shut on you like a trap that breaks
    The soul, Faustine.

And when your veins were void and dead,
    What ghosts unclean
Swarmed round the straitened barren bed
    That hid Faustine?

What sterile growths of sexless root
    Or epicene?
What flower of kisses without fruit
    Of love, Faustine?

What adders came to shed their coats?
    What coiled obscene
Small serpents with soft stretching throats
    Caressed Faustine?

But the time came of famished hours,
    Maimed loves and mean,
This ghastly thin-faced time of ours,
    To spoil Faustine.

You seem a thing that hinges hold,
    A love-machine
With clockwork joints of supple gold –
    No more, Faustine.

Not godless, for you serve one God,
    The Lampsacene,
Who metes the gardens with his rod;
    Your lord, Faustine.

If one should love you with real love
    (Such things have been,
Things your fair face knows nothing of,
    It seems, Faustine);

That clear hair heavily bound back,
    The lights wherein
Shift from dead blue to burnt-up black;
    Your throat, Faustine.

Strong, heavy, throwing out the face
    And hard bright chin
And shameful scornful lips that grace
    Their shame, Faustine,

Curled lips, long since half kissed away,
    Still sweet and keen;
You'd give him – poison shall we say?
    Or what, Faustine?

J. A. SYMONDS
(1840–1893)

from *Ithocles*
Section 6

Ithocles alone on Ida, as before: to him Lysander

That night, when storms were spent and tranquil heaven,
Clear-eyed with stars and fragrant with fresh air,
Slept after thunder, came a sound of song,
And a keen voice that through the forest cried
On Ithocles, and still on Ithocles,
Persistent, till the woods and caverns rang.
He in his lair close-lying and tear-tired
Heard, knew the cry, and trembled. Nearer still
And nearer vibrated the single sound.
Yet, though much called for, Ithocles abode
Prone, deeming that the gods had heard his prayer,
And spake not. Till at the cave-door there stayed
The feet of him who one month since had trodden
Toward that path beneath another moon,
Then Ithocles, thick-throated, 'Who calls me?'
Cried, knowing well the voice of him who called.
'It is Lysander.' 'If indeed it be he,
Let him forgive; strike deep; I ask no more.
Thy coming, youth, long looked for, sets me free;
For now the storm of love and life is o'er,
And I go conquering and conquered down
To darkness and inevitable doom –
Conquered by Kupris who hath had her will,
But having slain within my soul the sin
That made a desert of her garden-ground.
Live happy in the light of holier Love:
Forget the man who willed thee that great wrong.'
'Nay, not so, Ithocles, if this hold good!
For I have left my kith and kin for thee,
And, pricked by sharp stings of importunate love,
Am come to cure thy hurt and heal thy soul.'
'Can this be true? for I do lie as one
Who long hath ta'en a dark and doleful dream:
Waking he shudders, and dim shadowy shapes

Still threaten and weigh down his labouring soul.'
'Rise, Ithocles, and we will speak of Love;
Fierce-eyed, fire-footed, yet most mild of gods
And musical and holy and serene.
Dear to his spirit are deep-chested sighs,
Pitiful pleadings of woe-wearied men,
And the anguish of unutterable things:
But dearer far when heart with heart is wedded,
Body with body, strength with strength; when passion,
Not raging like wild fire in lustful veins,
But centered in the head and heart, doth steady
Twin wills and wishes to a lofty end.
I come to save thee, Ithocles, or die:
Better is death than shame or loveless life.
I love thee as I love this land we tread,
This dear land of our fathers and our gods;
I love thee as I love the light of heaven
Or the sweet life that nourisheth my soul;
Nay, better than all these I love thee, friend;
And wouldst thou have me die, dishonoured die,
In the fair blossom of my April days,
Disconsolate and disinherited,
With all my hopes and happiness undone?'
'What will men say, Lysander, if we love?'
'Let men say what they will. Let us be pure
And faithful to each other to the end.
Life is above and round us, and her dome
Is studded thick with stars of noble deeds,
Each one of which with undivided will
And married purpose we may make our own.
Nay, rise: stand with me at the cavern door:
The storms are over and the skies are clear,
Trembling with dew and moonlight and still stars.
Heaven hears us and the palpitating air,
The woods that murmur, and the streams that leap
Regenerate with tempest-scattered tears;
Be these our temple and our witnesses,
Our idol, altar, oracle, and priest,
Our hymeneal chaunt and holy rite:–
What better need we? and before we die,
All Crete shall bless the marriage of tonight.'

Midnight at Baiae. A Dream Fragment of Imperial Rome

Darkling I steal, and with hushed footsteps slow
  Thread the dim palace, between painted walls
  And pillared aisles and perfumed plants a row.
Whither? O, where? Keen as a sword edge falls
  Light from yon slender portal. Onward still
  I am lured spell-bound through the noiseless halls.
Still onward. Sense and thought and shrinking will,
  Compelled by unresistible control,
  Grope toward yon shining slit that sharp and chill
Gleams like the lode-star of my shuddering soul.
  Yet would I fain draw back: all is so dark,
  So ominously tranquil; and the goal
Toward which I tread is but one steady spark,
  Clearing the dream-drowned twilight terrible.
  What noise? Nay startle not. The watch-dogs bark
Far off in farm-yards where men slumber well.
  Here stillness broods; save when a cricket chirrs,
  Or wheeling on slant wing the black bat fell
Utters her thin shrill scream. No night wind stirs
  The sleeping foliage of these stately bays.
  Forward I venture. On warm silky furs
My feet fall muffled now; and now I raise
  The latchet of the door that stands ajar.
  Light floods but dazzles not my frozen gaze.
What is within I reckon. Near and far,
  Things small and great, sights wonderful and strange,
  Alike in equal vision, on that bar
Of blackness standing, with fixed eyes I range.
  It is a narrow room: walls high and straight
  Enclose it. Yonder lamps that counterchange
Shadow with lustre, scarce can penetrate
  The fretwork of high rafters rough with gold.
  The lamps are silver: Satyrs love-elate
Upraising cressets; phallic horns that hold
  Creamed essence, amber oil. From gloom profound
  Lean shapes of mural heroes, lovers old,
Glimmering with shapes auroral on the ground
  Of ebon blackness. Hylas, Hyacinth,
  And heaven-rapt Ganymede: I know them: crowned

With lilies dew-bedrenched, upon a plinth
   Of jasper droops Uranian Love, a god
   Wrought out of bruised bronze for some labyrinth
Of Academic grove where sages trod:
   Bare, breathless, in his beauty, here love smiled,
   Making more dim the ghostly solitude.
Midward the chamber was a table piled
   With fruit and flowers. Thereon there blazed a cup,
   Carven of sardonyx, where Maenads wild
With wine and laughter, shrieking, seemed to sup
   The blood of mangled Pentheus. It was full
   Of dark Falerian; the draught bubbling up
From tawny into crimson, rich and cool,
   Glowed in the bowl untasted. Wreaths of rose,
   Pure as little shepherd lads in Paestum pull,
Circled two sculptured murrhine cups; but those
   Were void, no wine-spilth made their wreaths more red.
   Then was I ware how, neath the flaming rows
Of cressets, a flat ivory couch was spread.
   Smooth Tyrian silks and gauzes hyaline
   Clung draped with jewelled buckles to the bed.
Thereon lay stretched a fair nude form supine;
   An alabaster youth serenely laid
   In slumber. Honey-pale and sleek and fine
Were all his limbs: and o'er his breast there played
   The lambent smiles of lamplight. But a pool
   Of blood, low down, along the pavement strayed.
There, where blue cups of lotus lilies cool
   With reeds into mosaic rings were blent,
   The black blood grew and curdled; for the wool
Whereon his cloudy curls were pillowed, sent
   Thick drops slow-dripping down the ivory rim;
   Yet was the raiment ruffled not nor rent.
In trance I crept, and closer gazed at him.
   Ah me! from side to side his throat was gashed
   With some keen blade; and every noble limb
With marks of crispèd fingers marred and lashed,
   Told the fierce strain of tyrannous lust that here
   Life's crystal vase of youth divine had dashed.
It is enough. Those glazed eyes, wide and clear;
   Those lips by forceful kisses bruised, that cheek

Whereon foul teeth-dints blackened; the tense fear
Of that white innocent forehead; – vain and weak
   Are words, unutterably weak and vain,
   To paint how madly eloquent, how meek
Were those mute signs of dire soul-shattering pain.

GERARD MANLEY HOPKINS
(1844–1889)

The Bugler's First Communion

A bugler boy from barrack (it is over the hill
There) – boy bugler, born, he tells me, of Irish
   Mother to an English sire (he
Shares their best gifts surely, fall how things will),

This very very day came down to us after a boon he on
My late being there begged of me, overflowing
   Boon in my bestowing,
Came, I say, this day to it – to a First Communion.

Here he knelt then in regimental red.
Forth Christ from cupboard fetched, how fain I of feet
   To his youngster take his treat!
Low-latched in leaf-light housel his too huge godhead.

There! and your sweetest sendings, ah divine,
By it, heavens, befall him! as a heart Christ's darling, dauntless;
   Tongue true, vaunt- and tauntless;
Breathing bloom of a chastity in mansex fine.

Frowning and forefending angel-warder[1]
Squander the hell-rook ranks sally to molest him;
   March, kind comrade, abreast him;
Dress his days to a dexterous and starlight order.

How it does my heart good, visiting at that bleak hill,
When limber liquid youth, that to all I teach
   Yields tender as a pushed peach,
Hies headstrong to its wellbeing of a self-wise self-will!

Then though I should tread tufts of consolation
Dáys áfter, só I in a sort deserve to
    And do serve God to serve to
Just such slips of soldiery Christ's royal ration.

Nothing élse is like it, no, not all so strains
Us: fresh youth fretted in a bloomfall all portending
    That sweet's sweéter ending;
Realm both Christ is heir to and thére réigns.

O now well work that sealing sacred ointment!
O for now charms, arms, what bans off bad
    And locks love ever in a lad!
Let mé though see no more of him, and not disappointment

Those sweet hopes quell whose least me quickenings lift,
In scarlet or somewhere of some day seeing
    That brow and bead of being,
An our day's God's own Galahad. Though this child's drift

Seems by a divine doom chánnelled, nor do I cry
Disaster there; but may he not rankle and roam
    In backwheels though bound home? –
That left to the Lord of the Eucharist, I here lie by;

Recorded only, I have put my lips on pleas
Would brandle adamantine heaven with ride and jar, did
    Prayer go disregarded·
Forward-like, but however. and like favourable heaven heard these.

1. guardian angel

PAUL VERLAINE
(1844–1896)

Spring

Tender, the young auburn woman,
    By such innocence aroused,
Said to the blonde young girl
    These words, in a soft low voice:

'Sap which mounts, and flowers which thrust,
    Your childhood is a bower:
Let my fingers wander in the moss
    Where glows the rosebud.

'Let me among the clean grasses
    Drink the drops of dew
Which sprinkle the tender flower, –

'So that pleasure, my dear,
    Should brighten your open brow
Like dawn the reluctant blue.'

Her dear rare body, harmonious,
Fragrant, white as white
Rose, whiteness of pure milk, and rosy
As a lily beneath purple skies?

Beauteous thighs, upright breasts,
The back, the loins and belly, feast
For the eyes and prying hands
And for the lips and all the senses.

'Little one, let us see if your bed
Has still beneath the red curtain
The beautiful pillow that slips so
And the wild sheets. O to your bed!'

[ROLAND GRANT AND PAUL ARCHER]

Pensionnaires

The one was fifteen years old, the other sixteen
And they both slept in the same little room.
It happened on an oppressive September eve –
Fragile things! blue-eyed with cheeks like ivory.

To cool their frail bodies each removed
Her dainty chemise fresh with the perfume of amber.
The younger raised her hands and bent backwards,
And her sister, her hands on her breasts, kissed her.

Then fell on her knees, and, in a frenzy,
Grasped her limbs to her cheek, and her mouth
Caressed the blonde gold within the grey shadows:

And during all that time the younger counted
On her darling fingers the promised waltzes,
And, blushing, smiled innocently.

[FRANÇOIS PIROU]

Thousands and Three[1]

My lovers do not belong to the two rich classes:
They are the suburban and rural workmen.
Their fifteen and twenty years, unrestrained, and prodigious
With their brutal force and gross ways.

I sense them in their work clothes, overalls and shirts:
They do not smell of perfume, but blossom with health
Pure and simple; their heavy walk is nimble
For all that with youthful and grave elasticity.

Their frank and sly eyes crackle with cordial
Malice, and naïvely deceitful words
Flow – not without a gay oath to spice them –
From their mouths fresh with solid kisses;

1. The title refers to the catalogue of his master's conquests sung by Leporello in Mozart's
Don Giovanni.

Their vigorous ways and joyous manners
Gladden the night, and my soul, and my body
Under the lamp and at dawn, their joyous flesh,
Resuscitates my tired desire never conquered.

Body, soul, hands, all my being pell-mell
Memory, feet, heart, spine and ear and nose,
And the belly all cry out in a mad chorus,
Mingling in a frenzied dance amidst the frantic clamour.

A mad dance and a mad refrain, mad and stupid,
And rather divine than infernal, more infernal
Than divine, to engulf me, and I swim, and I fly
In their sweat and in their breath and at these antics.

My two Charlots: One a young tiger with the eyes of a cat,
Out of a choirboy to a soldier grown;
The other, a proud fellow, handsomely brazen, unruffled,
That my dizzy being towards him melts.

Odilon, an urchin, but developed like a man,
His feet love mine enamoured of his toes;
Or better still, but not better than the rest of him,
His adorable torso, but his feet are without comparison!

Lovers, fresh satin, delicate phalanxes
Above the souls, above the ankles, and on
The veiny arches: and those exotic kisses
So sweet, of four feet having but a single soul!

Antoine, again proverbial as to his sins
He, my triumphant king and supreme God,
Pierces my eyes with his blue pupils,
And my heart with his awesome passion.

Paul, a blonde athlete of superb shoulders,
White chest with hard buttons as sweet as
A good kiss: François, supple as a slender stem,
Legs of a dance, and as beautiful as his love.

Auguste, who becomes more masculine from day to day
(He was very pretty when he first came among us);
Jules, a little whorish with his pale beauty;
Henri, left me, the coward, to go with the others:

And all of you, in line or in mingled group,
Or singly: vision so clear of days that have gone,
Passions of the present, future that grows and unites
Cherished ones without number and never enough!

[FRANÇOIS PIROU]

A Bad Sleeper

He is a bad sleeper and it is a joy to me
To feel him well when he is the proud prey
And the strong neighbour of the best of sleep
Without false covers – no need – and without awakenings.
So near, so near to me that I believe he enflames me
In some way, with his overwhelming desire, that I feel
In my ravished and trembling body.
If we find ourselves face to face, and if he turns
Close to my side, as lovers are wont to do,
His haunches, deliriously dreamy or not,
Sudden, mutinous, malicious, stubborn, whorish,
In the name-of-God, his cravings, so gentle, will pierce my flesh,
And leave me girdled like a eunuch,
Or if I should turn to him with the wish
To soothe him; or, if peacefully we lie, his quietness,
Brutal and gentle, will suffuse my body in his;
And my spirit, out of happiness, will submerge and overwhelm him,
And prostrate him, infinite in that tack.
Am I happy? Totus in benigno positus!

[FRANÇOIS PIROU]

Ode: To My Lovers

My lovers
(Simple chaps,
But what constitutions!)
Please comfort me after my mishaps.
Refresh me after my literary endeavors;
You, my streetboy, let us play with each other in slang;
You, farmboys, let me hear in your country dialect a pitch
About cocks up the ass and eating dicks.
In the thick bushes we'll form a pigpile,
Have a gangbang.
We artists can use our tongues with such wile!
We'll shit on sad orations
Of pedants and pricks:
They're such a bitch!
(No, not 'bitch'; that word throws off on the opposite sex.
And, after all, women sometimes please
Even us, the fastidious, the elect,
The members of that grand sect
Whose leaders would be Plato and Socrates.
A woman now and then is correct,
And such concessions should pose no problem.
Besides, to each his due:
Women have a right to share in our glory, too.
Between moves let us be nice to them,
Then return to our business.)
My darling children, I revel in your caresses,
Your assholes, your cocks of a truly royal size.
Using them we'll take retaliation
Against those sad fellows who offer eloquence to shitheads,
Blowhards who don't know how to blow a hard-on –
No, let's not compose word-plays; let's screw!
Play with our balls until they're blue,
Then rinse our cockheads
And make a feast of shit and cum, of ass and thighs!

[J. MURAT AND W. GUNN]

EDWARD CARPENTER
(1844–1929)

From *Towards Democracy*

Through the Long Night

You, proud curve-lipped youth, with brown sensitive face,
Why, suddenly, as you sat there on the grass, did you turn full upon
me those twin black eyes of yours,
With gaze so absorbing so intense, I a strong man trembled and was
faint?
Why in a moment between me and you in the full summer afternoon
did Love sweep – leading after it in procession across the lawn
and the flowers and under the waving trees huge dusky shadows
of Death and the other world?
I know not.
Solemn and dewy-passionate, yet burning clear and steadfast at the
last,
Through the long night those eyes of yours, dear, remain to me –
And I remain gazing into them.

from *A Mightier than Mammon*

The love of men for each other – so tender, heroic, constant;
That has come all down the ages, in every clime, in every nation,
Always so true, so well assured of itself, overleaping barriers of age,
of rank, of distance,
Flag of the camp of Freedom;
The love of women for each other – so rapt, intense, so confiding-
close, so burning-passionate,
To unheard deeds of sacrifice, of daring and devotion, prompting;
And (not less) the love of men for women, and of women for
men – on a newer greater scale than it has hitherto been
conceived;
Grand, free and equal – gracious yet ever incommensurable –
The soul of Comradeship glides in.

The young heir goes to inspect the works of one of his tenants;
[Once more the king's son loves the shepherd lad;]
In the shed the fireman is shovelling coal into the boiler furnace. He
is either specially handsome nor specially intelligent, yet when he
turns, from under his dark lids rimmed with coal dust shoots
something so human, so loving-near, it makes the other tremble.

They only speak a few words, and lo! underneath all the differences
of class and speech, of muscle and manhood, their souls are knit
together.

The Cinghalese cooly comes on board a merchant vessel at
Colombo, every day for a week or more, to do some bits of
cleaning.

He is a sweet-natured bright intelligent fellow of 21 or so. One of the
engineers is decently kind and friendly with him – gives him a
knife and one or two little presents;

But the Cinghalese gives his very soul to the engineer; and worships
his white jacket and overalls as though they were the shining
garment of a god.

He cannot rest; but implores to be taken on the voyage; and weeps
bitterly when he learns that the ship must sail without him.

Ah! weep not, brown-bodied youth wandering lonely by the surf-
ridden shore – as you watch your white friend's vessel gliding
into the offing, under the sun and the sun-fringed clouds;

Out, far out to sea, with your friend whom you will never see again;

Weep not so heart-brokenly, for even your tears, gentle boy,
poured now upon the barren sand are the prophecy of amity that
shall be one day between all the races of the earth.

And here are two women, both doctors and mature in their
profession, whose souls are knit in a curiously deep affection.

They share a practice in a large town, and live in the same house
together, exchanging all that they command, of life and affection
and experience;

And this continues for twenty-years – till the death of the elder one –
after which the other ceases not to visit her grave, twice every
week, till the time of her own last illness.

And this is of a poor lad born in the slums, who with aching lonely
heart once walked the streets of London.

Many spoke to him because he was fair – asked him to come and
have a drink, and so forth; but still it was no satisfaction to him;
for they did not give him that which he needed.

Then one day he saw a face in which love dwelt. It was a man twice his own age, captain of a sailing vessel – a large free man, well acquainted with the world, capable and kindly.

And the moment the lad saw him his heart was given to him, and he could not rest but must needs follow the man up and down – yet daring not to speak to him, and the other knowing nothing of it all.

And this continued – till the time came for the man to go another voyage. Then he disappeared; and the youth, still not knowing who or whence he was, fell into worse misery and loneliness than ever, for a whole year.

Till at last one day – or one evening rather – to his great joy he saw his friend going into a public house. It was in a little street off Mile-end Road. He slipped in and sat beside him.

And the man spoke to him, and was kind, but nothing more. And presently, as the hour was getting late, got up and said Goodnight, and went out at the door.

And the lad, suddenly seized with a panic fear that he might never see his friend again, hurried after him, and when they came to a quiet spot, ran up and seized him by the hand, and hardly knowing what he was doing fell on his knees on the pavement, and held him.

And the man at first thought this was a ruse or a mere conspiracy, but when he lifted the lad and looked in his face he understood, for he saw love written there. And he straightaway loved and received him.

And this is of a boy who sat in school.

The masters talked about Greek accidence and quadratic equations, and the boys talked about lobs and byes and bases and goals; but of that which was nearest to his heart no one said a word.

It was laughed at – or left unspoken.

Yet when the boy stood near some of his comrades in the cricket-field or sat next them in school, he stocked and stammered, because of some winged glorious thing which stood or sat between him and them.

And again the laughter came, because he had forgotten what he was doing; and he shrank into himself, and the walls round him grew, so that he was pent and lonely like a prisoner.

Till one day to him weeping, Love full-grown, all-glorious, pure, unashamed, unshackled, came like a god into his little cell, and swore to break the barriers.

And when the boy through his tears asked him how he would do
that, Love answered not, but turning drew with his finger on the
walls of the cell.
And as he drew, lo! beneath his finger sprang all forms of beauty, an
endless host – outlines and colors of all that is, transfigured:
And, as he drew, the cell-walls widened – a new world rose – and
folk came trooping in to gaze,
And the barriers had vanished.

Wonderful, beautiful, the Soul that knits the Body's life passed in,
And the barriers had vanished.

Everywhere under the surface the streamers shoot, auroral,
Strands and tissues of a new life forming.
Already the monstrous accumulations of private wealth seem
useless and a burden –
At best to be absorbed in new formations.
The young woman from an upper class of society builds up her girls'
club; the young man organizes his boys from the slums. Untiring
is their care; but something more, more personal and close, than
philanthropy inspires them.
The little guilds of workers are animated by a new spirit: to have
pleasure in good work seems something worth living for; the
home-colonists turn their backs on civilization if only they may
realize a friendly life with Nature and each other; the girls in the
dress-making shop stand in a new relation to their mistress, and
work so gladly for her and with her; the employer of labor begins
to doubt whether he gets any satisfaction by grinding the faces of
his men – a new idea is germinating in his mind; even to the
landlord it occurs that to create a glad and free village life upon his
estate would be more pleasure than to shoot over it.
As to the millionaire, having spent his life in scheming for Wealth,
he cannot but continue in the web which himself has woven; yet
is heartily sick of it, and longs in a kind of vague way for
something simple and unembarrassed. He is pestered to death by
sharks, parasites, poor relations, politicians, adventurers,
lawyers, company-promoters, begging letters and business
correspondence, society functions, charitable and philanthropic
schemes, town and country houses, stewards, bailiffs, flunkeys,
and the care of endless possessions; and sees that to cast all these
aside and devote his wealth if possible to the realization of a grand

life for the mass-peoples of the Earth were indeed his best hope
and happiness.

The graduate from Cambridge is a warm-hearted impulsive little
woman, genuine and human to the core. Having escaped from
high and dry home-circles, she found curiously the answer of her
heart in a wage-worker of an East London workshop – a calm
broad-browed woman, strong, clearheaded, somewhat sad in
expression, and a bit of a leader among her trade-mates.

Having got into touch with each other, the two came at last to live
together; and immediately on doing so found themselves a focus
and centre of activities – like opposite poles of a battery through
which when in contact the electricity streams.

So the news and interests of the two classes of society streamed
through them. Through them too, folk from either side,
especially women, came into touch with each other, and
discovered a common cause and sympathy amid many surface
differences.

Thus by a thousand needs beside their own compelled, was their
love assured, their little home made sacred.

Everywhere a new motive of life dawns.

With the liberation of Love, and with it of Sex, with the sense that
these are things – and the joy of them – not to be dreaded or
barred, but to be made use of, wisely and freely, as a man makes
use of his most honored possession,

Comes a new gladness:

The liberation of a Motive greater than Money,

And the only motive perhaps that can finally take precedence of
Money.

'MICHAEL FIELD'
[KATHERINE BRADLEY AND EDITH COOPER]
(1848–1914 and 1862–1913)

from *Variations on Sappho*
33

Maids, not to you my mind doth change;
Men I defy, allure, estrange,
Prostrate, make bond or free:

Soft as the stream beneath the plane
To you I sing my love's refrain;
Between us is no thought of pain,
    Peril, satiety.

Soon doth a lover's patience tire,
But ye to manifold desire
Can yield response, ye know
When for long, museful days I pine,
The presage at my heart divine;
To you I never breathe a sign
    Of inward want or woe.

When injuries my spirit bruise,
Allaying virtue ye infuse
With unobtrusive skill:
And if care frets ye come to me
As fresh as nymph from stream or tree,
And with your soft vitality
    My weary bosom fill.

35

Come, Gorgo, put the rug in place,
    And passionate recline;
I love to see thee in thy grace,
    Dark, virulent, divine.
But wherefore thus thy proud eyes fix
    Upon a jewelled band?
Art thou so glad the sardonyx
    Becomes thy shapely hand?

Bethink thee! 'Tis for such as thou
    Zeus leaves his lofty seat;
'Tis at thy beauty's bidding how
    Man's mortal life shall fleet;
Those fairest hands – dost thou forget
    Their power to thrill and cling?
O foolish woman, dost thou set
    Thy pride upon a ring?

REGINALD BRETT, VISCOUNT ESHER
(1852–1930)

At Swindon

You touched my sleeve, and quickly spoke my name,
　　I turned, O friend, O love of long ago!
　　Amid the crush and hurrying to and fro
We asked where each was bound, and whence he came,

Then smiled, and said Good-bye. These ten short years
　　Have cooled the blood; why leaps my heart not still
　　At each plain word you speak? The veins grown chill
Make light of love, and check the trembling tears.

ARTHUR RIMBAUD
(1854–1891)

My mouth is often joined against his mouth
My soul! of fluffy and of jealous stuff,
That makes of mine its trough and nest of sobs.

'Tis the trembling olive and the flute of peace,
'Tis the tube where descends the celestial breath
Feminine Canaan in the protruding halves.

[FRANÇOIS PIROU]

The Tortured Heart[1]

Over the stern, my sad heart, drool;
My heart, spattered with soldiers' cum.
Each sprayed there the juice of his tool.
Over the stern, my sad heart, drool.
Beneath the taunts of troops so cruel
Who burst out laughing, all and some,
Over the stern, my sad heart, drool,
My heart, spattered with soldiers' cum.

Oh ithyphallic soldier lads
Whose taunting has depraved my heart,
A painting now the ship's helm glads

1. Written at the age of sixteen after an alleged rape.

Of ithyphallic soldier lads.
And, oh you waves where water mads,
Take, take and bathe away the smart
Of ithyphallic soldier lads
Whose taunting has depraved my heart.

When all of them had shot their bolt,
What could I do, my cheated heart?
The belching of each drunken dolt
When all of them had shot their bolt
Will make my sickened gorge revolt
If they corrupted every part
When all of them had shot their bolt.
What can I do, my cheated heart?

ARTHUR RIMBAUD and PAUL VERLAINE

Sonnet: To the Asshole

Dark, puckered hole: a purple carnation
That trembles, nestled among the moss (still wet
With love) covering the gentle curvation
Of the white ass, just to the royal eyelet.
Threads resembling milky tears there are spun;
Spray forced back by the south wind's cruel threat
Across the small balls of brown shit has run,
To drip from the crack, which craves for it yet.

Not wishing the prick to have its bent,
My mouth too has often mated with that vent,
My sobbing tongue tried to devour the rose
Flowering in brown moisture. The chute unmanned,
It's a heavenly jam-pot, the Promised Land
Which with other milk and honey overflows!

[J. MURAT AND W. GUNN]

HORATIO BROWN
(1854–1926)

A 'Kodak'; Tregantle

Where the wind attacks the downs,
   Where the fort Tregantle frowns
Over cliffs that curb the ocean in its glee;
   Where the gorse and heather quicken
   To a blaze above the lichen,
What a vision took the splendour out of down and distant lea!

For with comely, capless head,
   With a light, elastic tread
Came a trooper of some summers twenty-three;
   With his jacket all unlaced,
   And his belt about his waist,
And a ruddy golden colour from his bathing in the sea.

Though we went our different ways,
   And through all the coming days
We shall never meet again upon the lea,
   Yet he seemed the sum and glory
   Of the whole world's ancient story,
And I thanked the God that made him and the land and sea and me.

'Bored'
At a London Music

Two rows of foolish faces blent
In two blurred lines; the compliment,
The formal smile, the cultured air,
The sense of falseness everywhere.
Her ladyship superbly dressed –
   I liked their footman, John, the best.

The tired musician's ruffled mien,
Their whispered talk behind the screen,
The frigid plaudits, quite confined

By fear of being unrefined.
His lordship's grave and courtly jest –
   I liked their footman, John, the best.

Remote I sat with shaded eyes,
Supreme attention in my guise,
And heard the whole laborious din,
Piano, 'cello, violin;
And so, perhaps, they hardly guessed
   I liked their footman, John, the best.

A. E. HOUSMAN
(1859–1936)

'Look not in my eyes, for fear'

Look not in my eyes, for fear
   They mirror true the sight I see,
And there you find your face too clear
   And love it and be lost like me.
One the long nights through must lie
   Spent in star-defeated sighs,
But why should you as well as I
   Perish? gaze not in my eyes.

A Grecian lad, as I hear tell,
   One that many loved in vain,
Looked into a forest well
   And never looked away again.
There, when the turf in springtime flowers,
   With downward eye and gazes sad,
Stands amid the glancing showers
   A jonquil, not a Grecian lad.

'Shot? so quick, so clean an ending?'

Shot? so quick, so clean an ending?
   Oh that was right, lad, that was brave:
Yours was not an ill for mending,
   'Twas best to take it to the grave.

Oh you had forethought, you could reason,
    And saw your road and where it led,
And early wise and brave in season
    Put the pistol to your head.

Oh soon, and better so than later
    After long disgrace and scorn,
You shot dead the household traitor,
    The soul that should not have been born.

Right you guessed the rising morrow
    And scorned to tread the mire you must:
Dust's your wages, son of sorrow,
    But men may come to worse than dust.

Souls undone, undoing others, –
    Long time since the tale began.
You would not live to wrong your brothers:
    Oh lad, you died as fits a man.

Now to your grave shall friend and stranger
    With ruth and some with envy come:
Undishonoured, clear of danger,
    Clean of guilt, pass hence and home.

Turn safe to rest, no dreams, no waking;
    And here, man, here's the wreath I've made:
'Tis not a gift that's worth the taking,
    But wear it and it will not fade.

'The laws of God, the laws of man'

    The laws of God, the laws of man,
He may keep that will and can;
Not I: let God and man decree
Laws for themselves and not for me;
And if my ways are not as theirs
Let them mind their own affairs.
Their deeds I judge and much condemn,
Yet when did I make laws for them?
Please yourselves, say I, and they
Need only look the other way.
But no, they will not; they must still

Wrest their neighbour to their will,
And make me dance as they desire
With jail and gallows and hell-fire.
And how am I to face the odds
Of man's bedevilment and God's?
I, a stranger and afraid
In a world I never made.
They will be master, right or wrong;
Though both are foolish, both are strong.
And since, my soul, we cannot fly
To Saturn nor to Mercury,
Keep we must, if keep we can,
These foreign laws of God and man.

'Because I liked you better'

Because I liked you better
    Than suits a man to say,
It irked you, and I promised
    To throw the thought away.

To put the world between us
    We parted, stiff and dry;
'Good-bye,' said you, 'forget me.'
    'I will, no fear,' said I.

If here, where clover whitens
    The dead man's knoll, you pass,
And no tall flower to meet you
    Starts in the trefoiled grass,

Halt by the headstone naming
    The heart no longer stirred,
And say the lad that loved you
    Was one that kept his word.

'Half-way, for one commandment broken'

Half-way, for one commandment broken.
    The woman made her endless halt,
And she today, a glistering token,
    Stands in the wilderness of salt.

Behind, the vats of judgment brewing
  Thundered, and thick the brimstone snowed;
He to the hill of his undoing
  Pursued his road.

'He would not stay for me; and who can wonder?'

He would not stay for me; and who can wonder?
  He would not stay for me to stand and gaze.
I shook his hand and tore my heart in sunder
  And went with half my life about my ways.

'Oh who is that young sinner with the handcuffs on his wrists?'

Oh who is that young sinner with the handcuffs on his wrists?
And what has he been after that they groan and shake their fists?
And wherefore is he wearing such a conscience-stricken air?
Oh they're taking him to prison for the colour of his hair.

'Tis a shame to human nature, such a head of hair as his;
In the good old time 'twas hanging for the colour that it is;
Though hanging isn't bad enough and flaying would be fair
For the nameless and abominable colour of his hair.

Oh a deal of pains he's taken and a pretty price he's paid
To hide his poll or dye it of a mentionable shade;
But they've pulled the beggar's hat off for the world to see and stare,
And they're haling him to justice for the colour of his hair.

FREDERICK ROLFE, BARON CORVO
(1860–1913)

Ballade of Boys Bathing

I

As dainty a sight as ever I did see!
  In a drifting boat with an hour to spare
On the coast of the land of the kilted knee
  Under the sea-cliff's shadows, where
  A flash of boys, slender and debonair
    Laugh in a lovely disarray
  Fear they know not nor never a care
    The boys who bathe in Saint Andrew's Bay.

II

Deep blue waters as blue can be
   Rocks rising high 'mid the red clouds flare
Boys of the colour of ivory
   Breasting the wavelets and diving there
   White boys, ruddy and tanned, and bare
      With lights and shadows of rose and grey
   And the sea like pearls in their shining hair
      The boys who bathe in Saint Andrew's Bay.

III

A summer night and a sapphire sea
   A setting sun and a golden glare
.Hurled from the height where the rugged rocks be
   Wonderous limbs in the luminous air
   Fresh as a white flame flushed and fair
      Little round arms in the salt sea spray
   And the sea seems alive with them everywhere
      The boys who bathe in Saint Andrew's Bay.

Envoy

Andrea! Lay me out tinctures rare
   Set me a palette and while I may
I'll fix on my canvas if so I may dare
   The boys who bathe in Saint Andrew's Bay.

'ARTHUR LYON RAILE'
[EDWARD PERRY WARREN]
(1860–1928)

The Waning of Love

I

To love thee brings me sadness, for I know
each time the time will never come again, –
that every moment brings the darker stain
of riper manhood. Liker as we grow,
Love stirs his wings, impatient to remain.

II

Each night of love from such a love doth part
thy forward-looking self. At each remove
from boyhood thou art further from my love,
though nearer to the knowledge of my heart.
Love joineth us the closer to dispart.

III

Then thou and I to younger arms shall flee;
but thou, I think, in girlish form wilt find
what I, who know thee throughly, flesh and mind,
and never knew another like to thee,
shall never compass, leaving thee behind.

MARY COLERIDGE
(1861–1907)

Marriage

No more alone sleeping, no more alone waking,
    Thy dreams divided, thy prayers in twain;
Thy merry sisters to-night forsaking;
    Never shall we see thee, maiden, again.

Never shall we see thee, thine eyes glancing
    Flashing with laughter and wild in glee,
Under the mistletoe kissing and dancing,
            Wantonly free.

There shall come a matron walking sedately,
    Low-voiced, gentle, wise in reply.
Tell me, O tell me, can I love her greatly?
    All for her sake must the maiden die!

G. LOWES DICKINSON
(1862–1932)

I never asked for more than thou hast given,
The benediction of a brother's love;

Fairer to me than all the stars of heaven
That argent planet beacons from above;
And in thy spirit's ample firmament,
Where'er the orient sun may rise and shine,
Think not that I shall murmur or repent,
Craving a fuller light that is not mine.
Let but thy star of consolation lighten
Over the twilight meadows of my soul,
Larger across the gathering darkness brighten,
Surelier fix and fire the heavenly goal;
   Then though the dawn delay or fail me quite
   I am content to wait and watch the night.

C. P. CAVAFY
(1863–1933)

The Window of the Tobacco Shop

They stood among many others
close to a lighted tobacco shop window.
Their looks met by chance
and timidly, haltingly expressed
the illicit desire of their bodies.
Then a few uneasy steps along the street
until they smiled, and nodded slightly.

And after that the closed carriage,
the sensitive approach of body to body,
hands joined, lips meeting.

[EDMUND KEELEY AND PHILIP SHERRARD]

The Next Table

He must be hardly twenty-two. And yet
I'm sure that nearly as many years ago
That was the very body I enjoyed.

It isn't a kindling of desire at all.
I only came into the casino a minute ago;
I haven't even had time to drink much.
That very same body I have enjoyed.

If I don't remember where – one thing forgotten doesn't signify.

There, now that he has sat down at the next table,
I know every movement he makes – and under his
    clothes
Naked I can see again the limbs I loved.

[JOHN MAVROGORDATO]

Their Beginning

The consummation of their lawless pleasure
Was done. They rose up from the mattress;
Hurriedly dressed themselves without speaking.
They go out separately, secretly from the house; and as
They walk rather uneasily up the street, it seems
As if they suspect that something about them betrays
On what sort of bed they lay down not long ago.

But for the artist how his life has gained.
Tomorrow, the next day or years after will be written
The lines of strength that here had their beginning.

[JOHN MAVROGORDATO]

In Despair

He's lost him completely. And he now tries to find
his lips in the lips of each new lover,
he tries in the embrace of each new lover
to convince himself that it's the same young man,
that it's to him he gives himself.

He's lost him completely, as though he never existed.
He wanted, his lover said, to save himself

from the tainted, sick form of sexual pleasure,
the tainted, shameful form of sexual pleasure.
There was still time, he said, to save himself.

He's lost him completely, as though he never existed.
Through fantasy, through hallucination,
he tries to find his lips in the lips of other young men,
he longs to feel his kind of love once more.

[EDMUND KEELEY AND PHILIP SHERRARD]

The Twenty-fifth Year of His Life

He goes regularly to the taverna
where they'd met the previous month.
He made inquiries, but they weren't able to tell him anything.
From what they said, he gathered the person he'd met
was someone completely unknown,
one of the many unknown and shady young types
who dropped in there.
But he still goes to the taverna regularly, at night,
and sits there gazing toward the doorway,
gazing toward the doorway until he's worn out.
Maybe he'll walk in. Tonight maybe he'll turn up.

He does this for nearly three weeks.
His mind's sick with longing.
The kisses are there on his mouth.
His flesh, all of it, suffers from endless desire,
the feel of that other body is on his,
he wants to be joined with it again.

Of course he tries not to give himself away.
But sometimes he almost doesn't care.
Besides, he knows what he's exposing himself to,
he's come to accept it: quite possibly this life of his
will land him in a devastating scandal.

[EDMUND KEELEY AND PHILIP SHERRARD]

Days of 1896

He'd become completely degraded. His erotic tendencies,
condemned and strictly forbidden
(but innate for all that) were the cause of it:
society was totally narrow-minded.
He'd gradually lost what little money he had,
then his social standing, then his reputation.
Nearly thirty, he'd never worked a full year –
at least not at a legitimate job.
Sometimes he earned enough to get by
acting the go-between in deals considered shameful.
He ended up the type likely to compromise you thoroughly
if you were seen around with him too often.

But this wasn't the whole story – that wouldn't be fair;
the memory of his beauty deserves better.
There is another angle; seen from that
he appears attractive, appears
a simple, genuine child of love,
without hesitation putting
the pure sensuality of his pure flesh
above his honour and reputation.

Above his reputation? But society,
totally narrow-minded, had all its values wrong.

[EDMUND KEELEY AND PHILIP SHERRARD]

Two Young Men, 23 to 24 Years Old

He'd been sitting in the café since ten-thirty
expecting him to turn up any minute.
Midnight had gone, and he was still waiting for him.
It was now after one-thirty, and the café was almost deserted.
He'd grown tired of reading newspapers
mechanically. Of his three lonely shillings
only one was left: waiting that long,
he'd spent the others on coffees and brandy.
And he'd smoked all his cigarettes.
So much waiting had worn him out.

Because alone like that for so many hours,
he'd also begun to have disturbing thoughts
about the immoral life he was living.

But when he saw his friend come in –
weariness, boredom, thought all disappeared at once.

His friend brought unexpected news.
He'd won sixty pounds playing cards.

Their good looks, their exquisite youthfulness,
the sensitive love they shared
were refreshed, livened, invigorated
by the sixty pounds from the card table.

Now all joy and vitality, feeling and charm,
they went – not to the homes of their respectable families
(where they were no longer wanted anyway) –
they went to a familiar and very special
house of debauchery, and they asked for a bedroom
and expensive drinks, and they drank again.

And when the expensive drinks were finished
and it was close to four in the morning,
happy, they gave themselves to love.

[EDMUND KEELEY AND PHILIP SHERRARD]

The Mirror in the Front Hall

The luxurious house had a huge mirror
in the front hall, a very old mirror,
bought at least eighty years ago.

A good-looking boy, a tailor's assistant
(on Sundays an amateur athlete),
stood there with a package. He gave it to one of the household
who took it in to get the receipt.
The tailor's assistant,
left alone as he waited,
went up to the mirror, looked at himself,

and adjusted his tie. Five minutes later
they brought him the receipt. He took it and went away.

But the old mirror that had seen so much
in its long life –
thousands of objects, faces –
the old mirror was full of joy now,
proud to have embraced
total beauty for a few moments.

[EDMUND KEELEY AND PHILIP SHERRARD]

He Asked About the Quality

He left the office where he'd been given
a trivial, poorly paid job
(something like eight pounds a month, including bonuses) –
left at the end of the dreary work
that kept him bent all afternoon,
came out at seven and walked off slowly,
idling his way down the street. Good-looking,
and interesting: showing as he did that he'd reached
his full sensual capacity.
He'd turned twenty-nine the month before.

He idled his way down the main street
and the poor side-streets that led to his home.

Passing in front of a small shop that sold
cheap and flimsy merchandise for workers,
he saw a face inside, a figure
that compelled him to go in, and he pretended
he wanted to look at some coloured handkerchiefs.

He asked about the quality of the handkerchiefs
and how much they cost, his voice choking,
almost silenced by desire.
And the answers came back in the same mood,
distracted, the voice hushed,
offering hidden consent.

They kept on talking about the merchandise –
but the only purpose: that their hands might touch
over the handkerchiefs, that their faces, their lips,
might move close together as though by chance –
a moment's meeting of limb against limb.

Quickly, secretly, so the shop owner sitting at the back
wouldn't realize what was going on.

[EDMUND KEELEY AND PHILIP SHERRARD]

SAMUEL ELSWORTH COTTAM
(1863–1945?)

To G.R.

There is a club for boys where they
    By night can congregate,
Where many are the games they play,
    And each one meets his mate.

They are a rather rowdy crew,
    Rough diamonds at the best:
But those in charge will trust the few
    To influence the rest.

Now one would think this scarce the place
    Where Eros would intrude,
Or mix among the crowd to grace
    Their untaught manners crude.

Yet here I saw a fellow stand
    To read a notice on a door,
The while his chum with gentle hand
    On his left shoulder bore,

Who then so deftly kissed his neck,
    Embracing towards the right: –
A revelation! Just a speck
    Of friendship, love and light!

ANONYMOUS
(published 1866)

from *Don Leon*
lines 129–150

The anonymous poet in the character of Lord Byron depicts the birth of his gay feelings and then goes on to describe his first love affair and his time at Cambridge.

Then, say, was I or nature in the wrong,
If, yet a boy, one inclination, strong
In wayward fancies, domineered my soul,
And bade complete defiance to control?
What, though my youthful instincts, forced to brood
Within my bosom seemed a while subdued?
What, though by early education taught,
The charms of women first my homage caught?
What though my verse in Mary's praises flowed
And flowers poetic round her footsteps strewed,
Yet, when her ears would list not to my strain,
And every sigh was answered with disdain,
Pride turned, not stopped, the course of my desires,
Extinguished these and lighted other fires.
And as the pimple which cosmetic art
Repels from one, invades another part,
My bubbling passions found another vent,
The object changed, but not the sentiment.
And, e'er my years could ask the reason why,
Sex caused no qualms where beauty led the eye.
Such were my motions ere my teens began,
And such their progress till I grew a man.

lines 164–384

Among the yeomens' sons on my estate
A gentle boy would at my mansion wait:
And now, that time has almost blanched my hair,
And with the past the present I compare,
Full well I know, though decency forbad

The same caresses to the rustic lad;
Love, love it was, that made my eyes delight
To have his person ever in my sight.
Yes, Rushton, though to unobserving eyes,
My favours but as lordly gifts were prized;
Yet something then would inwardly presage
The predilections of my riper age.
Why did I give thee gauds to deck thy form?
Why for a menial did my entrails warm?
Why? but from secret longings to pursue
These inspirations, which, if books speak true,
Have led e'en priests and sages to embrace
Those charms, which female blandishments efface.
Thus passed my boyhood: and though proofs were none
What path my future course of life would run,
Like sympathetic ink, if then unclear,
The test applied soon made the trace appear.
I bade adieu to school and tyro's sports,
And Cam received me in his gothic courts,
Freed from the pedagogue's tyrannic sway,
In mirth and revels I consumed the day.
No more my truant muse her vigils kept;
No more she soothed my slumbers as I slept;
But, idling now, she oft recalled the time
When to her feeble reed I tuned my rhyme.
She knew how those midst song and mirth grow dull
Whose tender bosoms soft emotions lull.
As manhood came, my feelings, more intense,
Sighed for some kindred mind, where confidence,
Tuned in just unison, might meet return,
And whilst it warmed my breast, in his might burn.
    Oft, when the evening bell to vespers rung,
When the full choir the solemn anthem sung,
And lips, o'er which no youthful down had grown,
Hymned their soft praises of Jehovah's throne,
The pathos of the strain would soothe my soul,
And call me willing from the drunkard's bowl.
Who, that has heard the chapel's evening song,
When peals divine the lengthened note prolong,
But must have felt religious thoughts arise,
And speed their way melodious to the skies.

Among the choir a youth my notice won,
Of pleasing lineaments named Eddleston.
With gifts well suited to the stripling's mood,
His friendship and his tenderness I wooed.
Oh! how I loved to press his cheek to mine;
How fondly would my arms his waist entwine!
Another feeling borrowed friendship's name,
And took its mantle to conceal my shame.
Another feeling! oh! 'tis hard to trace
The line where love usurps tame friendship's place.
Friendship's the chrysalis, which seems to die,
But throws its coil to give love wings to fly.
Both are the same, but in another state;
This formed to soar, and that to vegetate.
Of humble birth was he – patrician I,
And yet this youth was my idolatry.
Strong was my passion, past all inward cure
And could it be so violent, yet pure?
'Twas like a philter poured into my veins –
And as the chemist, when some vase contains
An unknown mixture, each component tries
With proper tests, the draught to analyse;
So questioned I myself: What lights this fire?
Maids and not boys are wont to move desire;
Else 'twere illicit love. Oh! sad mishap!
But what prompts nature then to set the trap?
Why night and day does his sweet image float
Before my eyes? or wherefore do I doat
On that dear face with ardour so intense?
Why truckles reason to concupiscence?
Though law cries 'hold!' yet passion onward draws:
But nature gave us passion, man gave laws.
Whence spring these inclinations, rank and strong?
And harming no one, wherefore call them wrong?
What's virtue's touchstone? Unto others do,
As you would wish that others did to you.
Then tell me not of sex, if to one key
The chords, when struck, vibrate in harmony.
No virgin I deflower, nor, lurking, creep,
With steps adult 'rous, on a husband's sleep.
I plough no field in other men's domain;

And where I delve no seed shall spring again.
Thus with myself I reasoned; then I read,
And counsel asked from volumes of the dead.
Oh! flowery path, thus hand in hand to walk
With Plato and enjoy his honeyed talk.
Beneath umbrageous planes to sit at ease,
And drink from wisdom's cup with Socrates.
Now stray with Bion through the shady grove;
Midst deeds of glory, now with Plutarch rove.
And oft I turned me to the Mantuan's page,
To hold discourse with shepherds of his age;
Or mixed with Horace in the gay delights
Of courtly revels, theatres, and sights;
And thou, whose soft seductive lines comprise
The code of love, thou hast my sympathies;
But still, where'er I turned, in verse or prose,
Whate'er I read, some fresh dilemma rose,
And reason, that should pilot me along,
Belied her name, or else she led me wrong.
I love a youth; but Horace did the same;
If he's absolv'd, say, why am I to blame?
When young Alexis claimed a Virgil's sigh,
He told the world his choice, and may not I?
Shall every schoolman's pen his verse extol,
And, sin in me, in him a weakness call?
Then why was Socrates surnamed the sage,
Not only in his own, but every age,
If lips, whose accents strewed the path of truth,
Could print their kisses on some favoured youth?
Or why should Plato, in his Commonwealth
Score tenets up which I must note by stealth?
Say, why, when great Epaminondas died,
Was Cephidorus buried by his side?
Or why should Plutarch with eulogiums cite
That chieftain's love for his young catamite,
And we be forced his doctrine to decry,
Or drink the bitter cup of infamy?
  But these, thought I, are samples musty grown;
Turn me from early ages to our own.
No heathen's lust is matter for surprise;
He only aped his pagan deities;

But when a Saviour had redeemed the world,
And all false idols from Olympus hurled,
A purer code the Christian law revealed,
And what was venial once as guilt was sealed.
With zeal unwearied I resumed again
My search, and read whate'er the layman's pen
In annals grave or chronicles had writ;
But can I own with any benefit?
'Tis true, mankind had cast the pagan skin,
But all the carnal part remained within
Unchang'd, and nature, breaking through the fence
Still vindicated her omnipotence.
　　Look, how infected with this rank disease
Were those, who held St Peter's holy keys,
And pious men to whom the people bowed,
And kings, who churches to saints endowed;
All these were christians of the highest stamp –
How many scholars, wasting o'er their lamp,
How many jurists, versed in legal rules,
How many poets, honoured in the schools,
How many captains, famed for deeds of arms,
Have found their solace in a minion's arms!
Nay, e'en our bard, Dame Nature's darling child,
Felt the strange impulse, and his hours beguiled
In penning sonnets to a stripling's praise,
Such as would damn a poet now-a-days.
　　To this conclusion we must come at last:
Wise men have lived in generations past,
Whose deeds and sayings history records,
To whom the palm of virtue she awards,
Who, tempted, ate of that forbidden tree,
Which prejudice denies to you and me.
Then be consistent; and, at once confess,
If man's pursuit through life is happiness,
The great, the wise, the pious, and the good,
Have what they sought not rightly understood;
Or deem not else that aberration crime,
Which reigns in every caste and every clime.
　　Harassed by doubts, I threw my books aside,
Oh! false-named beacons of mankind, I cried,
Perdition's in your light! The gleam you show

Guides to a haven where no bark should go.
'Tis you that foster an illicit trade,
And warp us where a strict embargo's laid.
'Twere just as well to let the vessel glide
Resistless down the current, as confide
In charts, that lead the mariner astray,
And never mark the breakers in his way.
   But tell us casuists, were statutes meant
To scourge the wicked or the innocent?
What! if the husbandman, among the seeds
Of wholesome grain, detects unwholesome weeds;
What! if amidst the standing corn appear
Destructive tares, and choak the goodly ear;
Is evil, not prepense, a crime defined?
Are catiffs those, whose sin was undesigned?
   In vice unhackneyed, in Justine unread,
See schoolboys, by some inclination led:
Some void, that's hardly to themselves confest,
Flying for solace to a comrade's breast.
In lonely walks their vows of friendship pass,
Warm as the shepherd's to his rustic lass.
Their friendship ripens into closer ties:
They love. Then mutual vague desires arise.
Perhaps by night they share each other's bed,
'Till step by step, to closer union led,
Like wantons, whom some unknown feeling charms,
Each thinks he clasps a mistress in his arms.
Imperious nature's sensual prickings goad,
They own her dictates, but mistake the road.
Fond parents, speak! if truth can find her way
Through fogs of prejudice to open day.
Is there a father, when, instead of this,
His offspring sickens with a syphilis,
Who can unmoved his tender bantling see
Devoured with chancres, writhing with chordee,
His blooming looks grown prematurely old,
His manhood wasted ere its hours are told,
His means with harlots and in brothels spent,
His breath infected and his body bent,
And will not own that any means were good
To save from taint so foul, if save he could?

Reflect, and chide not errors that arise
Less from design than man's infirmities.
Shut, shut your eyes, ye pedagogues, nor keep
Too close a watch upon your pupils' sleep:
For though, in boyish ignorance they may
Stumble perchance on some illicit play,
Which looks like lechery the most refined,
In them 'tis not depravity of mind.
Ingenuous souls, oft innocent of wrong,
For some enjoyment yet untasted long:
'Tis ye who roused the latent sense of shame,
And called their gambols by an odious name.

lines 556–613

*Eddleston dies and the poet, leaving Cambridge, goes on the Grand Tour. In
Greece, while examining classical remains, he is invited to see more of the local
life.*

. . . A courteous man appeared;
And, bending low, with invitation pressed
To enter in, and on his sofa rest.
I crossed the threshold of the courteous man,
And smoked and chatted. Close by the divan
His son, as Eastern usages demand,
In modest attitudes was seen to stand
And smiling watched the signals of my will,
To pour sherbet, or the long *chibook*[1] fill.
Grace marked his actions, symmetry his form;
His eyes had made an anchorite grow warm,
His long attire, his silken *anteri,*
Gave pleasing doubts of what his sex might be;
And who that saw him would perplexed have been,
For beauty marked his gender epicene.
    Day after day my visits I renewed,

1. long pipe smoked by Turks

His love with presents like a mistress wooed;
Until his sire with dreams of greatness won,
To be my page made offer of his son.
I took him in my train, with culture stored
His mind, and in it choice instruction poured;
Till like the maiden, who some budding rose
Waters with care and watches till it blows,
Then plucks and places it upon her breast,
I too this blossom to my bosom pressed.
    All ye who know what pleasure 'tis to heave
A lover's sigh, the warm caress receive
Of some fond mistress, and with anxious care
Watch every caprice, and every ailment share,
Ye only know how hard it is to cure
The burning fever of love's calenture.
Come, crabbed philosophers, and tell us why
Should men to harsh ungrateful studies fly
In search of bliss, when e'en a single day
Of dalliance can an age of love outweigh!
How many hours I've spent in pensive guise
To watch the mild expression of his eyes!
Or when asleep at noon, and from his mouth
His breath came sweet like odours from the south,
How long I've hung in rapture as he lay,
And silent chased the insect tribe away.
How oft at morn, when troubled by the heat,
The covering fell disordered at his feet,
I've gazed unsated at his naked charms,
And clasped him waking in my longing arms.
How oft in winter, when the sky o'ercast
Capped the bleak mountains, and the ruthless blast
Moaned through the trees, or lashed the surfy strand,
I've drawn myself the glove upon his hand,
Thrown o'er his tender limbs the rough capote,
Or tied the kerchief round his snowy throat.
How oft, when summer saw me fearless brave
With manly breast the blue transparent wave,
Another Daedalus I taught him how
With spreading arms the liquid waste to plough.
Then brought him gently to the sunny beach,
And wiped the briny moisture from his breach.

JOHN GAMBRIL NICHOLSON
(1866–1931)

from *A Chaplet of Southernwood*

3

I love him wisely if I love him well,
    And so I let him keep his innocence;
    I veil my adoration with pretence
Since he knows nothing of Love's mystic spell;
I dare not for his sake my passion tell
    Though strong desire upbraid my diffidence; –
    To buy my happiness at his expense
Were folly blind and loss unspeakable.

Suspicious of my simplest acts I grow;
    I doubt my passing words, however brief;
    I catch his glances feeling like a thief.
Perchance he wonders why I shun him so, –
It would be strange indeed if he should know
    I love him, love him, love him past belief!

GEORGE IVES
(1867–1950)

A Message[1]

Ah, if I could, I'd dwell with you tonight,
And hold your hand in mine and pity you,
And smooth your prison pillow, and give you strength,
And bide with you till morning crossed the bars.

If I were Sleep, I'd fly to you this night,
And give you dreams, and such profound repose

1. Written to Oscar Wilde in prison.

That slavery were sweet, and that bare cell
A happy place to cradle you to rest.

And were I Death, I still would come to you,
Calm in my might and cold imperious sway,
And I would enter; who would stay my path?
And bend and kiss you, bid you follow me.

Once

They met in passion; Satyrs of the glade
Indulged not in a wilder carnival.
But at the end love came and all was changed,
They parted with a kiss quite cold and sad.

EDMUND ST GASCOIGNE MACKIE
(1867– ?)

from *Charmides*

Up leaps the lark. Delightful Spring once more
Returns, and Proserpine with sun-daz'd orbs
Steps from the underworld. Tell me, dark Queen!
Hast thou beheld my buried Charmides,
Or do the happier islands hold him – speak!
For I am stung with grief for Charmides:
The hillside and the echoing hollows mock me:
Vaguely I suppose he will return:
My questing gaze I bend, but his dear face
Is gone; nor find I comfort anywhere:
Thou could'st have known him well, because when sleeping
A frequent smile would hover round his lips,
As one who feels that he is greatly loved:
Ah, but thou hast not seen him: else methinks
Earth would have whitened to perpetual winter
Waiting thy advent, as I wait, in vain.

STEFAN GEORGE
(1868–1933)

The Lyre Player

How he advanced, with a white fillet twisted
Around his locks, a sumptuous garment weighing
His slender shoulders, how he struck his lyre,
Uncertainly at first with youthful shyness,
Astonished even the austere and aged.
And how he kindled cheeks to yearning scarlet,
How many women flung him strings of jewels
And priceless clasps, while he, who was still new
To such ovation, bowed – will be remembered
Wherever fruit grows on the holy tree.
The girls are full of endless eager talk,
And every boy in secret anguish, worships
The hero of his sleepless, starlit hours.

[CAROL NORTH VALHOPE AND ERNST MOROWITZ]

CHARLOTTE MEW
(1869–1929)

On the Road to the Sea

We passed each other, turned and stopped for half an hour, then went
    our way,
    I who make other women smile did not make you –
But no man can move mountains in a day.
    So this hard thing is yet to do.

But first I want your life: – before I die I want to see
    The world that lies behind the strangeness of your eyes,
There is nothing gay or green there for my gathering, it may be,
        Yet on brown fields there lies
A haunting purple bloom: is there not something in grey skies
            And in grey sea?

I want what world there is behind your eyes,
I want your life and you will not give it me.

Now, if I look, I see you walking down the years,
Young, and through August fields – a face, a thought, a swinging
      dream perched on a stile–;
I would have liked (so vile we are!) to have taught you tears
            But most to have made you smile.

To-day is not enough or yesterday: God sees it all –
Your length on sunny lawns, the wakeful rainy nights –; tell me
  – (how vain to ask), but it is not a question – just a call –;
Show me then only your notched inches climbing up the garden wall,
            I like you best when you were small.

            Is this a stupid thing to say
            Not having spent with you one day?
      No matter; I shall never touch your hair
      Or hear the little tick behind your breast,
            Still it is there,
            And as a flying bird
      Brushes the branches where it may not rest
            I have brushed your hand and heard
      The child in you: I like that best.

So small, so dark, so sweet; and were you also then too grave and
      wise?
      Always I think. Then put your far off little hand in mine; – Oh! let
      it rest;
I will not stare into the early world beyond the opening eyes,
      Or vex or scare what I love best.
            But I want your life before mine bleeds away –
                  Here – not in heavenly hereafters – soon, –
                  I want your smile this very afternoon,
            (The last of all my vices, pleasant people used to say,
                  I wanted and I sometimes got – the Moon!)

                  You know, at dusk, the last bird's cry,
            And round the house the flap of the bat's low flight,
                  Trees that go black against the sky
            And then – how soon the night!

No shadow of you on any bright road again,
And at the darkening end of this – what voice? whose kiss? As if you'd
say!
It is not I who have walked with you, it will not be I who take away
Peace, peace, my little handful of the gleaner's grain
From your reaped fields at the shut of day.

Peace! Would you not rather die
Reeling, – with all the cannons at your ear?
So, at least, would I,
And I may not be here
To-night, to-morrow morning or next year.
Still I will let you keep your life a little while,
See dear?
I have made you smile.

LORD ALFRED DOUGLAS
(1870–1945)

Two Loves

To 'the Sphinx'[1]

Two loves I have of comfort and despair
  Which like two spirits do suggest me still,
The better angel is a man right fair,
  The worser spirit a woman coloured ill.

                    SHAKESPEARE

I dreamed I stood upon a little hill,
And at my feet there lay a ground, that seemed
Like a waste garden, flowering at its will
With flowers and blossoms. There were pools that dreamed
Black and unruffled; there were white lilies
A few, and crocuses, and violets
Purple or pale, snake-like fritillaries
Scarce seen for the rank grass, and through green nets

1. the late Mrs Levesson

Blue eyes of shy pervenche winked in the sun.
And there were curious flowers, before unknown,
Flowers that were stained with moonlight, or with shades
Of Nature's wilful moods; and here a one
That had drunk in the transitory tone
Of one brief moment in a sunset; blades
Of grass that in an hundred springs had been
Slowly but exquisitely nurtured by the stars,
And watered with the scented dew long cupped
In lilies, that for rays of sun had seen
Only God's glory, for never a sunrise mars
The luminous air of heaven. Beyond, abrupt,
A gray stone wall, o'ergrown with velvet moss,
Uprose. And gazing I stood long, all mazed
To see a place so strange, so sweet, so fair.
And as I stood and marvelled, lo! across
The garden came a youth, one hand he raised
To shield him from the sun, his wind-tossed hair
Was twined with flowers, and in his hand he bore
A purple bunch of bursting grapes, his eyes
Were clear as crystal, naked all was he,
White as the snow on pathless mountains frore,
Red were his lips as red wine-spilth that dyes
A marble floor, his brow chalcedony.
And he came near me, with his lips uncurled
And kind, and caught my hand and kissed my mouth,
And gave me grapes to eat, and said 'Sweet friend,
Come, I will shew thee shadows of the world
And images of life. See, from the south
Comes the pale pageant that hath never an end.'
And lo! within the garden of my dream
I saw two walking on a shining plain
Of golden light. The one did joyous seem
And fair and blooming, and a sweet refrain
Came from his lips; he sang of pretty maids
And joyous love of comely girl and boy,
His eyes were bright, and 'mid the dancing blades
Of golden grass his feet did trip for joy.
And in his hands he held an ivory lute,
With strings of gold that were as maidens' hair,
And sang with voice as tuneful as a flute,

And round his neck three chains of roses were.
But he that was his comrade walked aside;
He was full sad and sweet, and his large eyes
Were strange with wondrous brightness, staring wide
With gazing; and he sighed with many sighs
That moved me, and his cheeks were wan and white
Like pallid lilies, and his lips were red
Like poppies, and his hands he clenchèd tight,
And yet again unclenchèd, and his head
Was wreathed with moon-flowers pale as lips of death.
A purple robe he wore, o'erwrought in gold
With the device of a great snake, whose breath
Was fiery flame: which when I did behold
I fell a-weeping and I cried, 'Sweet youth,
Tell me why, sad and sighing, thou dost rove
These pleasant realms? I pray thee speak me sooth
What is thy name?' He said, 'My name is Love.'
Then straight the first did turn himself to me
And cried, 'He lieth, for his name is Shame,
But I am Love, and I was wont to be
Alone in this fair garden, till he came
Unasked by night; I am true Love, I fill
The hearts of boy and girl with mutual flame.'
Then sighing said the other, 'Have thy will,
I am the Love that dare not speak its name.'

The Dead Poet[1]

I dreamed of him last night, I saw his face
All radiant and unshadowed of distress,
And as of old, in music measureless,
I heard his golden voice and marked him trace
Under the common thing the hidden grace,
And conjure wonder out of emptiness,
Till mean things put on beauty like a dress
And all the world was an enchanted place.

1. On Oscar Wilde

And then methought outside a fast locked gate
I mourned the loss of unrecorded words,
Forgotten tales and mysteries half said,
Wonders that might have been articulate,
And voiceless thoughts like murdered singing birds.
And so I woke and knew that he was dead.

PIERRE LOUYS
(1870–1925)

from *Chansons de Bilitis*

The Complaisant Friend

The storm lasted all night. Selenis, with her lovely
hair, came to spin with me. She stayed for fear of
the mud, and we filled my little bed, clasped close
to each other. When two girls go to bed together, sleep
stays at the door. 'Bilitis, tell me, tell me, whom
do you love?' To caress me softly she slipped her leg
over mine. And over my mouth she said: 'Bilitis, I
know whom you love. Shut your eyes. I am Lycas!'
I answered, touching her: 'Can I not see that you
are a girl? Your pleasantry is out of place.' But
she rejoined: 'I am really Lycas, if you shut your
lids. Here are his arms, and here are his hands . . .'
And in the silence she tenderly delighted my dreaming
with a singular vision.

[ANONYMOUS]

The Meeting

Treasure-like, I found her in a field
under a myrtle hedge, wrapped from her
throat to her feet in a yellow robe broidered
with blue. 'I have no friend,' she told me,
'for the nearest town is forty furlongs hence.
I live alone with my mother, who is widowed and

ever sad. If you wish, I will follow you. I
will follow you even to your own house, though
it is on the other side of the island, and I
will live under your roof until you send me
away. Your hand is tender, and your eyes are
blue. Let us go! I carry nothing with me
except the little naked Astarte which hangs
from my necklace. We will place it near yours,
and we will give them roses for each night's
reward.'

[ANONYMOUS]

The Breasts of Mnasidice

Carefully she opened her tunic with one
hand and offered me her warm soft breasts as
one offers a pair of living pigeons to the
goddess. 'Love them well,' she said to me,
'I love them so much! They are dears, they are
like little children. I amuse myself with them
when I am alone. I play with them and give
them pleasure. I sprinkle them with milk. I
powder them with flowers. Their little tips
love the fine hair with which I wipe them. I
caress them with a shiver. I lay them to
sleep in wool. Since I shall never have
children and since they are so far from my
mouth, kiss them for me.'

[ANONYMOUS]

Penumbra

Under the sheet of transparent wool we
slipped, she and I. Even our heads were sunk
under, and the lamp illumined the stuff over
us. Thus I beheld her dear body in a mysterious
light. We were closer one to another, more
free, more intimate, more naked. 'In the same
shirt,' she said. We remained with our hair up

in order to be less covered, and the perfumes
of the two women rose from their two natural
censers in the bed's narrow space. Nothing in
the world, not even the lamp, saw us that night.
Which of us was lover only she and I could tell.
But men shall know nothing thereof.

[ANONYMOUS]

Love

Alas! if I think of her, my throat becomes
dry, my hand falls back, my breasts harden and
hurt, and I shiver and I cry as I walk. If I
see her, my heart stops and my hands tremble,
my feet freeze, a redness of flame rises to my
cheeks, my temples beat in agony. If I touch
her, I grow mad, my arms stiffen and my knees
give under me. I fall before her, and I go to
my bed like a woman who is going to die. I feel
I am wounded by every word she speaks. Her love
is a torture, and those who pass by hear my
lamentations . . . Alas! how can I call her
well-beloved?

[ANONYMOUS]

The Agonizing Memory

I remember . . . (at what hour of the day
do I not have her in my sight?) – I remember
the way she lifted up her hair with her pale
and feeble fingers. I remember a night she
passed so softly with her cheek on my breast
that the joy kept me awake, and on the morrow
her face showed the mark of the round excrescence.
I see her holding her glass of milk and watching
me sideways with a smile. I see her powdered
and with her hair up, opening her big eyes in front
of the mirror and retouching the red on her lips
with her finger. And, above all, my despair is

a constant torture because I know minute by
minute she sinks into another's arms and what
she asks and what she gives.

[ANONYMOUS]

JOHN LE GAY BRERETON
(1871–1933)

Cling to Me

Cling to me, love, and dare not let me go;
Kiss me as though it were our time to die,
And all our comradeship had drifted by.
Who knows what face tomorrow's dawn may show?
All the night opens round us, dear, and lo,
Mysterious deeps wherefrom the unseen eye
Of formless dread is gazing sleeplessly!
Over our love what shelter can I throw?

How long have we been seeking, and how far,
With time and space betwixt us, till at last
Our instant life makes glory of my pain?
The awful Night is round us. Star on star
Calls us to wander, when our moment's past,
– Perchance upon that desolate quest again.

THEODORE WRATISLAW
(1871–1933)

To a Sicilian Boy

Love, I adore the contours of thy shape,
Thine exquisite breasts and arms adorable;
The wonders of thine heavenly throat compel
Such fire of love as even my dreams escape:
I love thee as the sea-foam loves the cape,
Or as the shore the sea's enchanting spell:

In sweets the blossoms of thy mouth excel
The tenderest bloom of peach or purple grape.

I love thee, sweet! Kiss me again, again!
Thy kisses soothe me, as tired earth the rain;
Between thine arms I find mine only bliss;
Ah let me in thy bosom still enjoy
Oblivion of the past, divinest boy,
And the dull ennui of a woman's kiss!

GABRIEL GILLETT
(1863–?)

Years and years I have loved you
    And dar'd not speak my love,
Your face was a light to lead my feet
    To the crown of the Heav'ns above;
(Lean closer, kiss me again, again,
    For *this* is the Heav'n of love).

Years and years I have waited
    And gazed at your face afar,
Set in the dim wide night of my soul
    A tremulous silver star.
(Lean closer, love is diviner now
    That the way to his shrine was far).

Years and years I have fear'd the shame
    And the cruel speech of the world.
But over our heads in the darkness now
    Is the banner of love unfurl'd,
(Lean closer, cling to me, kiss my lips,
    Our love can despise the world.)

AMY LOWELL
(1874–1925)

Madonna of the Evening Flowers

All day long I have been working,
Now I am tired.

I call: 'Where are you?'
But there is only the oak-tree rustling in the wind.
The house is very quiet,
The sun shines in on your books,
On your scissors and thimble just put down,
But you are not there.
Suddenly I am lonely:
Where are you?
I go about searching.

Then I see you,
Standing under a spire of pale blue larkspur,
With a basket of roses on your arm.
You are cool, like silver,
And you smile.
I think the Canterbury bells are playing little tunes.

You tell me that the peonies need spraying,
That the columbines have overrun all bounds,
That the pyrus japonica should be cut back and rounded.
You tell me these things.
But I look at you, heart of silver,
White heart-flame of polished silver,
Burning beneath the blue steeples of the larkspur,
And I long to kneel instantly at your feet,
While all about us peal the loud, sweet *Te Deums* of the Canterbury
   bells.

A Sprig of Rosemary

I cannot see your face.
When I think of you,
It is your hands which I see.
Your hands
Sewing,
Holding a book,
Resting for a moment on the sill of a window.
My eyes keep always the sight of your hands,
But my heart holds the sound of your voice,
And the soft brightness which is your soul.

Thorn Piece

Cliffs,
Cliffs,
And a twisted sea
Beating under a freezing moon.
Why should I,
Sitting peaceful and warm,
Cut my heart on so sharp a tune?

Liquid lapping of seething fire
Eating the heart of an old beech-tree.
Crack of icicles under the eaves,
Dog-wind whining eerily.

The oaks are red, and the asters flame,
And the sun is warm on bark and stones.
There's a Hunter's Moon abroad tonight –
The twigs are snapping like brittle bones.

You carry a lantern of rose-green glass,
Your dress is red as a Cardinal's cloak.
I kneel at the trace of your feet on the grass,
But when I would sing you a song, I choke.

Choke for the fragile careless years
We have scattered so easily from our hands.
They flutter like leaves through an Autumn sun,
One by one, one by one.

I have lived in a place,
I shall die in a place,
I have no craving for distant lands.
But a place is nothing, not even space,
Unless at its heart a figure stands

Swinging a rose-green lantern for me.
I fear the fall of a rose-green gate,
And the cry of a cliff-driven, haunted sea,
And the crackle of ice while I wait – wait!

Your face is flowers and singing sun,
Your hands are the cool of waters falling.
If the rose-green bars should drop between
Would you know that I was calling?

For the stars I see in that sky are black.
The kind earth holds me and laughs in my ear.
I have nothing to do with the planet's track,
I only want you, my Dear.

Beyond is a glaze, but here is fire,
And love to comfort, and speech to bind,
And the common things of morning and evening,
And the light of your lantern I always find.

One or the other – then let it be me,
For I fear the whirl of the cliff-wrung sea,
And the biting night. You smile at my fears,
But the years – years –
Like leaves falling.

GERTRUDE STEIN
(1874–1946)

from *Before the Flowers of Friendship Faded Faded*

21

I love my love with a v
Because it is like that
I love my love with a b
Because I am beside that
A king.
I love my love with an a
Because she is a queen
I love my love and a a is the best of them
Think well and be a king,
Think more and think again
I love my love with a dress and a hat

I love my love and not with this or with that
I love my love with a y because she is my bride
I love her with a d because she is my love beside
Thank you for being there
Nobody has to care
Thank you for being here
Because you are not there.

And with and without me which is and without she she can be late
and then and how and all around we think and found that it is time to
cry she and I.

ALEISTER CROWLEY
(1875–1947)

The Lesbian Hell

The unutterable void of Hell is stirred
  By gusts of sad wind moaning; the inane
Quivers with melancholy sounds unheard,
  Unpastured woes, and unimagined pain,
  And kisses flung in vain.

Pale women fleet around, whose infinite
  Long sorrow and desire have torn their wombs,
Whose empty fruitlessness assails the night
  With hollow repercussion, like dim tombs
  Wherein some vampire glooms.

Pale women sickening for some sister breast;
  Lone sisterhood of voiceless melancholy
That wanders in this Hell, desiring rest
  From that desire that dwells forever free,
  Monstrous, a storm, a sea.

In that desire their hands are strained and wrung;
  In that most infinite passion beats the blood,
And bursting chants of amorous agony flung
  To the void Hell, are lost, not understood,
  Unheard by evil or good.

Their sighs attract the unsubstantial shapes
  Of other women, and their kisses burn
Cold on the lips whose purple blood escapes,
  A thin chill stream, they feel not nor discern,
  Nor love's low laugh return.

They kiss the spiritual dead, they pass
  Like mists uprisen from the frosty moon,
Like shadows fleeting in a seer's glass,
  Beckoning, yearning, amorous of the noon
  When earth dreams on in swoon.

They are so sick for sorrow, that my eyes
  Are moist because their passion was so fair,
So pure and comely that no sacrifice
  Seems to waft up a sweeter savour there,
  Where God's grave ear takes prayer.

O desecrated lovers! O divine
  Passionate martyrs, virgin unto death!
O kissing daughters of the unfed brine!
  O sisters of the west wind's pitiful breath,
  There is One that pitieth!

One far above the heavens crowned alone
  Immitigable, intangible, a maid,
Incomprehensible, divine, unknown,
  Who loves your love, and to high God hath said:
  'To me these songs are made!'

So in a little from the silent Hell
  Rises a spectre, disanointed now,
Who bears a cup of poison terrible,
  The seal of God upon his blasted brow,
  To whom His angels bow.

Rise, Phantom disanointed, and proclaim
   Thine own destruction, and the sleepy death
Of those material essences that flame
   A little moment for a little breath,
   The love that perisheth!

Rise, sisters, who have ignorantly striven
   On pale pure limbs to pasture your desire,
Who should have fixed your souls on highest Heaven,
   And satiated your longings in that fire,
   And struck that mightier lyre!

Let the ripe kisses of your thirsting throats
   And beating blossoms of your breath, and flowers
Of swart illimitable hair that floats
   Vague and caressing, and the amorous powers
   Of your unceasing hours,

The rich hot fragrance of your dewy skins,
   The eyes that yearn, the breasts that bleed, the thighs
That cling and cluster to these infinite sins,
   Forget the earthlier pleasures of the prize,
   And raise diviner sighs;

Cling to the white and bloody feet that hang,
   And drink the purple of a God's pure side;
With your wild hair assuage His deadliest pang,
   And on his broken bosom still abide
   His virginal white bride.

So in the dawn of skies unseen above,
   Your passion's fiercest flakes shall catch new gold,
The sun of an immeasurable love
   More beautiful shall touch the chaos cold
   Of earth that is grown old.

Then, shameful sisterhood of earth's disdain,
   Your lips shall speak your hearts, and understand;
Your loves shall assuage the amorous pain
   With spiritual lips more keen and bland,
   And ye shall take God's hand.

RENÉE VIVIEN
(1877–1909)

Toward Lesbos

You will come, your eyes full of night and of yesterday . . .
And it will be by a beautiful sunset on the bay.

Frail like a cradle on the smooth waves rises,
Our ship will be laden with amber and spices.

The winds will submit, convinced of my right.
I will inform you, 'The sea is ours tonight.'

Your fingers will resemble the long fingers of the drowned.
We'll go forth at random, with full sails we'll be crowned.

You will ask me, eyes filled with wonder and charms,
'On what unknown bed will I sleep in your arms?'

The birds will sing, hidden in the sails.
We will watch stars appear, the first most pale.

You will say to me, 'The waves bow under my hand . . .
Where will we live tomorrow . . . what is this land?'

'The night waves are pale,' I will say,
'From the island I love we are still far away.

'Close your weary eyes from the voyage and abide
Sleep as in your room closed from noises outside . . .

'Like in an orchard a woman who smiles,
Happiness awaits us on this fragrant isle.

'Cover your pale face with your red hair.
The hour is calm and the peaceful sea is there.

'Don't worry about anything . . . I am aware
Of the risks of the sea and the winds, my fair . . .'

Under the protection of the silver crescent moon,
You will sleep until the approach of the dawn.

The beaches will mark on the horizon gray borders of sand,
. . . Your eyes will open upon the sea's expanse.

You will ask me, not without a little fear,
About the mysterious chants that will reach your ear.

You will say, blushing naively at the noises,
'Nothing is as moving as these unknown voices.

'Their sweet breath cools my weary face like a fan,
But the dawn is still dark and I do not understand.

'Will our black destiny be able to ignore us
At the height of this fearful morning I see before us?'

I will reply, closing your lips with a kiss:
'Happiness is over there . . . But we must take the risk . . .

'Over there, we will hear the supreme music . . .
And, see, we are landing on the island of magic . . .'

[SANDIA BELGRADE]

The Pillory

For a long time, I was nailed to the pillory,
And some women, seeing me suffering, laughed.

Then, some men took mud in their hands
With which to spatter my temple and cheeks.

The sobs welled up in me, swelling like waves,
But my pride made me choke back the tears.

No one said, 'She is perhaps less evil than
We suspect, she is perhaps a poor soul.'

The square was public and everyone had come,
And the women laughed in their naive way.

They tossed fruits back and forth to the tune of songs,
And the wind brought to me the sound of their words.

I felt the violent anger steal over me.
Silently, I learned to hate them.

Their insults cut deep, like the thorns of a nettle . . .
When they finally cut me loose, I left.

I went away at the mercy of the wind, and since then
My face is like the face of one dead.

[SANDIA BELGRADE]

Words to My Friend

Understand me: I am a mediocre being,
Not good, not very bad, peaceful, a bit cunning.
I detest heavy perfume and shrill voices,
And gray is more dear to me than scarlet or ocher.

I love the dying day which grows dim by degrees,
A fire, the cloistered intimacy of a room
Where the lamps, veiling their amber transparencies,
Redden the antique bronze and turn the gray stoneware blue.

My eyes drop to the carpet smoother than sand,
Indolently I evoke rivers flecked with gold
Where the clarity of the beautiful past still floats . . .
And nevertheless, I am quite guilty.

You see: I am at the age when a maiden gives her hand
To the man whom her weakness searches and dreads,
And I have not chosen a companion for the road,
Because you appeared at that turn in the road.

The hyacinth was bleeding on the red hills,
You were dreaming and Eros walked at your side . . .

I am woman, I have no right to beauty.
I had been condemned to masculine ugliness.

And I had the inexcusable audacity of wanting
Sisterly love fashioned with soft whiteness,
The furtive step that didn't trample the fern
And the sweet voice that comes to ally itself with evening.

They have forbidden me your hair, the look in your eyes,
It seems that your hair is long and full of odors
And it seems your eyes reveal strange longings
And grow agitated like rebellious waves.

They have pointed at me with irritated gestures,
Because my eyes searched out your tender look . . .
And seeing us go by, no one wanted to understand
That I had simply chosen you.

Consider the vile law that I transgress
And judge my love that knows nothing of evil,
As candid, as necessary and fatal
As the desire that joins lover to mistress.

They didn't read in my eyes how clearly I saw
The road where my destiny leads me,
And they have said: 'Who is this damned woman
Who gnaws blindly at the flames of hell?'

Leave them to the concern of their impure morality,
And let us imagine that dawn has the blondness of honey,
That days without spite and nights without malice
Come, such as lovers whose goodness reassures . . .

We will go to see the clear stars on the mountains . . .
What matters to us, the judgment of men?
And what have we to doubt, since we are
Pure before life and since we love one another? . . .

[SANDIA BELGRADE]

'MARIE MADELAINE'
[BARONESS VON PUTTKAMER]
(1881–?)

Foiled Sleep

Ah me! I cannot sleep at night;
    And when I shut my eyes, forsooth,
I cannot banish from my sight
    The vision of her slender youth.

She stands béfore me lover-wise,
    Her naked beauty fair and slim,
She smiles upon me, and her eyes
    With over-fierce desire grow dim.

Slowly she leans to me. I meet
    The passion of her gaze anew,
And then her laughter, clear and sweet,
    Thrills all the hollow silence through.

O, siren, with the mocking tongue!
    O beauty, lily-sweet and white!
I see her, slim and fair and young,
    And ah! I cannot sleep at night.

[FERDINAND E. KAPPEY]

Crucifixion

Nailed to a cross, your beauty still aglow,
    A fierce incarnate agony you seem;
Like purple wounds upon a field of snow
    My scarring kisses on your body gleam.

How thin your fair young face, your limbs how spare,
    How frail upon your breast the blossom lies!
But oh! the torch of lust is flaming there
    Through darkness and in triumph from your eyes.

When you, a virgin sword unstained, yet fierce
     To brook affront, came trusting unto me,
Your innocence was like a sword to pierce,
     And I desired to stain your purity.

I gave you of the poison that was mine,
     My sorrow and my passion – all I gave;
And now behold the depth of my design:
     A tortured soul too late for tears to save.

That I might now re-fashion from the dust
     My shattered altars, and redeem the loss!
Madonna, with the kindled eyes of lust,
     'Twas I who nailed you naked to the cross.

[FERDINAND E. KAPPEY]

The Unfading

The garden of my soul grows duller;
     But one sweet bloom scents all the air;
One scarlet blossom keeps its colour,
     The sinful flower you planted there.

In those cold winter days the willows
     Hung frosted by the river bank,
And virgin snow in drifting billows
     Along the margin rose and sank.

In those cold Winter days and frozen,
     When driving north-winds left their smart,
I – I of all the world was chosen
     To nestle warm against your heart.

And in your room it mattered little
     The cruel ending of the year,
The ice-bound Empire chill and brittle,
     Because I loved, and you were near.

And even to-day as life grows duller,
    The garden of my soul looks fair,
For one deep blossom keeps its colour,
    The scarlet sin you planted there.

[FERDINAND E. KAPPEY]

Moriturus

Upon your sunken cheek a hectic stain!
Upon your parted lips a cry of lust! –
Death stands beside your bed, and die you must!
You long to live, and know you long in vain.

Beneath the snow-clad earth your beauty soon
Shall unremembered be, – and you will sleep
While moaning winds above your grave shall sweep,
And forest-owls sit screaming at the moon.

Are you afraid of death? I know indeed
Your young and timid years the end resent;
Those lovely lips – once red – were never meant
To kiss and suffer kissing without greed.

For me what matters? I have understood
The pain and stress of strange idolatries;
Have wrought the nameless curse of desperate eyes,
And played with passion in an easy mood.

But I have kissed to-day, as never yet,
Your sinking bosom till my passions ache, –
And I would gladly perish for your sake,
My early star of love – so early set!

One little hour – no more – for breathing space!
Death stands beside your bed – and you must die!
One lessening hour – and still the moments fly;
I hear your clock tick out the hour of grace.

[FERDINAND E. KAPPEY]

The End is Now

The Autumn-pallid sun looks down
Upon your face that keeps the brown
Of Summer; and the yellow hair
    That sweeps your brow is palely lit,
And like a gold net cast to snare
    My soul, as if to capture it.
                            The end is now!

In poignant passion breast to breast
We stand, my arms about you lest
You lose my meaning – you who know
How loth I am to let you go.
That I might hold you ever thus!
It is the last hour left to us;
                            The end is now!

The symbolled bondage that you wear
Upon your hand I may not share;
It seems a fetter forged to hold
    Your spirit down, – a chain to weigh
Upon your life; a glint of gold
    From deepest hell; a curse to slay.
                            The end is now!

I mind me of the mountain wind
Whose healing fragrance left behind
So sweet a promise; and the flight
Of stags along the mountain height;
The dripping grass; the trailing mist;
The wooded vale where last we kissed.
                            The end is now!

[FERDINAND E. KAPPEY]

Vagabonds

Because mine eyes are fashioned so,
    Shalt thou forsake thy house and hearth,

And like a beggar thou shalt go,
  Despised of men and nothing worth.
Fair fame and fortune – all shall be
  As trodden dust beneath your feet,
              Because of me!

And we shall know the town at eve
  Where, in the gas-illumined street,
Unhappy people make-believe,
  And proven friends are few to meet –
Where lust and hunger, toil and hate,
  In noisy riot pay their due
              To cynic Fate.

Such bitter things and sweet shall fill
  Our souls like hydromel and rue;
The weary hours that others kill
  Shall wing about us strange and new;
No longer shall we need to guess
  Their meaning when poor mortals play
              At 'No' and 'Yes.'

For we shall sound Life's iron strings
  That do not yield to fingers gloved,
And gather from the heart of things
  The most abhorred, the best beloved.
We shall not shrink from bloody strife;
. Not we! Once tasted we will drain
              The Cup of Life.

Contempt will follow at our heel,
  And all will damn us – and in vain!
For us the solemn priests shall kneel
  In prayer again and yet again.
Into the world of night we go
  For ever cursed – because mine eyes
              Are fashioned so!

[FERDINAND E. KAPPEY]

JAMES ELROY FLECKER
(1884–1919)

The Hammam Name
(from a poem by a Turkish lady)

Winsome Torment rose from slumber, rubbed his eyes, and went his
    way
Down the street towards the Hammam. Goodness gracious! people
    say,
What a handsome countenance! The sun has risen twice to-day!
And as for the Undressing Room it quivered in dismay.
With the glory of his presence see the window panes perspire,
And the water in the basin boils and bubbles with desire.

Now his lovely cap is treated like a lover: off it goes!
Next his belt the boy unbuckles; down it falls, and at his toes
All the growing heap of garments buds and blossoms like a rose.
Last of all his shirt came flying. Ah, I tremble to disclose
How the shell came off the almond, how the lily showed its face,
How I saw a silver mirror taken flashing from its case.

He was gazed upon so hotly that his body grew too hot,
So the bathman seized the adorers and expelled them on the spot;
Then the desperate shampooer his propriety forgot,
Stumbled when he brought the pattens, fumbled when he tied a
    knot,
And remarked when musky towels had obscured his idol's hips,
See Love's Plenilune,[1] Mashallah, in a partial eclipse!

Desperate the loofah wriggled: soap was melted instantly:
All the bubble hearts were broken. Yes, for them as well as me,
Bitterness was born of beauty; as for the shampooer, he
Fainted, till a jug of water set the Captive Reason free.
Happy bath! The baths of heaven cannot wash their spotted moon:
You are doing well with this one. Not a spot upon him soon!

Now he leaves the luckless bath for fear of setting it alight;
Seizes on a yellow towel growing yellower in fright,

1. full moon

Polishes the pearly surface till it burns disastrous bright,
And a bathroom window shatters in amazement at the sight.
Like the fancies of a dreamer frail and soft his garments shine
As he robes a mirror body shapely as a poet's line.

Now upon his cup of coffee see the lips of Beauty bent:
And they perfume him with incense and they sprinkle him with scent,
Call him Bey and call him Pasha, and receive with deep content
The gratuities he gives them, smiling and indifferent.
Out he goes: the mirror strains to kiss her darling; out he goes!
Since the flame is out, the water can but freeze.
                    The water froze.

JOHN BARFORD
(1886–193?)

Toleration

Is it too much to ask that I should be
    Allowed to prove
God's gift of infinite variety
    In human love?

I do not seek that all should understand,
    Much less forgive;
But surely heed man's commonsense command
    'Live and let live,'

And, if the Greatest Lover's word divine
    Further can move, –
(Who had Himself all natures, even mine,)
    Love – and let love.

Serve Her Right

Gertie Green made eyes at me.
    Mother ought to slap her!
But I took her out to tea

Just to see if I *could* be
   Happy with a flapper.

But the base philanderer
   Ogled with another;
So, of course to despite her,
I decided to transfer
   Affections to her brother;

And I did! . . .

'Whom Jesus Loved'

Come, little John, tell me the lovely tale
Of your fine friendship with The Man, nor fail
   To whisper every detail that shall prove
   His glorious love.

Were things as difficult with you as now?
You were the younger, weren't you? Tell me how
   You met Him. Did his eyes so soft and sad
   Attract you, lad?

Or was it first the charm of that deep voice
That thrilled and made your boyish heart rejoice?
   I know He won you not by force or stealth
   But by Himself.

And did He recognize His image, you, in truth,
And revel in the radiance of your youth?
   And was it not a comfort when you came,
   Devoid of shame,

And held, for all the world to see, His hand
And whispered, 'Those poor chaps don't understand
   I am your friend; you, mine. I love you, see.
   Say you love me.'

Did men with muddy mind deride because
They'd fain imagine sin where no sin was,

Imputing to the Prince of Love and thee
Impurity?

But you two little plots and plans devised
For meeting unobserved, and so disguised
    Your love; for each the good name of his friend
    Swore to defend.

By simple codes and signs you'd seem to hear
In thickest crowds His soft 'I love you, dear.'
    And when His weariness at last He'd own
    Was He alone?

And did He love to watch you cleave the sea
And scamper on the shores of Galilee?
    And then rub down your back and ask for this
    Service a kiss?

And – for a treat for whom? – did you two dine
At His expense, and did the needless wine
    Add glitter to your eyes? Ah, the delight
    Of that 'good-night!'

And did He beg of you, His little John,
To write to Him, for He was going on
    A journey and might ne'er return? Ah, no,
    You could not go!

When sad and lonely did He haply seek
The solace of your smile and did you speak
    The words alone that could assuage His woe
    'I love you so!'?

And when He spoke of shame and agony,
Of sacrifice and its futility,
    You'd squeeze His fingers gently, would you not,
    And murmer 'rot!'?

And did He suffer gladly for your sake
And daily solemn resolution make

To guard with loving care against offence
Your innocence?

And, as o' nights your stripling limbs you spread,
Did he perchance come softly to your bed,
And did you feel beneath the shadowy vine
Cool lips on thine?

Oh happy John! Such love can never end.
Closer than brothers are is friend to friend.
You the divinity of it have proved,
'Whom Jesus loved.'

Sundered

O the aching pain of that long, long night
When we walked as friends, who are friends no more,
Side by side in the waning light,
By the ghostly cliffs, on the lonely shore!
O the aching pain of that long, long night –
And the void now the night is o'er!

I had marked a change, but it seemed so slight
I had thought, I had hoped I was wrong before,
Till a word and a look, like a flash of light,
Showed the friend I had loved was a friend no more!
O the aching pain of that long, long night –
And the void now the night is o'er!

If he came back now could it all come right?
Could I trust him again as I did before?
It is hard to tell. Who knows? I might –
But ah! I am sure he will come no more!
And the aching pain of that long, long night
Will last till my life is o'er!

Eric

Implacable, unmerciful, fulfilled
To overflowing with the sap of life,

A male in ev'ry muscle, ev'ry vein:
Contemptuous of weakness, proud, self-willed,
    And cruel in his ardour for the strife
        That steels his heart to his and others' pain:

Impervious to sickly sentiment;
    Clear-headed though hot-blooded; logical,
        And fain to follow Reason to the end:
Careless of creeds and convenance, content
    To trample under foot conventions all
        So he can slay a foe or serve a friend:

Hard-hearted – yes! hard, but not heartless! Nay,
    Afire with love, pure, passionate intense,
        But love that knows no pity – fierce as hate!
He seems a child of that heroic day
    Ere yet man bowed beneath Experience,
        And followed fettered in the train of Fate!

RADCLYFFE HALL
(1886–1943)

from *Forgotten Island*

32

As a lamp of fine crystal, wonderfully wrought,
Is the soul of the woman I love.
Behold the oil and the wick for the burning,
Yet the light of the lamp is absent.

How may I kindle the soul of this woman,
With what torch may I touch it to flame?
Since love himself hath no part in her beauty
Nor findeth abode in her spirit?

SIEGFRIED SASSOON
(1886–1967)

At Daybreak

I listen for him through the rain,
And in the dusk of starless hours
I know that he will come again;
Loth was he ever to forsake me:
He comes with glimmering of flowers
And stir of music to awake me.

Spirit of purity, he stands
As once he lived in charm and grace:
I may not hold him with my hands,
Nor bid him stay to heal my sorrow;
Only his fair, unshadowed face
Abides with me until tomorrow.

T. E. LAWRENCE
(1888–1935)

To S.A.

I loved you, so I drew these tides of men into my hands
  and wrote my will across the sky in stars
To gain you Freedom, the seven-pillared worthy house,
  that your eyes might be shining for me
            When I came.

Death was my servant on the road, till we were near
  and saw you waiting:
When you smiled, and in sorrowful envy he outran me
  and took you apart:
            Into his quietness.

So our love's earnings was your cast off body to be held
  one moment
Before earth's soft hands would explore your face and the

blind worms transmute
               Your failing substance.

Men prayed me to set my work, the inviolate house,
   in memory of you.
But for fit monument I shattered it unfinished: and now
The little things creep out to patch themselves hovels
   in the marred shadow
               Of your gift.

KATHERINE MANSFIELD
(1888–1923)

Friendship

When we were charming *Backfisch*[1]
   With curls and velvet bows
We shared a charming kitten
   With tiny velvet toes.

It was so gay and playful;
   It flew like a woolly ball
From my lap to your shoulder –
   And, oh, it was so small,

So warm – and so obedient
   If we cried: 'That's enough!'
It lay and slept between us,
   A purring ball of fluff.

But now that I am thirty
   And she is thirty-one,
I shudder to discover
   How wild our cat has run.

It's bigger than a Tiger,
   Its eyes are jets of flame,

1. teenagers

Its claws are gleaming daggers,
  Could it have once been tame?

Take it away; I'm frightened!
  But she, with placid brow,
Cries: 'This is our Kitty-witty!
  Why don't you love her now?'

Two poems from *ARTIST AND JOURNAL OF
HOME CULTURE*

J.J.W.
(1888)

Brotherhood

We must not sever, you and I,
  The world is cruel, friends are few;
Let us be steadfast faithfully,
                    I and you.

For we have heard the midnight wind
  Whisper the weary world to sleep,
And felt the stars upon mankind
                    Gently weep.

The quivering wonder of the morn
  Has been to us a sudden birth,
When all the world was overworn
                    And its mirth.

The stillness of the silent stream
  Has cried like some loud clarion
Within our souls, wrapped in a dream
                    Two alone.

And then we knew what seers have told
  In some half meaning mystic song,
And heard their cadences unfold
                    Right and wrong,

Till all the world grew bright again,
    And our new manhood too was free,
And each one clasped his friend again
                    Tenderly,

Knowing that he would never die.
    Thus is our kinship sweetly true
And we are brothers, you and I,
                    I and you.

G.G.
(1890)

To W.J.M.

Guessed you but how I loved you, watched your smile,
    Hungered to see the lovelight in your eyes –
    That ne'er can wake for me – Would wild surprise
Or sheer disgust at passion you deem vile
Be your response? For you are free from guile
    While I, enraptured foolishly or wise
    Long but for you, till even yearning dies
Save to be near, you loving me the while.

In all the world this thing can never come
    And tho' I die, no word your soul shall shame
    Mine be the punishment as mine the blame
And though in hopeless fear my heart is numb
At its renunciation, yet still dumb
    You shall not even hear me breathe your name.

F. S. WOODLEY
(1888–1957)

The Beautiful

Long years ago there came to me in sleep
    The vision of a boy divinely fair;
His eyes were moon-kissed seas, serene and deep,
    Elysian blossoms crowned his golden hair;

Light flowed around him, gently fell his voice
   Like a soft-singing shower of silver dew,
Long time he gazed, then smiling, spoke 'Rejoice!
   Seek only Me, for I alone am true!'

Straightway he fled upborne within a maze
   Of mighty wings and music wonderful,
Whilst all the air grew dizzy with the praise
   Of voices crying loud, 'The Beautiful.'
Heavenward he vanished – but his radiant face
   Still haunts me – a pure spiritual joy,
And well I know he makes his dwelling-place
   In the clear honest eyes of any boy.

*

I love this boy, not for his beauty only,
But just because my life that was so lonely
Knows in his presence some strange healing power,
An unfamiliar peace – as if each hour
Should pause a little in its swift-winged flight
And breathe a benediction. In his bright
Blue eyes his happy spirit sits and smiles,
And never evil dreams, or wanton wiles,
Or lusts o'ercloud their sweet serenity:
I dare not hope – but, when he looks at me,
Something half-shy, half-trusting, leaps therein
And shadows of dead passion and old sin
All dreadful haunting memories, take flight –
You think I'm happy? Well – Perhaps you're right!

JEAN COCTEAU
(1889–1963)

To a Sleeping Friend

Your hands, strewn on the sheets, were my dead leaves,
   And how my autumn loved your spring!
A door in the wind of memory heaves
   And banging, shuts on everything.

I left you, selfish, to your lying sleep
  Where dreams destroyed all trace of you.
But you believed in them. It's sad to creep
  About a dreamer's world untrue.

And how fully you became this other,
  Abstracted from your proper frame!
You were all stone. It's hard for a lover
  To cherish memory's mere name.

Awake, unmoved, I made my final call
  On every once familiar place.
Such fond returnings stirred me not at all
  Here with my hands cupping my face.

And I came back from voyaging so dead
  Drearily to rediscover
Your great and open hand, your eyes of lead,
  Night in the mouth of my lover.

And like that eagle with two heads were we,
  Or Janus of the double face,
Like Siamese twins gaped at for a fee,
  Or books by stitching held in place.

We were a beast called Joy made from love's play,
  Bristling with shaggy locks. He cried,
And, mad at being his own prey,
  With self-devouring slowly died.

But what are friendship's acres of despair
  Across which anxious lovers creep?
What is this labyrinth where all our care
  Is to rejoin ourselves in sleep?

And then, what have I found – and what's to be?
  I sleep, though not to sleep were due,
But if I rest I know I can be free
  Of dreams in which I'm losing you.

God, how beautiful the unsullied face
   Where sleep, death's copyist of old,
Embalms and polishes, repaints the grace
   Of Egypt's sleepers lapped in gold.

But as I watched you, masked by your own skin,
   Insensible to all our smart,
The remnant of your shadow grew more thin
   And hid itself within my heart.

Friendship divine is never of this world
   Which always finds it a surprise;
And ever in destruction's maw is hurled
   All friendship found, all loving guise.

Time counts no longer in our monastery.
   What is the time and what the day?
And when love comes, instead of subtlety
   We blab it quickly where we may.

I run; and you, you run another way.
   Where are you going and where I?
Alas, we're not a monster from Cathay
   A flautist from a Hindu sky.

Tangled as one in your climactic moan
   Ah, lovers, lovers, happy pain . . .
You are a monstrous gargoyle carved in stone
   Crouching on a medieval fane.

We are one body knotted by our hearts
   (Thus the body is asserted)
Our only hell's a hell where no flame darts,
   A void for all the stumbling dead.

Leaning nearer, I see your temples beat
   And show you are a thing of blood.
Your blood is that red sea where my soul's fleet
   Is moored. You don't look on that flood.

While I recrossed the ice of history
  You went to where your dreams behold
The sunlight glinting on the silken sea
  Reflected on the ceiling, cold.

And that is what your inner glance could see.
  I only had to shake your arm
To wake you and so ruin utterly
  Perfection built from sleeper's calm.

I sat in silence watching you: your knee
  On your elbow, chin in the air.
I could not have you, nothing welded me
  To your mechanic body there.

I dreamed, you dreamed, and all went round and round,
  Both blood and constellated stars,
While that false being Time was gaining ground
  And nations wrecked themselves with wars.

The creases of your clothes just idly tossed,
  The little folds where shadows run,
Were like those bodies which the holocaust
  Has changed to scarecrows everyone.

And there, far from the bed, a single shoe
  Though dying had a little life . . .
How such disorders showed the wounded you!
  What sleeper could repair such strife?

It extended you, it copied your way.
  I understood you from it. One
Just looking at your vest could really say
  It was going to fire a gun.

And when about us suicide or theft
  Turned a villa into a tomb,
Absorbing horror, your calm face was left
  A home for harbingers of doom.

And now I go my way as wracked with dreams
　　As when I sang *Monastic Chant*.[1]
My span of life contracts while sunlight seems
　　To lengthen out my shadow's slant.

I knew this shade in all that came to hand
　　And knew its gait as all I had;
And there before me on the desert sand
　　My shade at evening's stretched and sad.

The shade accuses now my body's plight;
　　But what can compensate its lack?
Unless the sun or moon with rising light
　　Can throw my shade behind my back?

The sky is riddled with chimeric stars,
　　With human eagles in alarm.
I will not rouse your self-destructive wars
　　But let the sunlight quiet your harm.

RALPH CHUBB
(1892–1960)

from *The Book of God's Madness*, Part 3

Liveliest effigy of the human race,
Loveliest in form, in spirit like a sword,
Boyhood! I weep to see you so disgraced,
From stream's and meadow's playground snatched away
To die on commerce' bloody altar-stone.
I weep for you alone; none cares beside.
What sort of love is that that loves you best
When you are least yourself? I love in you
The very wantonness which others hate.
I love the wilful animal in you;
Your wayward wickedness is my delight.
I love you as I love the squirrel wild,

1. a volume of poems by Cocteau

The wild wood-dove the gruesome sportsman murders,
The nightingale they slay to eat his tongue,
The playful seal, whose coat their females filch.
Youth, who of human kind can sing most sweet,
You dare not lift your voice for fear of scorn,
Because you know not friends from enemies.
There is an art in disobedience.
Rescue yourself, then save your sister dear,
Weaker than you, that ghouls have quite enslaved.
Ye ghouls, who worship mediocrity,
You clothe the beauteous flesh in ugliness,
Yourselves all paunch and rump from evil living
(Call it good living, wink, and all agree)
Turn you God's image to indecency?
Delicious form of youth I love your view,
Your feel, your sound, your scent, your taste, your all –
Your head, with crumpled hair, smooth cheeks and chin,
Soft lips and ears and nostrils, glowing eyes,
Lashes and eyebrows, throat and nape of neck,
Shoulders and armpits savoury with sweat,
Broad breasts with nipples, arms and wrists and hands,
Belly and navel, back and shoulder blades,
Caressing shapely buttocks, groins and hips,
Genitals dangling in a cluster down,
Thick thighs and knees, shins, ankles, calves and feet.
I speak to woman. – Here behold your king!
Lovelier than you, let flattering fools deny!
Mark his high glance, the swords of flickering light
That play about his shapely eager brow!
Whatever you have he has fuller store
Of good and bad, in flesh and spirit both.
In kind the same you are, in measure less –
Save in your *difference*. Glorious mother, how
My heart melts in your heart of ruddy flame!
The love of man and youth is as two fires,
Of mother and son two strong and gentle streams,
The love of man and maid a sluggish rill.
O! my mind swims; all images resolve
In dancing specks. Athwart a motley crew
Surges and glimmers; now a goodly youth,
Naked, triumphant, spurning with his foot

A heap of lumber, shattered instruments,
Books, broken statutes, tumbled palaces;
And women, babes and elder men
Bowing before him and all crying out, -
'Worthiest full life who fullest life enjoys!'
And he made answer on high, 'Is any here
Of fuller being than I? I'll bow to him!'

Song of My Soul, 3

The form of youth without blemish, is not such the form divine?
Children of love, today I will sing my song to you!

Under the sky in the hot noon-beam, in the water-meadow,
The sound of the rushing fall;
We two alone together screen'd by the trees and the thicket;
Naked the lecherous urchin, the slim beautiful boy,
Naked myself, dark, muscled like a god, the hardy enduring man;
He a fully form'd human being in his way,
Myself a fully form'd human being in my way;
No patronage between us, mutual respect, two equal persons;
He knowing the universe, I knowing the universe, equal together;
I having every whit as much to learn from him as he from me;
From him to me, from me to him, reciprocal sexual spiritual love.

No word needed, scarce ev'n a glance, mystically
Limbs interlace, bodies interpenetrate,
Spirits coalesce.
(He scarce needs to be there, 'tis in Imagination's realm true lovers
    meet.)
O burning tongue and hot lips of me exploring my love!
Lave his throat with the bubbling fountain of my verse!
Drench him! Slake his loins with it, most eloquent!
Leave no part, no crevice unexplored; delve deep, my minstrel
    tongue!
Let our juices flood and mingle! Let the prophetic lava flow!
Drink deep of love, the pair of us, O sacramental communion,
As our souls meet and melt!
The sweat of our armpits runneth down upon our breasts. -
Be our bodies seal'd together, part they with a smack!

I will be father and mother at once to thee, my son, thou shalt feed
from my bosom.
And you shall be mother and father to me, and give me to suck my
honey'd inspiration from your right nipple and from your left.
You shall leave no portion of me untasted, I will become fluid for your
sake.
I will feed you spiritually with a stuff that shall make a man of you.
With the milk of divine manhood will I satisfy your soul.
Quick, your lips under my poetic dug,
My own soul's calf, pull, pull. Well out the manly hymns!
For I am he that shall fill your young veins with the seeds of all
futurity.

from *The Sun Spirit*
lines 73–164

SPECTRE:
At the time of puberty I had obsessions.
I walk'd always with downcast eyes and blush'd scarlet to meet
anyone in the street.
I thought I harbour'd a secret vice which none had discover'd before
me.
I caught sight of my figure distorted in a shop window and
thereafter imagined that I had a physical deformity which others
ignored through kindness.
I believed that I stank.
If one raised his handkerchief to his nose even across the road I
thought it was to shut off my noisesomeness.
The schoolmaster with whom I had most to do was an ignorant
self-complacent tyrant. He did me great wrongs.
No one understood me. None explained to me nor relieved me.
All shunned me. I suffered in silence, alone.

SEER:
Poor wraith, I pity you! Speak on! Unbosom now your soul!
Altho' you are but an illusory reflexion of mine own past self.

SPECTRE:
As a babe I came forth from the womb and sucked at my mother's
breast with gurgling and deep satisfied sighs.

As an infant wee my fingers sought to my flesh unconscious happy.
Lying in my cot I caressed myself with innocent imaginings.
When I was now eight years old I went to the sea coast where I beheld
    the village boys romp and paddle in stark nakedness upon the
    beach.
Their forms were white and smooth like lilies.
My young heart ached with longing.
At about twelve years old I began to feel my sex.
One night on going to bed I stripped my skin bare before the glass
    and surveyed my parts in different attitudes back and front.
Behold I appeared lovely and I thanked heaven that I was a boy.
I straddled the rocking-horse with my fork I squeezed harder and
    harder upon the cushion-pad.
My face flashed my eyes sparkled. My heart beat faster faster.
Thrills passed through me. I had a movement of ecstacy.
   Suddenly a chill of disgust came over me.
Revolted at myself I got into my nightshirt and slunk ashamèd into
    bed.
My father came in the room to me with anxious face and said, What
    have you been doing little son? What have you been doing?
I replied, Nothing, papa, and he went away anxious.
I became surly nervous reticent by day, rejoicing in solitude by night,
    a butt for my school fellows, hearing them hint, from their
    knowledge at what I understood not, longing for explanation
    but kept out.
My lustful imaginings ran wild, I took part in orgies of phantasy.
Certain of my mates I loved passionately for their wayward beauty
    and yearn'd in secret for their caresses, but they rebuff'd me.
At night our invisible bodies met towselling in unlicensed intercourse.
As yet I knew nothing of the business of parenthood.
Nobody inform'd me. I long'd for relief, but none was vouchsafed me.
At eighteen years one Sunday in the mighty vaulted church I caught
    the glance of a dark-eyed chorister.
Instantly our souls flew to meet each other in wild embrace.
Had we not loved since the beginning with deepest love for ever
    and ever?
Such was the awakening of my spring. My eyes were open'd to love.
My friends perceived it and felt for me.
At this time I was exceedingly comely in both face and form and most
    happy and free from care.
My friends delighted in me and I in them.

We lay abed bestowing close kisses of comradeship.
Then providence fulfilled my desire and gave me as a lover a youth of
    fifteen years.
Idling we pass'd our sunny days bathing in sequester'd streams,
Sprawling with gold-brown bodies side-by-side beneath the noonday
    beam,
Fondling, spending, silently embracing.
The mounting heart, the shorten'd breath, the surging onslaught of
    desire,
Sweet pulsing short-lived agony seeking relief, the brimming
    consolation and flood,
The drooping languor, the heavenly listless content with bright
    swimming pupils gazing up seraphical at the azure vault . . .

VICTORIA SACKVILLE-WEST
(1892–1962)

from *The Land:* 'Spring'
lines 524–557

Once I went through the lanes, over the sharp
Tilt of the little bridges; past the forge,
And heard the clang of anvil and of iron,
And saw the founting sparks in the dusky forge,
And men outside with horses, gossiping.
So I came through that April England, moist
And green in its lush fields between the willows,
Foaming with cherry in the woods, and pale
With clouds of lady's-smock along the hedge
Until I came to a gate and left the road
For the gentle fields that enticed me, by the farms,
Wandering through the embroidered fields, each one
So like its fellow; wandered through the gaps,
Past the mild cattle knee-deep in the brooks,
And wandered drowsing as the meadows drowsed
Under the pale wide heaven and slow clouds.
And then I came to a field where the springing grass
Was dulled by the hanging cups of fritillaries,
Sullen and foreign-looking, the snaky flower,

Scarfed in dull purple, like Egyptian girls
Camping among the furze, staining the waste
With foreign colour, sulky, dark, and quaint,
Dangerous too, as a girl might sidle up,
An Egyptian girl, with an ancient snaring spell,
Throwing a net, soft round the limbs and heart,
Captivity soft and abhorrent, a close-meshed net,
– See the square web on the murrey flesh of the flower –
Holding her captive close with her bare brown arms.
Close to her little breast beneath the silk,
A gypsy Judith, witch of a ragged tent,
And I shrank from the English field of fritillaries
Before it should be too late, before I forgot
The cherry white in the woods, and the curdled clouds,
And the lapwings crying free above the plough.

R. NICHOLS
(1893–1944)

The Burial in Flanders
(H. S. G., Ypres, 1916)

Through the light rain I think I see them going,
Through the light rain under the muffled skies;
Across the fields a stealthy wet wind wanders,
The mist bedews their tunics, dizzies their brains.

Shoulder-high, khaki shoulder by shoulder,
They bear my Boy upon his last journey.
Night is closing. The wind sighs, ebbs, and falters . . .
They totter dreaming, deem they see his face.

Even as Vikings of old their slaughtered leader
Upon their shoulders, so now bear they on
All that remains of Boy, my friend, their leader,
An officer who died for them under the dawn.

O that I were there that I might carry,
Might share that bitter load in grief, in pride! . . .

I see upon bronze faces love, submission,
And a dumb sorrow for that cheerful Boy.

Now they arrive. The priest repeats the service.
The drifting rain obscures.
                          They are dispersed.
The dying sun streams out: a moment's radiance;
The still, wet, glistening grave; the trod sward steaming.

                    *

Sudden great guns startle, echoing on the silence.
Thunder. Thunder.
HE HAS FALLEN IN BATTLE.
(O Boy! Boy!)
Lessening now. The rain
Patters anew. Far guns rumble and shudder
And night descends upon the desolate plain.

WILFRED OWEN
(1893–1918)

Sonnet to My Friend, with an Identity Disc

If ever I had dreamed of my dead name
High in the heart of London, unsurpassed
By Time for ever, and the Fugitive, Fame,
There seeking a long sanctuary at last, –

Or if I onetime hoped to hide its shame,
– Shame of success, and sorrow of defeats, –
Under those holy cypresses, the same
That shade always the quiet place of Keats,

Now rather thank I God there is no risk
Of gravers scoring it with florid screed.
Let my inscription be this soldier's disc.
Wear it, sweet friend. Inscribe no date nor deed.
But may thy heart-beat kiss it, night and day,
Until the name grow blurred and fade away.

'Antaeus: A Fragment'

So neck to stubborn neck, and obstinate knee to knee,
Wrestled those two; and peerless Heracles
Could not prevail, nor get at any vantage . . .
So those huge hands that, small, had snapped great snakes,
Let slip the writhing of Antaeus' wrists:
Those hero's hands that wrenched the necks of bulls,
Now fumbled round the slim Antaeus' limbs,
Baffled. Then anger swelled in Heracles,
And terribly he grappled broader arms,
And yet more firmly fixed his graspèd feet.
And up his back the muscles bulged and shone
Like climbing banks and domes of towering cloud.
And they who watched that wrestling say he laughed,
But not so loud as on Eurystheus[1] of old.

J. R. ACKERLEY
(1896–1967)

After the Blitz, 1941
Invocation to a soldier reported missing

Observe! I turn the key in this new door
At which you have not knocked your gay tattoo;
Note the bright prospect down the passage to
The sunlit terrace (this conducted tour

Is specially for you) and disregard
The snake on that far threshold, it's a pigeon
Craning for crumbs: we need no admonition
That life's unstable and our due reward.

But praise me for my courage; could you tell,
Here in the ante-room, here in the parlour,
That all this newly-painted furniture
Three months ago was refuse raked from hell?

1. the king of Argos for whom Hercules executed his twelve labours

Though here and there some defect still reveals –
The clock strikes three but it is four,
Whose face stares back at me from the bright mirror? –
How life falls somewhat short of our ideals.

But now the forward view. Here we discover
The bedroom and the old familiar bed,
For love, or sleep, or death all sprucely spread;
It only waits the one thing or the other.

All's ready for you, see; neat as new pins
Carpets on floors, chairs upon carpets set;
The clock strikes four and it is five, and yet
The movement's onward, a new life begins.

Though as you may have noticed, standing here
In this triumphant scene of man's resilience
I find myself lacking, lacking in confidence:
Whence have I come? And I am going where?

For setting the sad mileage of the mind
Against the journey and the destination,
I ask myself, in all this preparation,
What lies ahead that is not lost behind?

But you who swept no brush, who drove no nail,
And never with your knock this silence shattered,
Will know, in spite of change, that in this scattered
And desultory life I should not fail:

All by itself your picture stands among
These foreign scenes, expectant bed and chairs,
A passport to your step upon the stairs,
Your knock smiting the silence like a gong.

FEDERICO GARCÍA LORCA
(1898–1936)

Ode to Walt Whitman

   Along East River and the Bronx,
stripped to the waist, the young men sang,

with wheel and oil, leather and hammer,
ninety thousand miners tearing silver from the rocks,
while children measured scales and perspectives.

But none would sleep,
none yearned to be the river,
none loved broad leaves
and none the blue-tongued shore.

Along East River and at Queensborough
the young men grappled with Industry,
the Jews sold to the river fauns
roses of circumcision,
and the sky poured out over bridges and roofs
herds of bison driven on by the wind.

Yet none would pause,
none would be a cloud,
none sought the ferns
nor the yellow ring of a tambourine.

And while the moon is rising
turning pulleys will tumble the sky,
a cordon of needles will surround recall
and coffins remove the ones who do not work.

New York of slime,
New York of wires and of death,
What angel is secreted in your cheek?
What pure voice will tell the truths of wheat?
And who the nightmare of your anemones' stain?

Not for a second, beautiful, aged Walt Whitman,
have I failed to mark your beard full of butterflies,
your corduroy shoulders worn thin by the moon,
your thighs of virgin Apollo,
your voice like a pillar of ash;
as ancient and as lovely as the mist,
you moaned like a bird
whose sex was pierced by a needle;
foe to the satyr,

foe to the vine,
and lover of bodies beneath the rough blanket.
Not for a second, manly beauty,
who in mountains of coal, in posters and railways,
dreamed of being a river and of sleeping like a river
with the comrade who would place in your heart
the small ache of the ignorant leopard.

    Not for a second, Adam of blood, male,
sole man of the sea, beautiful, aged Walt Whitman,
because on the terraces,
congregated in bars,
pouring in waves from the sewers,
shivering between the thighs of chauffeurs,
or spinning on stages of absinthe,
the faggots, Walt Whitman, dreamed of you.

    This one, also! Also! and they dive
on your chaste and numinous beard,
blonds from the north, negroes from the sands,
multitudes shouting, gesticulating
like cats, like snakes,
the faggots, Walt Whitman, the faggots,
turbulent with weeping, with flesh for whipping,
for the boot or the bite of the butch.

    This one, also! Also! Stained fingers
gesture to the edge of your dream
while a friend eats your apple
tasting slightly of petrol
and the sun sings round the navels
of striplings at play below the bridge.

    But you were not searching for those scratched eyes,
the pitchy swamp where children are swallowed,
the frozen spit,
nor wounds curved like the bellies of toads
which faggots carry in cars and on terraces
while the moon whips at the corners of their fear.

    You sought a nakedness that would be as a river,
bull and dream to join wheel and seaweed;

father of your agony, camellia of your death,
to moan in the flames of your secret equator.

    Because it is just that man does not look for delight
in the jungle of blood of the following day,
the sky has shores where life may be skirted
and bodies that must not come again to the dawn.

    Anguish, anguish, dream, ferment and dream:
such is the world, my friend, anguish, anguish.
The dead decay beneath the city clocks,
war goes by – a million grey rats weeping,
the rich give their mistresses
little illuminated geegaws,
and life is nor noble, nor holy, nor good.

    Man may, if he wishes, lead his desire
through the veins of the coral or celestial nudes.
Love by the morning will be as the rocks. Time's
but a sleeping breeze that creeps through the branches.

    That is why I cannot raise my voice, aged Walt Whitman,
against the little boy who writes
a girlie name across his pillowslip,
nor against the youth who drags up as a bride
in the darkness of his closet,
nor against the clubland solitaries
drinking with disgust the waters of shame,
nor against the men of green glances
whose love is for men and whose lips burn in silence.
But against you, faggots of the cities,
with tumid flesh and sluttish mind,
scum, harpies, enemies of the dream
of love that offers garlands of joy.

    Against you forever, who proffer to youth
gouts of rancid death, bitterly laced.
Always against you,
Fairies of North America,
Pajaros of Havana,

Jotos of Mexico,
Sarasas of Cadiz,
Apios of Seville,
Cancos of Madrid,
Floras of Alicante,
Adelaidas of Portugal.

    Faggots of the world, slaughterers of the dove!
Slaves of women, boudoir bitches,
blown across public places with the fever of a fan
or ambushed in frigid and hemlocked lands.

    Let no quarter be given! Death
teems from your eyes
and heaps grey flowers on shores of slime.
Let no quarter be given! Beware!
May the wondering, the pure,
the habitual, the noted, the supplicant,
bar to you the gates of the Bacchanal!

    And you, beautiful Walt Whitman, sleep on by the banks of the
        Hudson,
open-handed, with your beard to the pole.
Mild clay or snow, your tongue calls out
to comrades to guard your bodiless gazelle.

    Sleep on, nothing else is.
A dance of walls shakes the fields
while America drowns in machinery and tears.
I would the great winds of profoundest night
would tear the flowers and letters from the arch where you are
        sleeping;
that a negro boy would tell the golden Whites
of the coming of the reign of the ears of corn.

ELSA GIDLOW
(born 1898)

For the Goddess Too Well Known

I have robbed the garrulous streets,
Thieved a fair girl from their blight,

I have stolen her for a sacrifice
That I shall make to this night.

I have brought her, laughing,
To my quietly dreaming garden.
For what will be done there
I ask no man pardon.

I brush the rouge from her cheeks,
Clean the black kohl from the rims
Of her eyes; loose her hair;
Uncover the glimmering, shy limbs.

I break wild roses, scatter them over her.
The thorns between us sting like love's pain.
Her flesh, bitter and salt to my tongue,
I taste with endless kisses and taste again.

At dawn I leave her
Asleep in my wakening garden.
(For what was done there
I ask no man pardon.)

ERICH KÄSTNER
(born 1899)

Ragoût fin de siècle (with reference to certain cafés)

Here even experts can
hardly see clear:
the women are men,
the men are women here.

The young men are dancing here with zest
in evening dress with rubber breast
while talking in sopranos.
The women wear tuxedos
and talk like Santa Claus
while lighting big Havanas.

The men go to the powder room
to put cream on their hide.
No woman here has any groom,
each woman has a bride.

Here some tried so hard for perversion
that they returned to the norm.
And if Dante came here on an excursion
he would take chloroform.

Here nobody knows what is what.
The true are false, the false are not,
and all is mixed up in a pot,
and pain is fun, pleasure makes mad,
and up is down, and front behind.

For all I care, have an affair
with yourselves or a mastodon,
or every bird in Audubon.
I do not give a damn.

Only don't scream ad nauseam
that you are great.
That you prefer it from behind
does not prove an ingenious mind.

So much for that.

[WALTER KAUFMAN]

LOUIS SAUNDERS PERKINS
(?–?)

Genius

Lady,
You, who are pattering to your carriage door
In high-heeled shoes,
Your hat spraying delicate, white feathers,
Soft furs about your throat

And pointed designs, crusted with diamonds,
Pinned to your frail blouse –
Your coat was made by the best of tailors
Who patted and pinned and smoothed it with infinite care
So that it would give you 'long lines.'
And your figure has been stiffened rigidly
Into the proper shape.
You are hung with costly things,
You carry them about with you –
Even the intricate embroidery on your stockings is a cause for wonder–
And when you think of them
Your little, muffled mind glows with satisfaction.
But you are not half so beautiful
For all your trouble,
As the young workman who just went swinging down the street,
His body lithe and strong and free as a whip in the wind!

FORREST ANDERSON
(born 1903)

The Beach Homos

often you see them sitting, solitary, on a dune
with beach-grass making around them a light sawing sound;
for these are the wilfully alone – gazing moodily
out at the misty enigma of a far pacific blue

sometimes they look this way, at a group of handsome boys
cavorting in playful warfare – instinctively in training for
life's more serious battles soon to come. but not for long.
not for these eyes that golden flesh in still rosy bloom

seaward, instead, to swing their contemplation
over that salt-silken skin covering monsters very like their own
feelings. is this their true reflection: angels with diabolic visages
their real image: a fading concept, somewhat distorted, infatuate,
    maybe . . .
                    yet one floating forever free.

LUIS CERNUDA
(1903–1963)

Birds in the Night

The French government – or maybe it was the English – placed
a plaque on the house at 8 Great College Street, Camden Town,
London, where a strange couple named Rimbaud and Verlaine
took a room and lived, drank, worked, and fucked for a few short
stormy weeks. The ambassador and the mayor certainly
attended the dedication, along with all the others who scorned
Verlaine and Rimbaud when they were alive.

The house, like the neighbourhood, is poor and grim –
the sordid grimness that goes with poverty, not the funereal
grimness of spiritual riches.
When night begins to fall a hand-organ sounds from their sidewalk,
as it did in their time, echoing in the damp grey air,
and the neighbours, home from work,
take to dancing or head for the nearest pub.

It was brief that friendship between Verlaine the Drunkard
and Rimbaud the Unfathomable, brief and filled with conflict.
But even so we can assume that it had its saving moments,
if only in their remembrance of how one had freed himself from
an insufferable mother and the other had fled a boring wife.
Freedom in this world, though, is not for free, and they who broke
away were doomed to pay a terrible price.

They lived, the plaque says, behind those walls, prisoners
of their destiny – the impossible friendship, the bitterness
of separation, the scandal that followed; for one, then, the trial
and two years in jail for habits that society and its laws condemn,
at least for the time being, and, for the other, solitary
wandering from one obscure corner of the earth to another,
always in flight from our world and its vaunted progress.

The silence of one and the commonplace chatter of the other
balanced out. Rimbaud threw off the oppressive hand;
Verlaine kissed it, accepting his punishment. One carried
his gold in his belt; the other squandered his in absinthe

and cheap women. Both were hounded by the authorities and
frowned upon by the good people who grow fat from the labour of
    others.
Even the black whore had the right to insult them then.
But now, with the passage of time, their drunkenness and sodomy,
their contemptuous poetry, their wayward disordered lives –
none of these things matters anymore and France uses both names
and both works for the glory of France and her ordered art.
Scholars pry into their acts and retrace their footsteps,
baring the most intimate details of their lives to the world.
Nobody is frightened by them anymore; nobody objects.
'Verlaine? Oh, he was a smooth operator when it came to women,
just a regular guy like you and me. And Rimbaud? A good Catholic,
no doubt about it.' Then they quote bits of *Le Bateau Ivre*
and the sonnet about the vowels, but they skip Verlaine because
he isn't fashionable anymore, not like Rimbaud who gets done up in
deluxe editions with dubious texts while adolescent poets all over
the world babble about him, hidden away in their provinces.

Do the dead hear what the living say about them? Let us hope not.
Endless silence must be something like a balm for those, like Rimbaud
and Verlaine, who lived by the word and died by the word.
But the silence of the beyond can't blot out the farcical
and repugnant praise of the here and now.
Someone once wished that mankind had a single head,
to chop it off with a single blow.
In that wish he gave it more importance than it deserves:
better if it were a cockroach, simply to squash it.

[ERSKINE LANE]

WILLIAM PLOMER
(1903–1973)

The Playboy of the Demi-world: 1938

Aloft in Heavenly Mansions, Doubleyou One –
Just Mayfair flats, but certainly sublime –
You'll find the abode of D'Arcy Honeybunn,
A rose-red sissy half as old as time.

Peace cannot age him, and no war could kill
The genial tenant of those cosy rooms,
He's lived there always and he lives there still,
Perennial pansy, hardiest of blooms.

There you'll encounter aunts of either sex,
Their jokes equivocal or over-ripe,
Ambiguous couples wearing slacks and specs
And the stout Lesbian knocking out her pipe.

The rooms are crammed with flowers and objets d'art,
A Ganymede still hands the drinks – and plenty!
D'Arcy still keeps a rakish-looking car
And still behaves the way he did at twenty.

A ruby pin is fastened in his tie,
The scent he uses is *Adieu Sagesse*,
His shoes are suède, and as the years go by
His tailor's bill's not getting any less.

He cannot whistle, always rises late,
Is good at indoor sports and parlour tricks,
Mauve is his favourite colour, and his gait
Suggests a peahen walking on hot bricks.

He prances forward with his hands outspread
And folds all comers in a gay embrace,
A wavy toupée on his hairless head,
A fixed smile on his often-lifted face.

'My dear!' he lisps, to whom all men are dear,
'How perfectly enchanting of you!'; turns
Towards his guests and twitters, 'Look who's here!
Do come and help us fiddle while Rome burns!'

'The kindest man alive,' so people say,
'Perpetual youth!' But have you seen his eyes?
The eyes of some old saurian in decay,
That asks no questions and is told no lies.

Under the fribble lurks a worn-out sage
Heavy with disillusion, and alone;

So never say to D'Arcy, 'Be your age!' –
He'd shrivel up at once or turn to stone.

Ganymede

Crested and ruffed and stiff with whistling frills
Zeus as an eagle from the sky saw Troy,
Her waltzing towers and fast-impending hills,
Swerved plunging fieldwards gaitered with gold quills
To settle upon felspar and ogle the nude boy,
With plumage damascened and love-dance coy
To lure the lad, and promises of thrills.

The next day's headlines were the talk of Troy:
BIG BIRD SENSATION, MISSING LOCAL BOY.

CHRISTOPHER ISHERWOOD
(born 1904)

On His Queerness

When I was young and wanted to see the sights,
They told me: 'Cast an eye over the Roman Camp
If you care to.
But plan to spend most of your day at the Aquarium –
Because, after all, the Aquarium –
Well, I mean to say, the Aquarium –
Till you've seen the Aquarium you ain't seen nothing.'

So I cast an eye over
The Roman Camp –
And that old Roman Camp,
That old, old Roman Camp
Got me
Interested.

So that now, near closing-time,
I find that I still know nothing –
And am not even sorry that I know nothing –
About fish.

W. H. AUDEN
(1907–1973)

Uncle Henry

When the Flyin' Scot
fills for shootin', I go southward,
wisin' after coffee, leavin'
Lady Starkie.

Weady for some fun,
visit yearly Wome, Damascus,
in Mowocco look for fwesh a-
-musin' places

Where I'll find a fwend,
don't you know, a charmin' cweature,
like a Gweek God and devoted:
how delicious!

All they have they bwing,
Abdul, Nino, Manfwed, Kosta:
here's to women for they have such
lovely kiddies!

EDWARD JAMES
(born 1907)

from *Carmina Amico*

17

He had a many-coloured glance like flowers:
something of opals lay within his look:
and in the taper his strong shoulders took
was gleam and grace of tall and ivory towers.
He seemed as fresh as, after summer showers,
cool gardens seem. And as the hart the brook
thirsty I sought his mouth. Never was book

better perused than I his brow, long hours.
Two full carved rubies were his urgent lips.
Heavy as floating lilies on the Nile
hung the white waxen lids, behind whose smile
the jewels of Palmyra and of Spain
had tumbled to the windows of his brain.
Still past their lashes – still, the treasure slips?

19

You have returned. You have returned, my joy:
you have returned as polar morning comes
after a whole night winter. Throb the drums,
– yes, beat my blood to greet my darling boy.
My heart with wild delight shall now employ
both tongue and pen to reckon up the sums
of all my gladness. Pleasure almost numbs
my reason. I am shaken like a toy.
Like sunlight after storm, like flowers from ice,
yes, like a torch lit in oblivion
you have returned, and heaven bursts above.
No music mad enough can half suffice.
My heart shall paean like a clarion.
I am the bugle for the mouth of love.

STEPHEN SPENDER
(born 1909)

18

How strangely this sun reminds me of my love!
Of my walk alone at evening, when like the cottage smoke
Hope vanished into the red fading of the sky.
I remember my strained listening to his voice
My staring at his face and taking the photograph
With the river behind, and the woods touched by Spring:
Till the identification of a morning –
Expansive sheets of blue rising from fields
Roaring movements of light discerned under shadow –
With his figure leaning over a map, is now complete.

What is left of that smoke which the wind blew away?
I corrupted his confidence and his sun-like happiness
So that even now in his turning of bolts or driving a machine
His hand will show error. That is for him.
For me this memory which now I behold,
When, from the pasturage, azure rounds me in rings,
And the lark ascends, and his voice still rings, still rings.

To T.A.R.H.

Even whilst I watch him I am remembering
The quick laugh of the wasp-gold eyes.
The column turning from the staring window
Even while I see I remember, for love
Dips what it sees into a flood of memory
Vaster than itself, and makes the seen
Be drowned in all that past and future seeing
Of the once seen. Thus what I wore I wear
And shall wear always – the glint of the quick lids
And the body's axle turning: these shall be
    What they are now within the might of Ever.

Night when my life lies with no past or future
But only endless space. It wakes and watches
Hope and despair and the small vivid longings
Gnaw the flesh, like minnows. Where it drank love
It breathes in sameness. Here are
The signs indelible. The wiry copper hair,
And the notched mothlike lips, and that after all human
Glance, which makes all else forgiven.

JEAN GENET
(born 1910)

from 'The Man Sentenced to Death'

The murderers of the wall wrap themselves in sunrise
In my cell open to the chant of the tall pinetrees
That lulls it, hooked to fine lines
Knotted by sailors whom morning guilds.

Who carved a windrose in the plaster?
Who's dreaming of my home, from the depths of his Hungary?
What child rolled over my rotten straw
Remembering friends at the moment of waking?

Wander, my Madness, produce for my own pleasure
A consoling hell peopled with handsome soldiers,
Naked to the waist, and from their flowery skivvies
Pull up those heavy flowers whose odor strikes me like thunder.

Pull out from who knows where the worst acts of madness:
Kidnap children, invent tortures,
Mangle Beauty, batter her faces,
And give Guiana to the guys for their rendezvous.

O my old Maroni, O sweet Cayenne![1]
I see the bodies of fifteen or twenty hoodlums
Bending over a blond cutie smoking the butts
That the guards spit out into the flowers and the moss.

A wet butt is enough to depress all of us.
Alone, above the unyielding ferns, good and stiff,
The youngest is leaning back on his slender hips,
Passive, waiting to be anointed as bridegroom.

The old murderers rush to the rite
Where squatting in the evening they draw from a dry stick
A little fire nimbly stolen by the kid
Purer and more thrilling than a stiffening prick.

The toughest bandit, with his polished muscles,
Bows respectfully before this frail boy.
The moon climbs in the sky. A quarrel is settled.
The mysterious folds of the black flag waver.

Your lace-like gestures wrap you up so fine!
You're smoking, one of your shoulders leaning against

1. Cayenne is the capital of French Guiana, off whose coast Devil's Island is located. Maroni is a river in Guiana.

A reddening palmtree. The smoke in your throat falls
While the convicts, dancing solemnly,

Serious, silent, each one in turn, O youngster,
Come up to take a fragrant drop from your mouth,
Only one drop, not two, of the round smoke
Rolling off your tongue. O triumphant brother,

Terrible divinity, invisible and malevolent,
You sit there impassive, keen, made of shiny metal,
Thinking only of yourself, fatal bestower,
Raised upon the edge of your singing hammock.

Your delicate soul is beyond the hills
Still following the spellbound flight
Of a jailbreaker who, without a thought of you, lies dead
On a valley's floor, with a bullet through his lungs.

O kid of mine, rise to the air of the moon.
Come pour into my mouth a little heavy cum
Rolling from your throat to my teeth, my Love,
Finally fertilizing our divine wedding.

Glue your rapturous body to mine that is dying
From fucking the tenderest and sweetest of rascals.
Under your spell, as my hand weighs your round, blond balls,
My black marble prick spits you to the heart.

O take aim on him standing up in his burning sunset
That's going to consume me! I have so little time left,
If you dare, come to me, leave your ponds,
Your swamps, the mud you blow bubbles from.

The souls of my dead! Kill me! Burn me!
Like Michaelangelo, I've carved my life away
But as for Beauty, Lord, I've always served her,
My belly, my knees, my hands, roses of feeling.

The roosters in the henhouse, the Gallic skylark,
The dairyman's cans, a bell in the air,

A step on the gravel, my window white and bright,
A joyful light shining on the slate-gray prison.

Gentlemen, I'm not afraid! If my head was rolling
In the racket of the basket with your blond head,
Mine by good fortune on your slim hip
Or for greater beauty on your neck, my chicken . . .

Watch out! Tragic king with your mouth half-open
I have access to your sad sand gardens,
Where you're jacking off, alone, two fingers raised,
Your head wrapped in a veil of blue linen.

In a state of frenzy I see your look-alike!
Love! Song! My queen! Is this the male specter
I had a glimpse of in your pale eyes while playing
Now watching me so from the plaster on the wall?

Don't be so severe, let the morning-songs be sung
To your gypsy heart; let me have just one kiss . . .
My God, I'm going to croak without once being able
To hold you close to my cock and my heart!

[STEVEN FINCH]

PAUL GOODMAN
(1911–1972)

Lines

His cock is big and red when I am there
and his persistent lips are like sweet wine.
Then would I pause and breathe his closeness
a long time hungrily, for it is there.
Yet we dress in haste and friendly say good-bye
and do not intend, each for our own good reasons,
to commit ourselves to happiness together.
Our meetings are fortunate and beautiful,
he is chaste and I am temperate,
for I have learned by the unlikely way
of deficiency and excess temperance.

Long Lines: Youth and Age

Like a hot stone your cock weighs on mine, young man,
and your face has become brutish and congested.
I'd stop and gaze at it but drunk with carbon dioxide
we cannot stop snuffling each other's breath.

I am surprised you lust for a grayhead like me
and what a waste for me to grapple so much pleasure
with sliding palms holding your thin body
firmly while you squirm, till it is time to come.

Come, young man . . . I have come with him for company
to his pounding heart. We are wet. Wistfully
I play with his black hair while he falls asleep
minute by minute, slowly, unlike my restless life.

It is quiet on his little boat. 'He is a noisy lover,'
I notice idly – the April air is pure –
'but he has no human speech.' It's I who say
the words like 'I love you' or 'Thank you.'

TENNESSEE WILLIAMS
(born 1914)

Life Story

After you've been to bed together for the first time,
without the advantage or disadvantage of any prior acquaintance,
the other party very often says to you,
Tell me about yourself, I want to know all about you,
what's your story? And you think maybe they really and truly do

sincerely want to know your life story, and so you light up
a cigarette and begin to tell it to them, the two of you
lying together in completely relaxed positions
like a pair of rag dolls a bored child dropped on a bed.

You tell them your story, or as much of your story

as time or a fair degree of prudence allows, and they say, Oh, oh, oh,
    oh, oh,
each time a little more faintly, until the oh
is just an audible breath, and then of course

there's some interruption. Slow room service comes up
with a bowl of melting ice cubes, or one of you rises to pee
and gaze at himself with mild astonishment in the bathroom mirror.
And then, the first thing you know, before you've had time
to pick up where you left off with your enthralling life story,
they're telling you *their* life story, exactly as they'd intended to all
    along,

and you're saying, Oh, oh, oh, oh, oh,
each time a little more faintly, the vowel at last becoming
no more than an audible sigh,
as the elevator, halfway down the corridor and a turn to the left,
draws one last, long, deep breath of exhaustion
and stops breathing forever. Then?

Well, one of you falls asleep
and the other one does likewise with a lighted cigarette in his mouth,
and that's how people burn to death in hotel rooms.

SIR JOHN WALLER
(born 1917)

Goldenhair

Golden-haired boy on the edge of a street
In his tight blue jeans on his lonely beat.
Hush! Hush!
I'm rather afraid
Christopher Robin is looking for trade.

JAMES KIRKUP
(born 1919)

Gay Boys

Those two young men, dancing quietly together in a corner
To the slow fox of 'Moonlight on the Ruined Castle'
Are nice to watch – I don't know why – in this gay but ghastly bar.
Something in their close embrace's calm
Neutrality is more than moving: a perfect unconcern, their bodies'
Innocent conspiracy, appears to make them twins,
Their pale monkey faces mischievous and pure
Beneath the hair's black tomboy fringe.

Image of an ideal that is not only Greek,
They preserve an oriental poise, involuntary ignorance
Of private misery. Behind the sooty fans of their tilted lids'
Peculiar inclinations, their eyes dark ellipses slightly
Shift, like leaves glimpsed through holes in a paper screen.
Their pale mouths curve, flowers of blotted ink,
Into each other's cheeks. At the tips of their fine hands
The brown fingers make their nails bright pink.

Neither guilt nor passion moves them, neither do they think
Of happiness, a concept unnecessary to enjoyment.
Untroubled creatures of the spirit's jungle,
They neither smile nor weep, but turn their open masks
To look no further than the moment and each other,
Mirroring the long, cool record's easy play.
Knowing no reason why they should not be so,
They dance together, and are truly gay.

The Love That Dares to Speak Its Name

Gay News was successfully prosecuted for blasphemous libel
on publishing this poem. It therefore remains unavailable to the
British public.

The Love of Older Men

They are so moving in
their sadness, gentleness and longing –
all the sad old men who once
were all the sad young men.

How can you not be moved
by their loneliness and desolation –
their faint dreams and hopes
of love, a new love, a friendship?

The poorest and the ugliest still long
for just a passing warmth, a touch,
the clasp of hands, the feel, the joy
of another's nakedness and strength and grace
enriching all that poverty and emptiness and death.

Friendship is only for the young.
But it should be for the old also.
The old have more need of friends
than the young, who have too many.

When I was younger and better-looking
I always offered myself to old men.
I had young men too, sometimes, but
with the old I felt a special love.
I used to feel like a radiant blond angel
coming down to deliver them from
the darkness of their stinking cottages,
the weary wanderings of the parks, the baths,
patient waitings with aching backs and swollen ankles
in the dark at the back of the movies.

Fatuous youth! And yet my foolishness
came from the heart: I wanted them to be loved
as much as I was. And even more important –
I came to them, and they
never denied me, as the young so often did
in their caprice and frivolity and meanness.

The old are always serious. They have to be.
It was for that I loved them.

– Now I am older, I still love old men,
but there are no young angels
like the one I was in my golden days.

ROBERT DUNCAN
(born 1919)

The Lover

I have been seeing his face everywhere, the face of a former lover.
But it is not he. Passing, passing in the daily crowd,
an old ghost of the mind, of the heart, a starting up
of indelible pang. I said I would never forget.
 O the unknowing will of first love,
forcing a way, an eternity of feeling.

 Is it the time of the year? I cannot remember.
Memory will not yield his sure image, all clear trace
lockt at the springs of passion. Only old will
forces recall. All else forgotten. But the dead
turn certainly in the graves of our longing,
the dead belonging turns, seeking, unwanted.
He was once all of wanting, a need, an end
of youth! Now I am mistaken, often,
seeing his wraith in faces passing.

JAMES MITCHELL
(born 1920)

Gay Epiphany

In a culture where the aesthetic experience is denied and atrophied, genuine
religious ecstasy rare, intellectual pleasure scorned – it is only natural that sex
should become the only personal epiphany of most people . . .

                                                                GARY SNYDER

o sperm, testes, paradidymus! o scrotum, septum, and rectum!
o penis! o prepuce, urethra!

o prostate gland! o Dartos muscle! o spermatid and spermatocyte!

inguinal canals! seminal vesicles! seminiferous tubules!
prostatic utricles! efferent ductules! testicular lobules!
o male germinal epithelium!

o symphysis pubis! tunica albuginea! vasa efferentia!
corpus cavernosum et spongiosum! o ampulla of vas!

o meatus and bulb! o cutaneous dorsal vein! o lobulous
membranous convoluted pouch!

o glans penis, slightly bulging structure at the distal
end of the penis!

o Cowper's glands, secreting a slimy substance which functions
as a lubricant!

o seminal fluids, functioning to suspend and protect the
delicate spermatozoa during their stay within the male body!

o epididymis, a tube-like structure commonly attaining a length of up
to twenty feet!

Boy, at the lovely tip of your external urethral orifice, all my poetries
terminate

CASSIANO NUNES
(born 1921)

Episode

In the cheap room
he undressed completely
for the act called love.

He even
took off his socks.

This uncalled for gesture
moved me considerably.
I found in it a mark
of consideration and even a touch
of class.

[E. A. LACEY]

KINGSLEY AMIS
(born 1922)

An Ever-Fixed Mark

Years ago, at a private school
Run on traditional lines,
One fellow used to perform
Prodigious feats in the dorm;
His quite undevious designs
Found many a willing tool.

On the rugger field, in the gym,
Buck marked down at his leisure
The likeliest bits of stuff;
The notion, familiar enough,
Of 'using somebody for pleasure'
Seemed handy and harmless to him.

But another chap was above
The diversions of such a lout;
Seven years in the place
And he never got to first base
With the kid he followed about:
What interested Ralph was love.

He did the whole thing in style –
Letters three times a week,
Sonnet-sequences, Sunday walks;

Then, during one of their talks,
The youngster caressed his cheek,
and that made it all worth while.

These days, for a quid pro quo,
Ralph's chum does what, and with which;
Buck's playmates, family men,
Eye a Boy Scout now and then.
Sex is a momentary itch,
Love never lets you go.

PIER PAOLO PASOLINI
(1922–1975)

To a Pope

A few days before you died, death
    cast her eye on one of your own age:
at twenty, you were a student, he a working lad,
    you noble and rich, he a plebeian son of toil:
but those days you lived together illumined with a flame
    of gold our ancient Roma, restoring her to youth again.
– I've just seen his corpse, poor old Zucchetto's.
    Drunk, he was roaming the dark streets round the markets
and a tram coming from San Paolo ran him down,
    dragging him along the rails under the plane trees:
they left him there for hours, beneath the wheels:
    a few curious passers-by were standing staring at him
in silence: it was late, not many people in the streets.
    One of those men who owe you their existence,
an old cop, in a sloppy uniform, like any layabout,
    kept shouting at those who went too close: 'Fuck off!'
Then at last the hospital van arrived, to carry him away:
    the idlers began dispersing, but a few still hung around,
and the proprietress of a nearby all-night snack bar
    who knew him well, told someone who'd just come by
Zucchetto had been run over by a tram, it was all over now.
    You died a few days later: Zucchetto was one
of your vast apostolic human flock,

a poor old soak, no family, no home,
who roamed the streets at night, living as best he could.
     You knew nothing of all that: knew nothing either
of thousands of other christs like him.
     Perhaps we're crazy to keep on asking why
people like Zucchetto were unworthy of your love.
     There are unspeakable hovels, where mothers and children
go on existing in the dust and filth of a past long gone.
     Not too far from where you lived yourself,
within sight of the vainglorious dome of St Peter's
     there is one of those places, il Gelsomino . . .
a hill half ravaged by a quarry, and down below,
     between a stagnant sewer and a row of mansion blocks,
a mass of wretched shacks, not houses – pigsties.
     All it needed from you was a gesture, a single word,
for all your children living there to find a decent roof:
     you made no gesture, you spoke not a single word.
No one was asking you to give Marx absolution! An immense
     wave, beating against thousands of years of life,
separated you from him, from his beliefs:
     but does your own religion know nothing of pity?
Thousands of men under your pontificate
     lived on dunghills, in pigsties, under your very eyes.
You knew that to sin does not just mean to commit evil deeds:
     not to do good – that is the real infamy.
What good you might have done! And you did it not:
     there has been no greater sinner than yourself.

[JAMES KIRKUP]

NOTE: This poem was written in 1958 on the death of Pope Pius XII, and caused a literary scandal. I have taken it from the series of 'epigrams' published in Pasolini's *La Religione del mio Tempo* in 1962 by Garzanti, Milano. [J.K.]

JACK SPICER
(1925–1965)

Among the coffee cups and soup toureens walked Beauty
Casual, but not unconscious of his power
Gathering dishes mucked with clinging macaroni
Unbearable in his spasmatic beauty

Sovereign in Simon's Restaurant and wreathed in power
The monarch of a kingdom yet unruled.

Now regal at a table in the Starlite Club sits Beauty
Casual but not unconscious of his power
Kept by a Mr Blatz who manufactures girdles
Unbearable in his spasmatic beauty
Counting with kingly eye the subjects of his power
Who sleep with beauty and are unappeased.

Central Park West

Along the walks the sweet queens walk their dogs
And dream of love and diamonds as they pass
And I could be a statue or a stone
As they walk by me dreaming of their gods.
Beside their path, an apple's thrown away,
I see that old erotic garden where
Our parents breathed the wasteful, loving air
Before the angry gardener changed his will.
The park has no room for that memory.
Its paths are twisted like a scattered sky
Of foreign stars. The spinning queens go by
Within their orbits, leaving me alone.
What cosmic joy. The last companion here
Is Priapus, the gardener's ugly son
Who crouches in the bulbs with his shears
And hasn't got the hots for anyone.

ALLEN GINSBERG
(born 1926)

Maybe Love

Maybe love will come
cause I am not so dumb
Tonight it fills my heart
heavy sad apart
from one or two I fancy
now I'm an old fairy.

This is hard to say
I've come to be this way
thru many loves of youth
that taught me most heart truth
Now I come by myself
in my hand like an old elf

It's not the most romantic
dream to be so frantic
for young men's bodies,
as an old sugar daddy
blest respected known,
but left to bed alone.

How come love came to end
flaccid, how pretend
desires I have used
Four decades as I cruised
from bed to bar to book
Shamefaced like a crook

Stealing here & there
pricks & buttocks bare
by accident, by circumstance
Naivete or horny chance
stray truth or famous lie,
How come I came to die?

Love dies, body dies, the mind
keeps groping blind
half hearted full of lust
to wet the silken dust
of men that hold me dear
but won't sleep with me near.

This morning's cigarette
This morning's sweet regret
habit of many years
wake me to old fears
Under the living sun
one day there'll be no one

to kiss & to adore
& to embrace & more
lie down with side by side
tender as a bride
gentle under my touch –
Prick I love to suck.

Church bells ring again
in Heidelberg as when
in New York City town
I lay my belly down
against a boy friend's buttock
and couldn't get it up.

'Spite age and common Fate
I'd hoped love'd hang out late
I'd never lack for thighs
On which to sigh my sighs
This day it seems the truth
I can't depend on youth,

I can't keep dreaming love
I can't pray heav'n above
or call the pow'rs of hell
to keep my body well
occupied with young devils
tongueing at my navel.

I stole up from my bed
to that of a well-bred
young friend who shared my purse
and noted my tender verse,
I held him by the ass
waiting for sweat to pass

until he said Go back
I said that I would jack
myself away, not stay
& so he let me play
Allergic to my come –
I came, & then went home.

This can't go on forever,
this poem, nor my fever
for brown eyed mortal joy,
I love a straight white boy.
Ah the circle closes
Same old withered roses!

I haven't found an end
I can fuck & defend
& no more can depend
on youth time to amend
what old ages portend –
Love's death, & body's end.

      Heidelberg 8 AM 15 Dec. '79

Allen Ginsberg
for Gay Sunshine
& Winston Leyland
August 10, 1981
Naropa Institute
Boulder, Colorado

Please Master

Please master can I touch your cheek
please master can I kneel at your feet
please master can I loosen your blue pants
please master can I gaze at your golden-haired belly
please master can I gently take down your shorts
please master can I have your thighs bare to my eyes
please master can I take off my clothes below your chair
please master can I kiss your ankles and soul
please master can I touch lips to your hard muscle hairless thigh
please master can I lay my ear pressed to your stomach
please master can I wrap my arms around your white ass
please master can I lick your groin curled with blond soft fur
please master can I touch my tongue to your rosy asshole
please master may I pass my face to your balls,
please master, please look into my eyes,
please master order me down on the floor,

please master tell me to lick your thick shaft
please master put your rough hands on my bald hairy skull
please master press my mouth to your prick-heart
please master press my face into your belly, pull me slowly strong
    thumbed
till your dumb hardness fills my throat to the base
till I swallow & taste your delicate flesh-hot prick barrel veined Please
Master push my shoulders away and stare in my eye, & make me bend
    over the table
please master grab my thighs and lift my ass to your waist
please master your hand's rough stroke on my neck your palm down
    my backside
please master push me up, my feet on chairs, till my hole feels the
    breath of your spit and your thumb stroke
please master make me say Please Master Fuck me now Please
Master grease my balls and hairmouth with sweet vaselines
please master stroke your shaft with white creams
please master touch your cock head to my wrinkled self-hole
please master push it gently, your elbows enwrapped round my
    breast
your arms passing down to my belly, my penis you touch w/ your
    fingers
please master shove it in me a little, a little, a little
please master sink your droor thing down my behind
& please master make me wiggle my rear to eat up the prick trunk
till my asshalfs cuddle your thighs, my back bent over,
till I'm alone sticking out, your sword stuck throbbing in me
please master pull out and slowly roll into the bottom
please master lunge it again, and withdraw to the tip
please master fuck me again with your self, please fuck me Please
Master drive down till it hurts me the softness the
Softness please master make love to my ass, give body to center, &
    fuck me for good like a girl,
tenderly clasp me please master I take me to thee,
& drive in my belly your selfsame sweet heat-rood
you fingered in solitude Denver or Brooklyn or fucked in maiden in
    Paris carlots
please master drive me thy vehicle, body of love drops, sweat fuck
body of tenderness. Give me your dog fuck faster
please master make me go moan on the table
Go moan O please master do fuck me like that

in your rhythm thrill-plunge & pull back-bounce & push down
till I loosen my asshole a dog on the table yelping with terror delight to
    be loved
Please master call me a dog, an ass beast, a wet asshole,
& fuck me more violent, my eyes hid with your palms round my skull
& plunge down in a brutal hard lash thru soft drip-flesh
& throb thru five seconds to spurt out your semen heat
over & over, bamming it in while I cry out your name I do love you

HAROLD NORSE
(born 1926)

Behind the Glass Wall

behind the glass wall
    fluctuant   i see blue limbs
  crumble away   black fungus noses
    thighs kneecaps
                'i have the taste of the infinite'
ylem
        primordial squinch   the universe crushed into
                        a seed
nothing will satisfy me
           i write green ballets & hollow journeys
caught in the etheric web of yr crotch
        a hairy ocean of darkness

        dawamesc doors of pearl
        open to fiery radiance
majoun madness
    down marrakech alleys
  the   djemaa el fna
 squirming   with snakes
    in carbide glow

black gnaoua dancers!   lash sword!   flash teeth!
   under the barrow
    broiling in sleep mouth
& nostrils buzzing with flies
       genitals thick swollen out

of big tear in pants
               derelict 14 yr old street arab
         cameras   snapping
like teeth/great souk
       swarms for dirhams
and who
       are you little arab
              i shared my visions
                           and ate
           black hasheesh candy with
the doors of yr body   flung
       open we twitched in spasms
                 muscular convulsions
                   heavenly epilepsy on the bed
       in the hotel of the palms
           prolonged orgasm
             uncontrollable joy
                       of leaving the mind

Breathing the Strong Smell . . .

breathing the strong smell of each other
I want it to last forever
it is never enough
warming the coldness of the heart

we stood holding each other
two men locking eyes and lips
then your mind cut the flow
and it was abruptly over

yet I felt curiously healed
as if life were about to begin

FRANK O'HARA
(1926–1966)

Homosexuality

So we are taking off our masks, are we, and keeping
Our mouths shut? as if we'd been pierced by a glance!

The song of an old cow is not more full of judgement
than the vapours which escape one's soul when one is sick;

so I pull the shadows round me like a puff
and crinkle my eyes as if at the most exquisite moment

of a very long opera, and then we're off!
without reproach and without hope that our delicate feet

will touch the earth again, let alone 'very soon'.
It is the law of my own voice I shall investigate.

I start like ice, my finger to my ear, my ear
to my heart, that proud ear at the garbage can

in the rain. It's wonderful to admire oneself
with complete candor, tallying up the merits of each

of the latrines. 14th Street is drunken and credulous,
53rd tried to tremble but is too at rest. The good

love a park and the inept a railway station,
and there are the divine ones, who drag themselves up

and down the lengthening shadow of an Abyssinian head
in the dust, trailing their long elegant heels of hot air

crying to confuse the brave 'It's a summer day,
and I want to be wanted more than anything else in the world.'

RALPH POMEROY
(born 1926)

A Tardy Epithalamium[1] for E. and N.

You are proof that it can happen
and that it should.
There is as little hysteria

1. poem in celebration of marriage

attached to your household
as to that of the most 'normal' couple.

Because you are outlaw lovers though
I must salute you only with initials.
I hate this.

After eight years you still seem examples of clarity:
clear about looking at one another,
clear about getting up in the morning,
clear about people in relation to you,
clear about me when I arrive for dinner,
drink,
end up drunk.

All three writers, whenever we get together
we carp about careers and such.
We do this for some time, eating delicious
meals meanwhile, 'keeping it down' because of
the nosey neighbors (who express their
contempt by making love or fighting
with their shades up).

At regular intervals we seem – like deer
perked-up to the sense of something –
to stop and see the joke of it all,
and laughter comes barging in and takes over.

I, sooner or later, grow jealous of you
and begin to realize that I have to get up and go,
alone,
while you get to stay with each other.

This makes me blue and close to tearful
and defiant even. So I kiss you both gingerly
and head resolutely for the subway,
or resolutely for the bars.

Grateful for you
all the same.

The Leather Bar

Tonight, at the bar,
in the Members Only room,
the usual collection of aging 'cyclists'
lounge
wearing painfully tight jeans
elaborately arranged to show
maximum amount of cock and balls.
Even in summer a lot of them wear full leather.

Some are young – too young to be so pale,
so negative looking – and wear
that stupid expression resorted to
by those who try to appear indifferent.
They congratulate one another on some
new refinement in their get-ups –
a line of studs outlining their pockets,
a cleverly blocked cowboy hat, a pair
of real German Army boots.

Amid the greetings and badinage
a pool game goes: focus point –
because of the brilliant light bouncing
off its green field –
for involved nonchalance, exhibitions of
strained, tattooed muscles, 'baskets',
arching asses.

Cracks are made about someone wearing
mere shoes or – God forbid! – sneakers!
These are The Boys, The Fellas, The Guys.
So, if someone ambiguous enters, sunny
from a lucky weekend, rested from enough sleep,
not drinking at the moment, in a good mood
really –
and is dresed for the heat
in an old open-necked shirt, loose pants
and sandals –
they look up, stir uneasily.

To them, he doesn't project a butch enough image.
The masses of long golden hair don't help.
His smoking a small, delicious cigar is a
gesture too filled with the 'wrong' style.
Immediate alienation.

But those who know him,
those who have been to bed with him,
know what they know.
He exchanges greetings with them –
of varying degrees of warmth.
And the sly, furtive, taken gazes
will pass back and forth all night
through the dark smoke.

Sizing up. Sizing up. A puzzle pieced
together: 'If A's been to bed with C and
seems to like him, and I've been to bed
with C and we got on fine, then maybe A
would work out for me . . .
And he knows G whom I've always wanted
to make-out with . . . He could tell me
what G digs . . . Guess I better move
over to a better spot so I'll be more
directly in his line of vision . . .'

The clock, which advertises beer,
says half-past two. Tomorrow's a working day.
Yet the bar stays full with a Great Number
yelling from the juke box.
No one wants the night to end yet.
Most hope to connect with someone –
impersonally, in a group, or maybe
personally,
one at a time.

PHILIP BAINBRIGGE
(published 1927)

from *Achilles in Scyros*
'Chorus of Scyrian Maidens'

Oh, what can be more pleasant
  Than to live and die a maiden,

Without a man to bother
(When he isn't in the pub)?
Oh, I don't intend at present
To get gross and overladen
A fruitful faded mother
With a bouncing boy to tub!

It is very jolly, very,
In a solemn crocodile
To parade the town, & smile
To one's neighbour and be merry
Without a thought of boys.
Give a girl a girl to greet her!
Her figure is far neater,
Her sugared lips are sweeter
More daintily she toys.
Oh, infinitely meeter
Are homosexual joys!

One doesn't have to tremble
About waking in December
To the curious consequences
Of an afternoon in May.
One has nothing to dissemble
No dates one must remember;
And one gratifies the senses
In a much more gentle way.

We will not waste our beauty
On horrid hairy males;
And we laugh at old wives' tales
About the dismal duty
Of keeping up the race.
Eros – we do not fly him
But maidens all deny him,
Despise, dethrone, deny him,
And flout him to his face.
Let love-lorn lads ensky him;
We keep him in his place.

STEVE JONAS
(1927–1970)

Poem

It's a dull poem
    whose finish
        is sex

& whose climax
    is spoonful
of angelic
    gissom
  flush'd down
the drain
    in a men's room
where hopeful in-
    vitations come
at you from slabs of marble in-
viting
    Travel
        69
  or trips round the world!
just call this below number
    & we must assume
        centrally lo-
cated under 21
      white males
& i'll be yr slave.

THOM GUNN
(born 1929)

Fever

Impatient all the foggy day for night
  You plunged into the bar eager to loot;
A self-defeating eagerness, though – you're light;
  You change direction and shift from foot to foot,

Too skittish to be capable of repose.
    Like an allegorical figure of pursuit
Which can't reach the end toward which it points its nose
    And remain itself, you're unable to engage.

Your mother thought you beautiful I suppose:
    Perhaps that's half your trouble at this age.
Oh how she dandled her pet and watched his sleep.
    Here no one watches the revolving stage
Where, joints and amyl in your pocket, you keep
    Getting less beautiful toward the evening's end.
Potential of love sours into malice now, deep
    Most against those who've done nothing to offend
Except not notice you, for only I
    Have watched you much – though not as covert friend
But picturing roles reversed, with you the spy.
    We seem to you a glittering audience
Tier above tier viewing without sympathy
    Your ragged defeat, your jovial pretense,
From brilliant faces that seem to smile in boast.
    Time to go home babe, though now you feel most tense:
These games have little content, so if you've lost
    It doesn't matter tomorrow. Sleep well. Heaven knows
Feverish people require more sleep than most,
    And need to learn all they can about repose.

Modes of Pleasure

I jump with terror seeing him,
Dredging the bar with that stiff glare
As fiercely as if each whim there
Were passion, whose passion is a whim:

The Fallen Rake, being fallen from
The heights of twenty to middle age,
And helpless to control his rage,
So mean, so few the chances come.

The very beauty of his prime
Was that the triumphs which recurred

In different rooms without a word
Would all be lost some time in time,

Thus he reduced the wild unknown.
And having used each hour of leisure
To learn by rote the modes of pleasure,
The sensual skills as skills alone,

He knows that nothing, not the most
Cunning or sweet, can hold him, still.
Living by habit of the will,
He cannot contemplate the past,

Cannot discriminate, condemned
To the sharpest passion of them all.
Rigid he sits: brave, terrible,
The will awaits its gradual end.

ADRIENNE RICH
(born 1929)

from *Twenty-one Love Poems*

I

Wherever in this city, screens flicker
with pornography, with science-fiction vampires,
victimized hirelings bending to the lash,
we also have to walk . . . if simply as we walk
through the rainsoaked garbage, the tabloid cruelties
of our own neighborhoods.
We need to grasp our lives inseparable
from those rancid dreams, that blurt of metal, those disgraces,
and the red begonia perilously flashing
from a tenement sill six stories high,
or the long-legged young girls playing ball
in the junior highschool playground.
No one has imagined us. We want to live like trees,
sycamores blazing through the sulfuric air,

dappled with scars, still exuberantly budding,
our animal passion rooted in the city.

XII

Sleeping, turning in turn like planets
rotating in their midnight meadow:
a touch is enough to let us know
we're not alone in the universe, even in sleep:
the dream-ghosts of two worlds
walking their ghost-towns, almost address each other.
I've wakened to your muttered words
spoken light- or dark-years away
as if my own voice had spoken.
But we have different voices, even in sleep,
and our bodies, so alike, are yet so different
and the past echoing through our bloodstreams
is freighted with different language, different meanings –
though in any chronicle of the world we share
it could be written with new meaning
we were two lovers of one gender,
we were two women of one generation.

XVI

Across a city from you, I'm with you,
just as an August night
moony, inlet-warm, seabathed, I watched you sleep,
the scrubbed, sheenless wood of the dressing-table
cluttered with our brushes, books, vials in the moonlight –
or a salt-mist orchard, lying at your side
watching red sunset through the screendoor of the cabin,
G minor Mozart on the tape-recorder,
falling asleep to the music of the sea.
This island of Manhattan is wide enough
for both of us, and narrow:
I can hear your breath tonight, I know how your face
lies upturned, the halflight tracing
your generous, delicate mouth
where grief and laughter sleep together.

MAUREEN DUFFY
(born 1933)

Evesong

My love takes an apple to bed
apple, apple she puts the bite on you
or drops you, irresistible, to halt my chase.
As I pick you up and consider
your shape, texture
your virgin unblushed green
she is gone over the dream horizon
while I labour after with this
core, kore, mon cœur, half eaten
bitten fingernail of a poem
going down with the moon
these pips my teeth crack
for a taste of
bittersweet as almond skinned
cleft and dimpled
the apples she brings to bed

Sonnet

Afterwards there are dogends in
                        the ashtray
sheets heavy with her perfume and
                        our sweat
I don't want to change, rumpled, a
                        curled
about her attitude I imitate in sleep
the smell of her on my skin, a towel
                        awry
in the bathroom, the floor clouded
                        with talcum
with careful intaglio of two
                        footprints
all patched on this translucent
                        autumn weather
and its Veronese foliage, each leaf

outlined and brushed with decay I
                              interpret
as longing for a mythical landscape
all my fallacies are pathetic.

Sometimes I think I live only in my
                              head
where she walks in a Golden Age
                              I echo
with this lead shadow when we day
                              after
day made consort of each other's
                              smiles.
Yet I know it is just that those four
her hours were swift as Indian summer
this now has winter's black and
                              measured tread.

EDWARD LUCIE-SMITH
(born 1933)

from *Caravaggio Dying, Porto Ercole, July 1610, aged 36*

II

My own head. Seen in mirrors. Cleanly axed
By the frame's edge. Then in my pictures painted:
Young, wigged with snakes and screaming – staring gorgon
Made for a prince to stare at. Leering image

To freeze the great and mighty in their places.
Later, my own head for Goliath's painted,
Held in the tender hand of a young David,
Beard drenched with sweat, cheeks sunk, eyes fluttering open –
So I have looked, stumbling from a shared bed,
Humbled by the boy's easy, lewd surrender.

My vices. Framed on the walls. A naked urchin,
Mocking my namesake Michelangelo,

Sprawled on a cloth and insolently caressing
A ram, my lustful symbol. I got credit
For new invention, painting this St John –
At least my Baptist speaks of wilderness
(St John, St John, into what wilds you drove me,
Cursed me as Neptune did the wise Ulysses).

Another boy, one plumed with borrowed wings,
A Roman, offering wares, Giustiniani
Who bought it from me said he liked it best
Of all his pictures. 'Sir, a noble liking!'
Was what I told him. 'Lie in my soiled bed.
You know love-making makes me sweat in rivers.
Press your nose down upon that crumpled sheet
The boy bestrides. I think you'll smell sweat still.'
But still he bought it. Now this keyhole shows him
My conquest of *Amore Vincitore*.

EDDIE LINDEN
(born 1935)

A Sunday in Cambridge
(for William)

That Sunday was like an unfinished dream.
I've never been able to get it out of my mind.
You looked like Mary Magdalen
And I wanted to wash your feet.
The more I looked into your eyes
The stronger the pain.
Your thin body and small waist
Were all I wanted to possess
But a shadow hovering in our midst
Prevented a possible communion.

DAVID R. SLAVITT
(born 1935)

In the Seraglio

The maharani of midnight tresses,
jaded, silvered, and rustling silk,

smiles at her eunuchs and undresses,
bathes, and her black hair floats in milk,
bathes, and listens (a woman sings;
others play musical instruments),
emerges, and a servant brings
dusting powders and frankincense.

A dozen virgins, brought to serve
the maharani in her mood,
dry her with kisses; their smooth lips curve
with a sweet and tingling lassitude.

The maharani's half closed eyes
swim in their tawny bodies' grace.
She touches one of the delicate thighs
to delight in the blush on another's face.

(Thus had the maharani blushed
as the maharajah's fingers swept
over her body once and brushed
away the tears that she had wept.)

She kisses the naked, blushing girl
whose breasts are sharp and whose mouth is tart,
honey and jet and mother-of-pearl,
she holds the girl tight to her heart,
then sends her to the great lord's bed,
and pulls the girl with the delicate thighs
down on the cushions, a-tremble with dread
while the others hide their eyes.

PAUL MARIAH
(born 1937)

Quarry/Rock
A Reality Poem in the Tradition of Genet

I

O, Seeger, the night you tied the cabbie
to the tree
                and shot him, did you know

the shadow of the chair was waiting for you?
You, murderer, guillotined one,
You of the severed head,
You on death row for seven years,
You six feet seven taker of life,
you with the death shrouded head.

One night you walking in line
to your cell, swung and touched
hands with your love, Stevie.
You two walking in line
to your cells, swung and touched
hands. Swung hands and touched
the only way you could say good-night
swung hands and touched.

Later, that same night Stevie
lying in his 6 by 9 cell
in the quiet one-man cell
in the quiet of his only home
his desires became rampant
wanting you wanting
wanting you touching him wanting

(O, Seeger, what have they done to Stevie?
What have they done to Stevie?)

(The County had said his voyeur eyes
were too blue and should be
put away until the color changed to grey.)

wanting you wanting
wanting you touching him wanting

the broom became you
the broom became the strength of you
the broom became the anal worship of you
the broom became the regular stroke of you
the broom became the reality of you

until he fell off the bed
and broke
            the broom off, inside where
you were in the quiet of his night
he was visited by red horror
not withstanding, not waking.

II

O, Seeger, the night you tied the cabbie
to the tree
            and shot him, did you know . . .

that you would wait seven years
to be strapped in a chair?

that they would kill your love
in isolation, in lonely isolation?

that in the cubicle of a cell you
would want him, would want to love him?

It was the evening after you knew
Stevie had died that I heard

green tears whimper from your cell
and knew that in that severed head

you still had human tears.

(O, Seeger, what have they done to Stevie?
What have they done to Stevie?)

Later, Stevie was taken
to pauper's field where dandelions
grow in reverence to the sun.

When even his parents refused his body,
refused their son. It was then
I heard you rage like a wild tiger.

In the cold antigone of your dreams
I saw you in defiance go out
and bury the body. And in revenge
you took to the fields
looking for his parents
hiding in the forest of your dreams
in cabbie clothing.

O, Seeger, the night you tied the cabbie
to the tree
              and shot him, did you know
you still had green tears?

LEE HARWOOD
(born 1939)

Rain Journal: London: June 65

sitting naked together
on the edge of the bed
drinking vodka

this my first real love scene

your body so good
your eyes sad love stars

but John
now when we're miles apart
the come-down from mountain visions
and the streets all raining
and me in the back of a shop
making free phone calls to you

what can we do?

crackling telephone wires shadow me
and this distance haunts me

and yes – I am miserable
and lost without you

whole days spent
remaking your face
the sound of your voice
the feel of your shoulder

JUDY GRAHN
(born 1940)

from *Edward the Dyke and Other Poems*

in the place where
her breasts come together
two thumbs' width of
channel ride my
eyes to anchor
hands to angle
in the place where
her legs come together
I said 'you smell like the
ocean' and lay down my tongue
beside the dark tooth edge
of sleeping
'swim' she told me and I
did, I did

Carol, in the park, chewing on straws

> She has taken a woman lover
> whatever shall we do
> she has taken a woman lover
> how lucky it wasn't you

And all the day through she smiles and lies
and grits her teeth and pretends to be shy,
or weak, or busy. Then she goes home
and pounds her own nails, makes her own

bets, and fixes her own car, with her friend.
She goes as far
as women can go without protection
from men.
On weekends, she dreams of becoming a tree;
a tree that dreams it is ground up
and sent to the paper factory, where it
lies helpless in sheets, until it dreams
of becoming a paper airplane, and rises
on its own current; where it turns into a
bird, a great coasting bird that dreams of becoming
more free, even, than that – a feather, finally, or
a piece of air with lightning in it.
      she has taken a woman lover
      whatever can we say
She walks around all day
quietly, but underneath it
she's electric;
angry energy inside a passive form.
The common woman is as common
as a thunderstorm.

A History of Lesbianism

How they came into the world,
the women-loving-women
came in three by three
and four by four
the women-loving-women
came in ten by ten
and ten by ten again
until there were more
than you could count

     they took care of each other
     the best they knew how
     and of each other's children,
     if they had any.

How they lived in the world,
the women-loving-women
learned as much as they were allowed
and walked and wore their clothes
the way they liked
whenever they could. They did whatever
they knew to be happy or free
and worked and worked and worked.
The women-loving-women
in America were called dykes
and some liked it
and some did not.

> they made love to each other
> the best they knew how
> and for the best reasons

How they went out of the world,
the women-loving-women
went out one by one
having withstood greater and lesser
trials, and much hatred
from other people, they went out
one by one, each having tried
in her own way to overthrow
the rule of men over women,
they tried it one by one
and hundred by hundred,
until each came in her own way
to the end of her life
and died:

> The subject of lesbianism
> is very ordinary; it's the question
> of male domination that makes everybody
> angry.

ROYSTON ELLIS
(born 1941)

from *The Cherry Boy*

1

All my sex life, I had been drifting
in and out of bed with beauties
or old men who made it
furtively worth my while,
for kicks, through boredom, but coolly maintained,
until lying in the sun of a tropical isle
as one of the beach boys hustling
the tourists, masks melted, lusting
for every tan body, cartwheeling, lucky
strike, blatantly whispering *fucky, fucky*;
I saw this beginner, his small body
not even brown, bristling, facing
the hard horizon of sex beyond the beach –
thighs of the asthmatic Canadian,
wallet of the queen from Morecambe,
lips of the crewcut American plater,
hands of the frigid Brighton bookmaker –
nervously following the others.
                    Suddenly,
crushingly older, I carried him off the beach
in a vain attempt to save youth from the streets
for his innocence was worth more than those uncles could pay.

Now the season has faded, the tourists gone,
and the beach boys are taking each other
for free . . . In these months, I watched him evolve
from a cherry boy into a man, cool, a sexual
cashbox registering with a mechanical kiss
through pursed lips, the cost of short times.
For five more years, he'll be available as
my battered body once was.
Now I: shattered, the old man forced to pay,
He: the young body paid to oblige.

Retired, every night at his invitation, I feel
him stiff in my arms, on my lips, in my life;
and I find it so hard to believe that my youth was real.

6

It was an international rage
sweeping the youth of Europe, the world
of young men involved with music,
clothes, sex: a pursuit of enjoyment
as the only aim in a boredom of affluence.

It was a convenient kick,
more mature than drinking, keener than pills,
and a brotherhood from Istanbul to Puerto Rico
which turned us on to that softer life.
We smoked together confidently
appreciating the affection billowing around us.

And then, blow by blow, as the season months
stole by, you grew out of me
with visions and mind-blocked dreams
of a trip you must take to understand
the influence of your pituitary gland.

A Norwegian girl's hands groping on a car back-seat,
a French virgin succumbing at night on the beach,
an American widow, a typist who's Swiss,
an English air hostess, a German gym mistress,
a growling Dutch lesbian with contact lenses,
and a dozen Swedish whores in studied frenzies . . .

The cherry boy, once the sweetest prize,
was growing gnarled before my eyes.

Spiv Song

Where are you going, my spiv, my wide boy
down what grey streets will you shake your hair,
what gutters shall know the flap of your trousers
and your loud checked coat, O my young despair?

Have you been in a blind pig over whiskey
where bedbugs spot the discoloured walls,
did you play barbotte and lose all your money
or backroom billiards with yellowed balls?

It's midnight now and the sky is dusty,
the police are going their rounds in the square,
the coffee is cold and the chromium greasy
and the last bus leaves, O my young despair.

Don't you just hate our personal questions
with your 'Take me easy and leave me light,'
with your meeting your friends in every direction
– and sucking in private the thumb of guilt.

There are plenty of friends, my man, my monster,
for a Ganymede kid and a Housman lad
and plenty more you would hate to discover
what you do for a living, my spiv, my id.

And isn't it awkward, their smiles so friendly,
their voices so bright as they ask where you work:
a job in a store, or driving a taxi,
or baseball still in the sunlit park?

O why do you sit in the nightclub so sulky,
why so dramatic breaking the glass:
you've heard again that your mother is dying?
You think that you've caught a social disease?

Your looks are black, my spiv, my wide boy,
will you jump from the bridge to the end of the world
and break on the ice, my pleasure, my puppy,
your forehead so hot and your kisses so cold?

What desperate plan is this job that you talk of –
we'll read tomorrow what happens tonight . . . ?
and where are you off to, my son, my shadow,
with the bill unpaid, as the door swings shut?

SHARON BARBA
(born 1943)

Dykes in the Garden

One is an ex-professor of biology
the other is a stranger to us

but in their Saturday slacks
and old shirts
their hair cropped like Gertrude's

we would know them anywhere

Already we are their younger counterparts
In twenty years we will be indistinguishable

though I will go on writing my poems
and you will take my picture
under a trellis maybe

or with bare feet propped on a patio table
pencil in mouth
musing on the passions
of middle-aged Sapphics

By then we'll know how durable
the cunt is, or love itself
for that matter

working the garden together on Saturdays
stopping to talk, hands to hips
or gesturing with a spade

familiar as Gertrude and Alice
as Miss Lowell and Mrs Russell
in their greenhouse

By then we'll know all there is to know
about dykes and gardens

strolling arm in arm, perhaps with cigars
through our own American Beauties

DENNIS KELLY
(born 1943)

Chicken
after Harold Norse

my cock?
oh it just came
naturally big

I'm thinking
of being
a gigolo

I gotta lotta
come
(hot looks
in the direction
of big Cadillac
cruising
around block)

(dark blue
veins
along
his arms/biceps)

I'm gonna go off to
Miami & rent my
bod to some old rich
dragon (& he could
very easily with his
Michel Angelo looks
his big
Picasso prick)

I oughtta
be a foot long

when I'm 17.

FRAN WINANT
(born 1943)

Christopher Street Liberation Day, June 28, 1970

with banners and our smiles
we're being photographed
by tourists police and leering men
we fill their cameras
with 10,000 faces
bearing witness
to our own existence
in sunlight
from Washington Maryland
Massachusetts Pennsylvania
Connecticut Ohio
Iowa Minnesota
from Harlem and the suburbs
the universities
and the world
we are women who love women
we are men who love men
we are lesbians and homosexuals
we cannot apologize
for knowing
what others refuse to know
for affirming
what they deny
we might have been
the women and men
who watched us and waved
and made fists
and gave us victory signs
and stood there after we had passed

thinking of all they had to lose
and of how society punishes
its victims
who are all of us
in the end
but we are sisters and sisters
brothers and brothers
workers and lovers
we are together
we are marching
past the crumbling old world
that leans toward us
in anguish from the pavement
our banners are sails
pulling us through the streets
where we have always been
as ghosts
now we are shouting our own words
we are a community
we are a society
we are everyone
we are inside you
remember
all you were taught to forget
we are part of the new world
photographers
grim behind precise machines
wait to record
our blood and sorrow
and revolutionaries beside them
remark
love is not political
when we stand against our pain
they say
we are not standing against anything
when we demand our total lives
they wonder
what we are demanding
cant you lie
cant you lie
they whisper they hiss

like fire in grass
cant you lie
and get on with the real work
our line winds
into Central Park
and doubles itself
in a snakedance
to the top of a hill
we cover the Sheep Meadow
shouting
lifting our arms
we are marching into ourselves
like a body
gathering its cells
creating itself
in sunlight
we turn to look back
on the thousands behind us
it seems we will converge
until we explode
sisters and sisters
brothers and brothers
together.

RITA MAE BROWN
(born 1944)

Sappho's Reply

My voice rings down through thousands of years
To coil around your body and give you strength,
You who have wept in direct sunlight,
Who have hungered in invisible chains,
Tremble to the cadence of my legacy:
An army of lovers shall not fail.

Canto Cantare Cantavi Cantatum

I sing of a woman and summer
Of hot days within my limbs

July of months and blazing woman
Who comes before me, burning, burning
Whose eyes stir sulfer seas inside
To collide with the shores of silence.
I sing of a woman and summer
The woman loves another:
I burn as a lonely taper
In blackest night.

Dancing the Shout to the True Gospel
Or: The Song My Movement Sisters Won't Let Me Sing

I follow the scent of a woman
Melon heavy
Ripe with joy
Inspiring me
To rip great holes in the night
So the sun blasts through.
And this is all I shall ever know:
Her breath
Filling the hollows of my neck
A luxury diminishing death.

The New Litany

Compounded in confusion
A mute, prosaic Sappho, I pray
'Oh let me dumb be blessed with song
To fling at the metaphors of darkness
Cemented in silence of swift time
On this side of morning;
To bring the dawn and rein Time's ravenous mouth,
To spend the sacraments on sheets
Redeemed in a kiss,
To proclaim New Christmas
The carol chanted by her eyes.'
All this splendor, I pray
A groundling with face upturned
To the snow fallen down

In the night of her hair
Above me.
Deaf to my song?
Would she feign deafness
Or wave me away?
Ah, I'm left to pray,
As Venus in her ascendency
Draws triangulations on reality.

FELICE PICANO
(born 1944)

The Gilded Boys

The gilded boys are dancing
with their lover's brother's lover.
Those golden lads are having one fine time.
Swaying rather wildly
to the ever-present bass hum
from a hundred hidden speakers
within their platform heels.
As colored lights come screaming
to glitter off their denims
to glance on plastic pins.

The gilded boys are gathered
in a chic Morocco nightclub
from notime in the '30's
from noone's Garbo'd dream.
They meet there every weekend
to catch each other's numbers
to check each other's haircuts
to fill their lives with peergroup vibes
and dance their dance of mechanized trance
for the instant emulation
of their brother's lover's brother.

The gilded boys go on all night
sometimes till after sunrise.
They're always checking mirrors

and bitching at the DJ,
their Cardin shirts get sweaty
and their pills get ineffective
and the man they think they love
is sometimes leaving with another.
But they've always got each other
and their lover's lover's lover:
to dance with every weekend
to prove that they're alive.

The Heart Has Its Reasons

Not because you didn't call.
I almost half expected that.

Not because we set a date
you just couldn't make –
whatever your reasons.

Not because you never arrived,
never left a number to reach you.
For all I know you were hit by a car;
mowed down in some neighborhood war.

Not because the night I had planned
never got off the ground
never mind reach the heights.
We didn't have that much in common
except a good fit –
if you still can remember that fondly, that far.

No, not because you stopped a trip
never gave me the chance to decide
whether or not I'd take the ride,
whether I'd take the risk of true love or illusion.

But simply because
I straightened all day.
Washed all the glasses
changed pillows and sheets.

cleaned out the closets
even laundered the drapes.
Did everything that was needed
if a guest like you was coming.

Did, in short, what could wait,
For that I could never forgive you.

IAN YOUNG
(born 1945)

Double Exposure

At a party of university people
Jimmy and I sat on a bed
that seemed to be floating.
The whisky-drinkers
were making identical comments,
dancing ever so slowly,
and eyeing each other.
One girl had put Christmas ornaments
on her ears,
and a long-haired kid
read poems at the walls.

I was watching Jimmy –
his hands
holding a towel
and a book of Prévert –
his bare legs
and the curve of his prick
under the cut-down jeans.
The people all looked at us,
their mouths open,
and began to fade away
just as our bed drifted out of the window

They were waving goodbye
as I took pictures of Jimmy
with an imaginary camera.

Honi soit qui mal y pense

A boy of fifteen,
he wore a jacket, dark shirt, wool tie,
his bright eyes studying earnestly
Androcles and the Lion
in the Shavian alphabet . . .
His friend, a few years older,
blond and bundled in overcoat and scarf,
carried a flute
as they sat at the next table
of a café in Toronto.
My friend knew the younger boy
and I asked her who they were.
'He used to be a nice, ordinary kid,'
she said; 'Then he met *him* – Brett.
Brett took him to Montreal,
did things to him . . . I don't know . . .
they're fags . … you know . . . Music Room types.'
When they left, they were laughing,
planning how to spend Brett's paypacket.
I noticed they'd written in Shavian
all over the serviettes.
That's what corruption does for you.

WILLIAM BARBER
(born 1947)

Explanation

I am not gay by your definition.
I will not stand in the drab beige men's room
like a fern watered with urine,
and wait for penises. I'm sorry.
Morality will just have to change.

I speak directly to the sons of
your officials, under the moon,
with the professors listening.

We have burned the closet door in effigy.
There will be no more watching for the feet
of policemen under the partitions.
                                    Nor
the mediocrity of masses of shuffling gays
in the dark bars, ghettoed and ethnic.

I love men. I tell them so directly.
Wherever we encounter, there are no categories.

ELLEN MARIE BISSERT
(born 1947)

The Most Beautiful Woman at My Highschool Reunion

after 11 years
she is still as sleek as an unspayed siamese
charming everyone into her audience
she is a winner
rising to associate director of a department store
quitting to have 2 children
(1 for each of her husband's houses)
nothing has changed
she is still as leggy as a doe
her iris-blue eyes
her long smooth arms holding me in confidence
as she complains
motherhood hasn't done much
she's as flat as ever
glancing toward the table of husbands
I try to pick hers
nothing has changed
short smug & meaty
they are still the inert boys at the highschool dances
quietly pumping sperm into voluptuous moviestars
the way they force air into tires
she is a winner
moving beyond the mysteries of padded bras
still needing to offer herself like cut melon to the male eyes

opening her blouse
we will never be able
as i hold her cool thin fingers
i long to caress the silk of her nipples
into loving themselves
like the woman waiting for me tonight
does to mine

Another

you are a woman
i have no defenses in love against you
i cannot stop
i cannot love you less than myself
now as before someone calls
she is leaving you
i know
i know this despair
as sex burns love out
i hold you
loving the blood that drips like wine from our bodies
you kiss me hard
& go to her

ALICE BLOCH
(born 1947)

Six Years
for Nancy

A friend calls us
an old married couple

I flinch
you don't mind
On the way home
you ask why I got upset
We are something

like what she said
you say   I say
No

We aren't married
No one has blessed
this union   no one
gave us kitchen gadgets
We bought our own blender
We built our common life
in the space between the laws

Six years
What drew us together
a cartographer   a magnetic force
our bodies   our speech
the wind   a hunger

Listeners both
we talked

I wanted: your lean wired energy
control   decisiveness
honesty   your past
as an athlete

You wanted:
my 'culture'
gentleness   warmth

Of course that was doomed
You brought out
my anger   I resist
your control   your energy
exhausts me   my hands
are too hot for you   you gained
the weight I lost   my gentleness
is dishonest   your honesty
is cruel   you hate
my reading   I hate
your motorcycle

Yet something has changed
You have become gentler
I more decisive
We walk easily
around our house
into each other's language
There is nothing
we cannot say together

Solid ground
under our feet
we know this landscape
We have no choice
of destination   only the route
is a mystery   every day
a new map of the same terrain

PERRY BRASS
(born 1947)

I Think the New Teacher's a Queer

'I think the new teacher's a queer,'

I turned around
and saw that
they were talking about me,

one false move
and it would all be over,
I could not drop my wrists
or raise my voice.

so I stood there up against the board
arms folded
pressed against my chest
and looked without seeing
or hearing until
the children became a noiseless pattern

and all those years
from when I sat among them
stopped dead and I feared
that they'd beat me up

in the boys' room.

KATH FRASER
(born 1947)

Song (October 1969)

I love you, Mrs Acorn. Would your husband mind
if I kissed you under the autumn sun,
if my brown-leaf guilty passion made you blind
to his manly charms and fun?

I want you, Mrs Acorn. Do you think you'll come
to see my tangled, windswept desires,
and visit me in my everchanging house of some
vision of winter's fires?

I am serious Mrs Acorn, do you hear?
Forget your family and other ties,
Come with me to where there is no fear,
where we'll find summer butterflies.

I am serious Mrs Acorn, are you deaf?

ANONYMOUS AUTHORS
(1948–1976)

Twenty-five Limericks

There once was a warden of Wadham
Who approved of the folkways of Sodom.
    For a man might, he said,
    Have a very poor head,
But be a fine fellow at bottom.

That famous old pederast, Wilde,
Felt sure a boy stayed undefiled
   If you handled his penis
   With no trace of meanness,
Whenever you sucked off the child.

A well-bred young girl of Gomorrah
Would never let any man bore her:
   Neither back nor in front,
   Not in mouth nor in cunt,
And she viewed their stiff pricks with horror.

When Arthur was homeless and broke,
He would suck off his friends for a coke.
   The suckees would mutter:
   'Please bring some drawn butter –
We're going to have Artie choke.'

In a high-fashion journal for queers
A drawing by Dali appears.
   It depicts a June bride
   With three breasts on each side,
Caressing a penis with ears.

A Lesbian born under Pisces
Has dildoes of various sizes.
   The big one with warts
   Squirts several quarts,
And gives all her girlfriends surprises.

Our ambassador to Venus, Mz Abner,
Hoped the lesbian Veenies would be havin'er.
   But to her surprise
   They crossed all six thighs,
While the masculine Weenies were grabbin'er!

Though the music of love is Schubérty,
Love itself here is sordidly dirty.
   The men are all queer

Till their ninety-ninth year,
While the menopause strikes at pubérty.

A large, colored dyke from Atlanta
Said, 'If ya' mus' know dear, I plan tuh
   Finger-fuck Mother Hayes
   On Tahmes Squah fo' three days.
It's a project that's sponsored by ANTA.'

Aging old queers are no treat:
Sucking cocks, raping kids, smelling feet.
   They talk like a preacher,
   Pervert every creature,
And worry about being indiscreet.

Young Frederick the Great was a beaut.
To a guard he cried, 'Hey, man, you're cute.
   If you'll come to my palace,
   I'll finger your phallus,
And then I shall blow on your flute.'

Two dykes went their separate routes:
Said one, 'I just *don't* give two hoots.
   No common tie linked us
   Except cunnilinctus,
And a penchant for Brooks Brothers suits.'

A big bull-dyke, surly and sallow,
Cried, 'Pricks are just wicks without tallow!
   Why, all men admit
   They'd prefer a clit.'
(That's something I find hard to swallow.)

The S & M bar, oh my dears,
Is a place to get stomped on, for queers.
   To get beaten and spat on,
   And pissed on and shat on –
The *thrill* of your gayest young years!

A well-buggered boy named Delpasse
Was cornholed by ten in his class.
  Said he, with a yawn:
  'Now the novelty's gone,
It's only a pain in the ass.'

A smooth-bottomed fellow named Fritz
Contracted a case of the shits.
  Now with asshole distended
  His future is ended –
He can't find a penis that fits.

An anal erotic named Herman
Had a passion for buggering mermen.
  He'd lure the poor swine
  From their haunts 'neath the Rhine
With songs in exécrable German.

A hermaphrodite fairy of Kew
Offered boys something new in a screw,
  For they both looked so sweet
  On the front and back seat
Of a *bisexual built for two*.

There once was a Renaissance man
Who modeled his conduct on Pan.
  'I will' was tattooed
  On the tip of his rood,
And 'I will if I must' on his can.

A Fire Island pixie called 'Mary,'
Whose erogenous zones were quite hairy,
  Said, 'That last guy, I'll swear,
  Is still in there somewhere,
So I want to warn *you* to be wary.'

The treatment by old Mr Mears
Of small chubby boys and their rears

   Appears to his God
   As unnatural and odd:
Can it be he is one of those queers?

There was a young fellow named Nutz
Who would rut as the pederast ruts.
   His physician said, 'Solon,
   There's more in your colon
Than ever got in through your guts.'

A young fairy with habits perverse
Found that beatings made life just a curse.
   So each time he went hence
   He assured his defense
With a dildo he kept in his purse.

Said a gabby old queer in Saint-Lô:
'We sophisticates bugger and blow.
   Women just bore me,
   I need niggers to gore me –
I'm a bit of a *bisexual*, you know.'

A young Harvard man, sweet and tender,
Went out with some queers on a bender.
   He came back in two days
   In a sexual haze,
No longer quite sure of his gender.

OLGA BROUMAS
(born 1949)

Leda and Her Swan

You have red toenails, chestnut
hair on your calves, oh let
me love you, the fathers
are lingering in the background
nodding assent.

I dream of you
shedding calico from
slow-motion breasts, I dream
of you leaving with
skinny women, I dream you know.

The fathers are nodding like
overdosed lechers, the fathers approve
with authority: Persian emperors, ordering
that the sun shall rise
every dawn, set
each dusk. I dream.

White bathroom surfaces
rounded basins you
stand among
loosening
hair, arms, my senses.

The fathers are Dresden figurines
vestigial, anecdotal
small sculptures shaped
by the hands of nuns. Yours

crimson tipped, take no part in that
crude abnegation. Scarlet
liturgies shake our room, amaryllis blooms
in your upper thighs, water lily
on mine, fervent delta

the bed afloat, sheer
linen billowing
on the wind: Nile, Amazon, Mississippi.

PAULA JENNINGS
(born 1950)

Lesbian

Your petals open wet
to cradle my fingers

and I think tomorrow
I will scrawl
in red paint
on the town hall
that behind the word lesbian
stinking in men's mouths,
rhyming with perversion and revulsion,
was always this word
with a soft 'l' like in laughter and lilac
and an 's' that tenderness dissolves into
as your petals open wet
to cradle my fingers.

CHUCK ORTLEB
(born 1950)

Some Boys

When some boys
offer to dance
you can see how innocently
their cocks hang in their pants.
Pendulously, as they say,
connoting
horses, barns, liquor, hay.

some boys open up their shirts
and the beauty almost hurts.

some boys even undress in
rooms cluttered with Dylan on.

Some boys are evil.
They lure boys into deeper statements.
They take showers together,
they eat flowers together
and call each other studs.

Some boys, though, do take to sex like apes and monsters and their
      fathers.

They get hair-raising erections.
Pools of smegma collect near their beds.
Discarded condoms build up in their backseats
and dead pubic insects fall from their groins into
patches of vaseline.

The meat of rough alleys hangs in their underwear.
The kind of meat you pull out of the pants of muggers.
The meat in its American juice that lays in jeeps and B42s
I mean the meat
of all soldier boys who will bomb the hell out of heaven,
the meat
of all those high school cadets
masturbating in the twilight as though they were landing a 747.

E. A. LACEY
(published 1965)

Guest

If some boy were to come to me by night.
And say, 'I am chased. I was your lover. Let me in.'
And I, opening the door of a rented room,
Were to see him drunk, staggering, confusion in his hair,
With the perfection of the hunted animal.
And if I were to take him in – let's say from pity –
Strip him layer by layer, bathe him, spoon him, he
Falling gray and neutral on the clean linen and pillows.
And in bed he, who had bled, had plumbed me
Were to go soft and afraid and weep for a mother,
And I were to spend myself in his torn body
As morning gritted on his eyes.

Ramon

Seven years ago, almost to the month and day.

It is not hard to pick a sailor up at Retiro Station.[1]

1. the largest of the train stations in Buenos Aires

They come in, hot and penniless, from the sex prison of their
     ships and the time prison of the sea,
ready to sleep anywhere, or do anything,
to the great city, grave city on the silver river
– the city that hides its loneliness in eating.
Even out of uniform, you can pick them out by their air of guilt and
     expectancy,
as they arrive in pairs at the plaza, eye the prospects, then separate,
loll on the grass, sprawl on benches, prowl the marble station,
circle the British clock tower, round and round, like a ship's deck,
with faintly rolling gait.
Conversation is easy. Sit down beside one on the park bench.
Ask him where he comes from, tell him you once passed through
     there on a train, offer him a cigarette, offer . . .
Brown country boys, desert sailors most of them, drafted and
     recruited
from Tucuman, Jujuy, Saltá, towns of the mestizo north,
they come to the park because they are sick of the sea and afraid of the
     city and Retiro at least reminds them of home,
as it vomits out all day the hopeful brown faces arriving from the
     country
to the dark city, sad city, cold city on the silver river.
Once you have picked one up, the search for a room:
the good hotels have fastidious doormen who look at you
     unnervingly;
the alojamientos have stereos and mirrors for men with women;
the hospedajes demand many documents and show you sex-
     perfumed cots in rooms for five.
Finally, success. Inside the room. Alone.
The touching of bodies. The bedding down. Lifebuoyed
clean smell of white-and-blue crinkly uniform, soon cast aside, then of
     firm young body
trembling cock already rampant, casting its shadow on the hard
     brown belly,
and a desire for human tenderness.

O all night in that boy's arms I lay after the tumbling,
as he slept with an erection, and in the morning did him again,
for the price of a pack of cigarettes and a hotel room.
Eighteen years old, from Mendoza, in the throes of sex and life.

He had been a naval cadet for just five months.
Soon he would sail away – in a week – for the Antarctic; he was afraid;
        he had never been there; was it really cold?
And did I want to meet him again Sunday night?
And as we rode back in the subway, returning to Retiro,
morning light hurting our eyes, ill-humoured city faces all around us,
        we filled with sleep and peacefulness,
the question, almost whispered: 'Te gusté?' 'Did you like me?'

Sunday night I got stupidly drunk, did not go to Retiro;
alcohol ruins the best moments of a manic-depressive, or perhaps
        instinctively
I didn't want to spoil it. Never saw him again.
Seven years ago that sailor set forth for Antarctica.

Mesón Brujo

The boy brought in the logs to start the fire.
A gust of night and nature blew in with him,
of animals out prowling in the dark.
His cheeks were bright with cold; his skin was white;
black hair hung low across a narrow forehead.
From my cold bed I watched him stack the logs
in a kind of pyramid, the small ones under,
the bigger ones on top, then saw him stick
chips of pitch pine among them, strike a match,
and light a sliver; and the room soon filled
with the resinous odour of *ocote* smoke.
Then he blew on the spark of fire he had created,
till the chips burned brightly, wrapping in their flame
the smaller logs, which in turn would ignite
the larger, to the largest one, on top.
And the room blossomed roses. All the while,
crouched at his task, he had not spoken, not looked at me,
but fixed his gaze on his logs with a concentrated
beetling frown, across which light and shadow played.
Now he got up, asked awkwardly if the fire
was satisfactory, and prepared to go.

And I answered yes, the fire was satisfactory
and no doubt would burn for at least two hours more,
time enough for me to fall asleep, while I thought
there was something much more satisfactory than fire
which would warm me even more. He left. I dozed.
Or perhaps I slept; the fact is, some hours later
– how many, I don't know – I heard, at least
it seemed I heard a sound, a hesitant tapping
at my door, and I rose in the fire's ambiguous light,
glided half-asleep over the hard, flat tiles,
opened the door effortlessly, as one does in dreams,
and the log-boy came in, cheeks bright red with cold.
There in the fire's dim glow I watched him undress,
saw the white body define itself from layers of dark clothing,
saw him stand, legs apart, in the rosy dying light,
black hair ingathering round an opening rose,
felt his icy skin, glabrous as myrtle bark,
as he slid into bed beside me. He was an expert
at lighting fires, but now it fell my turn
to stroke for the first time that cold virgin skin,
caressing rubbing it to raise a spark,
blowing on that spark to fan it to a flame,
wrapping him in my arms and legs to warm him,
playing each trick of friction, till at last,
like wood still green, he caught . . . The hard logs crumbled
to white ash; the last embers closed their eyes;
and in the darkness we were our own fire.

All night the log-boy tossed there in my arms
in intervals of sleep and waking dream,
all heat and flame now, in a bed as warm
as roses. Till I heard, just before morning,
another distant tapping at my door,
and the fire-boy noiselessly, as one does in dreams,
rose and in the white light of the false dawn
donned slowly his dark clothing, slid across
the smooth tiles to the door, opened it effortlessly
and was gone. And I lay asleep in the half-light.

The next night, after dinner, when the hour
for the guests to retire and the fires to be lit

arrived, I lay in bed, awaiting him,
but a gray-haired old man came to light my fire,
place the pine chips, build the log pyramid
in my cold chambers at the Mesón Brujo.

Abdelfatteh

You put your hand on my shoulder
and n'aie pas peur you said.
Hot windless night. We were watching
a street-fight in Marrákech.
You smiled at me, young hill-boy
(who thought that you were twenty,
but you just might have been 18),
and you showed two broken teeth.
We drank tea on the corner,
where you taught me Arab letters,
and somehow we went to the hammam,
where you rubbed me down and fucked me.
Then you told me your life story,
all about your mountain village,
how you once had been a student,
but had fallen out with a teacher
(lost promise of your family)
and you'd been expelled, and, now
you slept nights in the cafés
and smoked kif all the hot day
and scoured the town for tourists.

I went with you to your village
in the mountains near Marrákech.
I saw the barren hillside
(but to you it was blooming).
I saw the bordj you lived in
with the stable underneath it
for the camels and the donkeys,
and the sheep, the goats, the turkeys.
I met your grave, stern father,
upright in his blue djellaba.
I drank tea and smoked kif there.

I met your other mother
(as you called your father's new wife).
And you washed my hands with water
poured from a silver pitcher
(the custom of the country),
and we slept on Berber carpets
that were woven by your sisters.

And so I came to trust you.
And so I took you travelling,
And then we fell in prison
in a town called Mogador.
And n'aie pas peur you told me,
maktoub, it was all written,
but, inchallah, we'll get out,
though you yourself were frightened.

For two long months we rotted
in a prison by the seaside,
where the gulls laughed every morning,
and the muezzin wailed at daybreak,
as the key turned in the iron door,
and the lice and bedbugs ate us,
and we lived on beans and lentils,
and you sold the shoes I'd bought you
and the blue shirt you were wearing
to get more food from the kitchen
so that I could eat 'European.'
And at nights you slept beside me,
(on the cold floor, rough wool blankets)
and you put your arms around me
to protect me from the others
(for there were forty others).

Days, we walked around in circles
in that courtyard with eight olive-trees,
hand in hand, like all the others
(the custom of the country),
sat and listened to the imams
(though of course I understood nothing),
while the armed guards prowled the rooftops.

The last time that I saw you
was as I was leaving prison
and we kissed each other on both cheeks
(the custom of the country),
while my police escorts looked on,
and you grabbed my hand and told me
'remember, I'm your brother,'
and I marched out of the doorway,
for I was being deported.

Now, back on your douar,
you send me Christmas cards and little letters
(decorated with calligraphy and flowers)
in your funny French, saying things like this:
Mon cher frère, si tu veux m'aider, aide-moi
à ce moment, n'importe de quelle chose,
de l'argent, si tu peux, ou des vêtements
anciens, ou une cartouche de cigarettes.
And I sometimes send you money,
and I hope it makes you happy,
for I won't be going back there.

And I wander
from country to country, purposeful, purposeless,
but sometimes
even now
at night
in my hotel-room of dreams
I hear across the darkness n'aie pas peur
feel
the small protecting body close to mine,
warm arms around my waist, quick, quiet breath,
the hard cock pulsing, saying 'let me in,'
brief spasm of union and separation.
Abd-el-Fatteh.
Servant
of the Open Door.

Hammam is a Turkish bath. *Bordj* is a fortified adobe house-castle, of a type common in
Southern Moroccan villages. *Douar* is a country village. *Mogador* is the other name of
Es-Saouira, a Moroccan coastal city. *Djellaba* is the Arab robe. *Maktoub* means 'it was written
(by fate)'. *Inchallah* – if God wills. All the 'Abd' names in Arabic mean 'Servant of Allah'.

Abd is servant or slave. The second part is one of the 99 names of God (the 100th fell into the sea and has never been found). *El Fatteh* means 'the open (i.e. illuminated, comprehending) way (door or mind)'. I'm of course punning most sacrilegiously on it here.

KIRBY CONGDON
(published 1966)

Daredevil

Hard helmets and high boots
tumescent in the sun,
got-up in rubber skin
and leather hide,
black, strapped, laced,
buckled with grommets,
chrome and brassy-eyed,
their dress itself is an act of sex,
as the body, used,
tumbles to its end
like jointed dolls we outgrew
and threw aside.
So the exalted race
to their base death
in self-abuse begins,
as the body's transient existence
sings its violent end,
to replace that dull, dull death
that waits upon the rest of us
behind a desk,
behind another desk,
behind the coffin lid
closing like an office door.

ANONYMOUS
(*c.* 1970)

'Lost lines from Chaucer's Prologue to *The Canterbury Tales*'

Ther was also a povre closet queane.
He was ryght olde and somdel balde, I wene,

But whilom had he bene a youth-leadere,
That is to seyn a manner scoutmastere.
To see his knaves naked in the streme
Was his felicitee and al his dreme.
He wolde han bene a proper sodomite
To live his dayes in lykorous delyght,
But could not beare that men should call him such.
Al myght he venture was a passing touch,
Ne wolde for anythyng his bent confesse.
He was a verray voyer as I gesse.
His studie was Dan Platoun and Socrate.
For wommens matters yaf he not a fart.
His fantasye was on lyf monastic
With divers choristerres pederastic.
It wer not good, thocht he, by copulacioun
T'encrees and eke to multiplye the nacioun.
His talk was al of bollock and of prikke,
Souning alway how longe and eek how thickke.
For lakke of younge lovyers whit and red
He had an eunuch cat hight Ganymed.

CAROLINE GILFILLAN
(?)

lesbian play on t.v.

there has been a play on t.v.
a voyeuristic lesbian tale
the leading woman has a hard unvarnished
face   flat tits   dirty hands
her fate is some cruel joke   dreamt up
in script rooms over beer-guts and smoke
stale coffee   and earnest liberalism

take a deep breath   for she is a
potsmoking christian artist lavatorycleaner
workingclass raped byherfatherattheageof11
bisexual motorbykeriding   lesbian
everything goes wrong for her all all all all

the wrong decisions   she has lost her
virginity her child lost her youth her freshness
her best (prostitute) friend her debby lover
her paintings her home even her oinkish sugar daddy

the love-making scenes are the funniest/sickest
the leading actress allbutch gets into bed
with her trousers on (no frank love scenes please)
when they kiss it is all violence on her part
hard mouth and smouldering glances

II

there's been some sort of mistake
the lesbian I know is
unsupported mother   printer
factory worker   barmaid   student
musician   van driver   waitress
mother   daughter   child   grandmother
fat   thin   spotty   smooth   beautiful
vain   hairy   timid   fucked-up
happy   angry   she is bullied
or pampered   loved or unloved
she touches other women sexually
sometimes in shame   mostly in joy
she dreams   she writes this poem

GENNADY TRIFONOV
(?)

For three swift days
You gave me solace
And on the fourth day
Your shadow vanished.

I didn't mind
That you accidentally
Broke my wing
when you said you loved me.

You were good for me
Like snow is good for winter.
You were obedient to me
Like growing grass to springtime.

And may God forgive me
That I, lacking the strength,
Have already forgotten you
The way the earth forgot peace.

Thus, all my life,
I'm not with him I love,
About whom I'm silent all night
And keep the candle burning.

[SIMON KARLINSKY]

MICHAEL RUMAKER
(?)

The Fairies Are Dancing All Over the World

1

The fairies are dancing all over the world
        in the dreams of the President
                they are dancing
    although he dares not mention this at cabinet meetings
In the baby blood of the brandnew
        they are dancing O most rapturously
    and over the graves of the fathers and mothers
            who are dead
and around the heads of the mothers and fathers who are not dead
        in celebration of the sons and daughters
            they've given the earth
The fairies are dancing in the paws and muzzles
        of dogs larking in the broad field next to the church
The fairies have always danced in the blood of the untamed
            in the muscular horned goat

in the blood of Henry Thoreau
    and most certainly Emily Dickinson
And they skip in the blood of the marine recruit
    in his barracks at night
        his bones aching with fatigue and loneliness
    and pure dreams of women
           and his goodbuddy in the next bunk
They are most lovely in the eyes of the black kid
      mucking in front of the jukebox

2

        at the local pizzeria,
more timorous in the eyes of his white friend
    whose hips are a bit more calcified
with hereditary denunciation of the fairies
    May the fairies swivel his hips
On sap green evenings in early summer
      the fairies danced under the moon in country places
    danced among native american teepees
and hung in the rough hair of buffaloes racing across the prairies
      and are dancing still
        most hidden
      and everywhere
in some, only in the eyes
  in others a reach of the arm
    a sudden yelp of joy
reveals their presence
The fairies are dancing from coast to coast
  all over deadmiddle America
      they're bumping and grinding on the Kremlin walls
  the tap of their feet is eroding all the walls
    all over the world as they dance
In the way of the western world
    the fairies' dance has become small
  a bleating, crabbed jerkiness
but there for all that,
  a bit of healthy green in the dead wood
      that spreads an invisible green fire
  around and around the globe

encircling it in its dance
   of intimacy with the secret of all living things

3

The fairies are dancing even in the Pope's nose
         and in the heart of the most stubborn macho
      who will not and will not
         and the fairies will
                  most insistently
      because he will not
In the Pentagon the fairies are dancing
         under the scrambled egg hats
         of those who see no reason why youths should live to old age
The fairies bide their time and wait
      They dance in invisible circlets of joy
         around and around and over the planet
They are the green rings unseen by spaceships
      their breath is the earth of the first spring evening
They explode in the black buds of deadwood winter
                  Welcome them with open arms
      They are allies courting in the bloodstreams
         welcome them and dance with them.

Index of Poets and Translators

NOTE: Figures in roman type refer to poets; those in italic type refer to translators.

Index of First Lines

FIND OUT MORE ABOUT PENGUIN BOOKS

We publish the largest range of titles of any English language paperback publisher. As well as novels, crime and science fiction, humour, biography and large-format illustrated books, Penguin series include *Pelican Books* (on the arts, sciences and current affairs), *Penguin Reference Books, Penguin Classics, Penguin Modern Classics, Penguin English Library* and *Penguin Handbooks* (on subjects from cookery and gardening to sport), as well as *Puffin Books* for children. Other series cover a wide variety of interests from poetry to crosswords, and there are also several newly formed series – *King Penguin, Penguin American Library, Penguin Diaries and Letters* and *Penguin Travel Library*.

We are an international publishing house, but for copyright reasons not every Penguin title is available in every country. To find out more about the Penguins available in your country please write to our U.K. office – Dept EP, Penguin Books Ltd, Harmondsworth, Middlesex UB7 ODA – unless you live in one of the following areas:

In the U.S.A.: Dept DG, Penguin Books, 299 Murray Hill Parkway, East Rutherford, New Jersey 07073.

In Canada: Penguin Books Canada Ltd, 2801 John Street, Markham, Ontario L3R 1B4.

In Australia: Marketing Department, Penguin Books Australia Ltd, P.O. Box 257, Ringwood, Victoria 3134.

In New Zealand: Marketing Department, Penguin Books (N.Z.) Ltd, P.O. Box 4019, Auckland 10.

In India: Penguin Overseas Ltd, 706 Eros Apartments, 56 Nehru Place, New Delhi 110019.